PRAISE FOR *NEW* *TIMES* BESTSELLIN THE GRIMROSE GIRLS

★ "Enthralling... Fans of empowering feminist fairy-tale retellings will love this."

—*Kirkus Reviews,* Starred Review

"Inclusive and fiercely feminist."

—*Publishers Weekly*

"Murder mystery laced with fairy tales...a chilling climax will keep readers engaged and anticipating the next volume."

—*The Bulletin of the Center for Children's Books*

"Mysterious and magical, *Grimrose Girls* turns classic tales upside down and then some. Fans of *Once Upon a Time* and anyone who likes their happily ever afters with a side of murder will love this fantasy thriller!"

—Rosiee Thor, author of *Tarnished are the Stars*

"*Grimrose Girls* takes the classic thriller story and fantastically twists it. For fans of classic murder mysteries, strong friendships, and shows like *Lost Girl* and *Grimm,* this is the series for you."

—Linsey Miller, author of *Mask of Shadows* and *What We Devour*

"Pohl weaves a suspenseful, thrilling tale full of all the dark magic, swoonworthy romance, and courageous heroines we know and love from our favorite fairy tales. Sink your teeth into this story and let it carry you through the woods."

—Roseanne A. Brown, *New York Times* bestselling author of *A Song of Wraiths and Ruin*

"A twisty, sapphic reimagining of all of your favorite fairy tales, *The Grimrose Girls* is darkly haunting and achingly romantic. In an exploration of grief and love, Pohl weaves a magical mystery of a murder most foul. These aren't the fairy tales you remember, and certainly not ones you'll forget."

—Ashley Poston, national bestselling author of *Geekerella*

"A contemporary take on classic fairy tales with a haunting setting, and a ruthless mystery at its core—perfect for lovers of dark academia vibes, fairy tales with a twist, or mini-Sherlocks in the making!"

—*The Nerd Daily*

ALSO BY LAURA POHL

The Grimrose Girls

The Last 8

The First 7

THE
WICKED
REMAIN

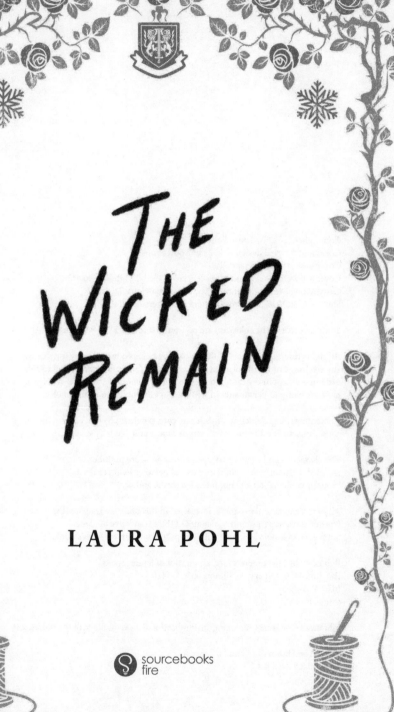

THE WICKED REMAIN

LAURA POHL

sourcebooks
fire

Copyright © 2022 by Laura Pohl
Cover and internal design © 2022 by Sourcebooks
Cover design by Ray Shappell
Cover art ©elkor/Getty, Kristina Velickovic/Getty, whiteisthecolor/
Getty, Wong Sze Fei / EyeEm/Getty, Nataleana/Getty, Djomas/
Shutterstock, Valeriia Myroshnichenko/Shutterstock

Sourcebooks and the colophon are registered trademarks of Sourcebooks.

All rights reserved. No part of this book may be reproduced in any form or by
any electronic or mechanical means including information storage and retrieval
systems—except in the case of brief quotations embodied in critical articles or
reviews—without permission in writing from its publisher, Sourcebooks.

Content warning: depiction of violence, gore, parental physical and emotional
abuse, and suicide attempt. Mentions of cancer and death by suicide.

The characters and events portrayed in this book are fictitious or
are used fictitiously. Any similarity to real persons, living or dead,
is purely coincidental and not intended by the author.

All brand names and product names used in this book are trademarks,
registered trademarks, or trade names of their respective holders.
Sourcebooks is not associated with any product or vendor in this book.

Published by Sourcebooks Fire, an imprint of Sourcebooks
P.O. Box 4410, Naperville, Illinois 60567–4410
(630) 961-3900
sourcebooks.com

Library of Congress Cataloging-in-Publication data is on file with the publisher.

Printed and bound in Canada.
MBP 10 9 8 7 6 5 4 3 2

To Solaine,

*Fairy godmother to this book, who has
helped me bury plenty of bodies.**

*fictional bodies. Just making that clear.

PART I

TALE
AS
OLD
AS
TIME

CHAPTER ONE

ELLA

The story started with Ella.

    She hadn't thought of it that way when she'd first picked up the fairy tale book last year, the one they now called the Black Book, but she realized it as soon as she explored the pages of its twin, the White Book.

The book's first tale was her own, "Cinderella," in nicely flourished writing. After its last page, there was a ink portrait of herself, Eleanor Ashworth, when she was a little younger than she was now, when her hair wasn't cut short to stay out of the way of cleaning, when there was a faint smudge on her cheek, which could have been ash, or something else, for those who knew better.

She didn't think that her tale being first was relevant. It didn't feel like the story belonged to her.

Yet when she'd opened the White Book, the one Penelope

had held on to, she couldn't help but fixate on this particular thing: The two books were almost exactly the same.

Except the White Book had the portraits.

And the happy endings.

As Christmas came and went, and then the New Year, there was not a single day where Ella did not think of the books hidden away in her friends' rooms in the castle at Grimrose Académie. Finding the White Book had changed everything.

After Ariane had died at the beginning of last year, they'd found the Black Book among her things. It had felt like the key to the mystery of her death. She'd written down a list of names that correlated with the tales in the book, and by the end, Ella, Yuki Nani and Rory had learned that each girl was represented inside—each of them had their fates written in those pages and were doomed to bad endings, unless they could find a way to break the curse.

Yet, on the first day of classes after Christmas break, Grimrose Académie felt as it always had. There was no sense of an imminent threat, no clock striking midnight, no hedge of thorns growing to imprison its students. There was nothing out of the ordinary in Eleanor Ashworth's last semester, though the ordinary was already extraordinary considering she was at an exceptionally exclusive boarding school inside one of the most resplendent castles in Europe.

Ella came in through the front hall, hearing the chatter of her classmates, several "nice to see you" spoken her way. There was no evidence that there had been deaths, plural, in the past year. The school grounds outside were still covered

4

in the relentless snow that buried the woods, the mountains, and the trees in blinding white.

When Ella stopped by a window, she could see the intact surface of the lake.

The memory came in a flash, and Ella swallowed it down, stopped her hands from shaking and losing composure. Blood, the white dress, the snow covering their tracks. Yuki's eyes, dark under the moonlight.

And drowning. Ella felt the choke hold of the lake on the back of her throat, as if it could pull her down if she wasn't careful, as if the black waters were still trying to claim her.

Someone put a hand over her eyes, and Ella jumped, her heart speeding up. She elbowed the person back instinctively.

"Ouch!" Freddie's familiar voice echoed through the hall. "Sorry!"

Ella immediately relaxed, breathing deeply through her nose. This was school, and for now, with Penelope gone, school was safe. There were no impending threats. No messages written in candy wrappers, no dead bodies waiting for them in the corridors.

There was still the curse, but Ella didn't know how to sort that away in a convenient box yet.

Ella looked up at Freddie's bright smile, which she hadn't seen since the ball. She'd told him she couldn't leave home, which was true, but it was more than that: She hadn't wanted to see Grimrose itself. She didn't want to be reminded of what had happened on the last day of school before break.

"What does that say about us, that the first words to

come out of my mouth are an apology?" Freddie said, taking her silence as a cue to keep talking. He leaned in for a kiss, and Ella's heart leapt as she felt the taste of the soft curve of his mouth against her own, something out of a dream. "So. Hello, beautiful."

Ella laughed. "Hello, tall stranger."

"I was expecting 'handsome.' Maybe 'attractive.' I would even accept a 'comely,' but I wouldn't like it a lot."

"I see you've been reading the thesaurus over the holidays."

"Affirmative."

Ella laughed, and Freddie leaned in for another kiss, smiling all the way through it.

"You elbowed me really hard, by the way," Freddie said, good-humoredly. "Didn't know I was dating a trained assassin. I'll be careful not to surprise you in the future."

It was the smallest mention, but Ella faltered, thinking about what happened to Penelope. Maybe she hadn't done the act, maybe she hadn't plunged the knife, but she was part of it all the same. She did it, and the worst part was that Ella wouldn't have changed anything. If Yuki hadn't done it, maybe Ella would have. She couldn't trust herself not to. Not when Ella had done what she did to protect all of them.

Ella promised to save them all, but she'd already started wrong. She hadn't saved Penelope.

She hadn't *wanted* to save Penelope, and now that decision would haunt her forever.

"You okay?" Freddie asked, bringing her back to reality, back to the laughter in the corridors, the swishing of uniform skirts and talks of holiday manors and skiing stations and island vacations and the beginning of the semester. All the students continuing on as if a few of them weren't missing. As if they were already beginning to forget because life went on. It always did.

That was part of the curse. Or maybe it was just normal life. Ella couldn't tell anymore which was which.

"Yes," Ella lied. "I'm fine."

CHAPTER TWO

YUKI

The darkness came mostly while she was sleeping.

It was creeping into Yuki's edges now that she'd let it in, now that her mirrors and perfection had shattered, and all her fears and wants had come spilling out. She'd kept them inside her for so long, afraid of where they might lead. Afraid of what she was capable of.

She knew it now, and the darkness did not let her forget.

It appeared in the shadows, in the broken mirrors, but mostly, it appeared in her sleep as a smile on Penelope's lips, tainted with her blood in the last seconds when Yuki had held her with one arm, and with the other, the knife that had killed her. Somehow, it had felt exactly right. In her dreams, the blood was the color of Yuki's lips.

You asked me what I wanted, Yuki had told her. *I wanted you dead.*

Penelope had smiled before staring into the void ahead of

her. Penelope, whose real name Yuki didn't even know. She'd replaced the real Penelope, taken her life and her belongings. She'd taken everything that the original Penelope had shunned and brought them into her own fairy tale. Except she hadn't gotten a happy ending, not when Yuki's hand had sealed all their fates.

The body of the real Penelope had been found near the train station, identified by the police. But by the time the police arrived at Grimrose to investigate, the girl pretending to be her was long gone. Everyone at school assumed she'd fled as soon as she heard the news, vanishing in the middle of the night without leaving a trace, exactly how she'd first appeared.

When Penelope's blood had been spilled into the lake on the night of the ball, Yuki had felt that it was fair, because Penelope killed Ari, because she'd killed the others and threatened Ella, and most of all, because Penelope had thought she was on Yuki's level.

Yuki could feel power that flowed in her veins. She'd feared it, feared losing control and showing her true self, but it was too late for that fear now—it had dissipated, just like Penelope's plots and manipulations, just like Yuki's illusion that she could still be perfect. She wasn't.

Yuki had killed someone, and she did not regret it.

Yuki knew she wasn't supposed to go back to the lake, but the darkness there seemed to draw her in. They'd promised to keep away, and with the Christmas holidays, Grimrose had been half-empty, since most of the students had gone back to their families. Ella had been shut inside her house, and Rory had gone back to her own castle. In their room at Grimrose, there was only Yuki and the new girl, Nani. Yuki hadn't spent that much time with Nani, though she was undoubtedly a part of their group now: she knew all their secrets and shared their story.

Instead, Yuki had walked around the lake. She'd forgiven Ari for what she'd said, and the ache felt resolved, dulled. Yuki watched out for any cracks in the ice, for any voice that could come back to haunt her, but the lake was always empty, spectral.

I won, she thought to herself, looking down at the thick layer of ice covering the waters. *I'm not afraid anymore.*

And yet, winning felt empty. Winning felt like nothing, because even though Penelope was dead and couldn't threaten them anymore, Yuki knew the threat went far beyond her. She had killed the others in the name of someone else, in the name of gaining *something.* Yuki had to find out what.

All that Yuki and her friends had gained was the White Book and even more questions.

Yuki couldn't deny the curse now, not when everything pointed to it. The ritual, the sudden appearance of her magic, and the things Penelope had said, hinting at a mysterious force behind it all, someone who was responsible for this curse. Penelope's killings had only accelerated the workings of the curse, but Yuki knew she couldn't escape forever.

"Aren't you cold out here?" a voice asked from behind her. Yuki snapped her head around, black hair whipping as her stepmother Reyna approached, huddled inside a black coat with a fur collar, her hands shoved inside her velvet pockets. "It's freezing."

Yuki didn't really feel it. "I'm okay."

Reyna walked forward to stand with her. Yuki knew she should go back upstairs to her room. Classes were starting again—another semester, her last one at Grimrose. She was supposed to do something after that, choose what life she was going to lead. But Yuki didn't know, because all her choices would end up disappointing the people closest to her. She'd grown tired of expectations and legacies. They were a burden she didn't care to carry anymore.

"It's a nice view down here," Reyna said, standing as close to Yuki as she dared, but the distance was always there. "I'm going to miss it."

Yuki turned sharply. "You're leaving?"

"Well, *you're* leaving for college too," Reyna pointed out, serene. "I'm sure we'll figure out our next destination when you make your choice."

Yuki sensed Reyna's big brown eyes examining her face. She didn't let herself hide or falter or turn away. Her heart beat a little faster, the darkness calling to her, knowing she was hiding. Knowing that even though she'd given in to it, Yuki hadn't really showed herself to anyone.

Nobody knew the vastness of it yet.

Nobody knew she was only one blink away from letting it all out.

"You shouldn't leave just because of me," Yuki managed to say. "I'm eighteen now. You don't have to take care of me."

11

"I know," Reyna replied. "But this is the most grown-up I've seen you. It's hard to get used to it."

Reyna shook her head, looking out into the lake. Yuki frowned slightly. Reyna was getting nostalgic. On the day of the ball, she'd seemed sad too.

Even if Reyna didn't realize it, Yuki knew all of it was going to come to an end, sooner or later. They'd have to break the curse, even if Yuki didn't know how.

All Yuki had was her hands, her will, her darkness.

They would have to be enough.

CHAPTER THREE

It was the first time Nani had spent Christmas away from Tūtū.

She'd always stayed with her grandmother in Hawai'i—it was less hot there than in summer, only a little drier than usual. They'd decorate the palm tree of the front garden instead of getting one from the tree barge, and Tūtū would make enough kālua pig and haupia to last them through the entire week. They would sit together outside, eating and watching the lights, hearing the distant music from the neighborhood and the other houses. When she was little, Nani could remember her mother sitting with them, and her father, on occasion, trying to help Tūtū with the pig only to get shooed away with a broomstick.

Christmas in Switzerland was like in the movies: covered in white and so cold Nani couldn't stop shivering, even with all of Rory's borrowed coats. The snow kept falling, and Nani hadn't even dared to step out into the gardens. She'd stayed inside, looking through fogged windows, waiting for classes to return.

Svenja had left the day after the ball. Nani had only seen her briefly after their kiss, and after that she had been too busy with the girls and the rush of that last night of school. Svenja had left her a message saying she'd gone home for the holidays and that they could talk after she returned. Nani's heart seemed to skip a beat every time she picked the note up again, trying to distract herself from more pressing matters.

Such as the fact that, apparently, they really were cursed.

Nani still had a hard time grasping it, even though now she held both books in her hands. Ariane's Black Book with the bad endings, which she had committed to memory last year. Penelope's White Book, with the happy endings and the portraits. Each book a mirror of the other.

She'd seen the portraits in the White Book, but now that she had the library to herself, she examined the pages, taking in every detail that she could memorize. Mephistopheles sat in front of her, his tail flicking from side to side like he was waiting for a moment of weakness to leap. She knew it wasn't a coincidence that most of the girls in the book were students at Grimrose. Maybe it was the castle that had been cursed, but the portraits also showed girls who hadn't set foot there, seemingly too young to be students. It was as if the Book renewed itself with new girls when other girls' tales were finished. Could it also predict the future? Would these girls come to Grimrose and meet their horrible fates? Or were they brought there *because* they were in the book to begin with?

Nani had too many questions, just like always.

Ariane, with the Black Book, couldn't have known the whole truth. She'd only seen the strange coincidences and the unhappy endings. Red Hood swallowed by the wolf, Sleeping Beauty thrown into the pyre. Cinderella with her sister's eyes bleeding raw, pecked out by birds. Macabre, raw, brutal.

The White Book showed a different side of the story. Nani knew the endings hadn't really changed, even if Penelope had hurried some of them along in the name of obtaining Ariane's Black Book for herself. Even if she had killed a few students, it didn't change where their stories were going to lead. It didn't change the fact that they had been doomed from the start.

Like the Black Book, the White Book couldn't be destroyed. Nani had run the same experiments just to be sure. She'd tried burning it, tearing pages, soaking it in the tub, but no matter what she did, there were no signs of damage. Nothing seemed to change at all.

The fairy tales were familiar, but Nani had no clue as to why they'd been chosen to be told over and over again. It was a cycle, that much was clear—the portraits of girls who had died recently, like Ari, were fading into the page, while the new, brighter portraits, in pitch black ink, showed younger girls who couldn't be more than five years old.

She'd faced the portrait of herself: Nani without glasses, Nani without looking like herself. Her cheeks seemed rounder, and she had a book under her arm, ever the book-worm. The title of "Beauty and the Beast" appeared in ample and sinuous calligraphy at the beginning of her tale. Nani had seen the other girls' tales, but when she'd turned to a page with a portrait of Svenja, she slammed the book shut.

Nani hadn't gotten any further than knowing the two books had to be connected and that Penelope had needed them both to buy her way out of some dark bargain she'd made.

"What am I missing?" Nani said out loud, and Mephistopheles' yellow eyes turned to her, his tail swishing against the cushion.

The cat had no answer. Nani didn't know why she should expect one. If Mephistopheles had an answer, she wasn't sure she wanted to pay the price of her soul for it, which is what the cat would ask for. Probably.

"I leave you for two weeks and you start talking to cats," a voice said from the library doorway. "Should I be worried?"

Nani jumped, slamming the books closed, shoving them back into her bag.

Svenja didn't look like she'd gotten much rest during the holidays. She seemed slimmer than before, her shoulder blades bony and her olive skin ashy, her straight dark brown hair falling past her shoulders. Still, there was that enthralling spark in her brown eyes as she watched Nani from the doorway, standing almost six feet apart.

A ridiculous distance, considering the last time they'd seen each other, Nani hadn't hesitated in pulling Svenja to her, kissing her like she meant it, their lips pushing together softly, and their heartbeats echoing the rhythm of the music in the ballroom.

Now there was the silence of the school, and Nani didn't know what to say. Words were tricky. They could define or break something. A kiss was a gesture, and it had been enough at the time, but it couldn't stand on its own.

"I didn't know you were back," Nani said, her voice hoarse.

Svenja raised an eyebrow, nonchalant. "I still go here, last time I checked."

"Yeah," Nani said. "You do."

Nani never wanted to be one of those girls who'd lose her mind over a boy—one of those who couldn't talk about anything besides their crush. Now she realized how arrogant she'd been to think she could be *better* than that. She deserved the punishment of thinking that she was so different, because in the end, she really wasn't.

Nani had pored over the fairy tale books to avoid poring over *this*.

"So, we should talk," Svenja said.

"Yeah," Nani repeated, hating the sound of her voice, the way her cheeks were heating. Svenja grinned, seeming to enjoy watching Nani squirm.

"Are you going to hurry up?" Svenja asked. "I don't want to be late for dinner."

Nani threw her an exasperated look. "I just thought this was going to be a lot easier."

Svenja's eyes narrowed. "Are you breaking up with me?"

"What?" Nani exclaimed. "No, I'm trying to get you to date me."

"I'll date you. You don't have to beg me."

Nani opened her mouth, shut it, then opened it again. She wasn't sure if Svenja was really saying yes or if she was just having a laugh at Nani's expense. Knowing Svenja, it could easily be both.

Svenja bridged the distance, putting a hand under Nani's chin, making her look up from her chair. "Don't tell me you had a speech ready."

"I didn't. But also now I'm considering pretending I never said a thing."

"I have something better than a speech," Svenja said.

And then Svenja's mouth was on hers again, and Nani realized she hadn't imagined that kiss in the winter ball after all and that even her own imagination didn't come close to what this felt like in real life. Svenja's hands held Nani in place, and Nani held her waist, her back pressed against the chair as her face tilted up, a growing heat in her veins and her belly. Even the slightest move of Svenja's tongue inside her mouth making her whole body shiver.

Svenja stepped away from the kiss, and Nani smiled like a fool, curls all over the place, glasses slightly crooked, face burning.

Now, in the library, Nani knew there were a thousand other things she should be thinking about: graduating in six months, the curse, and even her father still missing, still somewhere out in the unknown. However, the only thoughts that seemed to be filling Nani's brain were: girl hot, kissing good.

Svenja lowered herself until she was sitting in Nani's lap, and as Svenja's hands brushed against her neck, her hips, her collarbone, at the height of winter, Nani finally stopped feeling cold.

When the kiss ended, they were both out of breath. Nani's hands were trembling, scared, excited, wanting more, afraid of asking for what she wanted because she didn't know how this could be real.

"I don't know if this was better than my speech," Nani finally managed.

"Nani Eszes," Svenja said with a sigh, before leaning to kiss her again, "you'll be the death of me."

CHAPTER FOUR

ELLA

Ella made it through her morning classes as if she was just another ordinary student, living an ordinary life, and there had been nothing strange happening within the walls of Grimrose Académie. At home, she barely had any time to think, from shoveling the stables, scooping the snow out of the curbside, keeping the garden clean, and cooking and washing and mending and fixing, Sharon's voice always hovering in the background. Ella forgot who she was—what her life in school was. It always worked like that during the holidays because Ella was not really herself at home. She wasn't allowed the time to be anything at all.

It had helped.

It had kept her mind away from her friends, away from the school, away from the curse.

But being back at Grimrose meant she couldn't ignore it any longer. It meant maintaining the promise she had made when she opened the White Book and found a picture of herself staring back.

Ella kept fidgeting with her earrings, tiny stars pierced on her lobes, turning them over and over until she started feeling the metal rub her skin raw. She should have guessed it was going to be like this. The first day of school routine always hit the hardest. She should have taken double her usual dose of meds because there was no way she was going to survive with her anxiety gnawing and slowing down the seconds.

Ella spotted her stepsisters in the cafeteria line, and it felt like déjà vu from last year when Ari was missing from the lunch table. Ella looked over at her usual spot, and yes, Ari wasn't there, but Nani was.

Nani looked up from her book when Ella sat down, one hand holding the fork, another keeping her mystery novel propped on her fingers. "Happy New Year."

"I can't believe it's already the middle of January," Ella said.

"Yep," Nani agreed, chewing her lunch. "Time does fly when you're trying to figure out how to break a possibly ancient curse with magic you weren't sure existed until a month ago."

Ella smiled at Nani's sarcastic tone, glad to be back in some sort of familiar environment. During winter, the cafeteria offered soups, and Ella took a sip out of hers, the taste of sweet onions filling her mouth. She hadn't realized how hungry she was.

Nani's eyes narrowed. "I hate when people tell me anything like this, but you look...you look like you haven't been eating that much."

"I'm fine," Ella mumbled, hoping that her winter clothes—the big sweater she wore over the shirt uniform, the blazer, and everything else—hid how thin she'd gotten over the holidays. "No big deal. So what did Grimrose serve for Christmas dinner?"

"Turkey," Nani answered. "Some other stuff I didn't know. Mrs. Blumstein wore a Santa hat. It was the worst thing I've ever seen."

Even as Nani recounted this, she didn't seem especially ill-tempered. Nani's edges were hard, but Ella had always appreciated honesty, and even Nani's concern, as direct as it was, seemed like a good sign.

"You seem happy," Ella said. Nani looked more settled than she had been last semester. "Did something happen?"

Nani choked on her salad, her skin flushing. "How do you do that?"

"Do what?"

"You do it with Rory all the time," Nani replied, her eyes narrowing through the round lenses. "Like you can guess when she's—"

Ella blinked innocently. "When she's what?"

"Fine, Ella. Yes, Svenja and I are dating."

Ella beamed. She had noticed the glances between Nani and Svenja all semester long. Nani might think she could hide it, but Ella could read it earnestly in her face. "I'm happy you two worked it out. I know you and Rory play on the same team, but I'm glad you didn't end up with Rory's disposition."

"Don't you dare. I've never been in denial like her."

Ella smiled, ignoring her stomach's loud protesting as she downed her lunch. She looked around until she spotted Yuki's dark hair in the crowd. She was a full head taller than any of the girls in school and looked as pale as the snow on the roof of the castle.

"Hey," Yuki said, when she finally down.

Ella watched her best friend eat her lunch, trying to pick up on any sign of uneasiness. Ella's eyes kept wandering back to the lake, and she wondered whether Yuki's did the same. But Yuki's hands were steady. Yuki's hands didn't falter.

And that, somehow, relaxed Ella. If Yuki was fine, then Ella had to be fine.

That was the way of the world.

Ella took a deep breath, and then frowned at the empty spot beside her at the table. "Where's Rory?"

"Doesn't she have Latin first period with you?" Yuki asked Ella.

"Yes, but I thought she'd slept in," Ella replied, getting a sense of something wrong, her anxiety spiking. "But you did see her?"

"I left the room too early this morning," Yuki said. "I didn't see if she was back."

"Maybe her schedule was changed this semester?" Nani asked, her gaze flickering between the other two.

"You mean she didn't arrive last night?" Ella insisted, her voice pointed. "Or on Saturday?"

Nani shook her head. "No, her part of the room is surprisingly clean. If she'd arrived, I'd say we'd get at least the pile of clothes back in place."

"You mean the floor," Yuki corrected. "So she didn't return?"

Ella was already getting up. Her heart was beating faster now, and even though she knew it couldn't be something that terrible, even though the world wouldn't allow something of the kind to happen so soon, Ella still couldn't stop her mind from wandering to the worst, prickling at her edges, imagining devastating outcomes.

Ella got to the room first, Yuki and Nani catching up behind her. When Yuki opened the door, Ella's hands trembled and her breath hitched. Yuki's side of the room was tidy like always, Nani's side had a pile of open books, but on Rory's side, the bed was still miraculously made.

There was no sign of Rory Derosiers anywhere.

"So," Nani finally said, "where the hell is she?"

CHAPTER FIVE

RORY

Rory was supposed to have been back at Grimrose a week ago.

She was supposed to be in class, and no matter how much she hated classes, she was supposed to be *there*, and not *here*. Not stuck inside the castle walls.

Not stuck inside the castle walls, absolutely on *fucking* purpose.

When the door opened, Rory almost jumped as Éveline strode inside. Rory's room at home was four times as big as the bedroom at Grimrose. She had a private closet, a private bathroom with a bathtub the size of a double bed, a bed that could easily fit five people, a veranda where she could look at the gardens with an unobstructed view, and anything a person could ask for.

Anything but a phone, or a computer, or something she could use to get a message out to her friends.

Rory had gotten to the point of wondering whether she could capture one of the vagrant pigeons on the roof and train it into sending a note.

Rory didn't bother getting up from the bed, still in her pajamas. "Greetings, kidnapper," Rory said as way of hello.

Éveline rolled her eyes, walking over to the curtains and throwing them open to Rory's utter horror, blue eyes straining against the sunlight. "Good morning, Aurore."

"To you," Rory muttered under her breath. She checked the door. Éveline had come in, but the door had already been closed behind her, the security posted in case Rory decided to escape.

Again.

First, she had tried the front door, where she'd managed to put ten security guards on her tail, outrunning them all until her right knee gave in, and then her whole body had collapsed on itself.

The second time she went through the veranda, where she'd torn three Chanel dresses and tied them together like a rope to get to the garden—Coco Chanel had been a goddamned Nazi, anyway, good riddance—and she'd managed to get to the inner gates before Éveline dragged her back.

The third time, she'd faked a pain crisis. The doctor had come in, told the others to fetch supplies, and she'd gotten past the old buffoon as soon as he turned his back. Her pain wasn't made up—she was just used to it by now, and she knew how to take charge of it.

They changed the guards. Doubled the security. Rory didn't get cameras in her room, but it didn't make a difference.

They were all watching her. They were under strict orders to not let her out of their sight. To not let her out under any circumstances. Even prison wasn't as secure as Rory's room in the country estate.

"How are you today?" Éveline asked, leaning down against Rory's antique writing desk, which Rory never used.

"I would like to go for a run," Rory said.

"You know this isn't allowed yet."

"I would also enjoy going back to school," she said, her whole face grimacing as she forced the words out. "You have no idea how painful it is for me to say that."

"Actually, I have good news," Éveline said, and Rory sat up immediately, running her fingers through her cropped red hair. Her parents hadn't commented on it, but that would have required that they look at their daughter for more than five minutes, which seemed like too much to hope for. She'd fixed it, at least. Shaved off the sides, leaving the red waves only for her bangs and a bit on top. The hairdresser had come in from the capital and muttered under her breath the entire time about the cut. "We're already in contact with Grimrose, and you can take your tests here. Mrs. Blumstein kindly offered to send the content you've been missing."

"And have you told her the reason why I'll be missing it?" Rory asked, though she didn't know why she'd bothered.

Rory had gone home for Christmas, and the next day, her parents had sent her away to their other estate, and she hadn't been allowed to leave since. She didn't know if it was because of the fencing tournament, or because she'd flipped off Éveline last time, or because her parents had finally seemed to catch up with the news that girls had been dying at Grimrose.

They had decided, for her safety, that she couldn't leave the house.

Rory wished she could say she was surprised, but her parents were middle-aged white Europeans, so they were as unsurprising as people could possibly be. Still, she couldn't help but think of her own stupidity.

If only she had signed up for the tournament without telling them. If only she hadn't come back home. If only, if only, if only.

Rory's life was a big string of 'if onlys,' and she collected them like the fencing bruises on her body.

"It's only six more months of school," Éveline said simply. "It wouldn't have made much of a difference."

"It would have made all the difference in the world," Rory spit back. "Only you and my parents can't see that."

"You're safe here, Aurore," Éveline said. "After all that's happened, and with your eighteenth birthday coming soon. You'll have to take on more responsibilities."

"I can't do that if I'm locked up here," Rory said, and there was no argument against it. It infuriated her that it was the only solution they offered. If Rory was in danger, the best thing to do was to send her away. Keep her isolated, far away from anyone who could ever care about her.

Her parents wanted her to uphold their values, to represent them properly, and yet, she hadn't spent more than a week with them in her life because she was always being sent away. Always having to pretend she wasn't who she was.

She had stopped wanting to please them. She thought she couldn't stop living her life just because they wanted her to.

But of course they could stop her. They could keep her locked up inside her own house.

"As soon as we know you've adapted, we can start discussing new subjects," Éveline said distractedly, rearranging the papers on Rory's desk. Éveline's cell phone beeped, and she looked at the notification before setting it on the desk.

Rory saw the opportunity. She wasn't going to get a clearer sign than that.

She got up from the bed, yawning. "Okay, so what if I've adapted? You could give me my phone back."

"We're changing the communication system at the palace. You can't have anything until we've run through all the protocols."

"And even then, communications will be monitored," Rory muttered, inching closer to Éveline's phone, then sitting her butt right on top of it. Éveline didn't bother contradicting what she knew to be true.

"Aurore—" Éveline started, but Rory shook her head. "Rory. I'm not doing this to hurt you. We're doing what's best for you. What's best for everyone."

Éveline reached out a hand to tuck a wayward strand of Rory's hair out of the way, like a kindly, concerned parent.

Except Éveline was not her mother. Rory's mother wasn't here because she had delegated all motherhood duties to somebody else, after Rory had changed schools and changed names. And in the end, all of that had changed nothing at all.

29

"Get out," Rory said.

"I—"

"Get out!" Rory shouted, and the scream reverberated through the gigantic walls of her prison, echoing among the masterworks of renowned Dutch painters, couture clothing, and custom jewelry, among riches that Rory didn't care to name or have.

Éveline took back her hand, flinching, then straightened her shoulders.

"I'll be back with your lunch and your medicine," Éveline said. "We'll talk when you're feeling better."

The door opened, and Rory spotted the security guard's hands as they closed the door behind Éveline. She heard the lock click shut.

Éveline's phone was still on the table where she'd left it, underneath where Rory had sat. Rory couldn't believe her luck.

She had no time to lose.

She could only send one message, as Rory had never really bothered to learn any phone numbers. It was extremely embarrassing that there was only one she could recite by heart. Ella would never let her hear the end of it. Rory hated that she couldn't do this on her own.

Still, she didn't have a choice.

She typed the number and sent the message, then she wiped all evidence from the phone's history. To really drive the point home, she smashed the phone as hard as she could on the floor and waited for her rescue.

CHAPTER SIX

NANI

Rory didn't come back that first week, nor could they find a way to talk to her. Her phone went straight to voicemail. Their messages arrived, but the girls never got check marks to confirm they'd been read.

Last thing they'd heard from her was that she was at home with her parents—at least, that's all Nani knew because Yuki and Ella were always evasive when she asked about Rory's family. Nani could trouble herself with more research, but at this school, everyone had an important family, and Nani refused to let any rich person's business waste her time, not when she had other things to be troubled about.

Things that were surprisingly easy to forget, as Svenja was taking over every spare minute of Nani's life. Not that Nani minded, not when she didn't want to think of the curse or her own family at all. She also had the growing feeling, like thorns in her heart, that she was leaving her father behind, even when he'd given her the adventure he'd promised.

She couldn't help it. She'd examined her friends' lives against their tales, and it was so easy to see how they fit: Yuki, the most beautiful girl in school and her equally stunning stepmother, fit well into Snow White. Ella and her stepsisters—working at home endlessly made her story obvious. Rory and whatever her family was, trying to hide their daughter like she was a secret, like her life was in constant danger from perilous strangers.

But Nani was only a girl sent to a faraway place, and the tale meant nothing to her. She'd found a secret inside the castle, but not a monster. She had no idea how that fit with her tale at all.

Svenja made it easy to forget the castle was a prison with elegant walls. Their hands met in corridors after class; they pulled each other into dark passageways or empty bathroom stalls for kisses that made Nani's spine tingle, and there was the undercurrent of thrill that never ceased when they hid without really trying to hide.

Svenja had walked Nani to her room that evening, and Nani felt her heart flutter at every step they took, at the rush that persisted, because Svenja didn't ask for anything besides what they were doing right now.

They stopped together at Nani's door, Svenja's hands lingering against her waist. Nani half-heartedly checked to see no one else in the corridor. Their gazes locked, Svenja's breath soft against her cheek as she kissed Nani. It was like the first time all over again, Nani's toes tingling as their breaths commingled, as they spent long minutes together that only felt like seconds.

"I have to go," Nani said, her smile persisting even after the kiss was finished.

Svenja sighed, leaning her head against Nani's shoulder, the two of them embracing. Nani could feel Svenja's arm wrapped around her waist, her cheekbone grazing her neck. Every part of Nani touching Svenja felt like a bolt of lightning. Svenja breathed against her neck, kissed it lightly, and Nani's breath hitched.

"I have homework," Nani argued, only for the sake of it, because Svenja's hand was still against the back of her neck, half her body against the wall. "And if a teacher catches us..."

Svenja smirked. "I can take a 'Miss Niytrai, what is the meaning of this?' to get a few more minutes with you."

"Detention exists, Svenja."

"And? We'll both be in it together."

Nani adjusted her crooked glasses, her face burning. "You'll see me tomorrow."

Nani kissed Svenja again, finding her way quick into the room and closing the door, her heart in a haze.

"Oh, joy," Yuki said without looking up from her bed, where she was idly doing her chemistry homework. "I thought you were never coming inside."

Nani's embarrassment doubled; her pulse quickened. "I didn't know you were listening."

"I don't have a choice," Yuki said, lips wrinkling slightly in distaste. "You're obnoxiously loud."

Nani's face burned even more as she went to her bed, picking up her things so she could hide in the shower. "Are you always like that?"

"Like what?" Yuki asked, raising a single black eyebrow, her face impassive. "Pleasant?"

Nani snorted, and there was a shadow of a grin from Yuki, something that hadn't quite learned to turn into a full smile. Nani had watched Yuki carefully, from afar. Her tongue was as razor-sharp as her wits, but there was almost never any real enjoyment behind it.

But now there were those moments when it sparked, as if all this time, Yuki had been keeping herself far away, contained, and now, she was free.

"I was going to say like an asshole," Nani replied.

This time, Yuki's grin was real, her teeth flashing white. Nani felt a sense of eeriness, of the kind of warning in stories that she'd been so keen to pick out. She repressed a shudder.

Nani understood Ella. She understood Rory. They were the easy ones, the ones who held their hearts open like a book for her to read. Yuki was a book in the forbidden library section, in a dead language, written in an alphabet Nani didn't even know how to begin to decipher.

But still, Yuki was her friend. Wasn't she?

"Have you heard anything from Rory?" Nani asked, changing the subject.

Yuki shook her head, closing her homework, sitting tall on her bed. "Not yet. Ella sent her a letter."

"You mean an actual letter? By post? Like a caveman?"

Yuki snorted in response. "It returned unopened."

"That isn't a good sign."

"Nothing is a good sign," Yuki replied, and for the first time since the night of the ball, she looked tired.

Nani's memory was usually good, but that night was still a haze. She couldn't believe that she'd kissed Svenja the same night Penelope had been murdered. She couldn't believe that all of it had culminated at the same point, that her life had been changed forever.

Sometimes, Nani thought she had imagined all of it.

But Yuki was there, and Penelope was dead, and Yuki seemed...seemed more herself, even if Nani didn't really know what she was like before. She didn't know how to begin to unravel the girl who shared a room with her.

Thankfully, someone knocked before Yuki noticed her staring, and Nani jumped up to answer, running to the door. She opened it, expecting to see Svenja again, but instead there was another girl who Nani didn't know, but who she couldn't mistake. Her skin was a deep dark brown, and her eyes were equally dark, curls tied back into a single French braid, and her defined muscles were visible underneath her uniform shirt.

"Sorry to come over like this," the girl said. Nani didn't speak, and Yuki raised her head from the bed, peeking through the door. "You probably don't even know who I am, but—"

"Pippa," Nani and Yuki said in unison.

Pippa blinked. Her eyes darted inside the room. "Er.

35

Okay. Cool. I wanted to ask if you guys knew anything about Rory. Huh, I know we don't have practice until the teacher returns, but you know how Rory is, she'd forget. She wasn't in the training room when I checked, and I haven't seen her all week."

Concern was clear on Pippa's face, her thick eyebrows knitted in an elegant frown, her full lips slightly parted. Nani suddenly understood the attraction that Rory had been desperately trying to deny.

"We haven't heard from her either," Nani finally said, remembering her words.

"Do you think something happened?" Pippa asked. "She'd say something, right? She literally never shuts up. I mean. Don't tell her I said that." She laughed, shifting awkwardly, and Nani could guess she was blushing if it wasn't for her dark skin. "All I got from her was a message."

Yuki immediately got up and leaned against the door, peering over Nani's shoulder. "A message?"

Pippa nodded, looking up at Yuki. Pippa was a little taller than Nani, and consequently, a little taller than Rory, but she didn't come even close to Yuki's height. "It wasn't from her number, but it was signed by her."

"What did it say?" Nani asked.

"That she's fine," Pippa said, and Nani and Yuki exchanged a look.

"That's all?" Yuki pressed.

"She said hi, and that she wanted me to thank Ella for the book recommendation," Pippa said, voice filling with uncertainty. "Does that mean anything? I couldn't text the number back, I was blocked already for some reason."

"Oh, God," Yuki muttered, closing her eyes.

"Is it that bad?" Pippa asked, alarmed.

"Yes," Nani replied, catching on immediately. "I think we have to go get her."

CHAPTER SEVEN

ELLA

Ella didn't know how they'd ended up, the three of them plus Pippa driving, at a small roadside cabin along the border of Germany, praying for Yuki's GPS to work again, the weekend following Rory's message.

"Actually, I know," Ella snapped irritably, looking up. "We're lost."

"We're not lost," Nani replied. "It's only a miscalculation. Besides, you can't get lost in Europe. It's like getting lost in a kiddie pool. Each country takes only three hours to drive through."

Pippa walked out of the cabin holding four hot chocolates. They'd only stopped to ask someone for directions, but Ella was glad for the chocolate too. Pippa looked composed, even though Ella and the other girls had given her little time to consider their plan and hadn't waited for a positive reply before putting it into motion.

Ella had stolen the keys to her stepmother's car. Sharon thought she'd misplaced them and decided to go away for the weekend by train, taking Ella's stepsisters with her.

The problem was that Ella didn't know how to drive, and neither did Yuki—in Europe they technically had to wait till they were eighteen, and Nani only rode a bike back in Honolulu.

So Pippa was the only one who could drive them.

"Any luck?" Pippa asked.

"No," Ella muttered, the cold starting to bite at her toes. She took the hot chocolate gladly. "I mean, technically, we know where the place is, and they did tell us it was the right road."

Pippa rose an eyebrow.

"Found it," Yuki said in her low-pitched voice, her words accompanied by her breath turning to mist in the air. "I told you we weren't lost."

"Fine, then," Pippa said. "Give me the directions. How far away are we?"

"About an hour," Yuki said, shoving her phone in her pocket again. "Just need to follow the small road through the mountain path."

They got back into the car, and Ella was glad for its warmth. The car was relatively new—Sharon had bought it only two years ago, and its seats were impeccable. Ella kept glancing at the details, calculating to the smallest fractions, checking the gas, the lights, the mirrors. Ella hoped that Sharon wasn't going to look at the mileage, but if she did, Ella was ready to come up with a lie, or worse, face the consequences.

Pippa drove with an ease that Ella envied. She'd never really wanted to learn how to drive because it would surely be another thing to make her nervous. All the small rituals like checking the mirrors would make her easily fall into loops. It's how her mind worked, and she'd learned to ward herself against it.

But even with the snow starting, Pippa looked relaxed. Relaxed but attentive, her eyes never leaving the road as the car followed the winding path through the mountains. Germany and Switzerland were a lot different than England. Here, the winding mountain path went through the forests, through towns that hadn't changed since the twelfth century. Sometimes Ella spotted a smoke trail making its way above the mountain, as if it came from a witch's cabin.

The thought made her shiver.

"How did you learn how to drive?" Ella asked, trying to push the intrusive thoughts away.

"Me?" Pippa asked, checking on Ella through the rear-view mirror. Ella and Nani were sharing the back while Yuki was up front, her head resting against the window. "My dad taught me, summer vacation last year. He was tired of being the designated driver at parties." Pippa didn't particularly seek out conversation, but she seemed comfortable around the three of them.

When Yuki had told Ella about Rory's the message the next morning, Ella had understood the meaning. It was something that Ari had come up with, back in the first year they'd all met. Ari joked that if Rory ever said she was reading a book, it would be a secret call for help. Everyone who really knew Rory knew she wouldn't willingly pick up a book by herself.

Pippa drove quietly for almost an hour, but the snow was getting heavier, the flakes dropping with more frequency, the visibility starting to diminish. If it went on for much longer, they'd have to stop. Pippa shifted in the driver's seat, fingers gripping the wheel tighter.

"It's getting worse," Nani commented.

"Yeah," Yuki said.

"Can't you make it stop?" asked Nani.

Yuki gave her a wry look from the front seat.

"Do you know a magic spell that makes it stop snowing?" Pippa asked, eyebrows raised in question. "If you do, now's the time."

Ella gave Nani a nudge, who rolled her eyes. Yuki didn't bother answering.

"How are we going to know when we arrive?" Pippa asked, glancing sideways at Yuki. "You said there wasn't a real address."

"We'll know when we get there," Yuki said simply, in a way that made Ella want to hit her on the head. She was being obnoxious on purpose.

"How?" Pippa insisted.

Just as she asked it, the car curved around another bend in the road, and it was right there for all of them to see.

A palace rose out from the lower fields, beyond the forests and the mountains. There was an iron gate at the front, the trees almost bare from the winter. Only the pines still stood green, but the view was no less magnificent. The front of the palace rose elegantly, and there were over forty windows on the façade. The palace could be mistaken for an absurdly large house, but Ella knew exactly what she was seeing.

"There," Yuki said.

Pippa opened her mouth only to shut it again. The palace grew bigger as they approached, and Ella now realized that they were going to have to go inside to fetch Rory. That they had come out all this way for Rory without even second guessing, without even wondering if they should come, just because she'd given them a message. They hadn't hesitated.

Pippa didn't stop the car, even though the other girls hadn't told her what to expect. They'd asked for her trust, and she had given it to them.

Pippa trusted Rory, Ella realized.

"Do we have a plan?" Pippa asked, her voice even.

Ella looked at her friends.

"Yes," said Yuki. "Here's what we're going to do."

CHAPTER EIGHT

YUKI

Their plan wasn't great, but Yuki didn't have anything else. Yuki wasn't a mastermind criminal. She didn't know how to break into a palace filled with security. She didn't know how to distract the guards so that Rory could get out.

However, she was a bored teenage girl. A bored teenage girl with magical powers.

"Main entrance is open," Ella said, observing it from where they'd parked the car, the closest they dared to. "Would it be open to visitors?"

Yuki shook her head. If Rory was there, that meant the rest of the palace had to be closed; her parents wouldn't risk her safety. This was the country estate, much smaller and less impressive, according to Rory, even if it did have about forty different rooms.

"We have to find out where Rory's room is," Nani said.

"Probably not at the front," Yuki replied, examining the

palace. They weren't far enough away that they could go unnoticed for much longer. She turned around. "Pippa, take the car around to the back once we give you the signal. Rory will probably be trying to run if she sees us coming. Find her and get out."

Pippa blinked, looking uncertain for the first time. "You guys know for sure what you're doing?"

Yuki didn't, but she wasn't about to admit to it. She felt the snow all around her, and power jumped like an electric current through her bloodstream.

"Hide," Yuki ordered, and Pippa did, running for the back of the trees, staying hidden in her white clothes amongst the snow.

Yuki took a deep breath.

"Just so I'm caught up," Nani started, pushing her glasses back farther on her nose, the lenses slightly foggy because of the cold, "how many international laws are we breaking here?"

"A few," Ella replied. "But if it all goes well, we get pardoned."

Nani clicked her tongue against the roof of her mouth. "And if it doesn't?"

Yuki and Ella exchanged a look, but Yuki was glad to see Ella didn't falter.

"Okay, great," Nani said. "I'm so glad we had this conversation."

"They're coming," Ella said, and suddenly, the three girls were quiet.

Two security guards came in their direction, from the gates toward the road. Yuki was sure the security in the palace had more scrutiny than this, but this was also a remote

44

enough place that there wouldn't be many more guards. They didn't want to draw attention.

Yuki laid a hand against the front of the car, and once her fingers touched the metal, it grew cold, the freezing ice spreading through layers of the car.

Ella looked slightly concerned. "You sure it's going to work later?"

"It has to," Yuki answered.

She took her fingers off the car as soon as the two men approached, seeming less suspicious as they observed three teenage girls looking especially lost. The power in Yuki's blood continued to pulse inside her, a comforting rhythm that she'd learned to pay attention to. It didn't vanish like before, burning away in a single outburst of feelings; instead it was steady, constant. Now that she'd learned to accept it, learned what it meant, it was always present. A layer beneath her own mask, ready to spark.

"Hello," the first guard who approached them greeted in French. They were dressed for outdoor duty. "Can we help?"

"Hi, sorry," Ella said, in English, in a terrible exaggeration of an American accent that made Yuki groan inwardly. "Our car just broke down. It's all the ice, I guess? The motor just went cold. Like. Out of nowhere."

"What's the closest city nearby?" Nani asked. "I don't even know where we are."

Yuki waved her phone in the air, as if she was trying to get a good signal. The guards took a step closer, saw the car, the thin layer of ice covering its hood.

45

"Whoa, you've run into quite the storm," the second guard, a bearded one, said in a strong accent, but very clearly.

"We've just outrun it, but the car didn't last," Nani said smoothly. "Do you have a phone we can use? I have the insurance number for when the car breaks down."

The guards exchanged a quick look between them, and Yuki waited, her muscles tense, feeling her feet sink down into the snow.

"I think we can just jump start the car," the guards said. "You girls can stay inside while we take care of this."

"Oh, thaaaank you," Ella said with a big smile, and Yuki kicked her. "Really, it's so cold. I didn't know we could get lost like that. There's *literally* no one around."

Yuki kicked her again, and Ella coughed. Nani gave them both a piercing look.

"This shouldn't give you too much trouble," the first guard said, looking over at the car. "Half an hour to make sure the motor keeps running in the cold. Follow us, miss."

Half an hour should be their window. Yuki walked behind the girls and the guards, and when they were already a few paces ahead, she stopped. "Shit. I forgot the meds in the car."

"Again?" Nani said, her face serene.

Yuki rolled her eyes. "I'll be back in a few."

With the guards' backs still turned to the car, Yuki ran back, her fingers already working their magic. She could feel the coldness of the snow, and she could reach it, which meant she could also undo it. She touched the car, and the ice melted away like it was never there.

She found Pippa's eyes through the woods, and gave her a small nod, and then Yuki ran back to join back the girls. Now all Pippa had to do was drive the car to the back of the palace. They'd take care of the rest. She hoped Rory would see what they were doing.

Ella and Nani played their part in conversation with the guards, complaining about the weather, telling the guards effusively how sorry they were to bother them, and meanwhile, Yuki scanned the woods, the mountains, the palace.

There were more guards out there, she knew. They'd be patrolling the grounds. There were more cameras, more personnel. There was a lot more to this place than met the eye, but the same could be said for Yuki.

She felt it pulsing, the darkness, just beneath her fingers, begging to be let out again. Begging to be wanted, begging to be free.

The girls were led through the back door, the warmth of the palace greeting them. The small room led into the kitchen, and Nani tiptoed over to try to look inside, eyes moving curiously.

"Wait here," one of the guards said. Both guards left through another door, leaving the three girls unattended but unable to go farther into the palace. There was a pitcher of water on a table in the room, and Ella reached out to fill a glass.

Yuki texted Pippa and received confirmation that Pippa was driving to the back. Yuki didn't know how long the guards would take, but all the girls had to do was keep everyone busy and not let them back near the car.

"Are we going to talk about this?" asked Nani, casually leaning against the table.

"About what?" Ella asked.

"About Rory being royalty," Nani said.

Ella spluttered out the water she was drinking. "Pardon?"

"I may be gay, but I can do basic math," Nani deadpanned. "I know Rory's full of weird, wealthy secrets. I know we're not in Switzerland anymore. Or Germany, or France."

"Right. You're right in between," Ella said. "Another country altogether."

"God" was the only thing Nani said. "So many kingdoms. Europe is so stupid."

"That's something an American would say," Ella pointed out.

Nani gave her the finger. "I'm Hawaiian."

"Besides, this is not a real kingdom," Ella continued. "It's a principality."

"What's the difference?"

"None," Yuki replied. "It's just a synonym for monarchy."

"Great. How are death penalties over here? I'm guessing they aren't going to let us off with a warning for kidnapping the princess."

"It's your lucky day," Yuki said with a small smile, looking out at the door. "If you're going to commit crimes, might as well make them big."

Nani sighed, crossing her arms, and Yuki kept smiling. Her heart was beating faster in her chest, amazed that she'd gotten this far, that their plan only had to be simple to work. That they didn't even have to make a real effort.

Then, of course, the guards showed up again, more quickly than she could imagine, jumper cables in hand.

"This is going to be pretty quick work," the first one said, smiling straight at Yuki, and her own smile crumpled. "You girls can stay here in the warmth. We'll be back."

"Wait!" Nani exclaimed, before they could turn around to leave.

The girls knew Pippa was already in the car, driving it closer to the back. Yuki had said she was going to distract the guards. She had to come up with something big.

"Don't you need the keys?" Nani said.

"Well, yes," the second guard said. "You have them with you, I believe?"

Both guards looked at Yuki, and she drew a blank.

"I'd better come with you," Yuki finally said, trying to keep her voice even, each heartbeat more demanding inside her chest.

The guards looked at her, and she could tell that they were wondering if Yuki and her friends were more than just three lost girls with a broken car in the middle of a snowstorm.

Now that she'd spoken to the guards, her bloodstream seemed to pulse harder. She'd thought she needed to train this thing inside her, to control it, to tame it, but it was not made to be tamed. It worked in tandem with Yuki's heart, with her feelings, and there was no holding it back.

There was no need to train her powers—training was for those who didn't know themselves.

For Yuki, it was in her own heart from the moment she'd

accepted it. From the moment she realized she was not letting anything get in the way of what she wanted. That she
could have anything in the world if she only believed in it.

And Yuki *believed* in it.

"Here," Yuki said, taking out her keys and handing them
to the guards, hoping they wouldn't notice that it wasn't the
actual car keys. "Just be careful. The storm looks like it's
coming back."

The guards turned their backs, and Nani gestured to Yuki
wildly, like she was about to ruin the whole plan, like she
didn't know what she had to do.

Yuki knew what she could do.

She could call in the darkness. She could call in the storm.

"Yuki, what..." Ella's whisper found her, and Yuki turned
to her, already feeling half of herself lost to the power.

Ella shut her mouth, her jaw tight. There were words
still unspoken between them, but Ella didn't stop her. Even
if she knew what Yuki was about to do, she didn't take a step
forward.

Yuki turned her back to the door, and then she let all her
power pour out.

CHAPTER NINE

RORY

The storm came out of nowhere.

One moment, it was quiet, and then Rory heard it: a thunderous sound, like the clouds were being cleaved open by sheer force. It seemed to shake the palace like an earthquake, the crystal chandeliers rattling. She heard the commotion of the guards outside, running to the veranda door to check what was happening.

The snowstorm was covering everything. Rory couldn't see the gardens or the mountains and trees that were there a moment before. Now there was only tempest and cold and ice, all wrapped together in a snowstorm with no certain origin.

Except that, somehow, Rory knew what this was. She had felt the taste of this magic before, that night of the ritual, the night of the winter ball. The bite was electric, a thing that was sweet but heavy, dizzying her brain. She recognized it, and beneath the icy storm was the scent of Yuki's perfume, nutmeg and almond blossom, twisted into it until it became almost acidic.

They were here. They had come for her.

The wind shook the panels of the balcony doors, and Rory yelped as they banged against the room, the storm forcing its way inside. She couldn't see the garden ahead; she couldn't even see more than a meter in front of her nose. Everything was blurry and white. The curtains started billowing and knocked one of the ancient china plates off the wall. It broke with a shatter, and the door of her room blasted open.

"Your Highness!" the guard exclaimed. "Are you all right?"

"I can't close the door," Rory stammered as the storm seemed to get more violent. The guards both rushed to the veranda and the open door. Rory picked up a scarf from her dressing table, and when the wind caught it, she let it go. "My scarf!"

The guards, overwhelmed by the suddenness of the storm, watched the pink scarf blow out the door. Both ran after it at once onto the veranda, and luck smiled on her. Without hesitation, Rory took all her strength and closed the veranda doors, turning the lock.

The storm wouldn't last long, and it would probably break all the windows if it didn't stop. She picked up her bag and gathered a few of her things. There was nothing in this room that felt truly hers. She slung the bag over her shoulder and ran out into the corridor before the guards managed to break the veranda door down.

The corridor didn't have any windows, but Rory could still hear the storm—a thunderous fury, snow beating against the roof and the walls of the palace. Rory didn't look back. As she ran down the corridor, she checked for more guards, more security. They must have been busy with the sudden blizzard, locking up windows and doors, making sure nothing precious got broken. Out of all the things in the palace, Rory was the most secure, so she'd be the last to be checked on.

She couldn't escape through the front door; too risky. Guards were posted at the main entrance, but she might be able to go out through the library on the first floor. The library with books no one ever read, books that her ancestors had shoved into the walls, never bothering to even check the titles. Rory wished she could be smarter than she really was, better than she really was, so she could crack the spine of at least one of them.

The palace had grown cold. The storm was still deafening. She'd made it down three flights, moving through the stairwells and corridors filled with family portraits, antiques stolen or bartered from countries that did not own them, ancient china vases that were gifts from other royalty. Rory had almost reached the library when she saw a shadow move across the corridor.

A guard.

She was so close. She could get out of there, meet her friends, and then they could all go back to school, and even though Rory would have things to worry about that she did not in fact want to worry about, she would at least be in the right place. Not here. Not in this prison.

Rory checked the floor, closer to the stairs, and she picked one of the golden fireplace pokers off the nearest wall. The good thing about the guards was that their job was basically to do the opposite of hitting her, so she had the advantage. She picked the poker up silently, her muscles fueled with adrenaline, her grip tight, and she crept silently toward the shadow of the figure who stood between her and the way out.

Rory attacked, but the person was fast—faster than any of the guards. Her blow was stopped midstroke, and they stood, arm poised, holding a goddamned sword taken right off the palace walls, graceful and straight-backed and stunning. Rory let go of her poker and it clattered to the ground.

"It's—it's you."

Pippa Braxton smiled at Rory, her brown eyes filled with warmth. Rory couldn't say anything for a few moments. She forgot the storm outside. She forgot the palace. She forgot everything but Pippa, right in front of her.

And then realized that Pippa had no idea who she really was.

The thought struck her worse than the storm, and Rory knew that they had to get out, fast. Pippa was not allowed to get farther inside the castle. Rory didn't know what would happen if Pippa truly understood.

"You needed help," Pippa answered. "So I came."

Rory scowled, her heart beating nervously, and she looked behind her to see if anyone was coming. "I don't need rescuing."

"A likely story." Pippa gestured vaguely to the poker on the floor, and Rory hated how all of this looked. It had to have been Ella's idea to come. Why would they bring Pippa along? Rory was going to murder Ella and throw her body in the lake.

She immediately regretted the thought, remembering the very real body at the bottom of the lake that they'd put there at the end of last year.

"Now's not the time to argue," Rory said, turning toward the library and gesturing for Pippa to follow. "How did you all arrive?"

"We have the car waiting," Pippa said.

"Who the hell is driving?"

"Me," Pippa answered. "I don't think we can go out that way—"

"Come on," Rory said, and without thinking, she took Pippa's hand.

Every step of the way, Rory thought of how Pippa's hand felt. The way her fingers were shorter than Rory's, rounder, even if Pippa was taller. Her skin was soft, and even though Rory's palm was sweaty, Pippa didn't let go. Rory took them through the library to a passageway that led directly to the lower rooms of the palace and the door outside.

The storm in Rory's ears was nothing compared to the beating of her heart. "What's the plan?" she asked Pippa.

"I need to get the car back up front and pick the girls up," Pippa said. "We used it as an excuse for stopping here. We told the guards it had broken down."

Pippa left the last bit hanging, as if waiting to see if Rory would explain the guards, but Rory didn't. She knew the price of her secret. She knew the price Pippa would pay if she knew too, and she didn't want to give that burden to her. No, it wasn't a want: Rory would not *allow* Pippa to suffer through that.

Rory's secret bound her to the family, to these estates, to this country, to things that had been hers even before she was born. She belonged to this secret more than anything had ever belonged to her.

Anything, except maybe Pippa.

Rory found the door to the outside and opened it. She couldn't see anything except for the snow still blowing. Pippa looked concerned as she surveyed the storm, and Rory couldn't imagine what she was really feeling, or why she'd even chosen to come. Rory had texted Pippa because it was the only number she knew, the only number she'd clicked on her phone more than a hundred times. It was seared into the back of her eyes. She could recite it in her sleep, knocked unconscious, her lips forming the numbers that led her to the other end, that led her to Pippa.

"This is the way out," Rory said, her voice calm. The storm was roaring, but Rory paid no attention to it. She only looked at Pippa.

She made a list of all the things she wanted to say. Kept the list a secret and her lips tightly closed because she couldn't open her mouth.

"All right," said Pippa.

Pippa stepped out into the storm first, but she didn't let go of Rory's hand.

CHAPTER TEN

ELLA

The winds battered the palace until the windows shattered.

Ella stood in the doorway of the palace's back entrance and heard the commotion inside as if it were miles away. Guards and servants were shouting, roaring instructions from the kitchen and elsewhere. The impossible storm was raging, cold and ice rolling in the air. Yuki stood outside, her arms open and eyes closed, because she was the cause of all of it.

Ella and Nani stayed in the doorway, hovering, waiting.

"It's time," Nani said, looking at her phone.

Yuki kept her eyes closed, and the storm only seemed to grow louder.

"Pippa gave us the okay," Nani called again, louder. "Yuki, are you even listening to me?"

Nani stepped forward toward Yuki, but the force of the storm almost thew Nani back inside.

"Yuki?" Ella called out from the doorway.

She knew she should be scared, she should be terrified, but the storm kept going, and it was still only Yuki.

"We have to go!" Nani told Ella. The sensation was overwhelming, the storm otherworldly.

"Come on," Ella called out to Yuki.

Yuki didn't reply. Ella's heart twisted, like it had the night of the winter ball, and she swallowed it all down. She'd felt the danger that night too, but she'd thought it was only Penelope she'd feared, and not the girl who was standing in front of her.

Not her best friend.

For a moment, there was no answer.

Then Yuki opened her eyes, and they were entirely white. Ella couldn't see a thing beyond the stark devastation of Yuki's magic.

"Yuki!" Ella cried. Yuki's long black hair flew behind her, whipping in the winds like a current of lightning. Everything around her seemed static.

"We don't have time for this," Nani said, but once she stepped closer to Yuki, the wind slammed her back against the wall. Nani fell with a cry, and Ella ran to her, crouching. Nani cradled her arm, but otherwise, she looked okay.

The wind was still going strong, and it seemed like the storm was all that existed in the universe. Yuki's feet rose slightly above the ground, her arms extending open, her eyes and skin the same white of the snow, her hair deep and black, and her mouth, red, always red.

There was thunder in the background, the sky cracking open with the weight of pure magic, and Yuki didn't move, didn't respond. Ella felt her heart climb to her throat, beating faster and faster.

Ella didn't have to understand the full extent of Yuki's magic to know its consequences.

"Go," Ella said, turning to Nani. "Find the other door."

Nani looked at her like she'd lost her mind.

"Go," Ella repeated, and her voice was calm as she looked at Yuki.

"Ella..." Nani's voice was a warning.

Ella knew Yuki wasn't going to hurt her. And there was no stopping it: no stopping this storm, this magic, this raging force of nature, and anyone stupid enough to try would die trying.

But Ella wasn't just anyone.

As Nani moved away, Ella squeezed her shoulder before turning back to Yuki. She couldn't recognize her friend anymore in this shell of power that looked like her. It was like looking into the ocean and thinking it was only a puddle. Ella had no choice but to drown.

She watched Nani move away from the ongoing storm, and Ella steeled herself into place, her hands curled into fists, her thin blond hair blowing back. She took a step forward.

The winds made it harder to walk, harder to breathe. With every step she felt herself sinking back into the snow, the cold ever growing within her bones, until the moment she thought she'd freeze from the inside.

"Yuki!" she called out, but her voice didn't seem like it could reach her, even though Yuki wasn't that far ahead. "Yuki, stop!"

Ella took another step, and another, and still, none of Yuki's barriers hit her. But it was getting harder to get to Yuki, who was in the eye of the storm, the source of everything. Ella couldn't see anything, covering her eyes so the ice didn't get into the pupils, even as the wind was trying to lift everything around her.

"Yuki!" she screamed again. "You need to stop!"

As the storm raged on, Ella felt herself growing stiffer by the second. She couldn't feel her legs anymore, but still she walked, her bones brittle and limbs numb, until she was almost to Yuki, until the wind was unbearable.

The storm ripped through her, merciless, bleak, but Ella still wasn't close enough yet. If she stayed where she was one more second, she wouldn't be able to hold on. One more second, and it was all over.

Ella launched herself at Yuki, stumbling, and then wrapped her arms tight around her best friend.

"Please stop," Ella whispered, her voice hollow against Yuki's chest. "Please."

And then, suddenly, the world around them went quiet.

Ella was still holding Yuki, icy cold and grip firm, her tears and fear half-frozen on her face. Yuki blinked, and her eyes returned to the usual black, still no color in her cheeks.

Around them, the world was completely and utterly silent.

Yuki stepped away from Ella's embrace, trembling slightly

as she looked down into Ella's face. Ella opened her arms, blinking away the icicles of her tears. Yuki's face sparkled like her skin was made of snow, and she frowned, looking at Ella, and then at the devastation she'd wreaked.

Trees had been overturned. Windows were broken. The roof of one of the castle wings had collapsed. Everything was still, and there was no sound but the gasping breaths of the two girls.

Yuki peered into Ella's eyes, and Ella didn't let the fear show on her face.

"Come on," she told Yuki. "We have to go home."

CHAPTER ELEVEN

NANI

Nani didn't ask questions as Yuki and Ella got into the backseat of the car. The storm had frozen midair, small fragments of icicles hanging stagnant, defying gravity, before all of it shattered to the ground at once. Nani still didn't say anything once Pippa started accelerating through the icy roads, and then Rory popped her head out from the trunk, making jokes like nothing was wrong.

And when night came and they were back in Grimrose castle, Nani closed her eyes and pretended everything was all right, but her dreams wouldn't let her forget what she'd seen. Yuki appeared, eyes white, rising in the air like an ancient goddess, hair almost to her feet, and everything around them was fire and ice. Nani woke up in the middle of the night, sweating, and if she hadn't believed in magic until now, there was no going back. If that was what Yuki was capable of, Nani didn't want to find out the power of whoever they were up against with the curse. All she knew was that it was someone who could cast a curse to keep more than a hundred girls as prisoners.

Rory, of course, was the only one who was fine. She hadn't seen Yuki and her powers. Her parents had phoned her at Grimrose the day after they rescued her, and Rory had taken the call as if nothing had happened, daring them to try to force her back home. Rory's parents couldn't do anything without making a fuss, and the school had assured them Rory was fine. Three days later, Rory got her laptop and phone back, and their little excursion went unpunished.

Ella and Yuki didn't mention what had happened on purpose, and Nani found herself settling back into a routine with classes and studying, hanging out with her friends, and kissing Svenja. Although she was now comfortable with her roommates and Ella, it still felt like they were all avoiding particular subjects when they should have been doing everything to untangle the mess they were in.

When February rolled around, and the gardens outside were still covered in a snow that didn't relent, Nani knew she couldn't ignore the matter of the curse forever. They'd all spent the whole past month as if they were in a hazy state of sleep, waiting for something to wake them. Nani knew nothing would happen unless they went looking for answers.

So at the end of the first week of February, she'd slammed both books on her bed, making Rory jump.

"All right, we're not getting out of this room until we have some answers," Nani said.

Rory blinked again, swiping her fringe out of the way. Her haircut had managed to grow out into something that didn't look like it had been snipped at home with a pair of blunt scissors during a mental breakdown—precisely what it had been. Nani thought it suited Rory's face, and she looked more like herself than the princess that other people were trying to make her out to be.

Nani couldn't comprehend that kind of duty. Even with Tūtū, her only responsibilities had been studying hard and doing her house chores. While she was at home, she knew that one day, her father had promised her an adventure. She'd never know the type of burden Rory carried. Nani's duty was to her family, not a country.

"Why me?" Rory asked. "Call Yuki back here. I bet she's just in the library hiding. She's the one who knows reading and stuff."

"Every time you call yourself stupid, I'm hitting you with this book," Nani warned.

"Why is your pep talk so aggressive?"

"It's efficient," Nani said, and she handed Rory the Black Book. Rory put it on her lap, the spine cracking open, and Nani bit back a wince. "We have to find something we've overlooked. Clues we've been missing. Something."

"We've looked at these four billion times," Rory complained, leafing through the pages, looking bored, turning all the earrings in her right ear. "Ari didn't find anything."

"Ariane knew something was strange, but she didn't know the curse was real. We do."

"And what difference does it make? I can't—" Rory was interrupted when the White Book hit her head. "Ouch! What the hell, Nani?"

"I told you," Nani said coolly. "You're going to sit there and read and look at the pictures or whatever until we have at least something new to turn over."

Rory grumbled under her breath, but apparently understood that Nani meant business. Nani knew that *Rory* knew she was smart enough for this. She'd been the one to find the clue in Ari's bag that had led them to Penelope, after all.

Nani sat down with the White Book that had belonged to Penelope while Rory turned the Black Book pages over, sitting opposite each other on the bed, their knees touching. The room was warmer than outside, and Nani felt comfortable. She'd always loved reading because it was an activity that she could do alone. It was strange seeing that she could do it with company too, but the experience didn't lack anything for it.

Rory leafed through the pages, sighing loudly from time to time, rubbing her eyes. "What if we don't find anything?" Rory asked, seemingly distracted, but Nani could feel the weight of the question.

"We have to," Nani answered.

Rory glanced over at Nani's bed. Nani knew her bed was where Ariane used to sleep. It was where Rory's best friend used to be, and now wasn't anymore. Even though it had only been six months, it felt like ages.

"I miss her," Rory mumbled, and then looked at Nani again. "You never told us why you decided to help us."

"Why, besides overhearing clearly the only interesting conversation in the entire school?"

"Oh, so you thought we were *interesting*."

"Rory, shut up."

Rory grinned at her, blue eyes bright. Nani felt glad that it wasn't just that she considered these girls her friends, but that they also considered that she was their friend. It was a strange sensation that made her heart bubble with warmth, and then she felt stupid for even thinking it.

"I'm serious," Rory said, her voice dropping a little lower. "You can tell me."

Nani hesitated a moment. After all this time, she hadn't said a word about her reasons. It was something that Nani had kept guarded, and she still hadn't found the right words to tell them. It was almost as if she was afraid of being dismissed, that her story wouldn't matter in their list of priorities. That Nani's story wasn't as important as everyone else's.

"My father's missing," Nani finally said.

Rory's eyes widened in surprise. "What? Since when?"

"I don't know," Nani said. "Remember how you all asked how I ended up here? He used to work as head of Grimrose security. He worked here for two years, and then when I was sent tickets to come, he vanished. Reyna said he wasn't even on their payroll anymore." Nani swallowed, hard. "He left before I arrived. Let's be honest, I clearly don't have the money to even breathe inside this castle. So my father got me a place, and then I never heard from him again."

Nani's throat felt raspy, and she bit her lower lip to stop

the tears from coming, from even saying out loud what she'd been suspecting for a long time now.

Her father had gone missing because of her.

If she weren't a part of this curse, nothing would have happened to him. He would have been safe.

"I'm sorry," Rory said. "Fuck. I had no idea."

Nani looked down at the book again, leafing through another page distractedly and landing on a portrait at the end of a tale. "I thought it was just some coincidence, but nothing can be a coincidence here. Not when this is basically my story."

Beauty had exchanged places with her father for his mistake, but Nani had no idea where her father could be.

"It isn't your fault," Rory said, her tone sincere. It was the most serious Nani had ever seen her. "It's not as literal as that."

"You don't know that."

"I know this may pain you, but you *also* don't know," Rory replied haughtily. "We've seen some weird shit, fine, but it's not meant to be taken literally. It's—a metaphor."

Rory nudged her, and Nani felt comfort blooming in her chest. "That's a big word you're using. Careful there."

This time, it was Rory who hit her with the book. Then her expression sobered again. "We're going to find him. You're going to see him again."

"You can't make that promise."

"Watch me," said Rory. "Besides, Ella said it first. We're going to save all the girls. That includes you."

Nani looked up at Rory, seeing Rory's bright blue earnest eyes, her apparent confidence that never faltered, that brave face she put on. Nani wished she could be a little more like that, even if she thought it was stupid most of the time.

"How can you be so sure?" Nani asked.

"I'd like to see anyone who thinks they can stand in the way of Ella Ashworth," Rory told her. "Including an ancient curse."

Nani smiled, and then she looked down at the page she'd turned to. The portrait looked like all the others at first glance.

It had the same frame of vines around the woman's face, around her dark curly hair that fell past her shoulders, her eyes boring directly into Nani's. But her face was gaunt and elegant, and there were slight wrinkles around her eyes, marks of aging that the others didn't have.

Because all the other portraits were young girls. All but this one.

"Rory," Nani called. "Rory, look at this."

Rory looked down at the page in Nani's lap. "What? I don't see anything. Just some old lady."

"Exactly," Nani said. "She's old. She's not supposed to be old."

All the girls died young. They'd died before their tale was complete, before they got to the happy ending. Yet here this woman was.

Here, finally, was a clue.

CHAPTER TWELVE

L iron Heyman," Nani said, tossing the iPad Rory had lent her on the cafeteria table. Rory saved her glass of juice just in time.

On the screen was an old newspaper article.

"I'm sorry, who?" Yuki asked, frowning at the picture and the date on the newspaper.

"The woman in the book," Nani said, sitting down impatiently across from Rory. She adjusted the golden frame of her glasses, her hair pulled back into a loose ponytail over the back of her head. "The one that survived."

Rory glanced at the iPad, and Ella leaned in from the other side. The four of them were sitting at their usual table in the cafeteria for lunch. Rory brushed her hair past her eyes, the copper bright, looking at the picture accompanying the headline. She could vaguely recognize the features, though the girl shown in the picture looked much younger than the one in the book, probably close to the age they were now.

"How did you find this?" Ella asked, looking half-mesmerized as she twisted in her seat to read the page.

"Way too much time on the internet," Nani replied. "And a couple of true crime podcasts."

Rory looked over at the page: Liron Heyman, sole survivor of a family tragedy back in the early nineties. Eleven older sisters and her father were all found dead at their house. Police arrived in the scene and found the youngest daughter still breathing and managed to save her. The investigation ruled the deaths as a possible murder-suicide committed by the father, who had died not realizing his youngest daughter still lived.

Rory's stomach twisted as she read the words, the tragedy growing familiar in her bones. She supposed it was because she'd gotten used to death with Ari and the other bodies that came after. Rory had barely seen Penelope's, but she remembered the hilt of the knife sticking out from her chest—it had seemed like all you needed to do was take it out for Penelope to start breathing again.

Rory darted her eyes at Yuki but said nothing. She knew what had happened with Penelope was behind them, that there was no other way around it. But something had changed because the whole world had changed.

"This is horrible," Ella muttered, looking up from the screen, shaking her head.

"That's from thirty years ago," said Yuki. "It's older, like the deaths in the archives."

"Yeah," Nani said, brown fingers drumming the cafeteria table. "Took me a while to find it, but I guessed that the number of sisters would be the same. Found the story, found her name."

Rory had read the tale of the twelve dancing princesses with Nani. Rory thought she remembered watching a Barbie movie version of it one night when her pain had woken her up, her body screaming, and the only thing she could do to keep herself distracted was following whatever was on screen, the badly animated dance moves, the tale of sisters who loved each other and stayed together no matter what happened. Rory had always wished she had a sister, because at least then, the burden would be shared. At least then, she'd know that she wasn't her parent's only hope.

"What do we do?" Ella asked. "Should we talk to this woman? Does she even realize she's part of this?"

"Probably not," Yuki said. "Not unless she has seen the books, and why would she?"

"She could have seen it for all we know," Nani said. "We don't know where these books came from, or where they'd been before Ariane and Penelope had them. The problem is Penelope didn't tell us anything. So we don't *know* anything."

Rory didn't dare breathe for a second, eyeing Yuki sideways, fleeting.

"It doesn't matter," Ella cut Nani off before she could complain about their lack of clues, which Rory had only heard about a few million times. "We don't even know what her ramblings really meant. She was scared, and she wasn't making sense. It's no use wasting time thinking of that now."

"Yes," Yuki agreed, her dark eyes meeting Ella's. "Ella's right."

"At least Penelope had some clue," Nani muttered. "She knew about the two books. How did she know there were two and that they were connected?"

"Can we not waste time on speculation?" Yuki said, her eyes narrowing.

"It's our responsibility," Rory replied.

Yuki scoffed. "Interesting *you* should be the one to mention that word."

Rory snapped her attention to Yuki. "What the hell is that supposed to mean?"

Yuki didn't even blink. "You texted Pippa, of all people, to come get you. We had to go all the way to pick you up and bring someone who had no idea what they were getting into."

"I didn't either," Nani muttered lamely, and Yuki glared at her.

Rory felt her blood start to boil. It wasn't her fault that her parents thought it was better for her to be locked up instead of coming back to school. It wasn't her fault that she was stuck with the role she had been born into, the role she didn't even want. She hated that she had to ask for their help.

Hated.

"This is not my fault," Rory said.

"None of it ever is," Yuki shot back. "But if you want to talk about responsibilities, maybe you should try assuming yours first."

"You know I can't," Rory said, feeling her muscles tense up in a way she didn't like, feeling herself get hurt by words that she couldn't shield herself against. Yuki *knew* this. "I can't let anyone else know."

"Well, then, keep lying to Pippa about who you are. I'm sure it's all going to work out."

"You think *you* can give me advice on this?" Rory asked, and Yuki held her fork with a steel grip, tensing like Rory had never seen before, and only then Rory realized that the fork itself was covered in ice.

"That's enough," Ella said evenly. She hadn't raised her tone. Hadn't even looked away from her plate, but both Yuki and Rory stopped immediately at the sound of her voice, like the breaking of a spell.

"We don't need to fight over this," Ella said, as if there were no tension still electrifying the air. "We have bigger issues at hand. That's what we should be focusing on, not Rory and Pippa's relationship."

"I don't have a relationship," Rory snapped.

"Rory, we all know how you feel about Pippa."

"I don't—" Rory stammered. "It's nothing like that. We train together. We fight, and then—"

"You dream of her kissing you passionately against a wall?" Ella asked, and Nani snorted.

"I don't!" Rory protested, blushing furiously, even though that was, in fact, what Rory had envisioned many times when she closed her eyes after training.

Ella smiled, taking a sip of her water with a smug expression.

"Take that smile off your face or I'm taking it off for you," Rory said, her blush still burning.

"Can we get back to this?" Nani asked, tapping the iPad on the table before them.

"Yes!" Rory replied, turning to Nani, more than happy to find a new subject, trying to ignore the sting of truth contained in Yuki's words. "So, what do we do?"

"I think we should talk to Liron," Nani said. "Ask her how she survived. It's the only clue we have."

Rory looked around the table at the rest of her friends, and reluctantly, Yuki nodded.

"Right," Rory said. "Where does she live?"

"Salzburg," Nani said. "Not too far from here."

Coincidences, piling up. Rory had never believed in them, but now, all her life seemed to be dictated by them. She was starting to doubt whether she had a choice in anything at all.

CHAPTER THIRTEEN

ELLA

The girls had to wait for a weekend when Sharon and Ella's stepsisters would go out of town and Ella could sneak out of the window. March was already blossoming when it finally happened. Yuki bought the train tickets, handling most of the German with her almost perfect accent. It had taken a while until they figured the exact address, but apparently Liron lived above a small clothing shop that she ran.

Ella had never been to Salzburg. The only trip she'd taken since coming to Grimrose was to Paris and only because school organized it. Now she sat on the train, Yuki across from her wearing headphones. Ella kept working on her crochet just to have something to do with her hands, to stop herself from looking at Yuki and wondering when she would break again. If she was controlling her powers, or the magic was controlling *her*.

But if Ella asked Yuki about it, if she told Yuki that she was still dwelling on Penelope's body beneath the lake, that would mean she didn't have enough faith in Yuki. Ella believed Yuki had done what she'd needed to protect them. Ella *had* to believe her.

As a group, they looked like they were headed to entirely different places. Nani sat by Ella's side wearing one of her floral dresses with bright white and red flowers, woolen leggings, and a long white cardigan Ella had knit for her. Her hair was bound in a half-ponytail, and her nose was stuck inside a book she'd bought at the train station, already on page 100.

Rory, opposite Nani, was wearing combat boots, ripped black jeans, a backwards black hat, and a pink sweatshirt with the words WOMEN WANT ME, FISH FEAR ME. Ella had no idea what that meant. By her side, Yuki looked like a literary prodigy attending a university seminar, with knee-high socks, a high-waisted skirt, and a red tweed coat with elbow patches. Ella herself was wearing an oversized rainbow sweater, her warm denim overalls, and a pair of baby pink and blue trainers Rory had gifted her that looked too big for her feet.

Ella had spent a lot of time thinking about friendships when she'd started figuring out how to name her feelings: the differences between loving a friend and loving someone romantically and how she could find someone attractive only after she'd spent enough time to get to know them thoroughly, after they'd already wormed their way to her heart. By all accounts, the four of them were all too different to *be* friends—they had different opinions on everything, they didn't all enjoy the same activities. But still, here they were, together despite all their differences. She'd heard more than once from the adults that friends made in school were only your friends because you were forced to spend time together, and as you moved on, it was normal to drift apart and find like-minded people.

Ella didn't think that was particularly true. There was nothing that defined friendship except wanting to spend time together and choosing to care for each other.

Rory turned to look at Ella, perhaps feeling Ella watching her. "What is it?"

Ella shook her head, pushing her scatterbrained thoughts away. "Just wondering if Liron will even talk to us."

"She has no reason not to," said Nani, listening to the conversation even though her eyes were still glued to her book. "Unless someone else figured that Grimrose is cursed first, which I doubt."

"Point," Rory said.

Not that there weren't people who enjoyed mysteries at Grimrose—it was a castle, after all, with a hundred years of history and secret passageways.

"The only other people interested would be that study group," Ella considered. "You know, the ones spending more time in the library than us, speaking only in Latin and whatnot."

"Half of those idiots are on my fencing team," Rory grumbled. "Stuff doesn't have to be in a dead language to be mysterious. They're all *academia this* and *hermeneutics that—*"

"I'm surprised you even know how to pronounce that word," Yuki remarked.

"—the curse could hit them right in the face," Rory continued, ignoring Yuki altogether, "and they'd still be too busy obsessing about who got a higher grade on the stupid philosophy essay."

"You're complaining because you didn't have time to copy mine," Nani said behind her book, without looking at Rory.

Rory gave Nani the middle finger.

"Yuki could easily fit with them." Rory elbowed her. "You already dress the part."

Yuki looked amused. "Oh, they tried inviting me."

"What?" Ella said, tilting her head. It was the first she heard of this story. "What did you say?"

"I told them I had better ways of wasting my time," she replied savagely, and all four of them cracked up laughing.

When they got off in Salzburg, the streets were cramped with cobbled stones and rising church towers, the river cutting the city in half. They found the shop easily. It was open, but Ella hesitated at the door. Rory brushed past her first, and as the rest of them followed her in, a bell on the door ringing to announce their arrival. At first the shop seemed empty, but finally, a woman appeared behind the counter.

Compared to her portrait, her curls were brighter and the wrinkles more evident around her eyes. Ella knew the woman must be in her late forties, and a few white hairs gave away her age. Her cheeks were hollow, and the most striking feature were the depths of her eyes. She narrowed them, examining the girls' clothes, probably taking them for tourists.

"I'm sorry," Liron said in English, though her German accent was on the heavier side. "We're closing in a moment."

"Actually, we're not customers," said Yuki. "You're Liron Heyman."

Something danced across her eyes, and she gave the smallest nod. "Yes. I'm not sure how I can help."

"We just want to talk," Ella said.

Liron's eyes narrowed even more, and her shoulders tensed.

"This is about what happened to your family," Nani said.

Ella saw the change in Liron. She straightened her back, and her face grew defiant. "I'm not going to talk to you girls. Leave immediately."

"Please, Ms. Heyman," Ella said, trying to keep her voice calm. This was the only chance they had. "We know what happened, and we think you can help us. What happened to you was—"

"None of your business," Liron finished, walking to the door and holding it open. Her posture was adamant, and the girls had frozen in place, not knowing what to do, but then Ella stepped forward.

"We came from Grimrose," Ella said, hoping that it meant something.

Liron blinked, and Ella could see that she could barely contain her shock. And then it was Yuki who took over—she stepped up and put her hand on the metal frame of the door. The metal bristled under the force of cold, and Liron let go. Yuki held in her hand a frozen snowball, her fingers curled like claws, the scent of magic in the air. Liron stood with her mouth agape as she stared at the four girls inside her store.

"We won't waste your time," Yuki said. "This is important."

"I want no part in this," Liron said.

"You don't have a choice," Nani said, taking the White Book out of her bag and showing Liron her portrait. "You're already here."

They all entered Liron's small living room. Ella sat in a chair, and Yuki kept standing behind her, leaning her arm protectively in the back of Ella's chair, her hand resting just above Ella's head. Ella looked around and noticed there were no photographs on the mantelpiece or on the walls. There was a single crochet quilt covering the sofa and no vases.

Liron brought them all tea, her eyes darting over at Yuki. Ella could still feel the shiver of magic, even though Yuki had snuffed it out. Nani sat on the love seat with the White Book on her lap, stroking the edges. Next to her sat Rory, the only person in the room who didn't look nervous. At least this was typical.

Liron sat down opposite Nani and Rory, her fingers gently tapping her cup of tea. "I don't know what else I can tell you that wasn't in the newspaper at the time. It's not something I enjoy talking about. It's been thirty years, and I've turned down anyone who tries to interview me about it."

"We're not just anyone," Rory said. "We showed you your portrait. And we're in the book too."

Liron shifted in her seat. "I'd like an explanation for all of this."

Ella felt her friends' eyes all snap back to her because she was always the one to talk. They didn't know how much they could actually share, but Liron had already seen what Yuki could do. She'd been freaked out by the portrait, and there wasn't any other explanation for any of this besides what it was: magic.

"What do you know of Grimrose?" Ella asked.

"Only that someone had mentioned the name to me before," Liron said. "Someone who came to see me."

"Ariane?" Rory snapped up, her blue eyes wide. "About a year ago, red hair? Nice voice?"

"No," Liron said. "This was a long time ago. Almost twenty years."

Ella looked over to Yuki, but Yuki's face remained impassive.

"There was a girl," Liron began, glancing over at Yuki, pausing for a moment too long. "She was very—strange, if I had to describe it. She said she attended a school in Switzerland, Grimrose Académie. I'd never heard of it before. But she asked me how I'd survived. The same thing you ask of me now."

"Who was she?" Nani almost snapped.

"She didn't give me a name," Liron said. "But I remember her because she was the most beautiful girl I'd ever seen." She darted her eyes at Yuki again, and then Ella understood.

It wasn't just another girl. It had been someone Liron recognized, somehow.

Someone from a past cycle.

"What was she like?" Ella asked, almost too afraid to hear the answer.

"The blackest hair," Liron said. "Pale white skin."

"And lips as red as blood," Ella muttered.

81

Liron nodded. Ella didn't dare to look over to see Yuki's face. A chill climbed up her spine.

"There are many girls whose portraits are in the book," Ella started explaining, slowly. "Each girl's life corresponds to a different fairy tale."

Liron frowned. "A fairy tale? Such as...'Schneewittchen?'"

"Yes," Yuki replied, and Ella recognized the name of "Snow White" even in German. "Exactly."

"We believe the book is tied to—a curse," Ella explained, her voice hesitating a little. "A curse that makes us repeat fairy tales without getting to the real endings."

"The real endings being?" Liron asked.

"Happy ones," Rory said.

The room was silent as Liron looked back and forth to all of them. Ella could see Liron struggling to believe it. Ella couldn't blame her. To anyone else, it would seem like madness, but Ella recognized the hesitation—that she knew all that had happened couldn't be just normal, that maybe there was another explanation to what she had been through.

"And I'm in this book?" Liron asked. "Which tale is mine?"

"'The twelve dancing princesses,'" Nani said.

Yuki was quick in translation. "Die zertanzten Schuhe."

A look of recognition seemed to come over Liron's face. She looked at Nani. "Can I see it?"

Nani handed her the book, opened to the fairy tale that was hers. Liron seemed reluctant to read, but she turned the pages. When she appeared to be close to the ending, her face paled, and she closed the book vehemently.

"I don't want to see this," she flared. "Why do you want my help?"

"The other girls all died," Ella said. "At the end of your tale, you're supposed to die. But you're different. You're the only one in the book who's older than we are."

Rory nodded. "What's the secret? What did you do?"

Liron turned sharply to Rory. "I don't understand what you mean."

"You lived. The others died. Something had to be different."

Liron peered at each of them, her eyes lingering on Yuki again for only a moment. Ella looked over at Yuki, and their eyes met. Yuki's softened, just a bit, and Ella smiled before she turned back to Liron.

"I have never seen this book before," Liron said. "The girl who'd come from Grimrose wanted to know the same thing you're asking, but I couldn't tell her."

"What happened?" Nani said. "What was your story?"

Liron looked away from them a moment, and Ella could only imagine what painful memory she was reliving. They had only just begun their own stories, and already they were filled with grief.

"I was the youngest of twelve," she said. "My mother died when I was young. We were left with only my father taking care of us. He was very...controlling. My eldest sister was only eight years older than me. My father used to lock us inside the house so we couldn't go out. So we didn't embarrass him."

Liron looked away, but none of the girls moved. They all stayed still, waiting for what would follow.

"So my sisters, the older ones, started sneaking out of the house during the night," she said. "My father locked us up, but our room was the biggest in the house. We all shared it. We sneaked out through the basement."

"You too?" Nani asked.

Liron nodded. "I was fifteen when it happened. My eldest sister had a boyfriend, but my father didn't approve. She didn't tell him, but she and my sisters had sneaked out so many times that they started getting sloppy. My father started to suspect something was wrong. Then one day, he caught us."

"And?" Rory asked.

"And then he poisoned everyone," Liron said, looking straight at Rory, "and killed himself. I was lucky enough to survive. That's all it was. Luck."

Ella took a deep breath. "You must have done something different. You didn't die. No new face appeared in your tale."

"What do you think happens if you don't follow the story through?" Liron asked, her voice harsh.

"A happy ending."

Liron closed her eyes, and Ella could see an unrelenting, terrible grief written all over her face.

"I did not get a happy ending," Liron said. "Do you not understand? I may have survived, whatever you call it, this curse, but it was not a good ending. I have not lived happily. I lost eleven of my sisters. I've spent thirty years remembering their faces, seeing them while I sleep. Do you call that happy?"

Ella felt the tears blinking in the back of her eyes.

"But you survived," Nani said, her voice becoming heated. "All the other girls who were cursed died."

"Surviving is not the same as living. I could have died, and it would have been the same. There is no difference for me. The tragedy remains."

Ella tried to keep her composure, but every single word felt like a hammer. The thing Ella had not told anyone, the thing that only she had realized, was that she had almost no time left.

In six months, her birthday would come, and she would be free of Sharon and her stepsisters.

In six months, she would have her freedom. In six months, she would have her happy ending.

But in six months, if she couldn't break the curse, she knew she'd get the bad ending.

It wasn't the same for Yuki, Rory, or Nani. They didn't have a due date. The curse was hanging over their heads, but Ella had spent the last five years of her life looking forward to the day when she would be free, knowing all her suffering was coming to an end. Now that it was near, it didn't feel like a liberation.

It felt like a deadline.

"I'm sorry to bother you," Ella said, choking on her words. "Thank you for your help."

Ella stood up and rushed down the stairs before anything else could snag her remaining hope.

CHAPTER FOURTEEN

Ella ran out of the house, and Rory and Nani went after her, though Nani glanced back at Yuki for one second too long before leaving. Yuki stayed behind and stood calmly, a chilled stillness in her bones. She turned in Liron's direction.

"You're lying," Yuki said simply, switching to German. She was as comfortable speaking in German as she was in English, both rougher languages on her tongue, both lacking any nuance.

"Excuse me?" Liron's shoulders tensed, her attention snapping sharply from the door to Yuki.

"You're lying," Yuki repeated. "Something did happen. Something that you think was the reason you were spared."

Yuki had watched Liron the whole time as she told her story, eyes never wavering from her. Liron's small gestures, the trembling fingers on the teacup. The way she'd closed the book too fast when she got to the ending, where all her sisters died.

"You're different from the other girls," she said.

Yuki shrugged.

"Your magic," Liron said, "do the others have it too?"

Yuki shook her head.

"So that makes you special," said Liron. "It already makes your story different."

"Perhaps. We don't know for sure."

"And yet you talk easily about the curse," Liron continued. Yuki knew the other girls were waiting outside for her, speculating if she was going to get more from Liron than they could. Yuki could almost hear Ella, wondering if they should come back in.

Yuki and Ella hadn't talked about the storm. They hadn't talked about how Yuki's power could cleave the world in two. She felt it, running through her veins, ready for the reaping, ready to bring it all crashing down.

The thing about this power was that even though it was ice, all it did was scorch everything in its path, everything that Yuki had built for herself over the years. She enjoyed the power of tearing herself down. By now, Yuki had burned too big a bridge for the flames not to bite at her heels. And if she wanted to avoid it, she had to keep running, lest the fire consumed her when she turned her back to watch what she'd left behind.

All she could do was burn, and burn brighter, until there was nothing else left on their path to salvation.

"I'm in the book too," Yuki replied. "I may have magic, but it doesn't help me break the curse."

"But maybe it helps you escape it."

Yuki shifted slightly where she stood. She should go outside, turn her back on this woman. There was something about her, though, something that felt to Yuki like a misplaced memory, something she'd already seen.

Liron had described a girl who looked exactly like Yuki, or exactly like the girls Yuki had seen reflected in her mirror. Another version who had gotten close to escaping, but still died so that Yuki could be born in her place.

"What happened the day your family died?" asked Yuki.

Liron sighed, her shoulders sagging. "I can't give you good answers. I didn't want to tell this to your friends. They look like nice girls. They may want a way out, but this isn't a fairy tale. I didn't know about any kind of curse, and it makes no difference to me now. It wasn't easy. It wasn't pretty."

Yuki felt her blood draining from her face, and she was sure what Liron was going to say before she uttered a single word.

"You killed them," Yuki murmured. "It wasn't your father. It was you."

Liron's eyes showed no regret. She held Yuki's gaze and didn't flinch. "I did. I loved my sisters, but they were too willing to believe in salvation. My eldest sister kept going on about how her boyfriend was going to get us all out, but it wasn't true. It couldn't be true, because we'd spent our lives locked up, forbidden from truly living, and if we ever escaped, my father would kill us all."

Liron bit the inside of her cheek, and Yuki listened.

"Sarah had an idea," Liron continued. "She set up a date

with her boyfriend, and he was going to sneak us out, but then my father discovered the plan. He told the boy to run and never look back, or my father would kill him. And do you know what that boy did?"

"He didn't come back," Yuki said.

Liron laughed, but it was an empty laugh, all teeth and no mercy. And suddenly, Yuki realized what she'd recognized in Liron. It was the same sort of determination that Penelope had, the same willingness to do something terrible just to get what she wanted.

"And I realized that's what was going to become of me," Liron said, looking at her. "All my life, that's what I'd be waiting for. An outsider to rescue me, and I would stand like my sisters, numb and innocent and waiting for something. I killed them because I wouldn't become like them. I refused to."

Liron got up. Her hands were steady as she collected the teacups left behind, shoulders straight. Yuki was sure it was the first time she'd ever made this confession. She wondered if Liron had recognized in Yuki the same thing that Yuki saw in her. The hunger. The want. The refusal to go down quietly, and the willingness to take what she deserved. Whatever the cost.

"You want my advice on how to escape the curse?" Liron hissed. "Swallow your heart. Take any kindness and any softness that's left in you, and you gobble it down. It's the only way you'll survive."

Yuki nodded. She felt her own bones responding to that call, eager to forget those things. To have her own goal to break the curse and be free. She was not bound by the same rules as the others, not anymore.

She hadn't lost control of the storm. She knew exactly what she was doing.

Ella had brought her back to herself, and Yuki had let her. Because in the end, if Yuki couldn't save Ella, then there was no point. If she couldn't save Ella, the one good thing in her life, the person she both loved and envied, who had been twisted and carved into her heart from the day they'd met, then it didn't matter how much power she had. It didn't matter what she wanted because it would be for nothing.

Yuki turned to leave. "Thanks for the advice," she said.

Liron gave her one last look, her chin raised and defiant.

"Those girls don't have what it takes, but you do. You are like me. You'll survive."

Yuki nodded again, and then she shut the door.

CHAPTER FIFTEEN

NANI

By the time Yuki finally joined them outside, Ella had already calmed down. Nani had asked why Ella had run out of the room, but Ella had said only that she was anxious and needed fresh air. Nani didn't buy it, but she didn't press.

"What took you so long?" Rory complained when she saw Yuki.

"Nothing," Yuki said coolly. Her eyes swept over the three of them, measuring. "I just wanted to ask her a few more questions."

"Did she tell you anything else?" Nani asked.

"She was very slippery," Rory said.

"She has reason to be," Yuki replied. "It's a delicate subject."

"Well, shit, then," Rory grumbled. "It got us nowhere. She doesn't know about the curse, and her answer was useless."

"We'll find out something," Ella said, speaking for the first time. "It's not over yet."

As the girls set out to catch their train back to Grimrose, Nani couldn't help but notice that Yuki had never answered her question.

With their only lead turning out to be a dead end, Nani didn't feel like going back to the books. The only thing she'd found had led them nowhere, though Nani knew she shouldn't have expected too much.

There was something else bothering Nani too. She remembered what Liron had told them about the other girl who had come from Grimrose, years ago, to ask Liron how she'd survived. This meant that others had tried to investigate the curse before.

When they finally arrived back at the castle, Nani didn't want to be the one to bring up the subject of the curse again.

Instead, she went to Svenja's room.

The door was already open, and the room was dark. Svenja's room had a different view than the one she shared with the other girls. Their room faced the gardens; Svenja's overlooked Constanz's rooftops. Svenja's back was to Nani, hair tied up in a ponytail, as she searched for something on the desk.

"Hey," Nani said. "You're doing homework on the weekend? What an exemplary student."

Svenja jumped and turned around, and only then Nani realized it was not Svenja, but Odilia staring back at her.

Her eyes were darker than Svenja's, but the resemblance was uncanny enough to make a shiver run down Nani's spine. Odilia recognized Nani too. Before Nani could say a word, Odilia ran out of the room.

Nani, stunned, heard the bathroom door open. This time it was the real Svenja, wrapped in a towel, the hot steam engulfing her. Nani was still standing frozen near the door.

"Hey. I left the door unlocked after getting your text saying you were back. What happened?" Svenja asked, noticing Nani's expression.

"Your cousin," Nani said. "She was just here. I thought—" Nani shook her head, rubbing her tired eyes. Her mistake had been so obvious. "Never mind. Why was she here?"

"How should I know?" Svenja answered nonchalantly. "She didn't tell *me*."

Nani looked at the door again, still cursing herself for mistaking the two of them.

It was a simple mistake. A stupid one. It wouldn't happen again.

Nani had seen Svenja's face in the White Book, next to the tale of *Swan Lake*. As far as she knew, there was no happy ending to its original version—the heroine transformed and the prince danced with the wrong girl, dooming her to be cursed and tragically die while the villain took her place.

Nani couldn't afford to make that mistake if she wanted Svenja to survive this curse.

Svenja looked at Nani, knitting her eyebrows. "You sure you're okay? I'm sure she was just here to get a hairbrush or something. I stole some of her makeup last week, so she's just getting revenge."

It was no use talking to Svenja about this; Nani knew her concern would be dismissed. For all Svenja complained about Odilia, she always thought her cousin was harmless, albeit irritating.

Nani closed the door and then stared back at Svenja, remembering that Svenja was only wearing a towel. She cast her eyes down, unable to hide the heat rushing to her cheeks.

"Oh, please, don't say you're embarrassed," Svenja said. "I'm the one not wearing any clothes."

"Maybe you should put some on?"

"Maybe you should take some of yours off?" Svenja teased.

"I'm leaving."

Svenja sighed, throwing her hands up, and her towel slipped down a little, and Nani wanted to both look and turn away at the same time, her cheeks still burning. Svenja went to the bathroom and came back a few moments later fully clothed, her hair still dripping wet, her white shirt transparent where the water soaked through.

"I'm your girlfriend, you know," Svenja said, shoving Nani's shoulder slightly. "You're allowed to look."

"Svenja, you're going to make me die of awkwardness."

"Nani, you're a grown girl, you know how relationships work."

The problem was that Nani knew, but she didn't want to think about it. It was disconcerting to admit that all her knowledge of any relationships, ever, came out of books.

She had always been a lesbian in theory, but not exactly in practice.

And while at first Svenja's kisses were mindless and made her giddy, Nani realized that wasn't *all* there was to it. Not just physically.

Nani's stomach twisted. She was keeping secrets from Svenja and not only about the curse.

Svenja sat down on the bed, gesturing for Nani to come sit with her. Nani snuggled against Svenja's flat chest, and though she was bigger than Svenja, she still felt protected under that hug, and not self-conscious about her body. Well, she was conscious about her body, about the heat she felt every time she kissed Svenja, but she never had to worry about her appearance or her size. She was self-conscious about what it could do. She didn't exactly know how to decipher what her body wanted.

Besides, there was the curse to consider.

Was Svenja a part of Nani's tale—and was Nani a part of Svenja's?

Svenja's words from their fight last year echoed back to her. *Don't make me into a monster I'm not.*

Nani had always liked the monsters and the villains and the morally gray characters in stories, but she wasn't ready to unravel this part of her own tale.

The truth was that Nani didn't want any more trouble. And if things with Svenja went further than this, if she let herself truly stay, it would definitely be trouble.

CHAPTER SIXTEEN

ELLA

At the end of March, the winter weather relented and gave way to the new breath of spring. Plants shyly began to bloom as the bleakness that had hung over Grimrose for so long was banished from their kingdom. However, Ella couldn't enjoy the coming of her favorite season because she was crossing out days on the calendar—feeling dread with each red X.

Their visit to Liron had been fruitless, but Ella couldn't stop thinking about the way Liron had looked at Yuki, the way she described the other girl who had come before from Grimrose. Whoever she was, she must have certainly known about the curse. She must have made the connection at the time, after Liron had just survived her tragic ending.

Ella went back to her notes, to the things she had wondered about last semester. She knew both the Black Book and the White Book by heart now, could recite their words in her sleep. She knew each of the girls who had attended the school. Could count the number of portraits, could see the faces as she turned the pages in her mind. But instead of the counting keeping her calm, like numbers usually did, the effect was the opposite.

The only thing Ella still had was Penelope's warning. *You don't have a chance with them.* Ella didn't know what Penelope meant, and every time she tried to recall more details of that night, all she remembered was the knife, the blood, her nails caked with dirt.

And every day, she looked at Yuki, searching for signs, but Yuki never faltered. She was like the normal Yuki from before, and Ella had to trust her. There were moments, though, when Ella thought something else was about to break through. Something unknown. Something dangerous.

She couldn't name her fear, because if she did, it meant she'd lost faith in Yuki. Ella Ashworth never lost faith in her friends.

"I'm going to break the curse," Ella muttered under her breath, searching her notes. "I made a promise. Ella Ashworth doesn't let her friends down."

There was a knock on her door in the attic, and Ella pushed the papers aside, hiding them under a heavy chemistry book.

"Ella?" a hesitant voice asked as the door opened. Ella's room didn't have a lock on the inside. Silla stood in the doorway, a less confident version of her twin Stacie. "Sorry, I know it's late."

"I'm not asleep," Ella said, but she didn't dare raise her voice. "Is there something Sharon needs?"

"Not Mum," she replied. "I tore the buttons on my uniform blazer. I was wondering if..."

Her voice trailed off as she looked down. Ella extended her hand, and with another wavering step, Silla came in, handing off the periwinkle blue blazer. It had Grimrose's beautiful coat of arms embroidered on the left pocket, a G and A intertwined. Silla stood as Ella examined the blazer.

"You can sit down, you know," Ella muttered, gesturing to her bed. Silla sat down almost immediately, but she didn't look like she was enjoying it.

Ella picked up the sewing kit, the one she used for fixing things around the house—not the good one, not the one she kept hidden under the bed with her mother's old sewing machine— and for a moment, she was taken back to the days after the ball, where she'd spent three whole nights awake, sewing Yuki's white dress to replace the bloodstained fabric. She'd shed a single drop of blood on the white tulle as she finished, prickling her thumb. In a frenzied panic, she'd torn it all out and began anew, afraid that the red stain would be a reminder. The dress was white, and it had to stay white, bright as snow, the same shade of Yuki's skin. White, clean, unblemished.

Ella blinked and cleared her mind, picking up the thread and needle to mend the blazer. As she looked up, she noticed Silla watching her. Silla and Ella almost never talked—Silla was always in Stacie's shadow, and for better or for worse, that's where she usually stayed.

"You won't tell Mum, will you?" Silla's voice was only above a whisper.

"Tell her what?" Ella asked.

"About this," Silla said. "I was just trying it on. I didn't mean to rip the button off. And you know what she'll say, because the button wouldn't have popped off if I was in shape."

Anger bubbled to Ella's throat. "I'm not going to tell her anything."

Silla shifted again, seeming to be not entirely trusting, as Ella did her work. Sharon hovered over her daughters, ready to tear them down at any change in their bodies. The only compliment Sharon ever gave Ella on her appearance was that she was thin. That was only because Ella was almost never allowed to eat a full meal if she wasn't in school.

As she worked, Ella could see Silla was looking around the barren room. Ella's uniform was laid on her chair, her textbooks and notebooks on the table. Out the small window they could see the tallest tower of Grimrose castle. Every morning when Ella woke up, it was the first thing she saw. Her freedom, and now, her curse.

"Do you think things here will be different," Silla said, so quietly that Ella almost thought she was imagining it, "when we leave?"

Ella looked up from pressing the button, the needle slipping from her grasp for a minute.

"I know you're going to," Silla said, not looking at Ella. She was staring straight out at the castle, her brown eyes fixed on the point of the horizon. "Goodness, we all want to. Stacie has all the plans. We talk about it, but—but we never really include you."

Ella wasn't hurt by this statement. The last thing she'd expect was for the twins to include her in something, not when they and Ella had spent the last five years carefully avoiding each other, meticulously staying out of each other's lives, painstakingly ignoring the hurt on each other's hearts.

"What are your plans?" Ella asked.

"They're Stacie's," Silla corrected. "I'm just following her."

Ella finished the stitch gracefully, tucking the end of the thread inside the blazer. She offered it back to her stepsister, who took it gingerly, biting her lower lip. As Silla got up to leave, Ella turned around in her chair.

"Don't you want something of your own?" Ella asked.

Silla stopped and shrugged. "Who knows. Maybe when we break this cycle, I'll find something. Maybe I'll even find something I'm good at."

"You're good at riding."

Silla smiled, and Ella could tell it was genuine. "Yes. But not good enough."

"That's Sharon talking."

Silla sighed. Ella had never paid attention to how Silla was different from Stacie. Stacie had always been the prettier twin—the one with the glossy hair, the arched eyebrows, the elegant cheekbones. Silla had round cheeks, her mouth fuller, her hair always tucked limply behind her ears. "Maybe. Maybe when I leave there'll even be a day when I don't hear her voice in my head before I hear mine." She held up the blazer. "Thanks, Ella."

She closed the door behind her and left Ella alone.

Ella repressed a sigh. She already had plenty to worry

about, but there was something about the way Silla called their lives a *cycle*. An idea struck her, her heart beating faster, her head swimming as she made the connection.

All the fairy tale deaths that had come before had the same *stories*. The stories were always repeated, forever and ever, the girls stuck into the same positions. They had always been fated to live the same way, to die the same way, and she was repeating the cycle.

How many times had Ella already lived through this?

How many times had she lived in a place that hated her, where she had to work every single day just so she could eat, where every second was spent dreaming about the day she would get out? Was this her whole existence, the only one she ever got to have? Working until her hands were open scabs bleeding raw, until her own mind was screaming at her to stop, so she'd not realize the extent of the prison she was stuck in?

Ella thought of Ari again, sinking to the bottom of the lake. Her portrait would disappear, its edges would fade, and a new one would appear in its place, but it wasn't going to be the same Ari. Ella had searched newspapers and historical records for other girls that had drowned, and there they were—forty years before, sixty years before. Girls who had been poisoned by their food, girls going to sleep and never waking up. While she did her research, Ella didn't look at any pictures, because she didn't want to see the similarities between her and her friends.

She also never looked for her own story in these old records because her story was so much like the stories of countless other young girls in the world. Not just the girls who were fated to retell Cinderella, but girls who were prisoners in their homes, held captive in the darkness, until the day they vanished. No one noticed them, and no one would remember their names.

There were a hundred thousand other little Cinders out there, but only Ella got to be named for what she was.

She curled her fists, suddenly angry, rage beating through her heart. Rage that her mother had died, her father had left her in this position. Rage at the injustice of it all, at how much was asked of her every single day, at how much had been taken from her without her consent.

Ella brushed away her tears.

She had made a promise.

She was going to keep it.

CHAPTER SEVENTEEN

RORY

For almost the entire winter, the fencing hall had been closed until their teacher returned. Rory had waited every moment since she'd come back to Grimrose. She knew there were other things that were worth her attention—the damned curse, for one—but Rory wanted to get back to the one thing she knew how to do.

Out of all the things that had gone wrong in Rory's life in the past year—having a dead best friend, being cursed, being forced by her parents into house arrest, suffering from a chronic illness that made it seem like her whole body was trying to obliterate her—the one thing that had always stayed right had been training on Friday afternoon.

So when the teacher had finally returned, and the fencing hall had opened again, Rory had practically catapulted into the place.

But she had not thought of what would happen once she saw Pippa again.

Pippa was already there, dressed in her practice uniform, dark blue shorts and a white shirt, her hair braided, her dark skin radiant. Pippa seemed as surprised as Rory to see her there, and Rory dropped her bag on the bench.

"Hi," Pippa said. "Didn't think you'd come."

"It's Friday," Rory said.

"Yeah. But you know, we haven't exactly talked since..." Her voice trailed off. "I was hoping you'd come."

Rory looked down, embarrassed, dropping her bag. Out of habit she went to tie her hair back, except she didn't have long hair anymore. So she ruffled it up, giving a small smile. Rory felt bad that after all that they'd faced together at the country palace, she hadn't even talked to Pippa afterwards.

Well, Rory knew why she hadn't. Because Pippa was already too involved, and Rory couldn't afford for her to know too much.

And yet, she couldn't resist digging herself in deeper, either.

"I never said thank you," Rory said, her words coming out rushed and hot. "For coming with the girls to get me."

Pippa looked at her. "I never did ask you why you sent me the message."

"Yours is only the number I actually remember."

Rory's eyes met Pippa's, and there was a flustered silence. Rory looked away quickly again, feeling the heat get to her cheeks. She couldn't be back where she'd started, in the path she knew exactly where it would lead her.

It was a trap, and she was going to walk into it willingly. She supposed that's what made it a good trap.

"I was happy to help," Pippa finally said, brushing her braid behind her back. Both of them stood facing each other. Rory wanted to say something, but she wasn't sure she wanted to be the first one to breach the silence. "So, we're doing this or what?"

Rory was glad that Pippa moved to grab their practice swords before she did. Pippa held out a sword to Rory. Her hand was warm when it brushed hers, and Rory bit the inside of her cheek so hard that she thought it was going to bleed.

Pippa walked first to the floor. When she got to the middle, she turned around, holding the practice sword as a perfect extension of her arm, and cocked half a smile. This time, Rory was ready, her muscles in position.

"*En garde,*" Pippa said, and then she attacked.

Rory parried off the first blow, flicking her wrist, twisting Pippa so she was at her back, spinning around and catching her from the other side. Rory missed the way her body knew what to do when it was in its full power, when there wasn't something holding her back.

And just like that, they were back, and there was no tension of the last year—at least not the same way, the anger, the underlying conflict. It was only Rory and Pippa, their swords clashing, zipping past each other as they twirled, both hands on their swords, trying to elbow each other out of the way, cutting arcs in the air.

It was silent but for the steps they took, the sound of the

wood beating, the swooshing of the air as the strikes were made fast, the grunts as they adjusted their stances.

"I like your hair," Pippa told her, and Rory almost tripped. She narrowed her eyes toward Pippa, holding the wooden sword tighter in her hand as she felt her muscles cramp. She wouldn't lose her balance for such a little thing. "I didn't tell you then. But you look..." Pippa grinned. "Well."

Rory shook away the fringe from her eyes, hoping her blush wasn't as deep as she was feeling it. She hated that her skin was that kind of marble white that colored at the slightest compliment.

"I cut it the night of the ball," Rory said as she parried against Pippa. "It's a pity we didn't meet then. Yuki spent the whole night throwing up in the bathroom, so I only stayed five minutes."

"I wouldn't have seen it anyway. I didn't go."

Rory's blow had too much force, and Pippa's arm flew back, but she didn't lose her grip on the sword.

"What? Everyone went to the ball."

"I didn't."

"Why not?" Rory asked, and even though she thought all balls were stupid, there was something about Pippa not going to one that made her feel outraged. Pippa should go everywhere, even when no one was really deserving of her company.

Pippa shrugged. "I just don't like them that much."

"Well, I'll say, from my experience in balls, I'd agree with you," Rory said, "but this is school. It's supposed to be corny. And being corny makes it a lot better."

Pippa muttered something under her breath that Rory didn't quite catch.

"What?"

"I don't dance," Pippa said, their eyes meeting over the next parry. Rory pivoted for a last-minute blow, but Pippa was just as fast, throwing her off before she got too close.

"Like, your religion forbids it?"

Pippa laughed. "Rory, sometimes I think you do it on purpose."

Rory cocked her eyebrow. "Do what?"

Pippa opened her mouth, her tongue rolling against her teeth, and then she shook her head. "Piss me off."

"Honestly, it's not personal," Rory replied, liking the way Pippa's smile came out in the end, the way they still tried to search for each other's weaknesses. "That's what everyone tells me."

"Should I be glad I'm not special?" Pippa tilted her head, and this time, Rory was ready for it, for the faltering of her stance.

This time, Rory didn't fall for Pippa's feint. She went in for the attack, and Pippa had to jump back in time to counter another blow.

"You are, though," Rory said. "I wouldn't be talking about dancing with anyone else."

Pippa snorted. "All right. I don't dance because I don't know how."

"I doubt that."

"I've always focused on fencing more than anything else," Pippa said, twirling her sword as she engaged again, positioned for Rory's next attack. "By the way, are you going to fight, or just talk? I kind of miss real battle?"

"Oh, you want real?" Rory said. "I'll give you real."

Pippa was ready for her, but not for the force that Rory was coming with. She parried the first blow, but her footwork was slightly off balance, her legs a bit more open than they should have been, and Rory knew she couldn't hesitate. The second blow came in full force, but it was only meant for Pippa to step back without regaining equilibrium. When Rory made the third cut, twisting her sword at the last minute to get in at an angle Pippa wouldn't be able to blow off, Pippa went crashing to the floor, her sword clattering, but not before pulling Rory down with her.

Rory's face was just centimeters above Pippa's. She looked down at Pippa's sweat-covered brows, and then cursing herself for it, dared to look at Pippa's parted lips and ragged breath.

She lingered in that moment for longer than she should. Then she scrambled back up and brushed herself off, her face flushed, her lungs gasping for air with a stab of pain that warned of an oncoming wave. "I think you'd be a good dancer," Rory said, finally.

She offered Pippa her hand.

"Why?" Pippa asked, still on her back, gasping. As she took Rory's hand, their fingers grasped together for what felt like only a second. Electricity jolted through Rory's body.

"Dancing is like fighting," Rory said. "And you're good at fighting."

CHAPTER EIGHTEEN

YUKI

Yuki spent the whole month turning Liron's words over inside her heart, knowing the truth within them. She wondered, every time, if she should just tell the others, but she knew it was futile. Liron hadn't given her an answer; she'd only given a way out.

Swallow your heart.

Yuki couldn't fall prey to that kind of thinking, not when she still felt the rising turmoil of her powers within her, knowing what she could do. Yuki was different not only because of who she was, but because of her powers. She couldn't save only herself.

Could she?

As she sat across from Reyna for their Saturday lunch, Yuki still thought about the curse, and how all her friends refused acknowledge that sooner or later, they would have to dig deeper for answers, push aside that feeling of helplessness.

Or maybe Yuki was the only one feeling this. Ella didn't seem helpless with Freddie by her side. Yuki watched her friends closely in their interactions, even if she didn't have patience for them—Nani with Svenja, the way Rory acted around Pippa, and most of all, Ella. Ella never seemed anxious by Freddie's side. Maybe he had that effect on her, and Yuki envied that.

Yuki didn't want to be jealous. Ella deserved good things; she deserved someone who loved her. It hadn't changed their friendship, yet there was a part of Yuki that still felt the stab inside her. Everything that Penelope had said about Yuki echoed within her deepest fears. Yuki hated that she didn't know if Penelope had truly understood her, or if she had just been manipulating Yuki all along to get what she wanted.

Except it hadn't worked all that perfectly. Penelope had threatened the wrong person, made the wrong move. And Yuki's blade was as unforgiving as her heart.

"What is it?" Reyna asked from across the table. "You're unusually quiet."

Yuki looked up to see one of the few pictures Reyna had put up on her shelf. Yuki, her father, and Reyna, all side-by-side. Probably the only picture Yuki had seen where her father was smiling, and she felt a pang in her heart.

"How did you know?" Yuki asked, turning back to Reyna. "How did you know my father was your true love?"

Reyna looked at her, blinked, and then burst out in laughter. The sound made her seem younger, and Yuki was reminded that Reyna was barely twenty years older than she was. The almost imperceptible wrinkles around her eyes vanished, and her hearty laugh echoed around the room in a breathless giggle.

"There's no such thing as true love, Yuki," Reyna said, the smile still wide on her face but her eyes kind and patient. "True love implies that all the other love you feel is false and that you cannot love more than one person at once. It's not something to be measured or balanced in an equation. I never believed in something like that. I don't think your father believed in it either, if we're being honest."

Yuki didn't understand this because Reyna had seemed like the last person in the world her father would marry. He'd married Yuki's mother, and they had Yuki, and they had been the perfect picture of a traditional family. Reyna was a foreigner, so different from Yuki's mother in both appearance and demeanor.

"Why, then?" Yuki asked. She'd wondered before, but she'd never pried. "What happened?"

Reyna reached forward and took a sip of her wine. "When we met, I thought he was an interesting man. He was intelligent, perceptive. And he cared about what I felt, which I always appreciated. I wasn't sure I'd ever marry him, though."

"Why?"

Reyna shrugged. "It's more complicated than wanting a relationship. I liked him, but for me, that romantic feeling— it's elusive, to describe it as best as I can. I told him so. He told me he didn't care, as long as I liked him. And that, I did."

Yuki opened her mouth, and strangely, it was like staring into a mirror of herself. She had never considered that Reyna could be like *her*. She always imagined that Reyna and her father had lived a maddening and short-lived epic love story, that something had swept over them both and that it had ended too soon when he was gone.

"So why did you?" Yuki asked, unable to stop herself. "If you didn't feel the same way, why did you marry him?"

"Because of you."

Yuki blinked, taken aback. "What?"

"That was your father's condition," Reyna explained. "If he was to marry someone else again, he wanted someone who could take care of you, just as he did. He wanted to make sure you wouldn't feel alone."

Yuki's eyes darted back to the picture of her father, feeling an echo of pain. Because it hadn't really mattered. She was still alone.

Except that Reyna felt the same way. Reyna seemed to know what it was like. Her marriage had been one of convenience, one of liking more than loving. Yuki felt like she'd been looking at the picture wrong the entire time.

"I always wanted to be a mother," Reyna continued, still staring at Yuki from across the table. "I didn't have a mother, and everyone told me what a special child I was. I didn't feel special. All the other girls had a mother, and I didn't."

"I didn't know you were an orphan too."

"Yes. I always hoped to find a love that would overwhelm me, that would sweep me off my feet, but I never did."

Reyna took a moment as if to search for the right words. Yuki could understand. It had taken her years too, and she never exactly found words that were enough to describe the depth of all that she could feel, even when the world told her that the way she felt was not enough. That her feelings didn't matter. For the longest time, Yuki thought that she was a frozen statue, unable to show her feelings in an adequate manner.

But it wasn't that Yuki didn't feel a thing; instead, she felt too much, too much all at once, and it was terrifying.

"A mother's love is unconditional," Reyna said. "It's the most powerful thing in the world, and I thought that if maybe I got to nurture it for someone, I'd understand. I'd get a small fraction of it in return. I would know what a love so devastating feels like."

Yuki felt the lump in the back of her throat growing, and she swallowed. Her heart beat steadily, but she didn't feel cold. Yuki had liked Reyna, but Reyna always felt so distant.

Yuki realized that she was to blame for that too. She'd always kept everyone at arm's length, not trusting anyone to get too close, feeling they would turn away as soon as they realized that the perfection was only a farce. That as soon as they saw the real Yuki, the Yuki who felt the darkness within her, the cruelty and the twisted gnawing bones, they'd turn away.

"I don't think I've been a good mother to you, Yuki."

"I'm not dead yet," Yuki whispered.

"I know," she replied quietly. "Being your mother is not as easy as I thought it would be, but I'm glad you gave me a chance to try."

Reyna could have chosen a different life. She didn't have to marry Yuki's father, and then she didn't have to stay. Still, she did. Even at their distance, with a table between them, Yuki realized that Reyna had always been there for her. Whenever she had to listen, whenever she had something to say, Reyna was there.

And in that moment, Yuki felt a little bit less lonely.

Yuki thought she should say something, maybe say something that felt real for once, because she was scared. No matter what the future held, it wasn't even the curse that bothered her. She'd made her mistakes, knew who she was, but still it didn't seem like enough, because soon enough, everything was going to change.

She was supposed to be enjoying her last year, but everyone was too busy worrying. About the curse, about the people they loved romantically, but Yuki felt like she was still stuck in the same place where she'd began. Everyone would move forward, and she would always stay here.

Everyone was going to leave her.

In that moment, before Yuki could manage any words at all, Reyna's phone rang. Reyna jumped, murmuring an excuse. She picked it up, and her expression changed from relaxed to concerned, her face going pale. Her brown eyes became sadder, her head shaking.

When she finally put the phone down, she looked at Yuki, studying her.

"What happened?" Yuki asked, but somehow, she knew what Reyna was going to say before she said it out loud. Yuki knew it had been coming, from the moment they did the deed.

"The ice melted," Reyna said. "They found a body float-ing in the lake."

Sooner or later, the curse would catch up.

Time had just run out.

PART II

BRING ME HER HEART

CHAPTER NINETEEN

ELLA

It took only three days for the body in the lake to be identified as Penelope's.

Or rather, the girl who had passed herself off as Penelope. The news picked up the story again—*Girl who pretended to be Penelope Barone for two years finally found*—and the remaining details became clear. This dead girl had all of Penelope's documents, and she certainly was the one responsible for killing the real Penelope in the first place.

For two years the false Penelope had kept the pretense up, working her way around the various difficulties such as not returning home on breaks, giving the excuse of a typical rich girl upset at being sent somewhere she didn't want to be. The news showed pictures, but they were of the real Penelope, not the one erased at the bottom of the lake. Ella almost felt sorry when she looked at them because now, with the sham discovered, it was as if the girl who had lived with them had never been real at all.

Grimrose was, of course, responding to the inquiries. Ella heard the whispers of investigators coming in. She went over her story of what she'd done that night, again and again and again, repeating it like a mantra. The lake would have washed fingerprints away. The fake Penelope wasn't wearing anything but her dress for the ball, and the girls had taken her purse. But no amount of concealed evidence would change the knife wound in Penelope's heart.

Nothing could mark them as being responsible. No one had seen them at the lake, far too cold for anyone else to be out on a stroll. The girls could all cover each other's alibis. Nani had been seen with Svenja at the ball. The lake had been covered with ice.

They were going to be okay. They had to be.

Gossip at the school ran rampant. Whispers followed throughout every corridor. According to the rumors, the fake Penelope surely had been behind the attacks last year— she had to be. Micaeli must have discovered the truth, and Penelope killed her first. The guesses were close enough to make Ella worry. Her eyes had dark circles, and she'd put her straight blond hair hastily into a tiny ponytail at the back of her head, held together by several colorful mismatched hair clips. She looked like she was falling apart.

"You should rest," Freddie told her by the end of the day. "You look tired, El."

His concern was genuine, and Ella was glad he worried about her, but it didn't make her feel better. "I just have insomnia, that's all."

Freddie looked at her like he wasn't buying it. "Come on, I'll take you home."

"I can't," Ella said. "Group project."

Just as she'd said it, Yuki appeared on the corridor outside their classroom as if on cue. Yuki looked the same as she always did—her beauty ethereal, hair black and luscious, skin luminescent. She didn't look one tiny bit anxious.

"What subject?" Freddie frowned. "Am I forgetting one? God, why do I do that?"

"History," Yuki said curtly. "Come on. We don't have much time."

Ella smiled apologetically at Freddie, rising on her tiptoes to give him a goodbye kiss. His lips found hers and Ella closed her eyes, feeling the tingling warmth and reassurance that Freddie always gave her.

When Ella opened her eyes, Yuki looked like she'd rather be thrown out of the tallest tower fifty times in a row than watch them.

"Sorry," Freddie said.

"For what?" Yuki said coolly, straight-faced.

"I know how annoying it is to be the fifth wheel," he said good-humoredly.

"I'm not a fifth wheel."

"I don't want you to feel like I'm stealing Ella from you," Freddie said jokingly, and something dark flashed in Yuki's eyes.

"You couldn't," Yuki said sharply, looking over at Ella.

There was a time when Yuki had kept the world away,

but now Ella could read everything on her face. Penelope's death had changed it. Yuki had been guarded, even with Ella. Ella had listened and tried to open Yuki like a fragile rose that needed encouragement to grow.

Except the rose hadn't grown into a flower. It had simply grown thorns.

"Very funny, you two," Ella replied, trying to keep her tone light. "No need for escalated hostilities."

"Don't want to be killed in my sleep, ha-ha," Freddie said.

Yuki gave an amused smile, her lip curling, and Ella's heart skipped a beat. "Oh, I wouldn't dream of it."

Ella grabbed Yuki's arm, yanking her before she gave any more away. Yuki waved politely, her face defiant and sharp.

"You didn't have to be so rude," Ella murmured as they walked off. "Don't you like him?"

"I have nothing against him."

"That's not the same as liking him," Ella said.

"He's your boyfriend, you're the one who has to like him."

"Don't be such a child."

"It's not personal," Yuki said. "You can ask Nani how I feel about Svenja."

Ella sighed, resigned, but she was glad that this was a normal conversation between them. They arrived at the group's usual spot at the library; Mephistopheles was already at his favorite place on the window seat. He looked even bigger than usual, his fur spiked, yellow eyes bright.

Nani didn't waste a moment. "What do they know?"

Yuki took a breath before moving to her usual seat. "The

bare facts. They know it's Penelope, they know she's been killed. They don't have a date."

"Any chance they'll let this go?" Nani asked, getting up, pacing around the room. Her curls were kept away from her face with a ribbon of periwinkle blue that matched their uniform, her glasses falling over the bridge of her nose.

"The others were deemed accidents," Yuki said, sounding almost bored.

"They won't find anything," Ella said, her voice assertive. She had been over this. She repeated, to assure herself, "They won't find anything."

"Are you sure?" Nani asked.

"Very sure," Ella repeated, glancing at Yuki.

Yuki did not look back at her.

"Does anyone feel weird that we're discussing murder like it's what we're having for lunch?" Rory asked, putting down her mirror after she'd popped a pimple on her chin.

"Rory, please," Ella said, feeling a headache coming on. "Do you even remember our story?"

"Of course I do," Rory replied, annoyed. "Yuki threw up, everyone went back to the room. No one saw anything."

"Then we do nothing," Ella said, determined. "If they ask questions, we answer them. We know what really happened that night."

When Ella's eyes met Nani's she quickly avoided them, as if those strong browns were ready to bore down into her, making her squirm. Ella didn't want to talk about what happened.

123

It was in the past. It was over.

"Fine," Nani finally said. "We still have to figure out what this means for us."

"There's only the body," Ella said.

"I'm talking about the curse," Nani said. "Penelope did what she did for a reason. She knew that there were two books, so how the hell did she know? What did she tell you?"

Ella frowned slightly, trying to rack her memory for answers, but when she closed her eyes, all she remembered was cleaning Penelope's body, her hands red with blood.

"She said she wasn't meant to find the book," Yuki said. "And that we all would have died anyway. She knew about the curse and how the tales ended."

"So does that mean she connected the dots by herself," Nani wondered, "or did someone else tell her?"

Ella's eyes opened again. "She said the book bought her way out. As long as people were dying, she could stay here. She was—she was rambling. She said she made a bargain to stay alive."

Nani's pacing was relentless. "What kind of bargain?"

"Why does it matter?" Rory said. "We have the books now."

"Yes, but it's too much of a coincidence. I don't want to be doing this any more than you do," Nani said with a sigh, finally pulling a chair to sit down. She massaged her temples. "I know we don't have a lot of answers. Honestly, we don't have a single fucking answer, which is great because I have a blank sheet and it can be filled with all our suggestions. But we have to start somewhere. It isn't ideal, but maybe

Penelope's body coming back puts things in motion again. It moves us forward."

Ella could only wish the body would have stayed buried for longer so that she didn't have to think about what had happened that night. She felt Nani's helplessness from across the table. She wanted answers, but wanting answers had cost them everything already.

Ella's eyes darted to Yuki again, thinking of the night of the ritual, how they'd pushed too far, and Yuki had come out a wholly different person.

Well, not different. Maybe she had just been hiding who she was all along.

"There's always the option of bargaining with the cat," Rory said, trying to cheer them up. Her eyes narrowed in the direction of Mephistopheles, who meowed nonchalantly. "The Prince of Hell holds all the answers. Do we have any spare souls?"

Suddenly, Nani got up from the table again. "Rory, you're a genius."

Rory blinked. "Wow. We're really *that* fucked?"

"Shut up," Nani said. "Look, if Penelope made a bargain, and she got to stay alive, the other person had the upper hand. Whoever it was knows about the curse. Not only that, but Penelope was supposed to make sure that the deaths kept happening, right?"

Nani looked at Ella, waiting for confirmation. Ella nodded, slowly.

"The only person who doesn't want to break a curse is

someone who benefits from it," Nani said. "Someone who wants it to keep going."

"The person who cast it," Yuki concluded. "But Penelope was trying to get away from that."

"Well, when you blackmail someone, there are only two options. You keep getting paid unless the other person gets fed up and finishes you off."

"I'm concerned about where this conversation is going," Rory said.

"Penelope wanted the book," Nani concluded. "The book is the key! And now that Penelope's body has been found, whoever bargained with her knows she isn't in the game anymore. That she doesn't have the books."

"This is so confusing," sighed Rory.

Ella knew that whoever bargained with Penelope would realize someone else had the books in their possession. The danger was coming for them. Again.

"So there's nothing we can do," Ella said. She got up, brushing her skirt. "We have to put this past us and focus on what we can still learn about the book and the curse."

"We can't just brush this off," Yuki said, meeting Ella's gaze from across the table. Ella stared at her best friend, willing her not to say anything, willing Yuki not to acknowledge it. Neither of them moved. "This is what brought us here."

"Don't say it like that," Ella whispered.

She knew what Yuki was going to say next. She knew it because it's what she'd been doing her best to ignore, to pretend, to lock it away in her mind and never see it again.

Please, Ella thought, *please don't say it.*

"We can't pretend that this has nothing to do with us," Yuki said. "We can't pretend it's not our fault."

"Why not?" Ella asked brusquely, and begging, begging in her mind for Yuki not to say it out loud, because that meant she had to admit that it was real. "Why not?"

Don't. Yuki. Don't.

"Because *I* killed Penelope!"

CHAPTER TWENTY

YUKI

The words had come out impulsively.

It reminded Yuki too much of the last time she'd exploded. This time, though, there was no rising of her voice, no feeling of loss of control, because Yuki did not need to be in control anymore. She was free, and calm, and she'd killed a girl because she wanted her dead.

Ella stared at her from across the table, the light from behind the window creating mosaics in the hazel of her irises.

"I know," Ella finally answered, her voice quiet. She didn't avoid Yuki's gaze. "I was there."

There was a silence following Ella's statement. Rory and Nani chose to look anywhere but at the two girls facing each other across the table. Yuki couldn't blame them; in the end, it hadn't been their choice. They weren't the ones who made the decisions; Ella and Yuki had. And now the consequences had caught up to them.

Penelope's body had emerged, and their sin was exposed like an open book.

"It doesn't change things," Ella said, taking a deep breath. "We did what we had to. Penelope killed our friend, and she killed other people in school too. She wasn't innocent."

If she wasn't innocent, Yuki wasn't, either.

Her actions were as deliberate as Penelope's.

"But she was being manipulated," Nani pointed out. "What would happen if she'd gotten the two books? Would that have given her power over the people who cast the curse? And were they willing to destroy her if she didn't help their plan along?"

"But the deaths happen either way," Rory said, frustrated.

"Liron didn't die," Nani pointed out. "And she didn't break the curse."

"She didn't get a happy ending either," Ella said, and Yuki kept herself quiet. If Yuki told them about Liron's choice, it would break them in half.

Penelope's body hadn't broken them, but the next thing might.

Yuki would have to be the one to bear it to the end, knowing the price of surviving the curse without truly ending it.

A last resort.

"So what else can we do?" Rory asked, exasperated, throwing her hands in the air. "We don't know who was manipulating Penelope, and unless we can talk to the ghosts of all those girls who came before, we aren't getting anywhere."

Yuki narrowed her eyes in Rory's direction. Her mirror

visions were less frequent now, but she'd spotted different versions of herself. Yuki hadn't stopped thinking about Liron's description of the other girl from Grimrose, the one who looked like her. White skin, black hair, red lips.

Yuki didn't understand what it meant.

"We don't need their ghosts," Nani said. "We have the book."

"What?" Ella asked, frowning.

Yuki caught Nani's meaning fast enough. "We use the portraits in the book," Yuki said. "Like we used it with Liron. Her story was over, but most of the others aren't."

"Exactly," Nani said, offering a smile in Yuki's direction. "Look, we can do this. Ariane could only guess who was who, but we have both books, we know our classmates. We know how the story can go wrong. If we keep a close watch on these girls, we'll know when the end is coming."

"How does that help us break the curse?" Rory asked.

Nani's smile was apologetic. "I don't know if it does. But if the book changes, we'll learn something new."

"We can break them into groups," Ella said, nodding along. "This way we can at least see how far along everyone is. And if anyone else tries to interfere in a story, we'll know who the culprit is."

Ella had waited for Nani and Rory to go back down the stairs before she pulled Yuki back into the library. They'd collected the books and assigned the fated girls between themselves, all in the name of having something new to do, whatever that was.

Ella's hand was warm on her arm, but Yuki quickly brushed away the touch.

"You're okay, right?" Ella asked, voice subdued.

"Yes. Why?"

Ella searched Yuki's face. "I'm worried, that's all."

"You don't need to worry about me," Yuki told her flippantly. "You know that."

"These last months have been hard," Ella said. She reached out to scratch behind Mephistopheles' ears, and the devilish cat purred contentedly. "Some things change."

"And some don't," Yuki replied. "I know you don't want to talk about it either."

Ella's looked away, her eyes blinking rapidly, looking hurt. Yuki knew had gone straight to the sore spot. Ella wouldn't talk about it, but she didn't want to pretend nothing was happening to Yuki. Except that what was happening to Yuki was intricately connected to the murder she'd committed.

Yuki observed the familiar lines of her best friend. In the past, this conversation would have ended at this point out of kindness and from trying to be more like Ella. Except she wasn't that girl anymore. If Ella was good, she was so effortlessly, and no matter how much Yuki tried, Yuki could never be enough.

So Yuki wasn't going to try at all.

"We have it under control." Yuki's voice hardened. "Isn't that what you said?"

Ella hesitated for a moment again. Yuki could almost see her mind working. Trying to approach Yuki without scaring her away.

"You know I'll be here if you need it," Ella replied, and there was something else in her voice that Yuki heard: an echo of the moment when the blizzard was all around them, when Yuki had unleashed everything so she could test the limits of where she could go. To see whether she could come back at all.

"Thanks," Yuki replied, "but I don't need it."

"Everyone does," Ella countered.

"Don't do that," Yuki snapped. "Stop trying to make me say something, because you won't like what you hear."

Ella's mouth was a determined fine line, her eyes firm. "Why not?"

"Because I'm not you!" Yuki exclaimed. "Because the answer you want is not the one I can give you. That's not who I am."

"I don't want you to be anyone else," Ella said, gentle. She reached out again, and this time, Yuki purposefully drew back.

"Really?" Yuki asked, her voice exasperated. "Because this is who I am. The girl who killed Penelope. Do you understand that?"

I would kill for you, Yuki thought, *and I have.*

It made it sound like a sacrifice, deliberate and careful, but Yuki didn't think Penelope's killing had been either of those things. She hadn't sacrificed herself to do it. She'd just let go. Became who she was meant to be.

Yuki wasn't perfect, and she was never going to be.

She was ice and cold and darkness; she was sharp and scared and lonely, and there was a hunger so deep within her to be accepted, to be loved, to be embraced for who she was.

She wasn't better than Penelope. She was exactly like her.

And if Yuki accepted herself, all her friends would turn their backs on her.

Ella took her hand at that moment, gave it a squeeze. The touches were becoming more frequent now. Yuki had grown up without any, and they usually made her jolt. But Ella's hand fit over hers, and it was the only thing Yuki was sure of anymore, even when she was desperate for Ella to really look at her.

Ella wasn't going to like what she saw, and Yuki was terrified of the day she would finally see it.

"I do," Ella said, "and it's all going to be okay."

Ella wasn't a very good liar.

CHAPTER TWENTY-ONE

NANI

Nani hadn't given the others a chance to claim Svenja.

Svenja's face in the White Book was Nani's problem because Svenja was her girlfriend. She'd considered giving Svenja a clue, finding a way to talk to her about the curse, but she'd given up on the idea as soon as it occurred to her. Nani would take care of Svenja's story as if it were her own, because it probably was. If falling for Svenja meant that Nani's cursed and beastly prince didn't exist, or if Svenja was another version of it, then that meant Nani, too, was playing a part in a tale that wasn't her own.

She owed Svenja. Or at the very least, following Svenja's story would be a gift. Nani could give her that.

She took her list with her, observing the girls' names on it, trying to figure out where they were in their stories. Nani knew each of the girls in Grimrose by name now, if not by story. The curse weighed heavily on her heart as she walked through classes, did her homework, and tried to remember that there was a life to live that wasn't folded within the pages of the Black Book.

Nani sat to do her homework on one of the library window seats, watching the other students in the garden below, when her phone rang. She picked it up. The librarian was used to her now, and she didn't mind Nani talking as long as she was quiet.

"Hi, moʻo."

Hearing Tūtū's voice was a comfort, but it also created in Nani a wave of sadness and longing that she thought she'd never get over.

"Hi, Tūtū," Nani said, closing her eyes for a moment, the call taking her miles away from the castle. "I miss you."

"Soon enough you'll be home," Tūtū said cheerfully on the other side of the line. "And then you'll tell me all about it. You're not giving the rich kids a hard time, are you?"

Nani snorted. "They wouldn't know a hard time if it punched them in the face."

"Nani," her grandmother said in a warning tone. "You play nice. I won't hear someone say my granddaughter across the world hasn't got any manners."

"I do. Too many manners if you ask me."

Tūtū sighed through her nose. "Sometimes you are too much like your mother. Your heart was born out of an argument, and it's only happy whenever it's in one."

That got a smile out of Nani, even if it wasn't meant as a compliment.

"You haven't heard from dad, have you?" Nani asked, already knowing what her grandmother's answer would be.

"Not yet, moʻo." Nani liked the *not yet* her grandmother always used. As if the next day would somehow turn out miraculously different. "You enjoy that fancy school of yours before he comes to drag you away. The other day I was talking to what's her name, the nice daughter of the owner of the market, not the one across the street, the other one—"

Nani was only paying half her mind to the overly complicated story, and it all seemed too far away. Nani looked around at the library just before she saw Svenja make her way over.

"Tūtū, I gotta go," Nani said, cutting off her grandmother. "I'll call you later."

"You take care, moʻo. Study hard. Eat well, you hear? I saw that last picture you sent me. They don't know how to cook over there."

"Bye, Tūtū!"

Her grandmother was still talking when Nani pressed the red button just as Svenja sat down. She planted a kiss on Nani's cheek and adjusted her uniform skirt as she leaned against the opposite wall of the window seat.

"Your grandmother?" Svenja asked, and Nani nodded in reply.

Svenja sat quietly across from her, contemplative. That wasn't like Svenja. Svenja was usually the opposite—where Nani was quiet and introspective, Svenja was provocative, unnerving, trying to always get a rise out of Nani. And most days, she did.

Still, it was hard to know what Svenja was really thinking. There was always an aura of mystery around her, and even though she'd asked Nani for her secrets, she still seemed to keep some of her own.

"Can I ask you a question?" Svenja said, looking Nani straight in the eye.

"You already—"

"Yes, I already did, thank you *so* much for that insight, it's particularly clever," Svenja said, interrupting her. "Look, my mom is coming to Switzerland for Easter, and I was wondering if you'd like to come with me to meet her."

Nani froze. Of all the things she was expecting, this was at the very bottom on the list of conversations she'd thought she'd have with Svenja.

"I don't celebrate Easter," Nani said, the first thing that crossed her mind. Sure, they did *Christmas* at her house, but Christmas was Christmas because she got gifts and they stayed together with family, but it wasn't really a celebration of the religious part of it.

Svenja laughed outright, a shrill and delighted noise, which earned them a look from the librarian. Nani put a hand over Svenja's mouth to muffle the sound until she finally was in control again.

"So that's a no?" Svenja said lightly, crossing her legs over Nani's lap. It was only a small contact of skin, but it was still electrifying. Nani looked around, almost sure that the librarian would expel them for their next transgression.

"I just..." Nani wanted to find the right words. For a girl

137

who had read so much, it figured that she should have been better at them. "What do you want me to do?"

"Nani, it's an invitation, not a death sentence. I want you to do whatever you want to do. That's it."

Somehow, it didn't seem like the truth.

Nani hadn't even told Tūtū about Svenja yet because that meant there was a certainty in the future, and with the curse, even Hawai'i and its shores felt like something she wouldn't see again. The more she thought about it, the more she thought that Grimrose was the only real thing, and everything else was a lie.

The thing was, Nani was sure Tūtū would invite Svenja over as soon as she heard about Nani's relationship. She'd make a big fuss about the visit, insist on taking Svenja to see her favorite parks, showing Nani's baby pictures, maybe even going on a boat tour, even if Tūtū feared and hated boats. ("My ancestors settled on the island for a reason, mo'o. Somebody has to stay indoors while the other fools get in the water.") Her grandmother would love to have people over; she always did.

Nani just didn't know if she was ready to make all these plans yet. She didn't know what she wanted. That had always been the problem.

First, she wanted family. Her father home, her mother alive. Then she wanted comfort, which she found in books because her family had been too hard. And then the books had offered her adventures and a place where she wanted to belong, a place that was real and true, and where Nani could find her home.

And even that wish seemed too unattainable.

"Can you let me think on it?" Nani asked.

Svenja shrugged. "Sure. Take your time. I just thought it'd be a good idea."

Nani could see that Svenja was expecting her to reply that she agreed and that she'd been just taken by surprise— but Nani wasn't going to lie to Svenja. And if she accepted the invite, then what did it mean? She didn't want to dream of things that couldn't be. Nani was far too practical for that.

Nani closed the book on her lap. She hated change. She hated things that were out of her field of control, and ever since coming to Grimrose, it was all her life had been. Her father was missing, she'd tumbled into a relationship in which she didn't know the rules, and now there was ominous magic in the air controlling her fate and pulling her strings.

Nani had always been stubborn enough to turn her back on all the rules. She hoped it'd be enough to carry her through the end.

CHAPTER TWENTY-TWO

The conversation with Yuki replayed in Ella's mind for a long time.

Because this is who I am.

Ella didn't know how to answer that. Not when she'd spent so much time in her life loving her best friend and only now suspecting that she didn't know who Yuki was at all.

They'd split all the girls in the books among themselves. Ella had Alethea, the student body president that was in a lot of her classes; Ivy, the shy girl who wore her long hair in a braid down her back, the thick strands of light brown interwoven like a rope; and Emília, a girl two years younger who hailed from Brazil. None of their stories seemed too complicated, and Ella was glad she could keep an eye on how things were going, letting herself feel useful. In truth, even with all of Nani's brilliant deductions, Ella wasn't sure she and her friends had made any real progress.

Luckily, her work was not that difficult, mostly because it was impossible to miss Alethea, for one.

"Eleanor," Alethea had called to her as soon as she walked into their classroom that Thursday morning, "are you volunteering?"

Ella headed straight for her chair. Her hair was dripping from the rain outside, her uniform soaked. She'd ran all the way to school, but she hadn't escaped the weather. "Volunteering for what?"

"Alethea needs more minions to boss around for the graduation party committee," Rhiannon explained.

"I'm not bossing people around," Alethea replied haughtily. "I'm directing. It's different."

Rhiannon shook her head at Ella. Alethea shot her best friend an awry look.

"Ella can't stay after class," Stacie cut in, offering an excuse. Ella looked at her stepsister and gave her a faint smile. "I'm sure you don't need more people."

Alethea groaned, doodling with her pen. "I don't want prom to be less than perfect. Besides, some people who volunteered are already trying to back out. Ivy, for one."

Ella's ears perked up. Micaeli might have been the original source of gossip in Grimrose, but she hadn't been the only one.

"Ivy?" Ella asked. "What's wrong with her?"

"Wrong wouldn't be the word I'd use," Rhiannon said in a half-whispered tone as the others leaned in. "She's just been acting strange lately. Sleepwalking a lot. Delilah was telling

141

me about it. She could have sworn she saw Ivy trying to sneak off the school grounds through the eastern gate tower."

"But that's off limits," Ella said. "And she's graduating. We can all leave the school without permission, through the front gate."

Alethea raised her eyebrows, just to say that a point had been made. "Who knows what's in her head? She's always been strange, in my opinion."

"You think that about everyone," Stacie said, bored, and Alethea glared at her as well.

"Do you think it could be serious?" Ella asked.

Rhiannon shrugged. "It can't be worse than what we had last year. She doesn't look like she's about to kill anyone."

"Neither did Penelope," Alethea said darkly. Ella offered a sympathetic smile. Alethea had lost a friend too, when Micaeli was killed.

Nani walked into the classroom at that precise moment, and Alethea immediately hassled her. "Hey! New girl! Volunteer for the graduation party!"

Nani looked like she'd rather be struck by lightning. "Not in ten lifetimes."

Ella snorted while Alethea was put off by Nani's bluntness. Ella turned around in her seat. "Any progress?"

Nani shook her head. Then she frowned. Her hand reached out, but she stopped. "You have something on your face."

Ella checked herself in the mirror in her bag, and her whole body went cold. "I have to go," she whispered, picking up her bag and running to the bathroom.

She got to the closest bathroom, and because the bell had already rung, she was thankfully alone. In the mirror, she saw the dark stain that covered the left side of her face. Her foundation had melted in the rain. A novice mistake.

Shuddering a sigh, Ella washed her face and dried it with paper towels, her hazel eyes staring back from the mirror. Mousy-looking, Sharon called her, and Ella could see why. She was small, bony, underfed. Her shoulders were all angles, but beneath the skin, she had muscles from all the house chores.

She took out her makeup pouch for emergencies and reinforced the mascara and eyeliner, applied a pinkish lipstick to seem healthy, and foundation over the heavy concealer. When her bruises were fresh, she used green concealer, and as they faded, she changed to an orange kind to counteract the yellow-greenish haze. She was almost done when Nani came in after her, stopping and staring right at Ella.

At the bruise that was still visible.

"You left in a hurry," Nani said. "I was worried."

Ella had been in this spot more times than she would have liked. She could brush it off and act naturally, quickly putting off the suspicion.

"It's nothing," Ella said, her hand hovering over the yellowish bruise on her jawline. "I fell down the stairs."

For a moment, Ella thought Nani was going to let it go.

She didn't.

"I've seen people fall down the stairs," Nani said quietly. "It doesn't look like that."

Ella felt the lump in her throat taking form, threatening to consume all her words before she could think up of an excuse.

"I have it taken care of," Ella managed to say, her voice coming out half-choked, slathering on even more foundation until her skin was covered by a thick layer that made her seem like her face was made of concrete. "Really, I do."

Nani said nothing, her arms crossed over her chest, looking down slightly, and Ella felt vulnerable standing there. Usually, she was the one in Nani's position. She was the one listening and offering help because she knew what it was like to need it and not know how to ask for it.

"Do the others know?" Nani finally asked.

Ella nodded. She finished tidying up mechanically. She washed her hands, stained by the black of her mascara, until they came out clean. A ritual she had gone through many times.

"It's okay," Ella reassured Nani, wanting to apologize for the whole inconvenience of having to listen to her sorrows. "It doesn't...it doesn't get worse than this."

Except sometimes, it did. Sometimes she'd have bruises on her face that she couldn't hide with makeup. A broken arm, a broken wrist. Yuki had called Reyna once, when she'd learned what was happening, but Sharon only made it worse—making sure Ella didn't leave the house for two weeks, at risk of her scholarship being taken away. After that, Yuki had never mentioned it again. Ella's bruises were hers to take care of and hers to tend until she healed.

She didn't want to burden anyone else with her sob story.

"You can't be serious," Nani said, her tone full of barely

contained rage as she adjusted the round frames of her glasses. "There must be something we can do."

"Yes," Ella said. "I wait. My birthday is in June. When I turn eighteen, I'm free. I get my father's money back. All I have to do is survive until then."

Ella hadn't meant to say the last words, but they slipped out before she could stop them. She'd been thinking it ever since the visit to Liron's house, and every week that had passed was part of the countdown.

"So that's why you ran that day," Nani said, the realization dawning on her face. "June is when your story ends."

Ella's shoulders sagged in relief, glad there was at least one person who understood. Even if Nani hadn't mentioned what they were both surely thinking—that her tragic end would be waiting for her if they couldn't stop the curse.

"I don't have much time," Ella whispered.

Nani nodded, her face serious. Ella had liked Nani's face from the moment she'd met her. There was a determined aura about her that reminded Ella of her first school crush, when she was nine, a tall Indian girl who had been in her class and collected butterfly wings. Ella had spent the whole summer trying to catch butterflies with her. Once, they'd spent five hours in the same spot, determined not to leave without a catch. Nani had the same reassurance: the way she carried herself proudly, how she didn't let anyone step on her.

"We're not going to fail," Nani said. "I have a stake in this too."

They both stood looking at each other, and Ella brushed

the last of her hair behind her ear, taking a deep breath, stopping her body from shaking. She'd been through too much already. She wasn't going to give up now. She couldn't let herself be defeated or pulled into hopelessness. She was better than that.

She offered hope when no one else could. It's what she'd always done.

"Your father is out there," Ella told Nani. "And we're going to find him. Because it's part of your story, but also because you deserve to find him. You don't have to do this on your own."

Nani nodded, smiling back. Ella pushed any concerns she had aside. She couldn't get caught up with the bad things.

She had a curse to break and people to save.

CHAPTER TWENTY-THREE

Yuki wasn't keen on the idea of following other girls' stories, and she'd never been one to take interest in people's lives. Still, for the sake of trying to study how the curse worked, Yuki made an effort. Delilah and her sister Sienna didn't seem to be showing any signs of having a story; Lana, a Russian girl who was a year below them, seemed to have a story that was too similar to Ella's; and So-dam, who Yuki had exchanged only brief conversations with during their years of school, didn't seem to be out for blood every night as her story would have her.

It's not that Yuki didn't try hard enough, but there seemed to be no point. When a story was on the brink of coming to an end, that's when they would know who was in danger. They couldn't predict where lightning would strike before it did.

It was like trying to stop destiny itself.

Yuki thought they had nothing to worry about until she was called to Mrs. Blumstein's office.

Mrs. Blumstein's office was in one of the other towers of the castle, a secluded place in the western wing. There was a spiral staircase all the way up, one that was tricky to climb.

Along with Mrs. Blumstein, Ms. Lenz and Miss Bagley, two of the oldest teachers in school, stood in the room, one thin and with sharp eyebrows, the other stout and short.

"Please sit down, Miss Miyashiro, we'll talk in a moment," Mrs. Blumstein said almost absentmindedly across her desk, but Yuki didn't move to take a seat.

"What's this about?" she asked, looking at all three teachers.

Ms. Lenz and Miss Bagley exchanged a look, which wasn't lost on Yuki.

"We'll leave you to it," Miss Bagley said in her high-pitched voice. "Be seated, Yuki. It should only take a moment."

Yuki watched with narrowed eyes as the two teachers turned their backs and closed the door, their steps echoing down the stairs. Yuki sat down, finally, her posture erect, her black hair falling over her shoulders as Mrs. Blumstein finished typing something.

"I'm so glad you could come," she said, smiling to Yuki behind her square lenses.

"I thought it was a summoning rather than an invitation."

Mrs. Blumstein smiled politely. Yuki didn't let herself worry.

They'd found the body, but not the weapon, and even if they had, no one could prove anything.

"This is just routine, my dear," Mrs. Blumstein said. "I wanted to ask a few questions about Livia Ricci."

Yuki blinked. "I'm sorry, who?"

"The girl who impersonated Penelope Barone while she was at Grimrose," the teacher clarified. "She has been identified at last, and I'm asking a few questions to those who were closest to her."

Yuki trained her face not to move a single muscle. She'd had years of hiding her anger beneath the surface, remaining impassive when she'd only felt storms.

"We're looking for anything that could help us figure out what happened to her," Mrs. Blumstein said. "We know now she was likely responsible for the murder of the real Penelope. Other than that, she was an exemplary student who never got into trouble. We want to know what happened."

Yuki breathed through her nose, thinking of all the possibilities and the questions Mrs. Blumstein could ask, but she knew better than to say anything. She hadn't even understood Penelope's motivations in the first place.

This fake Penelope had been a better Penelope than the real one could ever have been. The imposter had been puppet and puppeteer, and Yuki couldn't be sure if that had been all there was between them.

Maybe Penelope had been her equal, and Yuki had failed to see it.

"You girls talked," Mrs. Blumstein said gently, wrinkles forming next to her eyes. "Unfortunately, Penelope's only other close friend in school was Micaeli, and she's gone too."

"And Ari," Yuki said. "Ari was her friend."

Mrs. Blumstein tilted her head, and Yuki didn't move. She didn't like being examined this closely. She'd never drawn much attention from the teachers, even though her grades had always been perfect and her posture impeccable. Yuki had stayed quiet, blended in, and this way, she had disappeared into the shadows.

Mrs. Blumstein was trying to get her back into the light.

"So many losses this past year," she said, shaking her head sadly. "It's become hard to keep track."

Yuki wasn't suffering a debilitating grief. All she understood were the words of her wanting, of the darkness that lurked in the corners of her soul, and the fact that she'd not hesitated when it was time for her to choose.

Maybe she'd made a mistake. Maybe it would be marked forever on her soul.

But it had been *her* mistake to make.

Yuki refused to atone for it.

"So did you see Livia before the holidays?" Mrs. Blumstein asked, her eyes scanning Yuki's.

"Only at the ball, I think," Yuki said, feigning concentration. "I spent the better part of the evening in the bathroom. I may have seen her briefly."

"May?" Mrs. Blumstein raised an eyebrow.

"The ball was dark, full of people," Yuki replied. "I wouldn't count on my recollection of the evening."

"What happened?"

"Stomachache," Yuki said, the lie they'd been telling to

themselves coming out easily. "Rory and Nani were with me, if you want to verify."

"We're not asking for alibis, Miss Miyashiro," Mrs. Blumstein said with a reprieving tone. "We think that was the night she suffered her accident."

"So it was an accident," Yuki stated, her voice cutting in quickly.

"An accident means many things, even an untimely encounter with death," the teacher replied. "The police aren't going to ignore all the events in campus this past year, and Livia's no exception. When too many coincidences happen, we can't help but to start questioning their truth."

"Maybe you should have questioned a little earlier when the first body showed up in the lake," Yuki said.

Mrs. Blumstein didn't answer her, her lips sealed tight until they were an almost invisible line. Just at that instant, the door behind them opened, and Yuki turned around to see her stepmother, looking as if she'd just run up the whole flight of stairs. Her hand was on the doorknob, and her eyes flashed dark as she saw Yuki sitting there.

"Oh, Reyna," said Mrs. Blumstein, her tone strained. Reyna had never really hidden her dislike for the teachers, complaining that running the school was only subject to the school board and no one else. "Is there something you needed from me?"

Reyna seemed to take an instant to recompose herself, her features schooling back into polite coldness. "I'm not sure any further investigations are necessary unless the police require them. I'd rather you let Yuki get back to her studies."

Mrs. Blumstein gave the smallest sigh through her nose. "Yes, of course."

Reyna looked at Yuki, and Yuki got up.

"Well, if you remember anything at all that Livia might have said," Mrs. Blumstein ventured, "I'm sure the police will appreciate it."

"I'll let them know," Yuki replied pointedly. "But as I said, Penelope wasn't my friend. Is that all?"

Mrs. Blumstein looked at Reyna, but Reyna's face betrayed nothing. Yuki watched the apparent tension between the two women. Finally, it was Mrs. Blumstein who broke.

"Yes," she said. "Be careful on the way down. We don't want any more accidents."

She offered Yuki a smile, but her eyes were staring straight at Reyna.

"What was that about?" Yuki asked as soon as they were out of the stairwell and once again in the larger corridors of Grimrose.

Reyna shook her head. Yuki noticed her red nail polish was peeling. Reyna was never less than perfect, and that single detail bothered Yuki.

"You've noticed that there's an investigation," Reyna said. "The police say the cause of Livia's death is inconclusive."

"So it was an accident?"

Reyna paused. "No. They think she was murdered."

Yuki didn't know how to react—if she were to feign shock, an exaggeration might give her away. She stayed still as a pine tree in winter, bracing herself.

"They don't have any suspects," Reyna continued. "And it's not likely that they will considering how they've been turning in circles."

"What are you going to do?"

Reyna blinked, and once again, Yuki watched as her stepmother looked not quite herself, as she too was used to wearing a mask of perfection that never slipped. Only now her edges were coming undone.

"I don't have the power to do anything at all," she said. "The school board is deciding whether to call for my resignation."

"What?" Yuki exclaimed, caught by surprise.

"Yes. It is—harrowing, to say the least. Clearly, I haven't been handling things as well as I ought. As long as we don't have any other accidents, we should be able to make it through the rest of the school year."

No more accidents, or Reyna would be gone. No more accidents, or Yuki's own story would be spiraling in a way that would take her far away from Grimrose. Wasn't that what she wanted? To escape? Her heart beat with a sudden spike of magic, a sudden uncertainty that wasn't there before.

"Do you want to tell me anything else?" Reyna asked.

"No."

Reyna searched her face, and Yuki felt as if her stepmother was looking through her, through her mask, into the depths of her very soul. Yuki stood her ground.

"You'll tell me if you need anything," Reyna said, "won't you?"

"Of course," Yuki said.

"Good. No more accidents."

Yuki knew the words were supposed to be assuring, but all she heard was the underlying threat.

CHAPTER TWENTY-FOUR

RORY

Rory had just returned to her room when she heard something crash in the bathroom.

Rory ran and opened the door, and there was Yuki, her face unreadable, the mirror smashed into a hundred thousand different pieces on the floor. Yuki was gripping the sink basin.

When she turned to face Rory, Rory involuntarily stepped back. Yuki's eyes were all black, her hands so white that Rory felt the cold emanating from them in a rising mist from where she was standing, fogging the pieces of the glass.

"You okay?" Rory asked.

Yuki's eyes softened. "Yeah. It was an accident."

It didn't look like an accident. She'd smashed the mirror with her own hands, but where Rory stood, there was no sign of blood. Yuki's hands were white and spotless.

"Don't tell Ella," Yuki said, her black hair a curtain over half her face. "She'll think..."

Yuki didn't finish the sentence, but Rory knew what she meant. It would worry Ella more than was necessary; by all appearances, what they had done hadn't really changed them.

Except it had. Of course it had.

Especially Yuki.

"I'll get the dustpan," Rory said instead, trying to remain practical. "We'll clean this up before Nani gets back."

Yuki gave her a grateful look, pushing her hair behind her ears, standing in place until Rory got the dustpan and broom. Rory handed the broom to Yuki to get the smaller pieces of the broken glass, picking up the larger pieces carefully in her hands. Yuki swept the pieces into Rory's dustpan.

Rory lifted the handle to carry it away, but her fingers cramped suddenly in a bout of pain, and she dropped the dustpan, the pieces falling to the floor again. Rory cursed.

"Let me do that," Yuki said, crouching.

"I'm fine," Rory snarled, snatching the dustpan again before Yuki could pick it up. This time, her fingers obeyed, her body dutiful once more as she cleaned the mess up.

Sometimes, Rory forgot that her body was never going to obey her entirely. It would always betray her when she least expected it, even when she'd honed it as much as she could. When she looked up, Yuki was watching her, but instead of judgment, there was sympathy, as if she understood what it meant to lose control.

And of course she did. Rory still remembered the sharpness of the icicles in their room. Yuki's magic was heavy and dangerous, and all it took was one second for Yuki to lose her grasp and hurt someone.

"What happened in Mrs. Blumstein's office?" Rory asked finally.

"They know Penelope was murdered," Yuki replied, without looking at Rory. She examined a piece of the mirror, holding it up between two of her long fingernails. "The school board is thinking of calling for Reyna's resignation."

"Are you serious?" Rory asked. "They don't mean that."

"Rory, people are *dying*," Yuki said, emphasizing the word. "That's not supposed to be normal."

"You'd think the only concern the board would have in a Swiss school would be tax fraud or something."

Yuki shot her a look, her lips curled in distaste. "Rory."

"I know, I know. Be serious."

Yuki snorted, and Rory shot her a grin. Rory finished the floors, and then they wrapped up the glass, ready to throw it in the trash. There was no sign of broken reflections anywhere, and it was like there had never been a mirror there at all.

"What happens if Reyna leaves?" Rory asked.

"I don't know," Yuki replied. "It's my last year of school. I think I'd have to stay."

Rory noticed the choice of words, the way Yuki was always careful and deliberate about anything that she said. It wasn't lost on Rory.

"You mean you *could* leave," Rory said, looking up at Yuki, hearing the possibility in her voice. "If you wanted."

"Yes. I think I could."

Rory fiddled with her hair, brushing it back from her forehead, trying to untangle her feelings. She leaned against the sink with her hands gripping the edges to keep herself propped up, facing Yuki.

Yuki could leave—Yuki could choose it. And her magic would probably help her.

"If Reyna resigns, you should take the chance."

Yuki blinked. "Isn't that just running?"

Rory shrugged. "I wouldn't blame you."

Yuki chuckled, her smile bitter. "You would. You aren't able to run, so why should I? Why do I get to be the one to turn my back on this place?"

There was another question Yuki didn't say, and the one Rory read between the lines, like she'd learned to do with Yuki from the start: Why did Yuki get to be the one to turn her back on her friends?

Rory looked down at her feet, and there was a truth in what Yuki said—she envied, just a bit, what Yuki had, that freedom that she'd acquired through her magic. Yuki could run away and be fine, probably. But even if Rory tried it, it wouldn't be enough. She couldn't hide from who she was.

But Yuki had paid the price too; she was just better at hiding her frustrations. Rory was supposed to see only the perfect image that Yuki had crafted, but now all she saw when she looked at Yuki were the cracks.

"Liron wasn't here, she didn't escape either," Rory said. "We don't know enough. But you know what? If one of us gets to escape the curse, that's more than enough. If one of us gets to escape—"

"Then it's Ella, not me."

Their eyes met, and Rory didn't remember the last time she'd seen such determination. Yuki had been offered a way out, but she wasn't taking it. Rory couldn't tell if it was stupid or brave, or maybe, like all things, it was both.

"Then it's all of us," Rory corrected. "Ella would kill us if we thought of giving up."

Yuki smiled. "Ella wouldn't kill anyone."

"Right. We'd get preached to death."

"I'd rather take my chances with the curse."

Rory laughed, because honestly, she felt the same. Still, when she looked at Yuki, she saw not only her friend for many years, but also something else entirely. Yuki was the one who truly looked right out of a fairy tale, conjured up right from of the page.

"We're good, right?" Rory asked, voice uncertain, remembering how tense it had been with Yuki, a tension Yuki seemed to have with everyone lately.

But maybe it was just Rory's imagination. Maybe everything would turn out fine, and they'd all get to see the other side of the end that was coming.

Rory glanced at Nani's side of the bed, thinking of Ari again.

"Yeah," Yuki replied. "We're good."

CHAPTER TWENTY-FIVE

ELLA

Spring arrived with little fanfare. Almost a whole month after the equinox, the flowers finally decided to bloom, fighting away the rest of the snow that still insisted on showing up, and the green of the grass conquered its territory slowly but surely. Once the landscape had been completely transformed, the students of Grimrose Académie flocked to the sunny spots around the water, sunbathing and laughing like nothing was wrong.

"It's not wrong," Ella said. "Not for them."

Frederick wrapped his arm tighter around Ella's waist as they walked to the bus stop after Friday's classes had ended.

"I know," Freddie answered. "We could have gone somewhere else. We don't have to sit by the lake."

"Where else? The abandoned owlery?"

"It's as good a spot as any."

"That place is full of cobwebs and the steps are all splintered. It's a death trap."

Freddie tilted his head. "You've been there?"

"What?" Ella said, pointedly ignoring his last remark.

Freddie studied his girlfriend's face, smiling to himself. "Sometimes, Ella, I think you're better at lying than you give yourself credit for."

"It was a stupid prank," Ella said. "But I'm not going up there again unless we get bleach and mops."

"That sounds like a lovely date," he replied, and Ella felt he was only being half ironic.

They continued their walk as Ella counted the steps down the path to the edge of the school. It was a routine that they'd established without Ella even having to ask him. Every Friday after class they'd walk to the bus stop together, and he'd wait around for her to get home safely. With his arm around her waist, Ella slightly leaning against his chest, she felt Freddie's heart beat steady underneath his shirt. She counted the beats, the numbers rising, and she knew she could count them for the rest of her life and they would keep rising, steady and sure.

The bus came on time, and Freddie boarded with her. He didn't mind paying, and plus Sharon had been leaving the house less often than Ella would like, so the only moments they could steal together were between classes and on the way home. Ella looked out of the window and thought she saw someone trying to climb over one of Grimrose's walls. A familiar face, with long brown hair.

"Did you see that?" Frederick asked. "I think that girl is in my class."

"That was Ivy, wasn't it?" Ella said, worried now. Ivy was the only one of her girls she hadn't really observed closely, and now guilt twisted in her stomach. She should have been paying more attention. Alethea had told her Ivy was acting strangely of late, but that could mean anything. Ella would have to make sure Ivy was all right.

Frederick took Ella's hand, drawing circles on the back with his thumb. They got off at Constanz. Before Ella could say goodbye, Frederick pulled her hand again, and Ella faced him.

"There's something I've been meaning to tell you," Freddie said, his hands still on hers. "I got accepted into Columbia for next fall."

Ella felt the words sinking in. She said, dumbly, "What?"

"I told you I was applying," Freddie said, tilting his head slightly, his warm brown eyes on hers.

"That means you'll be moving across the ocean."

"Ideally, yes," Freddie said. "Would be kind of hard to get a plane to class every day. I'm not sure I could afford the gas. I don't want to contribute to global warming."

Ella laughed, but the laughter was only superficial. Freddie was going to move because their school year was almost over. The panic started rising in her throat, and Ella looked around desperately for something that would stop her spiral.

"Hey," Freddie said, tilting her chin up so her eyes bore into his. "You're worried about what's going to happen to us, aren't you?"

Ella immediately felt guilty; the thought hadn't crossed her mind. She'd spent so much of the last five years waiting for the day her life with her stepmother would be over that she hadn't bothered to make any plans beyond those.

She wasn't even sure if all of this was part of the curse or if it was just her life. After all the washing, the cooking, the cleaning, when she lay down at night to sleep, she closed her eyes and wished only to survive it. To be strong enough to wake before the next day, and relive it, until she was free.

"You don't need to worry," said Freddie, kissing her lips lightly. "We'll figure something out."

Ella wondered if Freddie was also a part of the curse, part of the architecture of the tale. If her relationship, too, had been taken from the books and not something she had a right to make hers.

So she slipped her hand again in Frederick's, stood on her toes, and pulled him in for a kiss. Her free hand caught his red hair, and she could feel him smiling against her, even with her eyes closed. Maybe being with Freddie offered a false sense of security, but Ella was weaving hope from whatever fabric she had at hand.

When Ella slipped inside the house, Sharon was waiting for her at the door.

"Who was that with you?" she asked.

Ella froze in place and braced herself for what would come next. She'd have to make a ready excuse. What did Sharon see? Their kiss? Freddie leaving? She couldn't have seen too much; Ella was so careful, so deliberate, and now her own voice might betray her.

"Huh," Ella said, trying desperately to think of a lie that would make sense, her mind racing and coming up blank. She wanted to scream and cry, but neither of those things would help. She wanted to tell Sharon that Freddie was hers, and she had a right to him as much as any other girl had a right to a romance, to be loved, even if everyone around her was telling her that she didn't.

"Well?" Sharon asked again.

Just then, Stacie stomped down the stairs, crossing her arms impatiently.

In her most annoyed tone, Stacie said, "Did Fred give you the notebook?"

In a rush of gratitude, Ella nodded. "Yes. It's here."

Sharon continued to examine Ella, her eyes narrowing into slits. "What was he doing here?"

"I forgot my notebook in class and texted him to bring it. Ella just went to fetch it," Stacie answered. She didn't look at Ella as Ella handed her a notebook from her bag. She made it seem as natural as possible.

"Who is he?"

"Just some classmate. Silla is half in love with him."

"Am not!" Silla shouted furiously from their room. "Stacie is such a liar!"

Sharon looked at her daughter, amused. "Maybe we should invite him in sometime."

"No!" Ella and Stacie said in unison, and Ella froze again

on the same spot. It was Stacie who shook her head, rolling her eyes again. "He's not good enough for Silla."

Sharon raised her eyebrows, but finally, satisfied, she turned around and climbed the stairs back up to her room. Ella held her breath as she went, not believing her luck.

Stacie waited until they heard the sound of the door clicking shut in Sharon's room. Even then, she kept her voice low. "How long do you expect to keep this up?"

Ella wished she had an answer to that.

"Don't bring him home again," Stacie snapped. "I doubt we can fool her a second time."

Ella nodded. "Thank you, Stacie."

"Whatever," Stacie replied in a bored tone, but her eyes softened. "Silla told me you fixed her uniform without Mum knowing. So. We're even."

Ella smiled at her. Reluctantly, Stacie smiled back.

CHAPTER TWENTY-SIX

NANI

Nani couldn't believe it was already April. The sun was shining brighter now, the daylight lasting longer in the afternoon. Nani had picked up her pace following the girls she'd been assigned, but nothing seemed to change with their stories—Jannat was too boisterous, and Ophélie was inane, one of those girls who only ever talked about going to Disneyland during school breaks. At least Nani had Svenja. But every time she thought of Ella's time running out, she'd redoubled her efforts and gone through her notes again.

And life hadn't stopped.

Grimrose was preparing their graduating students to leave after the year was over; talk of college and travel filled the corridors. Nani had no idea how to answer any questions about her future, and she was glad no one had sprung them her way.

She would finish her last year at Grimrose—and then

what? Her father was still gone. Going back to Hawai'i to live with Tūtū felt like a step backward every time she thought of it, as if what she now knew couldn't contain her to a house on the islands anymore. Nani had left, but that hadn't been enough. She still wasn't on the right path yet to finding home.

Svenja hadn't pressed her for the Easter meeting with her mother, too busy with rehearsals for her final school performance. Nani had gone to watch a couple of rehearsals, but Svenja thought she was too distracting, so they would meet in Svenja's room instead.

Unfortunately, Easter was that weekend, so Nani couldn't avoid the conversation forever.

Nani headed to Svenja's room, a whole speech ready. Instead, when she got there and knocked, she found the door was locked already. Nani frowned, and when she spun around, she saw someone was behind her.

"Hello," the voice drawled, and Nani took out her glasses, cleaning them on her uniform skirt. It wasn't ideal, but Nani rarely lived under ideal conditions. She'd given up washing and cleaning her glasses properly when she was seven and on her third pair.

When she put them on again, she saw it was Odilia, smirking at her.

"A bit late, aren't you?" Odilia asked, tilting her head slightly to show the high cheekbones that she and her cousin shared. "Svenja already called her cab."

"What?!" Nani exclaimed, rushing to her phone, but there was not a single message from Svenja. "You're lying."

"Aren't you in a hurry to make a judgment," Odilia said, rolling her eyes. "Why would I lie? I'm just here to pick up her passport. That airhead forgot."

She brushed past Nani, haughtiness incarnate, and slipped a key into the lock, turning and revealing Svenja's room.

Nani hovered in front of Svenja's door, curiosity getting the better of her, not for the first time. Odilia's features were like a twisted mirror of her girlfriend, and she couldn't look away.

"Here to make sure I don't steal anything?" Odilia asked without looking at Nani, searching through the mess that was Svenja's bedside drawers.

Nani bit back the urge to snap. Even when her anger was getting the better of her, there was always that expectation, that whatever she said would always be misinterpreted as angrier than she was.

"Did she really leave already?" Nani finally asked, hating that she sounded so uncertain.

"Yes," Odilia said simply. "I told her not to wait for you. I was right, wasn't I?"

Nani's cheeks blushed.

"You have no business interfering in our life," Nani said. "She didn't even tell me she was going already."

"Unlike me, my cousin cares about your feelings and didn't want to pressure you." She opened the last drawer, muttering an "aha!" when she found the red passport there. "I'm just looking out for her."

"Really? Is that what you tell yourself when you follow her around the school and dress like her?"

Odilia snorted, lips curving into a sharp smile. The soft, heart-shaped mouth, the elevated cheekbones, the dark, thick eyebrows that marked both her face and her cousin's. She sauntered over to the door, her hips swaying.

"Don't pretend you understand what happens between us," Odilia said. "We're family. You think *you* have the right to say anything to me? What do you know of Svenja?"

This time, Nani actually rolled her eyes. "You'll have to get more creative if you want to manipulate me so badly."

"Creativity is overrated. Most people's issues are about basic things. Like lack of trust." Odilia gave her a pointed look. "Lack of commitment."

"Is that what you're here to do? Test me to see if I can be trusted?"

Odilia laughed, and Nani hated how the sound of her laugh was just like Svenja's. "No need to get so defensive."

"Well, it's my life. And she's my girlfriend."

"Then maybe act like it. You know, if it's just a physical thing..." She took a step forward, a hand lingering on Nani's shoulder. "There are other options available."

Disgust filled Nani's stomach, deep revulsion churning her insides as she shrugged Odilia's hand off her.

"Oh, fuck off," Nani said, finally losing her patience. Maybe her tale meant that Odilia was the monster, and Nani was about to kick the absolute shit out of her until she crossed the school gates. "You're welcome to be as creepy as you like, but spare me the lectures."

"Your choice," Odilia shrugged, looking bored. "You can

have your cake and eat it too. You just have to know what you want, and we can make it work."

Odilia's smile flashed hard, and Nani was left speechless.

"I'll tell her you send your regards despite not being brave enough to make it to the family dinner." Odilia waved a quick goodbye, blowing a kiss at Nani behind her shoulder as she sprinted down the corridor. "And if you get bored with her, you can call me! Ta-ta!"

Nani stood there, ashamed and stunned. She should send Svenja a message, but maybe it was better to wait and give her an apology in person.

There was truth in Odilia's words, but Nani always had a good reason for keeping to herself, for protecting herself. She couldn't afford to come undone. She couldn't afford to be hurt by other people's feelings.

If Nani couldn't afford the hurt, maybe that meant she couldn't afford the love, either.

CHAPTER TWENTY-SEVEN
RORY

On Friday, Rory went where no one would expect to find her: the library.

She was becoming fond of the quiet, and it was a good place to try to regain what she'd lost.

The truth was that Rory felt her fibromyalgia getting worse. It had been little things: Her hand cramping in fencing practice. Stumbling on the staircase. Dropping the mirror shards in the room with Yuki. Sleeping during class, trying to compensate for her lack of sleep during the nights, the haze that took over her mind when the pain was ebbing away. Little things that kept adding up, becoming more frequent. And she'd smile and pretend nothing was wrong.

She thought she'd conquered it by the end of last year, but the only thing she had stopped doing was lying to herself. And when she stopped, she realized that she was much worse than she thought.

She got down on the floor of the library. At least there she could lie down and feel like her body was straightened out, the hard marble helping her stretch. She stayed flattened to the floor until someone else walked in. Above her floated Nani's brown face and mass of curls.

"Everything okay down there?" Nani asked, tilting her head slightly.

"Fine," Rory said.

"Don't you train on Fridays?"

"Pippa's at the tournament," Rory replied absentmindedly. "What are you doing here?"

"I'm the one who reads," Nani reminded her. "What are *you* doing surrounded by books?"

Rory needed to get up from the floor. She willed her body to lift into a sitting position.

Except it didn't go as planned. Her back muscles spasmed, causing her whole spine to contort, shrinking so she could bear the pain.

"Here, I can—" Nani said, rushing to her side.

"Don't," Rory snapped, annoyed. "I can handle it."

Nani raised her hands defensively, and then sat down on the floor opposite her. "If you say so."

Rory wanted to be angry at Nani for offering to help, but she was mostly angry at herself. She wasn't weak, even if her body was trying to make her this way. She didn't need help.

"Is that why you're here?" Rory asked. "To check if I'm doing the things I'm supposed to do? Because I need constant supervision?"

Nani didn't rise to the bait, only crossed her arms over her chest.

"I didn't come here for that," Nani said, opening her notebook, still sitting on the floor. "I'm here because I'm going to drive myself up the walls if I have to connect one more dot about people I don't even know. I feel like Tūtū gossiping around town. I'm following one girl where I suspect if you knocked her on the head repeatedly, she'll maybe turn out to have a split personality."

"Do you want to hear mine?" Rory asked, raising an eyebrow. "Serefina has possibly done a deal with the devil and is keeping him chained inside her wardrobe, or maybe the bathroom. Rhiannon has lost her eleventh earring in the swimming pool this week, so if a frog doesn't come to give it back to her, the swimming team is going to drown her. Lastly there's Freya, who's certainly being catfished by her boyfriend, a guy on the internet who has a bear for a profile picture. Not sure if he's a pedophile or just weird. Probably both."

Nani looked at Rory with exasperation.

"Bearfished," Rory corrected, which made Nani sigh and turn her eyes toward the heavens. "It's not my fault all these fairy tales have girls falling in love with animals. You need to be careful."

"We're not going anywhere with this, are we?" Nani said, trying to keep a straight face, but then it was Rory who was grinning madly.

Nani started laughing too, and neither of them could help themselves, giggling like idiots.

It's not that Rory couldn't imagine how these stories could take a turn for the worse. She could because she'd seen it all. Blood and grief and waiting at every corner. At the same time, she couldn't help but see how stupid all of this was, how the tales changed shape and became absurd.

Nani adjusted her glasses, and for a moment, Rory remembered back to when she'd started at Grimrose, when Ari had sat with her in the library, in the same position. They'd complained about all the other bad choices being made around them at the school. The ache of missing Ari hit her like a lightning bolt. But instead of only sadness, there was a light there—that even if Ari was gone, there was always something of her left.

Rory looked up at Nani, at this girl who had come here less than a year ago and already fit in among them like she was meant to be there.

"What are your odds for solving this curse, Nani?" Rory asked, traces of laughter gone, wanting the sincere answer. It was the same question she'd asked Yuki the other day; Rory wanted confirmation. She liked being positive, but she didn't want to be oblivious.

Nani sighed, leaning her head back against the wall. "Who knows. We've only got the promises we made to ourselves."

She didn't want to admit it, but Penelope's body turning up had left Rory's insomnia even worse than usual. She remembered feeling the cold water, pulling her friends back from the lake, trying to hold on to what was left. Holding on to what was important.

"I'm worried about Ella and Yuki," Rory admitted.

Nani nodded in return. They hadn't talked about it, but there was a rift separating Ella and Yuki from the others. A fracture no one wanted to acknowledge. A torn seam that Ella was trying to hide with stitches but remained visible.

"It's different for us," Nani said. "We were there that night, but we didn't... It wasn't our choice. It's not the same."

"You're saying it's not our fault she's dead."

"I'm saying that it's different for Ella and Yuki. Whatever they're going through, we can't even begin to imagine it."

Rory agreed, reassured by Nani's words. Her body had stopped spasming, and she felt her muscles relax again. She breathed a deep sigh, loosening her shoulders.

"So what do we do until we figure it out?" Rory asked.

"I can give you cheesy advice," Nani said. "Live life to the fullest. Kiss Pippa or something."

Rory groaned inwardly. "Not you too."

"You want to know what I think?"

"You kiss one girl and now you're the expert?"

"Better than kissing none," Nani pointed out.

"For your information, I *have*," Rory said, puffing her chest, glaring at Nani. "Kissed girls, I mean."

It had been embarrassing enough then, and not only because it was Rory's first time kissing someone that she wanted. She'd almost kissed a guy once when she was thirteen, at one of the end-of-the-year parties at her uncle's castle, but she'd turned her cheek at the last minute and both of them almost died of embarrassment. At least she was certain that it was the right decision. Her next choices were equally questionable, made at other parties. One was during a game of truth or dare against another European heiress, kissing the American First Daughter against the bathroom door during a UN event, their breaths hot and mingled as they played with each other's hair, their hands running over each other's bodies.

But none of those kisses had led to anything. Rory was still living the half-life she was used to living, sticking to her parents' wishes, to the future she was meant to have.

"Then what are you afraid of?" asked Nani.

"Because if I kiss her, it's going to mean something."

Nani considered it a moment, and then said mockingly, "Awwww."

"You're horrible," Rory told her, a blush creeping to her cheeks and through her neck.

"It's the twenty-first century," Nani said. "It's time we get some gay princesses out there."

"I am but a poor baby dyke," Rory mumbled. This was the first time she had talked about this with another person without backing out. Yuki didn't indulge in anyone's romances, Ella was bi and that was great but it wasn't the same, and Ari had just been the straightest girl to ever be born on the face of the planet, so Rory never bothered talking to her.

But here was Nani, who was like her, and Rory knew she was understood.

"I thought you said you had practice."

"Nani, when I get up from here, not even the curse will stop me from killing you," Rory threatened.

"That said," Nani said carefully, looking up at Rory again, "the curse is happening either way. You might as well shoot your shot. Also, Pippa is, and I say this with the utmost respect, unbelievably hot."

Rory's face burned, and she looked down at her hands. "She is, isn't she."

Nani laughed out loud. "How can you even practice when you have to look at her?"

"I just insult her," Rory said truthfully. "So my brain gets distracted."

Nani snorted. "Excellent. I wonder how she hasn't noticed you're into her yet."

"Shut up."

"Seriously. What do you have to lose?"

"Huh, how about everything?" Rory quipped.

"That's what makes it worth it, doesn't it?" Nani got up, brushing her uniform skirt. She stopped midstroke, looking out the window, and her expression changed.

"What is it?" Rory asked, jumping up, her body suddenly tense.

"I think—I think there's a girl trying to jump off the balcony."

CHAPTER TWENTY-EIGHT

ELLA

Ella got the message just as she was about to head home. Frederick was chitchatting excitedly while Ella was guiltily only paying half-attention when she saw her phone.

It's Ivy, Nani's text read. She's outside the library tower.

Babbling an excuse to Freddie, Ella ran back into the school and climbed the stairs back to the library, her heart thumping against her ribs. Ivy was one of "her" girls. Ella didn't know when she'd started thinking of them that way, but Ella felt responsible for all their endings.

Except she had neglected her duties. She had been too selfishly worried about her own—about Freddie leaving for Columbia, about Sharon finding out about her and Freddie, about her own birthday approaching, doom on the horizon. She hadn't paid attention.

She should have. And now a girl would pay for it.

Ella arrived at the library tower and saw Nani and Rory staring out a window.

"What's happening?" Ella asked, her voice coming out in a gasp. Then she saw it.

Ivy was outside the library tower, in the outer balcony—an out-of-bounds place for students because it was too high, too unsafe.

"How did she get there?" Ella asked.

"The door is locked from the outside," Yuki's voice said behind her, and Ella turned to see her best friend standing there. "I just checked."

"Then what are we supposed to do?" Rory asked, voice urgent. "Should we shout? We have to call someone."

"That might make it worse," Yuki said. "People do stupid things when they're scared."

"She's going to do a stupid thing either way!" Nani snapped.

Ella examined the window. They could see the outer balcony wasn't too far. Ivy had not yet climbed over the ledge. Ella noticed the castle windows all had an outer stone sill that connected them to each other to the balcony.

"I can talk to her," Ella said. "I just need you all to help."

"Help how?" Rory asked. "There's no way to get on that balcony. Not unless you climb out the window."

Ella stayed silent.

"No," Yuki snarled. "Absolutely not. You're not going to put yourself into danger because of some girl."

"She's not some girl," Ella said. "She's one of mine. I can talk to her. I know what I'm doing."

"You don't," Yuki said, and suddenly, it was just the two of them in the room again, just like the night of the ball. The temperature that night was low, freezing, and they were the only two breathing beings in the room, in the castle, in the world. "You just want to save her."

"And is that so bad?" Ella asked. "She's my responsibility."

"No, she isn't. She's just a girl from the book. If she jumps—"

"If she jumps, we lose another girl!" Ella shouted, and Rory and Nani stood behind them, stricken at Ella's tone. Ella looked at Yuki, biting her lower lip. "If she jumps, then we failed."

Ella wouldn't fail Ari again. She had failed once. Failed Penelope too.

She looked at Yuki, staring straight into her dark eyes. Yuki's face was unrelenting.

"It's dangerous," Yuki whispered. "You could get hurt."

"That's not going to happen."

"How do you know?"

"Because you're right here," Ella said, smiling, and then before Yuki could protest some more, Ella opened the window and stepped onto the parapet.

Ella didn't look down. She had only a vague idea how far up she was. The stone was firm under her feet, and she kept herself tight against the wall as she moved to the outer balcony. It was just like climbing out of the window at home to sneak out.

As Ella slid her feet forward, one foot slipped, but she caught herself against the stone just in time, breathing hard, the wind whipping past her ears. Finally, the railing of the library balcony was in her reach, and she grabbed it with both hands, climbing over it. She was glad that her feet were on sure ground again, her knees trembling slightly.

"Ivy!" Ella called to the girl looking out into the mountains.

Ivy's head whipped back around to Ella, her expression half-angry, half-desperate. Her long reddish-brown braid fell down her back past her knees, and her uniform skirt swayed with the wind.

"What are you doing here?" Ivy barked, unmasked fury on her face. She looked behind her shoulder at the door. "How did you get here?"

"The window," Ella said. She took sure steps toward Ivy, her hands in front of her body as if she was trying to tame a wild horse. "It's the only way to get here if the door is locked."

Ivy's eyes widened in surprise. Still, she didn't move away from the edge of the balcony. Ella took another step.

"You don't have to do this," Ella told her.

"You don't even know what I'm doing here," Ivy replied. "You don't even know who I *am*."

"Of course I do," Ella said. As long as she could hold Ivy's attention, she wasn't likely to do something. "You painted that beautiful portrait of Alethea last year. You're very talented."

Ivy looked confused again, and Ella kept her voice soft, calm. The balcony wasn't big. The ledge only went up to their knees. There was a reason why it was always locked despite the view of the lake and the mountains.

"Whatever the reason you're here, it isn't worth it."

"How do you know?" Ivy spat. "Everyone keeps saying that. They don't understand. I can't go anywhere but here. This school is all I know. What kind of life is that?"

"It's ours," Ella said, not unkindly, and she got closer to Ivy. Closer to the ledge.

Ella didn't know how Ivy's story intersected with Rapunzel's tale. She didn't know Ivy's past or her problems. But she was willing to listen and try to understand.

"I hate it here," Ivy said, spitting the words to the air, but as Ella stood next to her, she didn't try to move away.

"I love it," Ella said, looking out onto Grimrose's grounds. "You know my best friend was found dead in that lake last year."

Ivy's face, blotched from crying, whipped around to look at Ella, but Ella didn't face her.

"And a part of me should hate this school," Ella said quietly, "because it ate up her suffering, and it did nothing for her. All that is left of Ari is an accident, a blemish on the school's record, and nothing else. Nothing was done. It's so unfair."

She took a deep breath, felt the helpless tears in the back of her eyes.

"But I can't hate it," Ella continued. "Even when it feels like I'm just stuck here forever, that maybe that this is all my life is going to be, I still can't help it. It's a beautiful place. And every day when I walk from Constanz to come here, I see the castle, and my heart does this little jump, because it never feels quite real."

Ella wet her lips, then finally looked at Ivy again.

"I know what it's like to be stuck in a place where you

182

don't think it'll get any better," Ella said. "I know what it's like to hear that voice inside your head, narrating things before they even happen, as if you can't control your own life. And you're right. I don't know you. Not really. And maybe I'm not the right person to be doing this, but if I'm the only one who is going to do it, then here I am."

Ella reached out for Ivy's hand and grasped it in her own.

"You're not going through this alone. And tomorrow will bring what it brings, but you'll still have another chance. You'll always have. As long as you stay alive."

Ivy looked at her, lower lips trembling, and then her body crumpled.

Ella caught her in her arms in time and took her away from the edge. Ivy broke down crying but didn't move from Ella's embrace.

"Come on," Ella said, pulling Ivy toward her, embracing the other girl as she collapsed into a pile of sobs. "You're going to be just fine."

CHAPTER TWENTY-NINE

I t didn't work."

Nani's voice rang loud and clear across their table in the gardens. Half of the students of Grimrose Académie had taken their lunch outside. They spread out over the benches and tables in the picnic gardens on the west side of the school, letting the sun soak through their skins, uniform sleeves rolled up, socks off, periwinkle blazers thrown carelessly on the grass. Nani could hear laughter and gossip around them, but no one paid any mind to them.

Rory looked up sleepily beside her, blue eyes blinking through the sunlight. "What are we talking about?"

Nani flipped the pages of the Black Book to Rapunzel's story. Ivy's story, which still contained the very clear bad ending.

"The book hasn't changed," Nani said. "The pages still look exactly like they did before."

Yuki didn't bother looking up at her. "We knew it wasn't going to change. Liron's story didn't change in either book."

"Liron didn't get her happy ending," Nani replied. "She said so herself. She merely survived. But Ivy was going to die, and Ella stopped her. The book should have changed. It's been two weeks."

Ella looked down at her food, and Nani felt her stomach knot. She knew Ella was the most aware of their deadline. Still, they had saved this girl, hadn't they? Ivy seemed okay. Ella had taken her away from the ledge, and her story had changed.

Or it was supposed to.

Nani had run through the book until the letters on the pages swam in front of her eyes. She'd picked the tales apart in her notebook, noting the smallest of sentences, the word choice, and everything that set the two books apart from each other.

And the words in Ivy's tale hadn't changed.

"Ivy's fine for now," Ella said. "I've talked to her. I'm keeping an eye on things."

"And what happens if you aren't there to keep an eye on things?"

Ella's eyes searched the garden, and Nani followed her gaze to see Ivy sitting among a group of girls. It seemed every student of Grimrose had taken time to enjoy the afternoon sun, everyone dressed in blue and white. It looked like how Nani imagined all schools should be.

Everyone seemed to have forgotten the deaths around them as if they were of no consequence.

"Is that Sabina making out with Evan?" Ella asked, and even Yuki looked up from her lunch to see.

"Is that allowed?" Rory asked, looking over her shoulder at the two students mashing their faces together. "Is that allowed?" Rory repeated louder, and Sabina paused just long enough to give Rory the middle finger.

"Just because you aren't doing it doesn't mean it's illegal," Ella said, taking a sip of her drink.

"Oh, shut up," Rory replied, blushing.

Ella shrugged, smiling to herself. And as much as Nani enjoyed moments like this, they also made her want to throttle the other girls. Also, she'd rather be kissing Svenja, but they were in a weird place ever since Svenja had come back from the Easter trip.

"Can we please take this seriously?" Nani said, concentrating on the matter at hand. "Our plan isn't working. We can't follow all these girls for the rest of their lives to make sure nothing drastic happens."

"What do you suggest?" Rory asked.

Nani's mouth frowned. "Why do I have to be the only one to come up with plans? We have four brains sitting at this table, last time I checked."

Nani knew she was being forceful, but sometimes they all needed a push. Nani had seen them make promises about a lot of things—including about her father—but she hadn't seen any of them come to fruition. She didn't want to be unfair to her friends, but she didn't want to be sitting on her hands, either.

Yuki finally set down her fork, tucking her long dark hair behind her ears. "I don't know what else we can do."

"Maybe you should try some magic," suggested Rory. "It couldn't hurt."

"On the books?" Yuki asked. "They don't get affected. Besides, the last time we tried anything with the books..."

Yuki's voice trailed off, but Nani knew what she was thinking. Yuki's power had begun manifesting after they'd done a ritual to try to talk to Ariane's spirit. Nani knew Yuki clearly had a stronger connection to the books than the rest of them had.

And this was another thing that was bothering Nani. She'd thought that the magic had chosen Yuki because Yuki tried to burn the book the night of the ritual. But Nani was starting to wonder if it wasn't the other way around. That if magic had been a part of Yuki's story all along.

"Why are you different?" Nani asked. "The four of us were there. You are the only one who got the magic."

Yuki shifted in her seat, suddenly uncomfortable. "I don't know."

"We were reading her story out loud," Ella said, but she didn't sound convinced of her words. Nani watched Ella's face. Ella had gotten good at not saying what she was thinking. "But I don't know how that would have made a difference. To be frank, I had no idea what I was doing."

Yuki pursed her lips in a thin line. Ella returned to her meal. Rory took off her thumb ring, twirling it on the table with her fingers like a fidget spinner.

"The curse makes its way through fairy tales," Ella said. "Maybe we should start thinking like them."

Yuki scrunched her nose in distaste, repressing a shudder Nani could see her eyes fixed on Rory's ring. "How do you suggest thinking in fairy tales helps? Should we dive to the bottom of the lake to fetch a golden ring? Should I get back into eating apples?"

Ella tilted her head. "You stopped? They were your favorite."

Yuki blinked, and for the first time, Nani realized how deeply the stress of the curse was affecting Yuki. She had put up a wall, and even though she wasn't hiding her magic from her friends, she was still as affected as the rest of them.

"Can't stomach them anymore," Yuki replied, then cleaned her throat. "There must be something else we're missing. Either with the books, or with us. Will you stop that?" she said to Rory, her tone sharp.

Rory looked up, her hands still playing with the ring. "I'm trying to help, but I'm out of ideas too."

"How is fidgeting helpful?"

"Maybe you'll get angry enough to curse me," Rory said. "Then at least we'll have an idea how this curse business works, since we can't exactly google a practical magic manual."

"Oh, yes, like it works that easily," Yuki said sarcastically, snatching Rory's ring. Rory yelped. "I curse you, Aurore, to speak only in French rhyme."

Rory laughed, a throaty sound. Then she opened her mouth, and all she said was, "N'importe quoi!"

All three girls sat open-mouthed, and Rory touched her own lips, eyes wide.

"Putain, ma foi," Rory tried again, amazed at the sound of her own voice. "Enlève ça, je veux mon choix."

Yuki suddenly started giggling, throwing her head back, laughter bubbling up from her throat. Ella snickered, trying to hide it, and Rory started a string of insults in French that only rhymed even more. Nani felt her own lips stretch into a smile, her cheeks hurting.

"Ici, donne-moi," Rory snapped, her face red, fingers reaching out for the ring in Yuki's hand. Just as she did, though, there seemed to be a force that pushed her hand back. Rory tried again, but she couldn't take the ring.

Yuki stopped laughing, and then, deliberately, she offered the ring across the table, holding it out between her long fingers. As much as Rory tried to touch it, she never seemed to grasp the object, as if there were a barrier between her and the ring. Nani reached out *her* hand—and the skin met metal just fine.

"I release you," Yuki said finally, and suddenly, Rory was cursing in English again.

Yuki and Nani eyed the ring curiously. Rory snatched it back, sliding it onto her thumb once more.

"That's all it takes?" Nani frowned.

"The curse on the castle is not so simple," Yuki said. "It must have taken a lot of magic. It connects dozens of different lives, and it's *old*. Breaking it probably won't be as simple as uttering the right words."

"Thank you, I *love* the idea of being cursed twice," Rory grumbled. "How did you do it?"

Yuki eyed her. "I think a curse needs some sort of connection. Somewhere to go to. I felt it in your ring, and it has a hold on you."

"So the books do hold the curse," Ella said quietly.

Nani examined it again. "But we can touch them. Why?"

Yuki, helpfully, shrugged. Nani stared daggers at her.

"Give me one of them," Yuki said with a tired sigh.

Nani turned over the Black Book to Yuki, still open to Ivy's page. Rapunzel hung from the tower, suffocated by a noose woven from her own hair. As Nani turned the page, Yuki caught the edge with her hand and the paper slit the skin of her index finger.

"Ouch," Yuki said, as a thin line of blood pooled red against her pale finger. It welled up and a single drop fell.

Yuki's blood dropped onto the open book, and then the drop shone like starlight as the pages turned completely black.

CHAPTER THIRTY

YUKI

W hat did you do?" Nani asked, jumping forward and snatching the book back.

Yuki looked at the small cut on her finger, the blood already diminishing. She hadn't meant to touch the page, hadn't meant for her blood to drop like that, and it felt like a strange out-of-body experience to see the blackened pages.

Nani touched the edge of the page, and the page shimmered before the words reappeared, the page returning back to normal.

Yuki stared, mesmerized. "It was just...blood."

She could not remember the last time she'd gotten hurt. Except the book had done that. The book had cut her open, just like her magic had.

"So the answer is to try magic, and I was right," Rory said. "Maybe we should try setting the book on fire again, just in case."

"Not on this lunch table," Ella warned. "Yuki, can you do it again?"

Yuki nodded, her lips pursed, and she pressed the paper cut again, squeezing another drop of blood as red as her lips onto the page. The blood spattered and spread in a pooling darkness, the words disappearing in a void. Nani touched the page again and it came back to normal.

"And the White Book?" Ella asked.

Nani took it out of her bag; she had been carrying both books. There were notes and papers stuffed inside the White Book, diagrams and notes that Nani had studied. She opened the White Book on the table. Yuki felt as if she was experiencing all this from a safe distance, her mind far away from her body, as if they were all in a parallel reality where dozens of students flocked to the grass to enjoy the sun, and they were discussing a curse as if it were the most normal thing to do.

The curse seemed different now to Yuki, when she looked at it the same way Nani did. Yuki considered her magic as a part of herself, a manifested will that she'd kept stuffed down for most of her life, a seed that had grown to take over her body when she couldn't hide who she was anymore. The magic and the curse were intertwined in her heart, spreading their roots to a point where Yuki couldn't tell if there had ever been a reality where she wasn't cursed.

Yuki knew that what Nani said was true: She was different. She just didn't know how.

Nani, on the other hand, had notes, spreadsheets,

diagrams. She had studied the curse like a scholar, under-stood it better than anyone else at the table. This girl who had arrived last, who had not been a part of Grimrose, was exactly who they needed to figure this all out.

"Try it again," Nani said, pushing the White Book in front of her.

"It's just a paper cut, it's not going to bleed more," Yuki said.

But somehow, Yuki knew the cut was going to give more blood anyway; this was the first time she had bled from a cut for as long as she remembered. She pressed her finger again, then dropped the blood on the White Book. But this time, instead of darkness, the words on the page disappeared.

"One mirrors the other," Ella said quietly.

Yuki looked over at Ella, whose forehead was furrowed, poring over Nani's notes, rearranging the papers. It's what Ella did, the way her brain worked. She took a mess and couldn't help but clean it.

"We looked at the books before," Nani said. "And when I tell you I've researched every inch of them, you had better believe it."

Nani sounded tired, and Yuki could feel Nani's exhaus-tion seeping into her.

"But you've been looking at the books separately," Ella said, her voice small as she tidied the notes. "What if they're just— what if they're just one thing? Two halves of the same whole?"

Nani narrowed her eyes across the table at Ella, and even Yuki was paying more attention now. She could see where Ella was going. The books were mirrors of each other, and they contained the same stories in the same order. Everything about them was the same, except for the endings.

"Maybe that's the curse too," Ella said. "The books offer a good ending and a bad one, but I can't help think of what Liron said. She said she didn't get her happy ending, but she didn't die. And in life—"

"You never get only the happy endings," Yuki finished for her.

"Maybe we're missing another element," Ella concluded, thoughtful. "Maybe if we find a third thing that unites them both, we can break the curse."

This sounded impossible to Yuki.

But Ella had just said they'd been thinking in a logical way, and the curse was anything but logical. Magic was anything but logical. It followed instincts and feelings, as Yuki had seen and learned. Magic was a battle of wills, of pouring the essence of self into the thing you wanted the most, making it real and concrete, letting it all out without guilt.

"Again, this is just a hypothesis," Yuki said. She pressed her cut, willing for it to heal, and suddenly it was like the blood had never been there at all.

Yuki searched the well of magic within her, that darkness on the horizon of her being, but this time, it was quiet.

Everything felt so quiet.

"Both Ari and Penelope found the books here at Grimrose," Rory said. "Which means that the third object has to be here too."

"Exactly," Nani agreed. "The curse has always been

connected to Grimrose. We're here. And whoever cast it is here. And then—then the books. Vessels of the curse."

Sometimes Yuki felt like the magic was wielding her and not the other way around. Something flashed in the corner of her eyes like golden blond hair. For a moment, Yuki thought she would see Penelope standing there, legs crossed, heart-shaped mouth pucked, expression mocking.

But it was just another student. Penelope was gone. Yuki had killed her.

Yuki had *killed* her.

Penelope couldn't hurt them anymore. Yuki would do anything to stop this curse—not only because Ella had promised it and because she believed in Ella. But because she would never let Ella fail.

She squeezed her fist tight, trying to get her concentration back. The sight of her blood had sent her spiraling, and she forced herself to be grounded again.

"I saw the secret passages last year," Nani was saying, and Yuki realized she'd missed part of the conversation. "And maybe we're not going to find anything there, but maybe that's where Ari found the book. We just have to explore more."

Rory and Ella nodded, and Nani tore out a page from her notebook to sketch something. Slowly, Yuki realized it was a sketch of Grimrose Académie, with clear lines. There were the gardens where they were sitting, the stables, the lake, the abandoned owlery. The four towers of the castle, the court-yard, the doors. Nani sketched with a precise hand.

"I had no idea you knew how to draw," Ella said, looking at the perfection of Nani's lines.

Nani blushed a little, adjusting her glasses. "I liked to draw maps from books as a kid," she mumbled.

Nani finished the sketch of the towers of Grimrose then began drawing lines to separate it into sections.

"There was nothing in the owlery, and I'm sure there's nothing in the stables," Nani said. "The gardens seem like a long shot. We could dig something, but I don't think the others had to dig anything at all to find what they were looking for. And if we're to believe what Penelope said, she took it from the person it belonged to. Which means it's inside the castle."

"Maybe the dungeons," Rory suggested.

"Grimrose has a *dungeon*?" Nani exclaimed. Then she sighed through her nose. "Of course it does. I don't know why I asked."

"It's sealed off," Yuki said. "They did it before Reyna's time. It's flooded with water from the lake."

Nani shook her head, circling parts of the drawing, Adding the numbers of floors to the towers. Yuki observed as the castle took shape: Grimrose as not just a home, but a place full of mystery and windows and towers, of hidden nooks and a thousand different secrets to be uncovered.

"We're never going to find this third thing, are we?" Rory said.

"We split up," Nani said. "Each of us takes a different part of the castle."

"This is the worst treasure hunt ever," Rory muttered.

"Ari found the book," Nani repeated. "If she found something, so can we."

Nani finished the last traces of her map. Yuki looked at the tall pine trees around the edges, the mountains topped with snow that kept them well-guarded and safe.

The more Yuki looked, the more she felt something twist in her stomach. For the first time since she'd let herself be open to magic, let herself be free of the expectations, she felt something akin to fear.

Before it could take root or shape, it was Ella's voice who cut through Yuki's thoughts.

"We're not giving up just because the castle is huge," Ella said, her voice sounding almost offended. "Nani, you've just arrived now, but we've lived here for five whole years. We know more about Grimrose than anyone else. We can do this."

Ella smiled at them, and then she looked at Yuki. Yuki could see worry in her eyes, but also Ella's earnest belief that somehow things would turn out to be just fine.

If Ella believed it, then Yuki had to.

There was no other way.

CHAPTER THIRTY-ONE

ELLA

So what's the treasure hunt for again?" Freddie asked from behind Ella, voice rising as they made their way through the ground floor of the castle and out onto the glass-walled conservatory.

The conservatory was small compared to the size of the castle and hadn't been in use for over ten years. There were trees with big roots, their branches rising to the glass rooftop, sunlight streaming through the leaves over the cobblestone path. The place was usually closed to the students, but Ella knew her way around it. Half of the panels on the roof were open, and the conservatory's path led from the gardens to the school administration's supply rooms.

"I don't think I've ever been here," Freddie muttered, looking up to where two birds were perched on one of the tallest branches of the tree.

"Students aren't supposed to be in here," Ella replied.

"So we're breaking the rules now. Oooh."

"It's not *not* allowed," Ella told him, walking a bit farther ahead, watching the birds chirping. On the opposite side of the door was another entrance to the castle, stairs that led up to the kitchens.

"I love your argument," Freddie said. "It's really solid."

Ella looked over her shoulder to glare at him. "I won't invite you next time."

"Are you kidding? I love going to potentially dangerous places we're not allowed in."

"Frederick, this is a conservatory."

"So? There could be poisonous plants. Dangerous vines. A bird that might shit on my head."

"At least it's not Mephistopheles."

"Truly, this school's lack of principles regarding the security of their students rivals Xavier's School for Gifted Youngsters."

Ella snorted, peering into the passage behind the kitchens, checking to see if it was empty. She wondered if she should climb upstairs. She'd been to the kitchens once already, and she knew some of the staff from Constanz, but she doubted that anything would be hidden in a place so busy.

The thing they were looking for had to be somewhere else, somewhere protected enough where it couldn't be discovered by accident.

But after checking the conservatory, pretty much all of Ella's options had been exhausted.

She kept going, crossing the path back from the door. The

conservatory wasn't even that big—it was like a long corridor with old trees and abandoned tables. She looked beyond the ivy-covered wall, sighing.

Freddie caught up to her, his hand catching hers before she marched on.

"You're doing that thing again," he said quietly.

"What thing?"

"The thing where you avoid talking to me for whatever reason," Freddie said, jerking his eyebrows up.

"I'm not avoiding you," Ella said. "I'm just distracted. I want to win the treasure hunt."

Ella turned again, but this time, Freddie pulled her back. She almost crashed into him, his height towering over hers. His grip on her hand was gentle but firm.

"I want to be able to see you more than just in between classes, El," he said. "And ever since I told you about Columbia, you just seem to avoid the subject even more."

The shortening of her nickname was a soft breath on his lips, and Ella felt her stomach sink. She couldn't get distracted now, though she wished she could.

Except Frederick wasn't just a distraction, was he? He was a safe option, a way to feel that someone would always be there to save her. And having a safe option was good. It was sensible.

"This is not how I want things to be either," Ella said. "But soon school's going to end, and then I don't know how it's going to be."

"I know. But you can talk to me about how you feel."

Ella smiled at him. "I want it to be better than this."

"Then let me try."

He inclined his head slightly, his lips grazing hers. Ella lifted up on her toes, her breath mingling with his, the scent of the conservatory mixed with his sweet perfume. His hand held hers, and then he slipped an arm around her waist. Ella threw caution out the window.

She grabbed his tie and pulled him into her, her lips pressing so hard against his mouth that she could almost feel his teeth.

The kiss deepened as Ella felt her back press against a tree. She held on tight to Freddie's collar as she pulled him closer, his tongue slipping through her mouth. Freddie's hand grazed underneath her uniform shirt, his touch softly caressing the skin of her belly. Ella felt like she was losing her breath, but she didn't want to stop—she breathed the air he gave her, her fingers grazing his neck, and Freddie lowered his kisses a little more as he opened the top buttons of her shirt with nimble dexterity. On her chin, on her jaw, on the space where her neck met her shoulder, trailing down her skin following the light line of her freckles. He kissed her neck again and Ella let out a satisfied gasp.

She'd missed him. She'd missed the skipped heartbeats in the beginning of their friendship, when she wanted his company, when he was always in her corner, when she wasn't even sure she'd wanted something other than friendship. She'd missed feeling that this was something she could enjoy too, that she didn't have to miss out on other things because the curse was coming. She didn't have to miss out on *this*.

Frederick stopped for a breath, their eyes meeting. She smiled back at him, true and sure, and then she pulled him back to her, unbuttoning his shirt with graceful fingers, kissing his neck as Freddie buckled underneath her touch. Ella kissed him harder, her hand around his neck, and Freddie's hand rose a little higher under her shirt, pressing against the skin of her ribcage.

Ella jerked away, lowering her shirt, a shudder running through her spine.

"You okay?" Freddie asked, letting go of her waist immediately. "I didn't think—"

"It's not you," Ella replied quickly. "Sorry, the tree is hurting my back."

The lie came out smoother than she intended, and Ella hated herself a little more for it.

"What is this?" another voice said, and Ella jumped in surprise.

Ms. Lenz emerged from the outer garden door, stopping in the middle of the cobblestone path. Ella's face went hot pink, and Frederick's matched his hair. Ella adjusted her uniform skirt, brushing a leaf that had stuck on her hair. Freddie's shirt was rumpled, and his tie was crooked, but even without their disgruntled appearances, there was the mark of Ella's lipstick right on Freddie's neck.

"The conservatory is out of bounds for students," Ms. Lenz said in authoritative voice, looking between the two of them. "I expected more from you, Miss Ashworth."

"I'm sorry," Ella muttered, though in a way, she was only

sorry she'd gotten caught. Freddie's kisses still burned down her neck and shoulders.

"I won't write you up this time," Ms. Lenz said. "But if I find either of you here again, there will be a note sent to your guardians."

She adjusted the half-moon lenses of her glasses, looking at them both with hawk's eyes. Freddie was so consternated that he couldn't even talk, so Ella just pulled him along and out of the conservatory door, back into the gardens.

"Sorry the treasure hunt didn't work out so well," Freddie said finally, when they were out of earshot and he seemed recovered.

Ella squeezed his hand. "I think I lost it for a good cause."

"I'll make it up to you."

"By distracting me even more?"

Freddie raised Ella's hand to his lips, a soft gesture, but his eyes were full of mischief. "I'm sure I can find more secret places in Grimrose where a teacher is not ready to jump on us. Next time we just go through the other door."

"Other door?"

"Yes," Freddie repeated. "The other door. The one not on the glass wall."

"There can't be a door there. There's nothing in the castle that leads up to it."

"There's a door there, Eleanor."

"It's a wall."

"God, you're stubborn. There's a door. I was kissing you right next to it." Ella narrowed her eyes, and then Freddie laughed. "Oh, I see. I was too good at my job, so you forgot your treasure hunt."

Ella elbowed him, looking back at the conservatory. Had she missed a door? Ms. Lenz was still standing next to the conservatory doorway opening, her eyes fixed on Ella and Freddie as they retreated.

"You can check it again," he said. "When Ms. Lenz is not looking."

Ella turned around, shaking her head. "Yes. I need to get home. Before you offer me any other distractions."

Freddie set his tie upright, sighing. "And here I was just getting started."

CHAPTER THIRTY-TWO

RORY

Rory was supposed to be searching for stuff inside the castle and thinking about the curse, but instead all she could think about was Nani saying she had to shoot her shot while they still had time.

Rory didn't do declarations of love, and with the people she'd kissed before, she had been relying more on her body than words. But Nani was also right. Rory had something to lose.

And the harder she tried denying it, the more she was ensnared back into it.

So on Friday, Rory got out of class earlier than she needed with an excuse, and she set about making the preparations. It wasn't much, but she'd picked up the suit Ella had sewn for her and combed her hair back away from her face. She still wore her uniform shirt, and she'd gone back and forth ten times whether to keep the two top buttons open or not, looking at herself in the mirror and fretting.

The training room was empty, like it always was on Friday. Rory sat down on one of the benches, two swords resting next to her. She was wearing a rose gold suit with a cloud of perfume surrounding her. She nervously kept checking her phone to look at every minute that had ticked by.

Finally, someone walked through the doors. Pippa, hair in her usual braid, T-shirt tugged inside her shorts loosely, bag slung over her shoulder.

"What's this?" Pippa asked, hovering over the entryway, looking around with large eyes.

Suddenly, Rory was extremely self-conscious.

She felt stupid for doing this. Rory should have asked before she made her plans, but no, she never did think anything through before she decided to jump headfirst, and of course it was stupid and Pippa would hate it.

"It's a dance," Rory finally said, meeting her eyes. "You didn't get to enjoy the winter ball, and then I thought..."

Rory's voice trailed off. She shoved her hands back in the pockets of her pants. It *was* too much. She didn't have to dress up for the occasion, didn't have to put on a suit. It's not like this was a date.

It wasn't. Even though there was a part of her that wanted it to be.

Pippa's eyes scanned the room, taking it in. The light of the sun glittered through the windows, naturally painting the floor in moving circles.

"Hold on," Pippa said, and Rory tried finding her voice to reply, but before she could, Pippa had turned her back to her and run out of the room.

Rory sat down again on the bench, and got up, and sat down, until she'd realized she was going to wear herself out. Was Pippa coming back? Why was she even *doing* this? She should just go. It had been a stupid idea, and now Pippa had fled, as she rightfully should, because a sane person wouldn't wait for them wearing a suit on a Friday afternoon without any explanation. Or with an explanation that included conjuring up a dance.

When Rory had finally gathered enough courage to go back to her room, shame burning her cheeks, Pippa walked through the door again, and Rory was stunned into silence.

Pippa hadn't let down her hair—but her braid looked different, more elegant. Rory knew from living with Nani all these months that curly hair couldn't be simply restyled without long hours, but Pippa had braided it sideways to fall over her shoulders. Her two-piece dress shaped her body and muscles like Rory had never seen before, showing off every one of her curves. Elegant straps tied the top behind her neck in a v-neckline of shimmering light blue with her midriff showing. The skirt had a slit, and Rory's brain was too overwhelmed to even take *that* into consideration.

Rory wanted to say something, but she was too afraid of what might come out, so she waited until Pippa came closer.

"I thought you didn't have a dress," Rory finally managed

as every single one of her other thoughts went out of the window, though she didn't have many of those.

"I just didn't go to the dance," Pippa said. "Might as well wear it now, or it's a waste of fabric." She looked at Rory, her gaze lingering at the base of her throat, where Rory had, in fact, left the upper buttons open. "The suit looks good on you."

Rory didn't know how to answer the compliment, so she followed the plan she'd seared into her mind as to not lose courage.

"Here," Rory said, offering Pippa the saber on the bench. It was different than the wooden swords they used against each other in training. This saber was thin and delicate, its edge sharp.

Rory offered with the blade turned down, and Pippa took it.

"I don't understand," Pippa said. "I thought this was a dance."

"You said you didn't dance. But you do fight. So I'm showing you something else."

Rory walked to the middle of the checkered floor of the room, where the sun's light was still glimmering. She stopped, sword down, hesitating and biting her lower lip.

"This is kind of..." Rory mumbled, without knowing where to start.

"I can't hear you," Pippa said.

"It's a ceremonial sword dance," Rory said louder, looking up to meet Pippa's eyes, even though she felt like her whole body was burning up, that she was as red as her hair and the pink suit only made it worse. "It's usually reserved for royal celebrations and such."

"But you know it."

Rory nodded. She remembered being bored out of her mind every time she had to attend a party, every time someone asked her to dance and the dancing made no sense, until she'd seen this one. It was traditional in the sense that not even fifty people in the whole of her country knew how to do it, but Rory had demanded to learn it, so her uncle taught her. They'd spent hours and hours in the empty ballroom, the two of them, dancing and dancing until Rory knew the movements by heart.

It was the first time Rory had fallen in love with something.

It was the first time her uncle had treated her as more than just a child, the first time he'd ignored her parents and listened to what Rory wanted. The first time he treated her as his successor.

Rory set up the music on her phone so it would start playing.

"Just mirror my movements," Rory said. "The beginning is pretty easy."

Pippa nodded, holding her sword in her right hand as Rory gripped hers tighter. She bowed with her head, and Pippa curtsied, but Rory couldn't even think of relaxing, hyper aware of every single one of her muscles and movements.

Rory stepped ahead and raised her sword in front of her in a vertical position, and Pippa did the same. Rory stepped to the left, Pippa to the right. Rory lowered the sword, reaching for Pippa, and their swords met in the form of an X. Rory stepped forward again, sword raised, and then down, until they'd done a circle around each other.

Rory put her right foot forward, blade lowered, and Pippa's foot met hers. They were both wearing white tennis shoes even in their fancier clothing.

Rory hesitated for the first movements, even when she'd rehearsed it more than a hundred times. Her first flicks of the wrist were skewered, her sword hand uncertain, but slowly, as the music flowed, Rory felt her body relaxing. Pippa's movements mirrored hers in such a natural way that she stopped worrying whether this was a bad idea. If it was, it was the grandest she'd ever had.

The ceremonial sword dance wasn't complicated. Uncle Émilien explained to her the first time that it was about recognizing the power in your rival, the person who danced with you. Acknowledging the power and the sway they held over your life and trusting them not to end it. Its movements were simple, the blades meeting and then dancing away from each other.

Rory let the music and the movements guide her in the mimicry she'd done all her life. When she stepped closer and raised the sword horizontally to the level of Pippa's throat, Pippa didn't even blink, raising her own sword so they'd balance.

The music picked up its final rhythms, and Rory raised her sword arm above her head, and Pippa raised hers too, keeping them both up. Shoulder to shoulder, they circled around the room, and then Rory did what she wished she'd had done many times: she slipped her arm in front of Pippa's waist, her hand brushing skin, and only a second later, Pippa did the exact same thing. With their arms intertwined across each other's body, they twirled. Rory stepped to the right, and Pippa gently moved along with her, and then when Pippa did the same, Rory let herself feel weightless, like she was walking on clouds.

They separated, swords crossed down, then up, the music only a distant sound to Rory's ears, her movements coordinated as they made their final twirls, as the swords finally crossed over their chests. Rory stepped closer, then Pippa too, the only thing between them was their blades.

The music stopped, but Rory hovered there for one minute longer, looking into Pippa's eyes, the way her braid hung over her shoulder, the way her eyelashes curled up, and Rory couldn't look away, couldn't blink, couldn't even breathe. Pippa's breath mingled with hers as they stood face to face, the blades held tight against their chests. If they moved one centimeter, they could get hurt, but both of them had control over their swords.

"I told you you'd make a good dancer," Rory said.

Pippa's eyes didn't leave hers. "Looks like you were right."

Rory was faintly aware of the music changing in the background, still echoing like it was coming from another world. Rory didn't remove her hand from Pippa's waist, acutely aware of their touch. She moved her thumb, just slightly, and Pippa's breath hitched. Pippa lowered her gaze to Rory's mouth, and then back up to her eyes.

The moment hung in a perfect and crystallized stillness.

Until it shattered.

Rory's phone started ringing. Pippa blinked, dazed, and Rory was forced to come back to reality.

"Sorry," Rory muttered, but those weren't the words she wanted to say. She wanted to tell Pippa to forget it, wanted to tell her to let go of the swords and just dance like normal girls. To pick up where her touch had left off, cup Pippa's face, brush her finger against her cheeks, trace her lips with her thumb.

Rory wanted to forget she ever had a life other than this one.

Her phone kept ringing, and reluctantly, hesitantly, if her whole hand was about to fall if she did it, Rory finally took her hand off Pippa's waist and walked away to pick her phone up where she'd left it on the bench. It pinged loudly with each message that arrived in their group chat. It could be important. It could be life or death.

"I—" Rory said, glancing apologetically at Pippa.

Pippa shook her head slightly, then stepped away, and the air went with her.

Rory had missed her chance.

CHAPTER THIRTY-THREE

NANI

The treasure hunt was going from bad to worse, in Nani's opinion.

They had scoured the castle from top to bottom, from the highest tower to the lowest room, from the smallest nook to the tiniest cranny, and it had yielded no results. No third magic book jumped out at them. No third magical object was miraculously conjured. All Nani got in return was a rather aggravating rhinitis crisis due to poking her nose in a lot of places that urgently needed a proper cleaning.

Not to mention they could only do all of that when they were *not* in class, and even though Nani had no trouble keeping up with all her subjects, there were still the literature essays she needed to hand in, the final biology experiment she needed to finish, and a lot of other annoying schoolwork. When she met her friends for lunch, they always looked tired and like they hadn't been properly sleeping, and Nani wanted to both scream that they couldn't wait forever and also hibernate for a week.

After lunch, instead of moving on to return to her searches—the lower-level classrooms *again* in case she'd missed anything the first and second time—Nani decided it was better to take a break. She decided to go to the auditorium to catch a glimpse of Svenja in her final rehearsals.

Watching Svenja dance was like watching the ocean rise with the tide.

Svenja's body surged elegantly, twisting from one side to the other, her arms reaching up and down again, her movement flowing like water. She was in control but effortless, like her body was fluent in a language known only to dryads and mermaids. Her chest rose and fell, her feet fluttering rapidly like a turbulent wave, then reaching to the floor like the foam on the ocean bed. Nani watched, mesmerized, as Svenja jumped and twirled. The music complimented her but never truly commanded her movements; it accompanied her as if it were obeying Svenja and not the other way around.

When the music ended, Svenja looked up. "Enjoying the show?"

Nani felt herself blush. "I couldn't resist looking."

"That's fine," Svenja said. "It's over anyway."

It had still been strange between them ever since Svenja returned from traveling with her family for Easter. Even the kisses they shared seemed to be more contrite. Nani didn't want to be the person to talk about it first, so she left it for Svenja, who seemed to consider ignoring problems a form of Olympic competition.

"When's the recital again?" Nani asked, distracted.

"After graduation," Svenja said. "My family will be coming to watch."

Svenja looked directly at Nani, and Nani felt the tension growing as Svenja started organizing her things, taking the phone out of the speaker docket, pulling her uniform shirt over the tight leotard.

"Oh" was all Nani could think of saying.

"Maybe then I'll get to introduce you," Svenja said. "I know I said mean things about my mom before, but she means well. She just doesn't really know how to act with everything. She's okay with me being who I am."

"That wasn't the reason I didn't go," Nani said.

Svenja pulled on her uniform skirt, closing it around her tiny waist.

"I know how it is with your own family, that you only have your grandmother," Svenja said, and Nani could feel almost a tad of condescension from her. "I just wanted you to know that, since you didn't tell me anything at all. Because I thought you'd at least tell me the reason why—"

"You don't have to know everything!" Nani snapped, her voice rising to a shout.

Svenja blinked, taken aback. Her bow-shaped mouth puckered, and suddenly, Nani was tired of fighting, and the words caught at her throat. She couldn't explode now, couldn't put Svenja in jeopardy. Svenja had to trust her, and that, ironically, meant that Nani had to lie and deceive.

"I'm not going to have this conversation with you," Nani said more calmly, and she watched as Svenja's eyes flashed with hurt. "Svenja, you're not entitled to every part of me just because you're my girlfriend. You're not entitled to all of my reasons why I'm not doing something."

"Except that thing involves me." Svenja set her jaw. "Maybe Odilia was right about you after all."

Nani's stomach sank. "What did she say?"

"That you don't care about me as much as I care about you," Svenja replied. "She told me you two talked. Why didn't you just say you didn't want to go?"

"Because you would have been upset."

"Well, I'm upset *now*," Svenja said ferociously. "You didn't have to ghost me because of a fucking invitation."

She sat down at the edge of the stage, unlacing her ballet shoes, the ribbons in pools around her feet. She raised her eyes to look at Nani again, and Nani didn't let herself falter—this was a fight, but they weren't saying everything they wanted to say.

"Look, I'm sorry," Nani managed. "But I think it's better if we just keep things as they are now. We're in school, and everything can change in the next three months."

Svenja snorted. "You think you're smarter than the rest of us, don't you?"

Nani looked at Svenja sideways, but Svenja's face was unreadable. A mystery that Nani kept getting dragged back into to solve, just like everything else in the school.

"Avoiding things that may hurt you is not being smart. It's common sense."

"If you try to build a wall around everything that might possibly hurt you, then you're not letting even the good things in," Svenja replied, her fingers running along Nani's cheek. "It's just a stupid wall, and you're alone, surrounded by it."

Nani said nothing to that. Her heart was always guarded, wanting to be certain before she ever did anything. She stayed closed up within herself, within the same security she'd created, never being challenged for it.

She didn't want Svenja to depend on her for her way out of the curse, and Nani didn't want to depend *on Svenja* to be a part of *her* ending. They had to stand on their own. That was how Liron had done it, in a way.

Nani couldn't rely on anyone anymore.

Svenja shouldered past her and left through the door, and Nani didn't follow her.

Luckily, Nani didn't have classes on Wednesday afternoon, so Nani marched straight up to her room. She opened the door, and to her surprise, found Rory and Ella there. Rory was in her fencing uniform, and Ella looked like she was ready to leave. However, as soon as Nani entered, they both turned to her immediately with looks of guilt on their faces.

"What is it?" Nani asked, impatient.

"I just did a sweep on the storeroom," Rory said. "And I found this hidden in the back."

Rory offered her a box. Nani didn't understand what it was until she saw the name stamped on the side of it.

Isaiah Eszes. Her father.

CHAPTER THIRTY-FOUR

ELLA

Ella watched as Nani took the box from Rory's hand as if it were the most precious thing in the world. She could understand the feeling—she had seen many boxes with her father's name, all those years ago, and she'd been the one packing them. She wished she could have kept at least one of them.

Nani set it down on her bed gingerly. She didn't open it.

"The storeroom?" she asked, and Ella could hear the strain on her words as she choked them out.

"Yeah, it's a mess in there," Rory said, trying to lighten the mood. "Just a bunch of stuff that people left behind."

Rory was not helping.

"This was all we found," Ella added apologetically.

Ella had asked around the security guards about Nani's father. Ella was friendly with all of them, passing them daily on her way to school; she even knew the names of their wives and children. They remembered Isaiah Eszes, of course—a man with presence, tall and broad-shouldered, who had been the chief of their security staff for a year, but there was nothing else they could tell Ella about him. He wasn't friendly with any of them—he lived at his own quarters inside the school and mostly kept to himself. When the school year had finished, he'd attended the small staff gathering, and then he was never seen again.

Ella didn't find anything beyond this, and Nani had done all the internet searches she could think of but encountered nothing. There was a possibility that Ella didn't like to entertain, so she never brought it up, but with the box there, it was impossible not to think of it.

Nani picked up the scissors from her desk and tore the tape that held the box together. Ella knew Rory was already late for fencing practice, and Ella herself had skipped her Gothic literature seminar for this semester, texting Yuki she wasn't coming. Both of them were there with Nani in case they were needed.

Nani seemed wrapped in her own world as she started taking things out of the box—a deep blue winter coat, which Nani wouldn't use anymore and looked far too big—old receipts, odd socks, some papers, which Nani cast aside after a quick glance, and lastly, at the bottom, there was a book. Ella recognized it as *Peter Pan* straight away, and it almost looked like a copy that her own mother read to her when she was a child.

Nani stretched the book out in front of her, examining it, and then sighed. "This was the only book I gave back to him."

Rory raised an eyebrow. "Why?"

"I hate Peter Pan," Nani said, still holding on to the book. "I thought the idea of not growing up was incredibly stupid."

"Glad to know you've always been like this," Rory replied, and that made Ella laugh.

Better yet, it made Nani laugh, and some tension left her shoulders. "Yeah. The most annoying kid in the world. I read it in a day and handed it back to him the next morning before he even left on the next assignment." Nani's lip tightened, and Ella could see the expression of someone trying not to cry. "He asked what I thought, and I said Hook should've skewered Peter."

Nani leafed through the pages, and Ella could see the hope there, waiting to find something; a letter, a last note, anything. When she had leafed the whole way through and nothing fell from between the pages, Nani put it down with a sigh.

"They wouldn't keep this here if he was dead, right?" Nani asked, trying to sound casual, but Ella felt every word like a stab.

Ella moved forward to hug and reassure her, but before she could, Nani stepped back again, and there was nothing Ella could do.

"Fuck that," Rory said, and Ella startled. "He's not dead. Okay? He's not dead."

"You don't know that."

"Being dead is a lot of bureaucracy. If he was dead, you'd know about it," Rory said. "This box probably just exists because some cleaning lady had to tidy up his room and didn't know where else to put his stuff."

"You thought it too," Nani accused, and Ella tried not to flinch.

They'd all made so many promises, and all of them seemed empty. Ella had promised to help Nani find her father, and she'd gotten nowhere, even when she'd thought she was digging deep. She'd promised to help the girls, and even though she stopped Ivy from throwing herself from the tower, that had changed nothing.

"He's still out there, Nani," Ella said instead. "You'll find him."

"When the time is right," Nani muttered. "When the curse comes for me, then I'll know, right? That's part of my story too."

Then, like a force of steel, she curled her hands into fists and shook her head. "Anything else? Anything useful?"

Rory shook her head. Nani turned to Ella.

"A door to the dungeon, I think," Ella said. "But it's locked. And if it's flooded..."

"Great. Another failed plan."

Ella knew Nani was needing to act out, and she didn't want to step in. Nani was obviously grieving for her father, worried about all of it—as they all were, with the end of the year approaching. And she wanted to offer to help, to let Nani know that she was safe here with them, but even after all this time, if Nani couldn't see it for herself, then Ella could do nothing.

All she could do was make promises on top of promises.

"I gotta go," Rory said. "Sorry this was everything I could find."

And then, like a storm, she left the room in a hurry. This left Nani and Ella. Ella, too, couldn't stay for much longer. It was best to get home.

Nani had picked up the book again. "You sure about this third thing?"

Ella wasn't sure of anything at all.

"It feels right," she said instead. "One book doesn't exist without the other. Something must bind them together."

Nani made a noncommittal noise. "What if we just ask Yuki to set fire to the school?"

"Yes, that seems the simplest and most straightforward solution," Ella agreed, and Nani snorted a laugh. "I know this seems hopeless, but it isn't over yet."

Nani tightened her lips, but Ella was glad she didn't say anything about her own deadline. The one that made Ella try to live like every day would be her last, because it could be.

Ella gave her a final small smile before heading to the door.

"We can still ask Yuki if it all goes south," Ella said, hand on the doorknob. "I'm pretty certain she'd agree."

CHAPTER THIRTY-FIVE

Yuki was going to burn the school to the ground.

It seemed like the simplest solution to her problem. Take down all the rooms, all the stones and the towers, each thing that got in her way as she made the search for whatever part was missing. Each room she searched and found nothing made her more irate, the answer simple. There was no need for menial work when she could find the needle by burning down haystack.

She wanted to deny that there was something calling to her—it would have been too easy to dismiss Ella's latest theory, but she could feel it in the school, something that was always present. Something that fed her magic, and that she fed in return.

Yuki walked through the corridors, again and again, her fingers touching the walls, walking through secret passageways. One way or another, she always seemed to end up in the same place. She always seemed to stop right in front of Reyna's tower, hovering on her stepmother's threshold.

That week, after Yuki had been through the castle three times, she saw the door was open and went in unannounced.

At first, she thought the place was empty, but then she saw Reyna with her back turned, facing the mirror on the wall. Her eyes were dark and clouded in the reflection, and she held a glass of wine in her right hand while her left hand gripped at something at her neck.

Then, suddenly, Reyna roared and turned around, smashing the wine glass against the wall. Yuki jumped back, stumbling against the table, and the noise drew Reyna's attention. Reyna turned her head, her face disfigured in anger, mouth open and contorted, clear rage stamped on her face.

Yuki felt her fingertips grow icy, and then Reyna's face smoothed.

"You weren't meant to see that," Reyna said, her voice cold.

Yuki blinked, a sharp emotion she couldn't quite name steeling her in place. Reyna took another breath, closing her eyes, and her features softened once more. On her neck, the ruby pendant she wore flashed bright.

"I'm sorry," Reyna said calmly. "It's been—it's been quite a week."

Yuki swallowed and felt something sinking to the pit of her stomach. She realized it was a fraction of fear.

"I didn't mean to interrupt," Yuki said.

Reyna stepped carefully away from the broken glass on the floor. A single stream of blood ran down her right hand, tinging the air with the deep scent of metal. Reyna didn't seem to mind it, but Yuki watched as the blood slipped down her fingers, leaving a scarlet trail on her light brown skin.

Reyna's face was impassive, her sculpted eyebrows sharp, her brown eyes attentive. Yuki had seen more than her fair share of parents at school balk and lose words at Reyna's undeniable beauty. As she was growing up, Yuki wondered if this was how it was going to be for her too. Yuki was beautiful, there was no denying that, but her beauty came from a place of coldness, whereas Reyna always seemed to be welcoming.

Except not this time. This time, it was like Yuki was looking at her reflection.

"You didn't interrupt anything," Reyna said, as if convincing herself. "The situation's not any worse than last year."

Yuki nodded, searching for words more carefully than usual. "Did the board say anything yet?"

"They've given me more time."

"Well, more time is good, right?"

Reyna's eyes met hers and Yuki realized that her stepmother looked exhausted. There was nothing in her outer appearance to indicate it—she still looked like she hadn't aged a day. In the depth of her eyes, though, was a fatigue that seemed older than Reyna herself. She brushed a strand of her hair back, finally seeming to notice the blood on her hand, watching it like a spider watches an insect on its web.

"You wanted something?" Reyna asked.

Yuki thought about the thousand questions she had locked within herself. "No. I was only walking to clear my head."

Reyna walked forward to the table and picked up a tissue so she could clean the blood off, holding it against the cut on her hand absentmindedly. Yuki didn't step any closer.

"Then off you go," Reyna said. "I have a meeting with the teacher's council in half an hour, and I need to be ready."

Yuki hovered for another instant there, lingering.

"And there's nothing else you can do about the board?" Yuki said, not knowing why she was pushing it, except maybe to see another frown on Reyna's face. To shatter once again her stepmother's image of perfection if only to understand the fury she saw before, an echo of her own.

Reyna didn't crack.

"There's nothing to be done," she replied, looking straight at Yuki. "Well, there is one thing," she added, their gazes still locked. Reyna took a deep breath, and Yuki almost shivered in place. "But I'm not sure it's time for that kind of thinking yet."

Yuki's fingertips buzzed just slightly, and she curled her hands into a fist, unwilling to let any magic out.

Finally, Reyna broke her stare, using the bloodied tissue to wipe her face. "If you'll excuse me, I need to clean this mess before I head to the meeting."

"Sure," Yuki said. "I'll see you Saturday."

Yuki closed the door behind her. As she left, she could have almost sworn that behind the door, Reyna was sobbing.

CHAPTER THIRTY-SIX

RORY

May arrived as the end of the school year approached, and the treasure hunt went nowhere.

Rory had combed over the part of the castle she'd been assigned to no avail, her muscles and bones tired from the walking. But she was sure they'd come up with something. Nani was good with questions. Yuki was good with answers. Ella was good at cheering them on.

Rory wasn't sure what she was supposed to be good at doing, so she tried to avoid feeling useless.

She hadn't expected the letter. She hadn't expected that the end to her tale was coming.

It'd arrived as priority mail, handed to her by Miss Bagley when she showed up to class that morning. It was enclosed in a white cream envelope issued by the palace, the letters golden. It was a message from her mother.

Figured they would send it in a letter, but Rory imagined it would be safer. No one could hack it; no one but her would read it.

It said only that Uncle Émilien's illness, a pulmonary disease, had gotten worse. That they were doing everything they could, but his lungs had begun to fail.

The letter said Rory had to go home.

Rory crumpled the paper in her hands, making a fist and throwing it in a drawer. They hadn't even given her a choice—hadn't needed to. She'd had never had a choice. She was a princess by birth, and when her uncle was gone, she'd become the heir apparent after her father.

The fact that it was her father filling her uncle's place, and not yet her, gave Rory her only hope, but she still wasn't free of the expectations that were created the moment she'd been born. Her parents had waited for her for a long time, paid for the most expensive fertility treatments, and what had they gotten? Rory, the family's disappointment.

And in a week, maybe more if she was lucky, she'd have to leave her life as she'd known it behind. This time, there was no use relying on rescues. Her prison door had closed. She was trapped inside.

Rory took a deep breath as she got ready for her usual Friday match with Pippa, but her heart wasn't in it. They hadn't talked about the dance, which had felt like something conjured out of a book. They'd gone back to normal—because they were still in school, because they were just students, and nothing was going to change.

When she got to the gym, Pippa was already there, stretching. She adjusted her posture as Rory came in.

"What happened?" Pippa asked.

Rory hated that Pippa could read it so easily on her face.

"Nothing," Rory replied.

"It's not nothing," Pippa said as her gaze followed Rory across the room.

"Why are you always so convinced you know better?" Rory barked back, immediately regretting it.

It wasn't Pippa's fault. If anything, it was Rory's fault. She'd spent all her life pretending this wasn't who she was, avoiding what she knew was inevitable, only for it to finally catch up to her.

"As you wish," Pippa muttered.

Rory hadn't picked up her sword. There wasn't any use picking it up now when she'd be forced to leave it behind. To leave Pippa behind.

And, suddenly, Rory realized *that's* what scared her the most. She'd danced around this feeling for the last three years, pushing it back with the blade of her sword, always keeping it at bay, thinking that if she admitted it, it would crush her. And now, the end was approaching, and she hadn't even gotten a taste of it.

Weak. Cowardly.

Rory wasn't going to let herself get beaten this time. She'd do the right thing.

Because if this was going to be her life, she might as well start with Pippa. The one important person she hadn't shared the truth with. Now there was no use protecting her from it. Not anymore.

"This is not what I'm here for," Rory said. "I haven't been completely honest with you."

"Rory..."

"That's not my name," she muttered, below her breath. "That's not my real name."

She had to say it before she lost her nerve. Before she regained her mind, before she lost Pippa in a way that wasn't her choice. She'd rather choose her own destruction. Face the consequences on her own without any outside help.

Pippa narrowed her eyes.

"There's no Rory Derosiers," Rory said. "Never was, never has been. It's just a name made up to conceal who I really am. To protect me." Saying it out loud felt wrong. She had chosen who she was. Rory *was* her name. But it wasn't all of it. "My real name is Aurore. Aurore Isabelle Marguerite Louise de Rosien. Princess of Andurién."

Pippa blinked.

For a long moment, they just stood there, facing each other, the truth heavy.

Then Pippa shook her head, incredulous. "You must think I'm an idiot."

"What?" Rory said. "No, I have—"

"You think I don't know that?" Pippa snapped, stepping forward, getting too close to Rory's face. "You think I didn't put two and two together? You don't think I did a fucking google search of your home country and figured it out?"

Pippa was close enough that she'd breached all of Rory's walls. Rory wondered if she'd let them fall. Willingly open the doors for the enemy to come within, to let them wield the power to destroy her. Because Rory knew how this would end. It was inevitable.

"I thought I ought to tell you," Rory said quietly. "I did lie."

Pippa rolled her eyes. "You lied maybe about your name. But you didn't lie about who you are. You didn't lie about anything else, and that's why this so *fucking frustrating.*"

Pippa half groaned the end of her sentence, cursing under her breath, and Rory stood face to face with her. She couldn't look away because maybe Pippa cursing was the hottest thing she'd ever seen, and she wasn't capable of moving a single muscle in case she missed any more of it.

"I *know* you," Pippa breathed, her voice hoarse, so near she could feel Pippa's gasps as her chest rose and faltered. "We've been doing this for so long that it became something out of a dream. I've watched every single flick of your wrist, every parry, every strike, every move you ever made, and I keep waiting for the moment I'm going to wake up."

Rory could not utter a word.

"I keep waiting for the day you won't show up. For the day you understand that this isn't what you wanted your life to be," Pippa said, her shoulders sagging. "I'm tired of playing this game, Rory. I know you, but I don't know what you want."

Rory hesitated, and her heart skipped a beat in her chest. "What are you saying?"

Pippa sighed impatiently. "I'm in love with you, you complete moron."

The silence echoed in the room as Pippa stared at her, waiting for Rory to say something. The words hit her like an arrow, and Rory didn't know how to respond.

So she did the only thing she could.

Rory grabbed Pippa's face and kissed her. It was a messy kiss, her face smashed against Pippa's, her lips thirsty and demanding. There was a moment of stillness, and then Pippa responded in kind, her hands pulling against Rory's waist, pressing her closer, devouring. Rory turned her head and parted Pippa's mouth open, and it was exactly like how they always fought, where each move could save her or doom her, but maybe it was going to be both at once.

Rory broke the kiss, her stomach dropping, every part of her body shaking.

"This isn't a dream," Rory said, gasping for breath.

"It better not be," Pippa replied, their breaths mingling. She touched Rory's lips again, softer this time. A flutter. "I've been thinking of doing this for the past three years."

Rory blinked at her, meeting Pippa's gaze. All this time waiting, dreaming for this moment, only for it to come true exactly as she'd imagined.

No. Better than she had imagined. Because once she opened her eyes, it would all still be true.

"Then maybe," Rory breathed, "you should kiss me again."

As Rory felt her own muscles melt in a good way for once, her knees growing weak, her body pressed against her wall and Pippa's mouth on hers, there was only one thought crossing her mind.

This was her destruction. This was her downfall.

And she was going to enjoy every moment of it.

CHAPTER THIRTY-SEVEN

ELLA

The weekend brought the unexpected blessing of Sharon leaving with the twins. Ella's stepmother had been hovering more than usual as of late, her hawk's gaze following her across the house. Ella kept her head down like she always had, listening to an audiobook or a podcast while doing the housework, trying to drown out all the other sounds that were filling her head.

Ella watched Sharon and her stepsisters drive off, observing the car from her window in the attic. Then she sat back on the bed. Before, she would have called her friends, spent another afternoon in town, or just hung out and talked. Now, it didn't feel the same. Now, every time the clock struck its hour, Ella felt her doom approaching.

Ella had promised Frederick a real date, so they went for lunch in Constanz. It was one of the most beautiful spring days yet, flowers blossoming in every flowerbed in town. Purples, pinks, yellows, and whites danced across their view. It was Ella's favorite season. Afterwards, they went out for ice cream and then walked slowly back together to Grimrose, hand in hand, and Ella couldn't remember the last time she'd felt this relaxed. The last time she'd let herself forget about everything and just enjoy one sunny afternoon with her boyfriend. They walked around Constanz until the sunlight started diminishing, until the sky started turning purple and they were finally back at the gates of the castle, hands intertwined.

"Thanks for this," Ella said. "I had a nice day."

"You're welcome," Freddie said. "I'd do it more often, but you know."

Ella offered him a half smile but said nothing. They both lingered near the gates of the school, and Ella didn't want to say goodbye. She didn't want to go back home.

"You don't have to go," Freddie said quietly, as if reading her mind. "You can come up to the room. You said they were spending the weekend out. You can stay with me."

Ella rolled on the balls of her feet near the gates, uncertain. It was true that Sharon wasn't coming back yet. She'd checked Stacie's Instagram just to be sure, her photos showing the nice hotel they'd booked in Paris. Ella could stay. Ella *wanted* to stay.

So for the first time, Ella didn't hesitate. "Okay."

The boys' and girls' dormitories were on different floors of the castle but in the same wing. A teacher would usually try to monitor any activities, but it was hard keeping up with all the students. Grimrose pretended not to take notice of their students' romantic endeavors, as long as they used protection and no scandals happened and the students tried not to flaunt it out in the open.

Freddie's room was in the south part of the corridor, and when Ella came in, she realized how different the boys' rooms were from the girls'. For starters, the boys shared rooms only in twos instead of threes because Grimrose had more female students. She could spot Frederick's side of the room, with three different movie posters along the wall and a stack of old DVDs piled with his schoolwork. It was a nice cozy sort of bedroom, simple but with personality.

"Where's your roommate?" Ella asked, looking around at the unmade bed on the other side of the corner.

"I kind of told him to find somewhere else to sleep tonight," Freddie said, giving her a smug smile.

"Oh, so this was planned," Ella replied, but there was a hint of amusement in her voice. Freddie blushed, turning to her, bending down to kiss her.

His kiss began slow and deliberate, but soon enough Ella was pushing harder, their hands intertwined, their clothes rumpled as they kissed more and more, until Frederick had stumbled onto the bed, taking Ella with him, and there they stayed. His hands started on her back, until they'd grazed the skin beneath her skirt, her calves, and Ella stopped.

"Can we..." Ella's voice trailed off. "I'm going to get the lights."

She got up quickly, pressing the switch. There was only Frederick's night-light on, but its glow was yellowish and faded, so Ella didn't mind. She sat back down on the bed, her heart beating fast.

Frederick kissed her cheek, and Ella turned to him again, her hands catching his hair, and this time, she didn't stop his hands from wandering beneath her skirt. She felt the warmth of his touch on her calves, his fingers stroking her delicately. She took off his shirt, her kisses trailing his collarbone, their hands wandering all over each other, calm and sure and with no hurry at all. Her heart was fluttering still, her own body growing heated but not uncomfortable, as their kissing rushed, and Ella tumbled on top of him. Freddie found the zipper down her dress and took it off, and Ella finally realized what she was doing.

She stopped kissing him, hovering just above his face. She didn't dare to look at herself, but Freddie said nothing, taking her in, a smile on his face.

"You're beautiful," he said. "It sounds awfully convenient saying it now, but it's still true."

Ella laughed. "You're not so bad yourself."

"What can I say, I work out."

Ella laughed harder, because if there was one thing that Frederick wasn't, it was full of muscles. His skin was soft, tender, and boyish, and Ella liked that she was the one with the hardened muscles. He tugged a stray blond hair behind her ear, his brown eyes searching her face as Ella leaned over him.

"Are you...?"

"A virgin? Yes," Ella answered truthfully. "Are you?"

Freddie shook his head. "Last time was a little different," he said, hesitating a little for the first time that evening. "I used to date a guy."

"Oh! That's nice," Ella said, feeling the tension dissipate a little more, her body relaxed even though her heart was still beating fast. "My first middle school crush was a girl. She used to collect butterflies."

"Good," he said, and then, awkwardly, "Not about the butterflies. That's weird."

Ella laughed, tracing the lines of Frederick's arm in the half dark. She didn't feel embarrassed, practically naked in another person's room, making her own confessions. For once, she felt comfortable.

Freddie must have interpreted Ella's silence in another way.

"We don't have to do anything. You can just stay here. We can share the bed. It's a single, so it'll be tight, but I don't mind sharing it at all, and you can just sleep—"

"Freddie," Ella said, thumb running down his lips, asserting for once what her heart told her. "I want this."

Carefully, Freddie brought her closer. She held his face with both her hands, and under the dim light, all the colors had faded into a deeper blue, and Ella wasn't afraid. She kissed him, and Freddie kissed her back, his hands on her waist, their hands brushing delicately along each other's bodies until they'd found each other. Freddie held her for a long, long time, until she fell asleep, her head resting against his chest.

The sunlight streamed through the curtains as Ella felt the warmth of Freddie's body next to her, his arm protectively wrapped around her waist. The bed was a tight fit, but Ella was small, and she wasn't complaining.

She moved quietly, trying not to wake him. Freddie was still half snoring, his eyes closed, and Ella slipped from beneath his hold, brushing sleep from her eyes. She had to be quick. She went to the bathroom, checked her back. She'd slept peacefully in one of Freddie's old T-shirts, and she took it off, folding it neatly over the back of his chair, finding her underwear and the dress.

She did it all very quietly, but it wasn't enough.

"El, what's that?" Frederick's voice was sharp. He didn't sound like he was asleep.

Ella turned, still holding her dress. Through the bathroom mirror, she knew what he hadn't seen last night in the darkness.

Yellowed bruises covered her ribcage. There was a red scratch on her arm, and her knees were so purple that only panty hose could hide it. Her makeup had rubbed off onto the pillow while she was sleeping, and there was the faint trace of an old mark beneath her left eye, a cut just above her eyebrow. She was covered in the marks of Sharon's hands.

Frederick's face was horrified.

"It's nothing," she said quickly, hurrying to put her dress on, covering what she'd been so careful to hide.

It had been a stupid idea to stay the night. If she had woken up earlier, none of this would have happened.

Frederick got up, wearing only his boxers, standing tall next to her.

"Who did this?" he asked, his voice firm.

"It doesn't matter."

His face only became angrier.

"Of course it matters," he said, his hand holding her chin so she would look at him. Ella didn't fight it.

"I lied to you," Ella said, feeling her voice catch in her throat. "I've been lying this whole time. I'm not like anybody else in this school. I don't have this perfect life."

"Who did this?" he repeated.

Ella felt the tears pooling in the back of her eyes, her arms protectively wrapped around herself. Admitting it out loud hurt so much more—she couldn't lie to herself once someone knew the truth. That she stayed, that she got beaten, and she had nowhere else to go. She had to stay with Sharon if she was ever going to inherit her father's money and be free.

That she was just a miserable, sad, and stupid girl who wasn't even smart enough to try and make her fate by herself. No one wanted someone who was like that. Someone to pity your whole life, to tread carefully around because they would always get hurt, too full of trauma and bad memories that couldn't be cured or forgotten.

Someone who couldn't be fixed.

"I don't want your pity," Ella said, pulling away. "Thank you. I had a nice night."

Then she turned around and left.

CHAPTER THIRTY-EIGHT

NANI

Nani had been on her way out of the library when Ella ran straight past her.

What was most bewildering was not that Ella was in Grimrose on a Sunday morning, but that she was also running, an activity that Nani had seen her do maybe once all year.

"Ella?" Nani called as she saw Ella rush down the stairs outside of the library.

Ella turned, one hand on the rail, and looked over her shoulder. "Hi. Didn't see you there."

Her voice was slightly off, and Nani noticed that Ella's usual makeup was gone, a bruise showing near her eye.

"You okay?"

"Fine," Ella muttered. Nani noticed her trembling fingers, the way her eyes darted to the pictures on the walls. Counting them to keep calm.

Nani stepped toward her. "Ella, you don't have to lie to me," Nani said. "I'm your friend, remember?"

That was all it took. Ella ran back up the stairs, her tears streaming, and then she wrapped her arms around Nani.

At first it was awkward, and Nani didn't know what to do. She didn't really hug people. But Ella was holding her so tight that Nani felt herself relax, wrapping her arms around Ella's back, Ella with her head on Nani's shoulder. There was the wetness of her tears against Nani's dress, but she didn't mind. She held Ella for as long as she needed.

"Let's go," Nani said, with an arm still wrapped around Ella. "Let's get you home."

There wasn't bus service on Sunday, but that didn't stop Nani from taking Ella all the way to her house. By the time they got there, Ella had stopped visibly crying, but Nani's thighs were painfully chafed from the long walk.

"Thanks," Ella said. They had stopped by the garden wall outside Ella's house.

"Shouldn't we go to the door?" Nani asked, raising an eyebrow.

"I don't have the keys," Ella said. "Sharon locks the whole place when she leaves."

Nani's face hardened as she understood the implication. She held out her hands for Ella to use as a step. Ella was almost weightless as she went over the wall. Nani found footing to climb it herself, swinging over and landing in the garden.

The house looked lonely from the outside. The windows

were all shut tight, heavy curtains over them. The only movement in the garden was the head of a horse that poked out of the stable door to neigh when Ella approached and petted its snout. Ella gestured for Nani to follow her, and she pointed to a single window open at the back of the house.

"I'll go in first," Ella said. "This one is jammed, so it never closes."

Ella slipped through the tiny gap of the kitchen window, and a moment later, she managed to open a bigger window so Nani could come inside.

The air was stuffy in the dark house, and there was no sign of anything that could even remotely belong to Ella. The pictures on the living room wall were all of Sharon and the twins; nothing indicated that there was another young girl living in the same house. Half of the windows were padlocked, the front door closed.

Ella shifted her weight as Nani took it in. "Sorry. It's all very dark. I don't get a lot of visitors."

Nani thought that this was an understatement.

"You don't need to apologize," Nani said. "Where do you sleep?"

"In the attic," Ella said. "It's lofty. Plenty of air up there."

Nani didn't know what to say. Even in the small two-bedroom house she shared with Tūtū, there was the feeling of home. Here, there was nothing of the kind. A prison of a different type. At least Nani had gotten the castle.

"I'll make you tea," Ella said promptly, and Nani let her, because that's how she took care of Ella: by letting Ella take care of her. Soon enough, the scent filled the living room and the kitchen, a citrus smell of lemon mixed with hibiscus and peach, and Nani suddenly felt like she was being transported straight into Tūtū's kitchen, drinking tea even when the heat on the street was unbearable.

Ella handed her a mug, a smile on her face.

"This tea smells like home," Nani said, taking it. "How did you know?"

"All your books kind of smell like it," Ella replied. "It's hard to miss."

"It's the plumerias," Nani said. "My mom used them as bookmarks. I just continued the tradition."

Nani took a sip of the tea, feeling the liquid burn the tip of her tongue. It was strong, good, certain. Ella smiled as she washed the rest of the dishes, her own mug forgotten at the top of the sink while her hands got busy.

"Do you miss her?" Ella asked, not looking at Nani.

"Sometimes," Nani admitted. "I think I miss the way it used to be when she was around. My dad came home more."

Ella gave her a knowing nod.

"Tūtū is wonderful," Nani found herself saying. "It sounds horrible if I complain about my grandmother. She raised me, raised my mom, and she taught me pretty much all I know. But when my dad came home, he brought me books. I didn't leave the house, but I didn't have to. The whole world was still right there."

"I'm sorry about your loss," said Ella.

Nani shrugged. "It's been a long time."

"So? You can still miss it," Ella replied. "I miss my family too."

"Should it bother us that almost all of us are orphans?" Nani asked. "Isn't that really weird?"

"You better not start thinking about our names," Ella said.

"God," Nani muttered to her mug. "The curse is fucked up, but it's also really tacky."

Ella laughed, finally turning off the water and picking up her own mug to sit side by side with Nani, sipping her tea. Nani found the silence with Ella comfortable, a strange thing since Ella always seemed to be moving, agitated, anxious.

And Nani wanted the comfort—Nani needed the comfort, after finding her father's box. She hadn't told the other girls, but one of the papers that she'd cast aside on the first glance had contained her father's papers for starting work at the school.

All of them had been signed personally by the headmistress.

Nani hadn't brought it up with Yuki. Hadn't told the others because they didn't need more tension. Because the curse didn't need to destroy the bonds they had created too, and Nani didn't want to be the one pointing fingers.

"You want to talk about it?" Nani asked instead. "Did something happen with Frederick back there?"

Ella sipped her tea, the lines of her mouth tense. "We— we slept together."

"Oh," Nani said, because she didn't know how to answer that kind of statement. "Was it that bad?"

245

Ella laughed, and the lines around her eyes cleared, her hazel irises warm. "No. It was good, actually."

"First time?" Nani asked.

"Yes. I mean, I always thought it would have to be some kind of big moment. That's what they all tell us, isn't it? That if I went through school without experiencing it, I'd be completely lost. I thought I'd feel all that pressure, but when it came to it, it was just...it was just good. Simple. I wanted it, and that's all that mattered."

Ella took another sip of her tea, both her hands holding the mug. Nani noticed she was doing it only so her hands would stop moving.

"So what's wrong?" Nani asked.

"He saw the bruises," Ella replied. "My plan was to get up earlier. Get dressed and leave, but I..." Her voice stopped. "He saw all of it, and I had to run."

Nani could almost imagine the scene, the same vision of Ella she had that day in the bathroom. Ella's skin not covered in makeup, all the yellow and purple stains underneath her clothes, invisible to anyone who didn't know where to look.

"You could have talked to him," Nani said.

"And then he would come with an intervention, trying to fix something that isn't fixable," Ella said. "Or worse, decide it's too much trouble in the first place. It's not his burden to bear. It's mine."

"You do know that burdens are for sharing, right?" Nani said.

Ella didn't look at Nani. She was the girl always trying to

save and spare everyone, and that took a toll. Maybe it had begun as a single gesture, but it was an effort she put forward all the time.

"Maybe that's not how he'll see it," Nani said. "You don't know until you give him a chance."

Ella snorted. "You're one to say."

The words echoed Odilia, the way she'd told Nani that she didn't know Svenja. And then Nani, proving her right, telling Svenja off and not sharing any of her secrets.

"How so?" Nani asked, sharply, if only to have confirmation.

"I just mean that sometimes I feel like you're not here at all, Nani," Ella said simply. "I think this is the first time in almost a year that we've had a real conversation."

Nani was too shocked to speak, and Ella looked up at her, eyebrows knitted in concern. It was the same expression that had lived on Tūtū's face while Nani grew up and tried to keep herself apart from everyone else.

Trying to keep herself safe, building castle walls around who she really was.

And here was someone, knocking on the door, asking to be let in. Asking to be led through the staircases and the dark dungeons, and maybe eventually, to a place filled with light.

That's what being a friend meant. It was crossing the dark and murky waters together, never afraid to see what would come out on the other side.

"I don't know how to be better than this," Nani finally said, wiping her eyes.

"I've had practice," Ella replied easily. "I know it isn't easy. But sometimes, it's worth a try."

Nani smiled, and Ella smiled back, and both girls stayed in silence, drinking the last of the tea, waiting for the taste at the end to turn just a little bitter, to balance things out.

CHAPTER THIRTY-NINE

YUKI

It was already late when Nani came back to the room.

Yuki hadn't gone up to Reyna's tower. She'd given the excuse of having to study for finals—which was true, even if it was so obviously a pretext—and she'd spent the day in the quiet but irritating company of Mephistopheles, feeling the cat's yellow eyes follow as she turned every page of her homework mindlessly, completing the exercises without thinking twice about them.

She'd rather spend her time on this than think about what she had seen.

Somehow, Yuki hadn't thought that the curse would get to her. As Nani had put it, Yuki was special. Yuki had magic. Yuki was different, and she was willing to do what it took. And so, her story wouldn't come true.

But as much as she avoided thinking about it, she couldn't stop seeing Reyna and the mirror, knowing that her own story had a dark turn, waiting for her to be careless. Liron's words hung around her, and Yuki tried not to listen to them. *Swallow your heart.* But, like the curse, they repeated over and over in her head.

It's the only way you'll survive.

Nani had come inside without stopping in the doorway, for which Yuki was glad. She looked around. "Where's Rory?"

"With Pippa," Yuki answered.

"It isn't Friday."

"I know."

Yuki watched as understanding dawned on Nani's face. "Oh, finally!" Nani exclaimed emphatically. "She finally did it! Are they—"

"Yes," Yuki replied evenly. "And before you can ask, like Rory did, I will absolutely *not* leave the room for either of you to use. Do it where I can't see or hear or even think about it."

Nani rolled her eyes, opening up Rory's laptop to look up something. Nani didn't have a computer, and Rory never worried twice about sharing anything of hers, her generosity an unspoken rule. Nani ran her eyes over a message she'd received, then she jumped up with her phone to take pictures of the Black Book and the White Book, both resting on her desk.

"What are you doing?" Yuki asked.

"I found something. An old man with a rare bookshop in Munich," Nani replied. "I'm sending him a couple of pictures of our own books."

"You're *what*?" Yuki demanded.

"I'm posing as a book collector's daughter," Nani said

defensively. "If I want to see pictures of what he has, I've got to send proof of some of mine. Otherwise, he'll just think I'm swindling him. Don't worry, it's not like I said our books are cursed."

Yuki took another breath, deeper this time, getting her emotions back in control. "And what did he say?"

"He might have heard of books similar to ours," Nani replied. "It's not confirmed, but it's the only lead I have."

"So why not tell the others?" Yuki asked, raising an eyebrow.

"I don't want to get their hopes up," Nani said.

"But you have no problem telling me."

"You aren't going to tell them either," Nani pointed out, and Yuki felt the understanding between them both, how they were both trying to approach this as logically as they could. "And you? Have you found anything?"

Yuki thought of Reyna in the tower, the way her face had changed. The way Yuki's body had become like ice, how she thought she wouldn't be able to move.

"Nothing physical," Yuki said instead. "But there is... something."

"Elaborate."

"Liron didn't attend Grimrose," Yuki said carefully, thinking how to phrase this, examining Nani as she said it, but Nani didn't seem to change her posture. "But most of the girls in the book—the ones alive, the right age, all of them are here. So there has always been something that brought them here. Something that connects them to this place. And I—I feel it. Sometimes."

Nani turned a curl of her hair curiously with her left hand. "Feel it how?"

Yuki thought of the faces she'd seen in the mirror before she understood her powers, before she kept trying to shut that part of herself out. Before she embraced herself fully, the darkness that lurked within, waiting for the right opportunity to come out. "As if my magic responds to it."

Nani narrowed her eyes, slowly coming to understand the meaning behind the words. "You don't think it's just the books."

"It can't be," Yuki replied. "You've seen my magic. You've seen its power. I've got nothing on this curse. I tried destroying the books too."

It was Nani's turn to exclaim in surprise. "What? When?"

It was the day Rory had caught her breaking the mirror. She'd tried everything. She'd hurled every feeling she harbored at the books, but nothing seemed to affect them. Nothing seemed to change. At last, she'd finally swung her hand at the mirror, smashing it into pieces with frustration, just as Rory had come inside.

She'd pretended that nothing had happened.

Just like Reyna had done with her.

"Even if we find whatever it is that is missing," Yuki said carefully, "I don't think it'll be as simple as destroying it."

"You don't think we'll be able to do it, do you?"

Yuki looked up sharply at her. "I didn't say that."

"It's all over your face," Nani replied, and then she laughed, a nervous laughter that she stifled with the back of her hand. "This is the first time I can actually see what you're thinking. Clear as day."

Yuki's face hardened. "You don't know what I'm thinking."

"You're right," Nani said. "I don't. I don't even know who you really are." Then she laughed again, biting her lower lip, and muttering, "Ella's right."

That made Yuki look up. "Ella's right about what?"

"It's like I'm not even here," Nani said. "But neither are you. Why do you hide so much?"

At that moment, Nani's brown eyes pierced through Yuki, sharp as spears. Yuki felt her edges coming undone; she didn't want to admit that both she and Nani thought the same way. Nani wanted proof of the curse as much as Yuki did. Nani wanted to figure out its workings, take it down from the inside, question it.

She could hear the other question in Nani's words. It wasn't a question of why she was hiding. Because as much as she could admit it to herself, everyone around her pretended nothing had happened. Everyone around her pretended they understood. Even Ella. Ella, who was so good, so forgiving all the time, who still refused to look Yuki straight in the eye.

It wasn't that Yuki was hiding. Only that the others refused to see her.

And that wasn't going to last long. The more time passed, the more she understood that the fire was catching up to her, that the fire she'd burned was going to consume her. The more she thought about Liron's words, the more they had taken root to the core, the more she knew her darkness would always be overwhelming, and soon, there would be no hiding anymore.

"I don't have anything to hide," Yuki finally said, facing Nani without blinking. "Why would I?"

There was a time when Yuki disliked questions.

There was a time she was afraid of the answers.

Before Nani could retort, the clock tower of Grimrose rang—but the bells weren't telling the time.

Yuki felt her body grow ice cold, exchanging one alarming look with Nani as they both ran to the door. Just as Yuki swung it open, she saw Rory in the corridor, looking disgruntled, her eyes wide, breathless as she stopped running.

"It's Ivy," Rory said. "She's dead."

CHAPTER FORTY

ELLA

Ella couldn't stand to stay in the assembly.

Her lungs felt filled with stones, and the more the teachers talked, the more she couldn't breathe. With her hands trembling, Ella ran out of the room, her feet taking her through the corridor and then down a set of stairs. She didn't turn around to see if anyone was following.

She needed a quiet place to think. She didn't want to go to the library, where she'd thought she'd saved Ivy, or even out to the gardens, where the beautiful day was shining outside. Finally, she realized there was one place she could run to—the old chess room.

It was in a neglected part of the castle, an old room off a remote hallway that had been converted for the chess club. There had once been tables, but the pièce de résistance of the room was a giant chessboard painted on the floor, with heavy sculpted wooden chess pieces lined up on either side of the board. The room had been abandoned ever since the chess team had been dissolved.

Ella let herself fall into the middle of the gigantic board. She sat in one of the squares, looking at the pieces that towered over her. Her heavy sobs moved her shoulders, and she tried to take deep breaths, controlling her crying, but at least here her sobs didn't echo to the rest of the assembly. At least here she was left to mourn in peace.

Except being alone, somehow, felt suffocating. It felt like she was sinking again to the bottom of the lake when Penelope threw her in, the darkness closing in around her. Ella counted the squares on the board; once, twice.

She heard someone else walk quietly into the room, and she looked up to see Rory standing in the doorway.

"Hey," Rory said, sitting down beside her. She looked calm, better than how Ella was feeling. "I came to check on you."

"I'm fine."

Rory gave her a look that said everything. Ella ended up smiling even when she didn't want to. She had wanted a quiet place, but being left with her own thoughts was worse.

"Ari hated this place," Rory said instead.

"I know," Ella said, sniffling. "She said it was vulgar."

"It's so cheap. Look at the size of that king piece. What the hell were they thinking?"

Ella smiled again as Rory traced one of the pawns sitting next to them. They used to spend hours here in the first year they came to Grimrose. Ella thought the giant game was comforting, but Ari always insisted it was tacky and had no place in a school as tasteful as Grimrose.

"I miss her," Rory said, saying out loud what Ella was thinking. "Sometimes I forget it was just a while ago that she died. Sometimes I wake up and feel like I've lived years."

Ella wiped away the rest of her tears. Rory's presence was a steady one, and this time, not too loud. It was comforting because Rory was always reliable. Whenever Ella needed something, Rory was there. She supported Ella in a less intense way than Yuki did, and sometimes, Ella was glad for that respite.

"Do you think we would have been happier if we hadn't found the book?" Ella asked, looking at Rory.

"I don't know. Dead-*er*, for sure."

Ella circled her fingers around the painted board, tracing the lines between one of the black and white squares.

"I keep going back to that question," Ella told Rory. "Whether maybe we should have just left it alone. Let Ari be at peace, and then we would just...quietly follow."

"You know there's no use thinking in what ifs," Rory replied. "I know this is part of your anxiety, but let me tell you, as a person who doesn't ever think too much, *what if* is a waste of time."

Ella broke into another smile. It was impossible not to around Rory. It was like the darkness was gone, and Rory had brought only light.

"I don't think it would have been easier, though, if we hadn't found the book," Rory mused. "Maybe we would have been more helpless. This way, at least we can control something."

"I didn't save Ivy."

"You couldn't have," Rory said gently, offering a hand to Ella. Ella's fingertips were red from rubbing them against the floor obsessively, and of course Rory had noticed. Ella took her hand, and Rory squeezed it. "It's not your responsibility. You can't save everybody."

"But I made a promise," Ella said emphatically. "If I can't save one girl—"

"Then you'll just give up and not try to save anyone else?" Rory looked pointedly at her. "Come on, Ella. I know you better than that."

Ella looked away, taking in the carved details of the chess pieces.

Rory was right, but Rory didn't know everything about Ella.

Rory didn't know that sometimes, when Ella woke up in the middle of the night, she was relieved that it was Ari who had died and not Yuki.

Rory didn't know that Ella was trying to do everything in her power to save everyone because if she lost *one* person— then she didn't know how she could go on living. She didn't know how to face the fact that she could keep on living when everyone was dying as long as Yuki was there.

Her guilt was overwhelming, so all she could do to compensate for this was break the curse.

"It doesn't change what happened to Ivy," Ella said.

"Ella, every time a new girl dies, I see Ari again," Rory

258

said, looking straight at her. Her blue eyes were intense, cheeks heated, red hair burning. "It's always Ari. Again, and again and again, and trust me, I get it. I understand. Because you lose one girl, and it's like losing her all over again."

Tears welled in Rory's eyes, and she blinked, making them disappear. Ella held Rory's hand tight; Rory would never let her see her tears on a good day.

None of them were having a good day.

"But if we stop," Rory continued, "if we think it's not worth it, then that's how we lose Ari once and for all."

The only way to honor these girls was to save them all.

Make them count.

Make it so that the next time their tales were repeated, reborn, they got the ending they so truly deserved.

"Now come on," Rory said. "Assembly is over. Let's go have lunch."

CHAPTER FORTY-ONE

RORY

Rory thought she should have been gotten used to the bodies by now, but they only made her think of Ari.

Ari was each and every one of them. It was Ari who had eaten the sweets. Ari whose head had been chopped off. And now Ari who had hung off the tower, her hair wrapped around her neck, and when they finally got her down, the body crashed into the briar bushes below, and her eyes had been gouged out by the thorns.

And when the curse got to Rory and her friends, it would be Ari all over again, even when they weren't there to remember her.

The girls sat in silence at lunch. Classes had been canceled for the day. The teachers had been standing by in case anyone wanted to talk about the tragedy, but no one seemed keen on taking the offer. They had managed to sweep the other deaths under the rug. Now, it was just one more.

One more body, one more on the trail they left behind.

"What do you think happens?" Rory asked suddenly, and Nani turned to blink at her. "To the bodies."

"Huh, why?" Nani asked.

Even though classes were canceled, Ella hadn't gone home yet, lingering. Yuki looked up from her own bowl.

"They have to keep them here," Rory said, trying to explain her train of thought, turning to the others. "Right?"

Nani seemed to consider it for a moment, and Rory liked watching Nani think because her concentration was stamped all over her face, in her smart brown eyes, in the slight crease between her eyebrows.

"They kept Ari's body," Ella said slowly. "Until her parents took it home. They have to keep all the bodies somewhere."

The three of them turned to Yuki, who was staring straight ahead. Her eyes seemed distant. "Why are you asking me?"

"Because you'd know," Nani pointed out.

Yuki hesitated. "They don't stay here. They are all transferred to the police morgue."

Rory heaved a sigh. Another idea, gone.

"But—" Yuki said, and she seemed to regret it almost immediately, "they did just find Ivy. The police were called, but I doubt they'll be transferring her before tomorrow."

"Great," Nani said, and then cringed at her own choice of words. "So her body is here, somewhere. Where would they keep it?"

"In the dungeons, probably."

"You told me it was flooded."

"Yes, most of it," Yuki said impatiently. "But it seems the likely place they would keep her. And even then, we don't know how to get down there."

"The conservatory door," Ella muttered.

Yuki looked up. "What door?"

"I forgot about it," Ella said, stronger this time, her hazel eyes frantic. "It's locked, I checked, but it doesn't make sense to lead anywhere else but below the castle."

The four of them exchanged looks. Rory didn't want to put the feeling into words, but they knew they were running out of time. Each new body increased the chances they'd be next.

And Rory hadn't forgotten her mother's letter yet.

"It might be another way in," Nani said, looking over at Rory. "Do you really think it's a good idea?"

Rory looked over at her, and for the first time that day, she offered a true grin. "And since when do I have any good ideas?"

They got in to the dungeon through the conservatory door, just like Ella said.

The four of them stood in front of the door, waiting expectantly as Yuki used her fingers to freeze the knob. The door opened into a set of stairs, and the stairs disappeared into the darkness.

Rory went down first. The steps were big, and they almost made her muscles cramp, but Rory ignored her body's protests. The stairs headed down, and then they turned to the right. Rory didn't turn around, but she could hear everyone's breath behind her. Yuki's, short and assertive; Nani's, deeper and slower; and Ella's, a little ragged from the exercise, much like all of Ella. Rory could hear her own breath, the way her lungs hitched just a second after she'd went down another step, waiting for a moment where she would crumble.

Rory took all her steps carefully and deliberately. There was lake water in the tunnels, and it soaked through her socks and tennis shoes. Rory knew this was risky—one wrong step and she'd go to the ground, and no number of pills could compensate a fall that bad if she slipped.

They walked quietly, phones turned downward with the flashlights lit up. The smell was musty and old, stuffy like the cellars of her uncle's castle. The light was low, but enough for them to see what came ahead. They kept turning in the endless corridor, going deeper. And there was the water, sloshing at their ankles.

"Where *are* we?" Nani asked, her voice piercing the coldness. "Are we sure there's another exit this way?"

"There's a current," Yuki said, pointing down. "The water is going somewhere."

Rory didn't like the tone of Yuki's voice, but she didn't say anything. The path veered to the right, but there were no doors. All Rory knew was that she was still underneath the castle, but she had no idea how far down. She could feel it in her bones, the way the wind cut through the old stones, the way they were going deeper with each turn into the heart of it.

The water was now nearly up to their knees. Rory didn't want to think of what was in that water. It was the same water from the lake; she could never look at the lake anymore without wondering how many ghosts had been left behind. How many other girls had drowned in these waters, just like Ari.

Her foot slipped a centimeter, and she stopped, clutching the walls. Behind her, Nani halted, but before she reached for Rory, Rory had already moved forward. She wasn't going to stop now. She didn't need the help.

"Can you do something about this?" Rory asked Yuki, annoyed at the waves rippling at her wet pants, trying to keep the fear out of her voice.

"Not unless you want to freeze to death," Yuki snapped.

When they turned once again, Yuki pushed past Rory, leading the way, turning left toward a door. Yuki stood in front of it for a moment, then put a hand on the knob. The wood creaked in its hinges, the water around them icy cold, and it swung open.

Rory was the first to go inside.

There was no body, and Rory didn't know if she felt relieved or disappointed.

The room was a vaulted chamber; the ceilings domed above them, painted in gold. It was a step above the water, for which she was glad. Her knees wobbled a little when she took the step, and Rory braced for the pain and moved forward. Shelves lined the three walls that comprised the room. The room was empty but for the small boxes piled up on the shelves, boxes with golden enamel circles on each of them.

Rory stepped closer to the wall, realizing the boxes weren't just boxes. They were chests.

The three girls followed her inside the vault, the marble floor extending below them in a dark swirl of black and white.

"What is this?" Ella asked, shaking her head in awe.

Rory's fingers grazed one of the boxes. It was warm to the touch, which surprised her, considering how the rest of the room was cold and austere. The box had no engravings, no markings, but there was a small device that kept it closed, not unlike a lock.

She'd seen the same kind of device before. Some of the old castle locks back home had been just like it. An ancient device that had a trick to it. Finally, this was something that Rory could do. She'd open this and solve the mystery.

Rory took the chest in her hands as the others turned to see what she was doing. Her fingers slid along the lock, and then a click resounded through the cellar room.

"Don't—" Ella said, dread filling up her white face, but it was too late.

Rory opened it.

Inside the box was a human heart.

CHAPTER FORTY-TWO

YUKI

R ory dropped the box, and the sound echoed against the marble floor.

For a moment, everything in the room stood still. No one breathed, no one moved, but as Yuki watched the heart in the box, she could have sworn it was still beating. Faint, distant, but still there, the pulse of life disrupting.

Then, finally, sound and movement came back. Ella opened her mouth in shock, gasping, her hands covering her mouth, and Rory jumped two feet back, almost smashing against the opposite wall and bringing down even more boxes with her.

"What is that?" Nani said, even though they all knew the answer to that question.

They couldn't mistake it for anything else. The thing was the size of Yuki's fist, the shape she'd seen in anatomy diagrams, but it wasn't covered in blood. It looked almost crystallized, like a fine web of glass was enfolding it.

Yuki bent down and picked up the box in her hands. The box felt normal. Wood, carved simply, the outside polished and lustrous. The lock was painted gold, but there was no other ornamentation.

"What are you doing?" Rory asked, voice half-strangled. "Don't touch that."

"Whoever comes back here will know it's out of place," Yuki said. "We have to put it back."

Her voice was calm, and she felt the same peace and stillness from after the night at the lake. After the worst had passed, after Penelope's body was in her arms, limp. That moment when everything had changed, but when everything also felt right. A second that lasted an eternity.

Because now Yuki understood what this curse was about.

It wasn't about dooming them. It was about conquering them.

"Do you think—" Nani's stronger, rougher voice spoke into the quiet. "Do you think that all of these boxes have hearts?"

Yuki closed her eyes, and she could feel it. The echoes inside the grim wooden caskets.

She didn't answer, and she didn't have to.

Yuki slid the latch closed. Yuki deposited the casket in the spot where Rory had picked it up. She put it back into place, heard a satisfying click as the box joined all its sisters along the walls. Yuki brushed her hands along their lines, but counting them would be pointless. There were far too many of them, and Yuki felt like this wasn't all this room could be. She looked up to the strange domed ceiling and then back to the center of the room, where the black and white marble in the floor held a pattern that formed a star.

Yuki crouched down again and brushed a hand against the floor, feeling her magic pour out.

She felt the overwhelming sensation of belonging as she understood that's what her magic had been calling to, all this time.

The star on the floor seemed to swirl underneath her touch. Then, the floor opened and out rose a pedestal that held yet another box.

This box wasn't like the caskets on the shelves. The wood was black, and on top of it, instead of the golden lock, sat a small mirror.

Impulsively, Yuki reached her hand out to touch it.

One moment she was there in the vaulted room, then the next moment her vision darkened, and she was somewhere else.

Someone standing on the edge of a dark wood.

A cottage, a girl bursting through the door, wearing a simple white dress. Sleeves covering her wrists, a long skirt. Yuki couldn't control her movements, couldn't look away.

When the girl looked up, Yuki knew who she was.

She had seen this version of herself before.

A rounder face. Shorter than she was but with more presence. Breasts, calves, belly, muscles. Her eyes weren't shaped like Yuki's; they were so round they looked like blackberries but still the same shade of black. With a shudder, she recognized the exact shade of her own lips.

As soon as the girl saw Yuki, she turned away.

"Snow," Yuki said. Yuki felt her mouth open, heard the sound of her voice, but she couldn't place it. Yuki was running toward Snow, arms outstretched, but she wasn't herself. Her skin was a shade darker. "Snow, wait!"

Snow stopped. Yuki didn't want to see her face, but she couldn't look anywhere else. Now that she didn't deny it anymore, it was jarring to see it so clearly. To see a version of herself this alive.

"I was going to tell you," Yuki said softly, reaching her arm to touch Snow. Snow stepped back, furious. "I never—"

"I don't care!" Snow shouted. "All of it was a lie!"

"Snow," Yuki repeated, as if it was the only word she knew. "Snow, please. You have to come with me. They'll find you."

"Never," Snow yelled, stepping back toward the forest. "Everything you touch withers and dies. That's what you and your magic do."

Yuki felt a sob catch in her throat. She'd made it worse. She'd made another terrible choice.

"You will never see me again," said Snow.

Snow ran.

Yuki reached for her, but there was only a blinding light. She felt the darkness of the magic course through her body as she reached out for Snow. Giant spears of ice rose around Snow, imprisoning her. Snow fell on the grass, clutching her belly where an ice spear had run her through.

Snow looked up, blood sputtering out of her mouth, and then she started melting—

The memory cut off with a jolt as Ella shook her shoulders.

Yuki was sure it was a memory. Maybe from before the cycle had started. Maybe from before they had been condemned to this fate.

"You okay?" Ella asked, and Yuki forced herself to look down, her hands still hovering over where she'd touched the box. Ella's hazel eyes were worried.

Yuki snatched back her hand and the pedestal retracted back into the floor, taking the black box with it. Around her were hundreds of hearts. Hundreds of memories trapped inside.

Hundreds of girls. The cycles had already gone through them all.

This is what happened to the bodies.

"There's nothing here for us," Yuki said bitterly.

She lifted herself from the ground. She didn't remember getting on her knees, but she must have. She brushed her skirt, feeling her fingers and magic freeze inside her, the darkness engulfing as she tried pushing back the memory of Snow running away from her. She didn't understand any of it.

"It's all right," Ella said gently. "We can still find something else."

A part of her found it almost tiresome, the way Ella would still believe in everything despite evidence to the contrary, the way she thought everything could be solved. That despite all that had happened, despite these deaths and their hand in them, Ella could still believe in *good*.

It was what Yuki always wanted. It was what Yuki could never have.

For the first time, though, she didn't feel guilty about not being good enough, for not being like Ella. Yuki closed her eyes, and all she felt was the flood of relief that she'd let all of that go. There was no place for kindness in these vaults, where the good were imprisoned. There was no place for belief when the wicked remained.

There was no place for forgiveness in the Grimrose curse.

"We should go," she said.

"We haven't looked around," Ella said quietly. "There may be something else down here—"

"Don't you understand?" Yuki snapped, her voice coming out cold and biting and ever so sharp. Her gaze was unflinching. "This isn't a secret place where we'll find our answers. It's a trophy room."

Ella staggered back from her.

When Yuki looked back at the girls, Ella wouldn't meet her eyes. There was a part of her that knew why she was pushing it with Ella. Maybe if Yuki made Ella leave, then there wouldn't come a time when Ella left her of her own volition. If Yuki forced it, then it'd be *her* choice. She watched with satisfaction as her friends looked at her and cowered.

Her true nature.

Everything you touch withers and dies.

Snow wasn't talking to Yuki, but she might as well have been.

CHAPTER FORTY-THREE

ELLA

Ella dreamed of the hearts all night.

She didn't have to look at the other caskets to know what they were. Somehow, deep in her soul, she knew that all the hearts belonged to girls who had come before them. Girls in the cycle of the curse, girls who had been in their place before. She wondered how many other Eleanors or Isabellas or Ellens or Elizabeths had lived through this, if they eventually found out what was destined for them.

Or if they died still dreaming of their freedom which never came.

She woke up sweating, and before she left for school, she took out the floorboard that hid her things. The money she'd kept for an emergency, all in smaller notes, money she'd gotten sewing things for others, cooking, and other services. Her mother's old button collection kept inside a giant glass jar, among other trinkets Ella had collected over the years—Ari's birthday notes, the tickets to the Eiffel Tower on the school trip two years ago—things she took out when she needed to remember that life was bearable. To remember that her life was more than the attic and the bruises that Sharon left in her body. One day, those too would fade.

When she got to school on Thursday, the only day all four of them shared class together, she found Nani and Yuki in a heated argument. Rory was staying out of it; she loved to pick fights with strangers but never with her own group.

"You can't deny it," Nani said, her voice hoarse. "You know what you saw. We know which story the hearts belong to."

Yuki wasn't looking at Nani. She was sitting still at her desk, her eyes turned to the pen she was holding. "Your accusation is baseless."

"There's no use pretending it's not your story," Nani said.

Yuki's hand clicked the pen, then clicked it again. Its surface was covered in ice. "I'm not denying anything."

"A box with a heart inside?" Nani asked, impatient.

Yuki's jaw tightened. "You want to accuse my stepmother of a curse that's taken hundreds of lives even before we came here."

"She's the one with access to the whole school," Nani said. "I know you don't want to think it, but it's time you stop thinking only of yourself."

"That is not what I'm doing."

"Aren't you? Isn't that what you've been doing ever since you killed Penelope, the only person who might have given us answers?"

Rory looked around, same as Ella, worried that they were being overheard, but none of the other students in class seemed to be paying mind to Nani's angry whispering.

"She wouldn't have told us anything," Yuki replied, finally turning to Nani, her dark eyes a turmoil. "Ella was in danger."

"If that's your excuse," Nani replied, her eyebrows rising above her glasses. "You know what I found in my father's things? The documents from when he was hired to work in the school. Everything was signed personally by *your* stepmother."

"You want to make accusations?" Yuki said, rolling her eyes. "Based on the way your story goes? What are you going to say next, that you're in love with Reyna?"

Rory looked sideways, shaking her head then narrowing her eyes as if genuinely taking this into consideration and finding that the possibility wasn't distasteful. "Well—"

"Be serious for once!" Nani said, elbowing her, hard.

Ella turned to Nani. "Is this true? About the papers?"

Nani took them out of her bag, shoving them in Ella's and Rory's direction. "See for yourself."

Ella took them, and she saw Reyna's signature stamped at the bottom. The same signature she'd seen when she'd gotten her own invitation to Grimrose, in an elegant red envelope, sealed with gold wax.

"Well, yes, poor you, Nani, who has to live in a castle and go to a decent school," Yuki snapped.

Nani flinched, her face growing darker.

Ella and Nani had both been invited to attend Grimrose

when neither of them had any money or connections. And yet, here they were. Ella used to think it was out of merit, but she knew better now.

"Our time is running out," Nani said, gritting her teeth. "Do you even realize that?"

"Maybe if we leave Grimrose—"

"Ella is not going to leave!" Nani said, her hand slapping against the desk. "Don't you realize that? Cinderella's story ends with her going off with the prince and getting away from her fucked up family forever. Ella leaves Sharon's house on her birthday at the end of the month. That's when her tale ends. *She doesn't have time.*"

Yuki's face paled a little and she blinked, stunned. Then she turned to Ella with accusation in her eyes. Betrayal too. Ella could read it, clear as day. She felt a lump in her throat as Yuki looked at her, an abyss stretching between them both.

"It doesn't matter," Ella said instead, trying to keep her tone even. She didn't meet Yuki's eyes. "We have to find a way out regardless. It's not about me."

She considered telling her friends about the cycle, the other girls coming before them, repeating the tales. But Ella understood how oppression worked—she understood what it was like snuffing someone's hope out, and if she told them that it was likely they themselves had gone through this already, that their own hearts had been stored down below in the vault, then what hope would be left of breaking it this time?

Rory and Nani were both staring at her, but Ella didn't want to look at them. She didn't want to see the pity in their eyes because she knew how stupid she sounded. She knew the judgment she got for wanting to believe.

Her belief had helped them discover the curse, and now her belief had to be enough to break it.

CHAPTER FORTY-FOUR

RORY

Two weeks before the end of the semester, Éveline showed up.

Rory was looking out the window of her classroom when she saw the cars approach. They came in a caravan, three black cars at once, and when first person stepped out, she recognized Éveline's blond head of hair.

Rory froze in her seat, her mouth dry. She hadn't answered the letter, she hadn't even acknowledged it. Of course it was no use ignoring it. They would come for her.

Rory's hand shot up in the air, and the teacher blinked, surprised at Rory's sudden interaction in class.

"Yes, Miss Derosiers?"

"Can I be excused?" Rory asked. "I need to go to the bathroom."

The teacher sighed and nodded.

Rory didn't go to the bathroom or to her room. Any of

those places would be easy to find her. Instead, Rory hid inside the armory at the fencing hall and sat there. She didn't know how much time passed; she hadn't brought her phone in case they tracked her, but finally, after what seemed like hours, there was someone else outside the door.

Rory peeped through the keyhole and saw who it was.

Without thinking further, Rory opened the door and caught Pippa by her waist, pulling her into the closet, shutting the door and locking it again. Pippa let out a yelp, turning around to face Rory in the darkness.

"What are you doing?" Pippa hissed. "The whole castle is looking for you."

Before Pippa could complain anymore, Rory kissed her. Their lips met with the same ferocity as always, and Rory's chest ached, feeling a burn in every place Pippa's skin touched hers.

Rory broke the kiss, and stood nose to nose with Pippa, She licked her lips, trying to concentrate, still lingering on the taste of Pippa's kiss. "I can't go out there. They're going to take me home."

"What?" Pippa asked, her voice softening to a murmur.

"My uncle got worse." Rory's voice was small, confessing the secrets. "If he dies...my father is next on the throne. And I become the heir."

Pippa blinked, her mouth slightly open, and then she let out a nervous laughter. "This is a new level of ridiculous for me."

Rory rolled her eyes. "Glad you're enjoying it."

"What are you going to do?"

"I don't know," Rory admitted. "I just...I can't go home. I can't."

"Maybe you should."

Rory looked up at Pippa.

"You can't run from it forever," Pippa whispered.

"You were the one who said to stop living halfway."

"Yeah, I did. But this is real life, Rory. As much as you want it to, this isn't going to change." Pippa turned her gaze away. "I mean, it was never meant to last, was it?"

She didn't need to gesture between them both for Rory to get her meaning. Rory's heart tightened again in her chest. "So you want me to go."

"I don't know what alternative you have," Pippa admitted. "You can't fight what you were born to be."

"So you never believed I could," Rory said. "If you don't want us to try, fine."

"Rory, that wasn't—" Pippa started to say, but Rory had already opened the armory door and run out.

Pippa didn't understand. It wasn't just that Rory couldn't fight them, but she couldn't leave Grimrose behind, not when they still had the curse. She had to stay by her friends.

Fine. Rory would handle it by herself, just as she always did, because she didn't need someone else pointing out her mistakes. Didn't need someone else helping her along, because Rory wasn't weak. She didn't need help.

She didn't need Pippa.

Rory dodged other students and teachers who were in her way and kept to the corners. She was so used to not calling any attention to herself in Grimrose that it was instinctive.

She found her way out of the castle through one of the side doors of the garden. She didn't know how long they would look for her, but she doubted Éveline would leave without her in tow.

Rory had to find the other girls—or they had to find her—and when she made a turn in the garden again, she almost slammed into two of her teachers.

Mrs. Blumstein and Ms. Lenz were outside, and Rory almost stumbled back into the briar bushes. The thorns rustled and prickled her uniform. Her heart was beating loud against her ears, blood pumping as her adrenaline levels climbed higher.

"Oh, there you are, Aurore," Mrs. Blumstein said calmly.

Rory stepped backward. "You can't make me go back there."

Neither of the teachers approached her, and Rory tensed, wondering if the two older women would grab her. But instead of shouting where she was, they stayed silent.

"Of course not," Mrs. Blumstein said calmly. "Why would we want that? You don't have to go anywhere you don't want to."

Rory's frown deepened.

"Éveline is going to take me back home," Rory said. "That's why she's looking for me. I can't go. I have to stay in Grimrose."

Mrs. Blumstein approached and gripped Rory's shoulder. The teacher was stronger than she looked. There was nothing frail about her, even when her hands were full of wrinkles. "We know, dear. You don't have to."

It was in that moment Rory realized she was trembling. Her fear was running through her body, her senses heightened. In the background, she could still hear shouts, but here, in this corner of the garden, she felt almost safe.

"I don't know what to do," Rory finally said, her words escaping her mouth before she could get a grip on herself. "They can't just make me go back. I can't abandon the others."

"There is always another way," Mrs. Blumstein said gently, but the hand did not leave Rory's shoulder. "If you want to escape, if you want all of this to be over. You don't have to do what anyone tells you. You can escape your own way, so they won't have you."

With a sudden jolt, Rory understood all of it.

The curse, the books, the girls. She hadn't known how all the pieces fit together, but now she could see the whole truth.

Slowly, she said, "What do you mean?"

"You don't have to do anything you don't want to," Ms. Lenz repeated. "Aurore, you know how your story is supposed to go."

That was all the confirmation Rory needed.

Mrs. Blumstein's grip was suddenly stronger, her nails clawing on Rory's shoulder. She needed to run, to tell her friends.

"You'll never get your hands on the book," Rory spat. "We'll break our curse."

"*Your* curse?" Mrs. Blumstein said quizzically. "It was never yours."

Rory struggled against the old woman's grip, but she

281

couldn't see a way out of it. Her fingers were like barbs on her arms.

"We're the ones who die," Rory said.

"Dying is easy. Anyone can do it," said Ms. Lenz. Her voice was calm and quiet, despite the absurdity of the situation. "You were never meant to live at all. It's payment until the path is set right."

Rory blinked in desperation, feeling her muscles cramp against Mrs. Blumstein's grip. She wouldn't be able to run back inside the castle. They would catch her, or Éveline would, and then it'd all be over. She had to run through the gardens. But it was too open, too wide.

She had to time it just right.

"Let me go." Rory struggled again, testing the grip on her shoulder.

"Ever so feisty," Mrs. Blumstein said. "I preferred your other versions. Naive. Much easier to deal with. You never questioned my authority."

She'd jump over the wall, find Ella in Constanz after she came home from school. She had to tell them who the real enemy was.

With a final twist, Rory turned around and slammed her knee against Mrs. Blumstein's crotch, breaking her arm loose. With a kick, she was free, and Ms. Lenz tried to grab her, but Rory was already running, her plan dizzy in her mind as she made her way.

"Aurore!" Someone shouted in the background, but Rory pushed past it. It didn't matter who it was.

The teachers, Éveline, they were all distractions.

All she could do was run. A sudden burst of strength and adrenaline raced through her body as she crossed the garden and went straight for the old owlery in the direction of the mountains. She'd cross the woods, climb the eastern wall, and head back into town. She climbed the steps running, two at a time, the path steep, the stair's stones slippery from the previous night's rain. She couldn't get caught now. Her friends depended on her.

They all depended on her.

Rory craned her neck to see if anyone was still pursuing, but there was no one on her trail. She moved past the steps and into the woods, the wind breaking in her face as she stretched her body to its maximum potential and ignored all the pain that was insisting on running through her body. She could do this alone; she would survive.

Rory turned and looked up, and her foot caught one of the roots on the old path, making her lose her balance. She tried to grab a low branch from the bushes around the path, but her hand only prickled their thorns, scratching her skin and drawing blood.

She rolled off the path, slamming against the stones, her ribs giving away from the impact, and suddenly she was slipping, tumbling, falling—

Rory hit her head on a rock, and she didn't wake up.

CHAPTER FORTY-FIVE

NANI

The commotion in the castle was a distraction for everyone.

Éveline had been shouting orders to Rory's security guards, trying to mobilize a search through the castle. Nani assumed Rory was fine and just buying time for an escape, or at least to negotiate a better deal. Rory couldn't go home yet, not when they were so close.

The thought turned bitter in Nani's mind. In truth, they weren't close to anything at all. That was just something she wanted to believe—that they'd progressed past a point, but it wasn't the truth. They were in the same place as the beginning, with two books in their hands, and no idea how to break the curse.

Nani believed there were people in this school who knew what was happening, and she was sure one of them was Reyna. If she wasn't to blame for all of it, then she at least had a guiding hand in the curse. And Nani was going to find out exactly what her place was in this story.

So when the commotion started, and half the castle was looking for Rory, Nani climbed the steps of Reyna's tower.

It was the tallest tower in the castle, the most distant and impractical, and by the time she'd climbed it, she was out of breath. She leaned against the door, wondering how she was going to get it open, only for the door to creak open by itself, unlocked. Nani set her shoulders she went in.

Nani expected something more dramatic. Maybe a dungeon, like the one below the castle, or at least something that would justify her suspicions. Instead, she was greeted by a normal, almost boring room and large, framed mirror on the opposite side of a wall, impossible to miss.

She didn't know how much time she had, and she wouldn't hear a thing this far up. She kept her phone in her pocket but left it on silent. Rory would extend the search for however long she had to, so Nani was going to use that time well. She started on the far side of the room, looking for hiding places in the floorboards, opening cabinets and drawers and rifling carefully through their contents. There was a part of her that wanted an obvious clue as to what happened to her father, when everything but her heart had already given up on the search.

Reyna had to know something. Reyna had to know she was inviting Nani by using her father. Her signature proved it.

Nani moved to the other side of the room, searching the shelves. There was the framed picture of a young Yuki with Reyna, and Yuki looked as serious ever, her black eyes staring straight ahead. There was nothing among the shelves, either, and the desk drawers weren't locked. Nothing in the room was locked or gave any indication of someone who wanted to hide something. There was nothing.

Nani sighed, frustrated. She looked at Yuki's small face in the photo, the only thing in Reyna's room that seemed to be personal. When she lifted the frame, there was a click as the shelf below it lifted, revealing a secret compartment brimming with files.

Nani shuffled quickly through them, her heart accelerating. She didn't recognize most of the names, until she saw—

Her father's name. A letter.

Addressed to Grimrose.

She heard a noise outside, and she shoved the letter in her pocket to read later and ran out of the room, closing the door behind her.

She wouldn't have the time to go down the stairs without encountering Reyna, so she adjusted her uniform skirt and tried not to look breathless as she leaned against the wall outside the door, looking as casual as possible.

"Nani," Reyna said as she came up the stairs, her heels echoing in her wake. "What are you doing up here?"

Even with all that was happening, there were no circles under her eyes. There were no marks of sleeplessness on her face—her heart-shaped face with perfect skin. Her hair hung past her shoulders in smooth dark chocolate waves, her makeup impeccable. The necklace glistened bright red on her cleavage, and now Nani felt like she had seen it somewhere else.

"I was waiting for Yuki," Nani lied. "I thought she was coming up to see you."

Reyna looked past her to the door. It was closed now, and Nani didn't inch closer to it.

"She didn't tell me," Reyna said. "I was busy with the search."

"Oh," Nani said, wishing she could say something smarter. "What search?"

Reyna frowned, and Nani thought that she had surely given herself away. Reyna opened the door, the light from her room flooding the corridor and hitting the necklace.

The crystal was deep red, and it looked almost alive and pulsing underneath its fine shell.

Nani knew where she had seen it.

The heart in the box, deep in the dungeons.

Reyna looked back at Nani, and Nani felt cold fear climbing up her spine. She wet her lips, heart pounding in her chest. She was almost afraid Reyna would hear it.

"You haven't heard, then?" Reyna said.

"I just heard shouting. I thought it was some game, or whatever."

Reyna's face fell for an instant, the mask gone. "No one told you?"

Nani shook her head, but she was too scared to move, too scared to even notice the tone Reyna was using was implying something much, much worse.

"They were looking for Rory," Reyna said. "She fell down the owlery stairs. I'm sorry. We don't know when she's going to wake up."

CHAPTER FORTY-SIX

ELLA

Ella didn't hear the news until the following day.

Rory was in a hospital bed in the private wing of the castle. Doctors had seen her, setting Rory's broken bones and bandaging her head. Rory lay with her eyes closed, chest rising and falling slowly. It was the first time Ella had seen her this peaceful in her life, and it felt wrong.

No one knew when she was going to wake up. The doctors decided it would be too risky to move her, and Rory's parents had finally come to be with her while she remained at Grimrose in full 24-hour care.

In the hospital bed, Rory looked like the princess she really was. She was wearing a light blue nightgown and her short copper hair had been washed and combed, all earrings and rings removed.

Ella had stopped in to see Rory on her way back home. All day in class she'd been worried, and now that she stood there, she didn't want to believe it. Rory's time had come before hers, and now she lay resting, asleep, and no one knew for how long. Or if she was ever going to wake up.

"How is she?" a voice asked behind her, and Ella turned around to see Yuki.

Ella felt the heavy weight of her eyelids and the sobs she was holding back. Her tears had been starting almost automatically now, the desperation growing in her chest.

"Stable," Ella managed. "That's what the nurse told me. They're not letting us stay long."

Yuki nodded, approaching the hospital bed gingerly. The curtains had been pulled back to show Rory asleep, her hands crossed over her chest. Yuki touched Rory's arm. "She's cold."

Ella nodded, and there was silence between them.

They had failed in everything they set out to do. Another friend lost.

"She's going to wake up," Ella said to herself. "This isn't over yet. If we can break the curse—"

"We won't," Yuki replied calmly, cutting Ella off. "I should have done something earlier. I should have—"

"Yuki, you didn't know. We've all got our hands tied."

"I don't," Yuki said angrily, and Ella could feel the rage that simmered behind the ivory skin. That familiar darkness Ella had been afraid of acknowledging, afraid that once she did, there would be no turning back.

Now it bubbled to the surface, plain for all to see.

There was a void in Yuki's eyes, the same as the night in the lake. Ella hadn't witnessed this intensity before, but now she was experiencing Yuki unfolding all her layers, shedding all the things that Ella was so used to seeing.

Except that what she was seeing hadn't always been the real Yuki. Yuki had told her that, but she'd just been too naïve, too stubborn to really look.

She had been too afraid.

"We haven't saved anybody," Yuki said, her voice sharp as ice. "Now Rory is gone."

And finally, as Yuki said it, Ella felt a weight lift from her shoulders, a truth she had been denying all along, because she wanted to save everyone, she'd wanted to make it all right.

But she couldn't. They'd started it all wrong, and Yuki had killed Penelope.

Yuki had plunged a knife straight into her heart and hadn't looked back, and as the darkness gathered, Ella saw the truth she couldn't deny anymore—that it had been a deliberate choice.

Yuki had been standing in the light all along and Ella had refused to see her.

"You're right," Ella whispered, and then Ella let go of her pretenses too. She put all her fears out in the open, facing Yuki. "I tried. I tried saving you, but I can't do it. I'm not the one who can do that. I close my eyes, and I see it, the blood I washed, the body I pushed, and I can't ignore it anymore. I've been trying because I thought ignoring it was the best way, but I can't."

Yuki blinked, and Ella could see that she was holding back tears. Yuki swallowed hard, pulling away, and Ella saw her face change again. One second emotion, and the next, she'd steeled herself in place.

"That's true," she replied. "You really can't. And maybe Liron was right all along."

Ella couldn't move, her heart in her throat. "What do you mean?"

"She didn't tell you," Yuki said. "But I stayed back, so I heard the real story. You want to know how she survived?"

Ella didn't say anything, but she knew Yuki wasn't going to stop before she was done, before the truth came spilling out, before all their truths had been shattered and there was nothing left between them.

"She killed her family," Yuki said. "That's how she survived. She killed them all before they let her die. She took her ending the only way she could. No attachments. No mercy."

Ella felt her throat catch again, her lower lips trembling. Liron had killed her eleven sisters. Her father. Everyone around her, so she could survive. The only way to get through.

Ella's throat constricted.

Yuki did not look directly at her. "Maybe if I'd been brave enough—I could have done it too."

Ella looked at where Rory was sleeping peacefully and unaware of how it was all coming undone. And then Ella looked up to see Yuki. Yuki, who was as beautiful and ethereal as ever. Yuki, who she had loved more than she had ever dared to love anything. Yuki, her best friend.

Yuki, the love of Ella's life.

"If you think that's how you survive." Ella's voice did not

dare rise above a whisper. "If you think that you can make it through, then I won't stop you."

Ella watched as the implications of what she'd said hit Yuki, and she stepped back. *Kill me,* Ella thought, and she didn't need to say it out loud for them both to understand. Ella was the weak link. Ella had been holding her back.

And maybe they didn't need salvation. Maybe they needed destruction.

Yuki's fist curled into ice, and the room around them suddenly grew cold.

"If you think this is the way you do it," Ella continued, trying not to choke on the words, "then you take your way out, Yuki. I will stand here, gladly."

Yuki had killed for her, and if Ella had to die to save at least one of her friends, she wouldn't hesitate. Maybe she couldn't save Yuki from making her own mistakes. Maybe she had been looking at the puzzle all wrong. Maybe there was no way for this love to survive in a way that didn't destroy them both.

But if she had to make a choice, and if it was all she could do, Ella would choose Yuki.

She'd always choose Yuki.

Yuki stepped back, hands still clenched tight into fists, eyes wide, and everything was wrong and upside down. Eventually, after what felt like an eternity, she walked through the door without looking back.

When she was gone, Ella finally let herself cry.

CHAPTER FORTY-SEVEN

RORY

CHAPTER FORTY-EIGHT

YUKI

Yuki stalked away from the infirmary in a blizzard.

Ella's willingness burned on her mind, the idea that all along Ella was trying to save her. All the while, Yuki was falling deeper into herself, letting all her darkness come to the light where there would be no more hiding because no one could save her from herself.

She had hidden for so long what she wanted, and Penelope had been the first to really see it. See Yuki's red vengeance for what it was, her desire to wreak havoc. If she wanted, she could tear the castle in half. If she tried, she could break the whole world apart.

It still wouldn't save them.

Ella was ready to die for her, Rory was gone, and Yuki didn't even know where Nani was. Maybe she'd escaped. Maybe she'd fled and left all of it behind. Maybe Nani could save herself, which was good because Yuki wouldn't save anyone. She had been created to destroy.

Everything you touch withers and dies.

Snow had known, spoken it out loud, cowered under Yuki's sight. Yuki was no fairy tale princess with kindness and bravery in her heart. Yuki was claws and thorns and ice; she was the hunger coming to take all of them to their graves.

Ella would die for her willingly, but Yuki wouldn't let her.

If Yuki was going to do one thing, she was going to make this right.

She had the magic, she had the mirrors. She had seen the memory, once, but she needed to know more. She needed to know all of it. She needed to know the truth behind the curse, the truth that had been hidden away. The curse was dark, so it was time they stopped trying to fight the darkness with light.

It was time for Yuki to free herself once and for all.

She didn't need her magic to make her choices. She had used a knife first, and she'd do it again. If the ending was to be claimed, she'd claim it. She'd destroy everything in her path.

She would make the curse *pay*.

Yuki climbed down the stairs almost in a run. The passages of the dungeon of Grimrose felt familiar and welcoming as she walked, the water freezing underneath her feet where she stepped. She didn't need any lights to make her way; she knew exactly where she was going. When she saw the door, she threw a ball of magic toward it, and it slammed open, cracking in half through her rage.

She saw the boxes on the shelves, feeling the quiet pulsing

of the lives that had been taken from the beginning. It didn't matter whose hearts they were now, from their past lives, from their past sentences.

It didn't change how things were. It didn't change that these girls would always suffer.

She slammed her hand against the ground, feeling her magic bursting through her whole body, shrouding her in cold. The floor opened again, and the black box rose from its hiding place, standing in the middle of the room.

She looked at the mirror on top of the box, but Yuki didn't see herself. She saw Snow as she'd died, blood spilling out of her mouth, black curls to the wind, skin melting. There was no jolt as she picked the mirror up, and she wondered if she was wrong, if her instinct had made her take a wrong turn. There was no mechanism to open the black box, but Yuki didn't let herself get deterred. She bit her thumb as hard as she could, focusing her magic, and then she smeared the blood on top of the box.

Something clicked, and the lid sprang open.

The black box was open, but no memories came to her. Inside it was another heart. It was unmistakable seeing it now—the same shape, the same size, the same glowing crystal enveloping it, as if to preserve what it was inside. She touched it, but there were no memories.

She couldn't be wrong about this. She had a feeling.

Yuki stared, remembering Liron's advice.

Swallow your heart.

Yuki took the heart in her hands, and then she took a bite.

The outer glowing part of it was like a shell, but beneath it, the meat was fresh. Yuki felt a gag in the back of her throat as a red liquid ran down the corner of her open mouth. She could feel the heart pulsing in her hand, but she closed her eyes, ignoring the wrongness, chewing the savory fibers, dissolving the muscle on her tongue, gulping it down.

After she swallowed the first bite down, it got easier. Yuki took bite after bite, the metal taste of the blood filling her mouth. She felt the magic spring up inside her, returning to its rightful place, responding to the darkness of her own well, of generations that had been living the tragedy. She ate her heart and swallowed it whole, and then she remembered everything.

PART III

TRUE LOVE'S KISS

CHAPTER FORTY-NINE

ELLA

Ella was still sitting in the same spot on the edge of Rory's bed, tears streaming, when Nani came in.

"What happened?" she asked, her voice breaking.

Ella looked up and shook her head. Nani ran to her and put her arm around her.

"Where's Yuki?" Nani asked this time, and Ella sniffed harder.

"I don't know," Ella said. "She came here, and we had a fight. I think she's going to do something stupid."

"Yuki? Something stupid?" Nani asked, her voice ironic, and then Ella snorted a laugh, the sound escaping her lips before she could stop it.

Ella wiped her tears from her eyes, taking a deep breath so her lungs would fill with air, trying to control it again. The beeping of Rory's monitors helped in a strange way—they were steady and constant, and she counted up to twelve beeps before she turned to Nani again.

"Liron was lying," Ella said quietly. "She escaped the curse because she killed her sisters first."

Nani blinked, her eyebrows drawn to the center of her forehead. "That explains a lot."

"How did we not see that?" Ella mumbled. "How did I think I could be the one to break it?"

Nani snatched Ella's hand. "Don't. It's not over yet."

"Rory's in a coma!" Ella shouted, and then she took another breath, trying to calm all her anger and frustration. For once, she didn't feel like backing down or that she was being unfair. It *wasn't* fair. It wasn't fair at all. "I thought I'd be the first one to go, but now Rory's here."

"And now we just have to break the curse for her," Nani said simply.

"What if we have this all wrong?" Ella asked. "What if there's no other way?"

Nani looked her in the eyes, and Ella was sure she was reading her like an open book. Nani was smart. Nani was smarter than all of them put together, and she only took a moment to measure and realize what was important.

"It's not your job to save her," Nani said, and Ella knew they weren't talking about Liron or Rory at all. "You did what you could."

"She's my best friend."

"Yeah," Nani agreed. "It's still not your job."

Ella sniffed again, feeling her jaw tighten, her heart

beating against her ribcage as if it wanted to grow wings and flutter away. Escape this claustrophobic feeling as the walls of Grimrose closed around them.

"Yuki's going to do what she can," Nani said. "It may not be the right thing. But she's—she's trying."

"And if she makes another mistake?"

The knife in Penelope's body. Yuki's hand, stained with blood. That all-consuming darkness, always at the edge, always at one hair's breadth of breaking the world in half.

Nani had no answer to that. Ella could still see Yuki storming out of the room, her black hair billowing down the stairs, her eyes cold and hard as ice. She looked prepared to do whatever it took, and Ella didn't know what that even meant for them.

Ella took Rory's hand, paler than hers, and squeezed it tight. Rory's breath didn't change.

For a moment, Nani looked like she was about to say something else, but then she shut it closed, her eyes at the infirmary door. Ella looked up and saw Frederick standing there. Nani exchanged a look with her, standing protectively in front of Ella.

Ella reached out for Nani's shoulder, giving it a light touch, letting her know it was okay. Nani stepped aside.

"I'm going back to my room," Nani said. "Text me if you need anything."

Nani headed to the door, not before exchanging a razor-sharp look with Frederick, putting her hands on her pockets and leaving without looking back.

Frederick approached Ella gingerly, standing on the opposite side of Rory's bed. He looked at the sleeping girl with sad eyes, then turned back to Ella.

"I'm sorry," he said.

"It's not your fault," Ella said automatically. She felt tired. She would face consequences when she got home, would see Sharon's wrath, but all of that was so far away. She couldn't get up from Rory's side, couldn't leave her friend there. "What are you doing here?"

"Checking on you," he answered, and Ella looked up. "I'm sorry if it was something I did. I didn't mean—"

"It isn't you," Ella replied, her voice cracking. "Of course it isn't you."

Freddie didn't approach her, standing on the other side of the bed, and Ella did not move, not letting go of Rory's hand, still trying to make Rory aware of something, anything, to let her know she was going to be there no matter what.

Ella stared up at Freddie's brown eyes, trying to find the words to explain the unexplainable. What made it worse was that there were so many other things that she wanted to tell him first: the curse, the cycle that kept it going, how there was nothing more she wanted than to find an explanation for what she suffered.

The reason didn't have to be supernatural, though.

Sometimes, these things were straightforward.

"It's Sharon," Ella said, simply.

Freddie's brows fell, his shoulders sagging. "Why didn't you tell me?"

"Because I didn't want you to worry."

"Ella, I worry either way," he said softly. "I've seen you jump over the walls of your house. I've seen you panic because you didn't get back home on time. I just didn't know how much I didn't know it was like that."

She saw him fidgeting in place, wanting to approach, wanting to reach out to her, but Ella couldn't move away from Rory's bed.

"It can't go on like this," Freddie said. "There must be—"

"There's nothing I can do," Ella cut him off. "Until I'm eighteen, Sharon controls whatever money my father left for me. Whatever I have, until my birthday, it's hers. I can't do anything."

"You can't live like this," he repeated, a sentence that didn't make sense to Ella because that's exactly how she'd lived. Learning how to survive, learning how to stay quiet and do the work, maneuvering carefully around the edges of Sharon's tempers.

She'd learned how to live, learned how to find the good things amongst the bleak.

"I know my way around," Ella said simply.

"What if she does something worse?"

"She won't," Ella said. She'd already argued this back and forth with herself for years. "She's not jeopardizing her part of the inheritance."

Freddie looked at her for a long moment. "There must be something else. I can—I can take you away. Say the word, and we'll leave. I'll take you wherever you want."

The offer hung in the air for a moment. Running away. Running away with Freddie. Being cared for, by him. Depending on someone else to mend her broken wounds because she couldn't stand on her own.

"And then what?" Ella asked, knowing where it would end.

"I don't know," Freddie said. "We could figure something out. Because even when your birthday comes, the process is not going to come pain-free."

"Do you really think I don't know that?" Ella snapped, letting her anger get the best of her. She'd been there for her bruises. She'd been there for her pain.

She was present during all of it.

"Of course not," Freddie replied. "I just think that you haven't considered how much it's costing you."

Ella felt the words sting her, felt it breaching the one place she'd locked away. She didn't want it to hurt as much as it did. She had always endured it. What right did she have to not endure it? There were people worse off than her. There were people who never had a choice at all.

She blinked away tears, and Freddie was on her side of the bed in a rush, wrapping his arms around her waist, his support silent. She leaned in against him, closing her eyes, breathing his scent.

"It's not your fault," Freddie said quietly, squeezing her tight.

Freddie kissed the top of her head. Ella wanted to live in a world where running away with him was a choice she could make. A choice she knew *how* to make. To leave the world behind, to be selfish for once, and to take what she deserved.

But that wasn't her true ending either. She couldn't leave anyone behind.

She'd make it right because that's what she always did. Because she took care of her friends, no matter what happened, and she would take care of them now. Not because she was good and kind or anything else that had been attributed to her all her life—because it had always been the other way around. She didn't love her friends because she was good. Loving her friends *made* her good. They were all that was worth fighting for.

They were all that was worth staying for.

None of them would want her faith to falter. She couldn't afford it to. She had to believe, even when none of the others did. Even if she was the last girl standing.

She squeezed Rory's hand again, and this time, she could almost swear that she'd felt the slightest squeeze back.

CHAPTER FIFTY

YUKI

Yuki had been so naïve.

She could almost laugh at her own stupidity, the sound escaping her throat before she meant to let it out. It was guttural, broken, the sound of her own soul cleaving in two. She knew who was to blame. She climbed the stairs, her feet certain, the magic rippling around her.

When she passed a mirror in the stairwell, it took Yuki a moment realize she wasn't seeing any other version of herself. Her hair was falling like a dark curtain, her mouth dripping with blood. Her pale face had black circles under her eyes, and she looked haunting but still beautiful.

Yuki climbed the stairs faster, and she barged into her stepmother's room.

Reyna jumped as Yuki came in. Reyna took in the sight of her, her brown eyes widening. She almost looked scared, and all Yuki could think of was: *good*.

"How long did you think you could keep this up?" Yuki asked, her voice even. She felt a surprising twist in her gut, but then—she had become more of herself after eating the heart.

She had seen the truth.

"What are you doing?" Reyna asked, blinking, regaining her composure. "Yuki, what did you—"

"Did you really think I wouldn't find out?" Yuki asked, and Reyna's hand flew to the ruby necklace at her throat, the red echoing what now pulsed inside Yuki's stomach.

"Yuki, I don't know what you're talking about."

"DON'T LIE TO ME!" Yuki roared, the icicles surging in her hands, making even sharper points. "I'VE SEEN THE MEMORIES!"

She had seen all of them. All the past versions of herself. The magic harbored them inside her now. In every version of her past, in every scene of her own death, there was the same person, over and over again.

Yuki always thought it was strange that Reyna hadn't aged a day since they met. She thought she might have been imagining it. Except Reyna hadn't aged a single day for the last three hundred years.

Reyna reached for her, and Yuki threw up a barrier of ice between them. It looked fragile and beautiful, but it wasn't a shield. It shattered as soon as Reyna touched it. Yuki felt the tears prickling her eyes, and then her rage grew again; she was not letting anything get in her way.

She was going to kill Reyna and end the curse.

Dozens of girls. Dozens of memories. Every lifetime, every *life*.

Yuki curled the magic around her like a fist, and every particle of air around her turned into a sharp dagger, reflecting her face around the room. She threw them in Reyna's direction and Reyna screamed, running for cover behind her desk. Yuki twisted again, flicking more daggers with her fingers as if the points of ice were a part of her.

The daggers shattered against Reyna's mirror, and the thing broke into a million pieces. Yuki ran after Reyna as she ducked, sending a wave of ice to slam her down. Reyna's scream filled the room again, but Yuki could barely hear her. She had the way out now, and she would do it.

"Yuki, please, listen—"

Yuki threw a gust of snow and wind in her stepmother's direction. Reyna was slammed against the wall, and her necklace dropped to the floor. Yuki swept it up, feeling its pulse echo her own. Before Reyna could react, Yuki closed her fists, letting the magic flow. A layer of ice covered her hands and stretched out to the wall, imprisoning Reyna. She looked up at Yuki, her eyes wide and afraid, and Yuki's heart echoed *good, good, good*.

"Nowhere to run now," Yuki said, her voice even.

Yuki picked up a shard of the mirror in her hands. She grasped it tight, but even then, her skin didn't break. Maybe the magic had always been a part of her, the magic that didn't let her break or blister. It only burned her from the inside out. She gripped the mirror shard tight and raised the cutting edge like a dagger toward Reyna's heart, and then she struck.

A kind of repelling barrier sent Yuki flying back from the wall. She fell to the floor, tasting the metallic tang of blood in her mouth. She could still feel the heart and its fibers inside her mouth, the meat threatening to rise back up.

"What is that?" Yuki growled, getting up, her hands curled into fists as she felt the magic growing around her.

She felt for the invisible barrier and pushed against it again, this time her hand grazing it gently until she'd almost touched Reyna's face.

Except she couldn't. There was a wall keeping them apart. Just like with Rory and her ring.

Yuki hammered her magic against the barrier, screaming again and again, hurling the ice and snow until her arms grew tired, groaning in frustration. She fell back onto the floor with the ice and broken mirrors, looking at her stepmother, who was silent and still fixed to the same place. But now, instead of confusion or hurt, there was only sadness in Reyna's eyes.

"This is part of the curse too," Yuki said, finally, her breath labored, and she sat down with crossed legs on the floor. Her anger had subdued but her rage simmered beneath the surface. "Isn't it?"

Reyna's shoulders fell. "So you know."

"I found your vault," Yuki said. "All those hearts. I found mine."

Reyna blinked in surprise, but she didn't move. The ice around Reyna was melting now, but Yuki realized she wasn't trying to do magic. She wasn't trying to escape. She was quiet, her face searching Yuki's. "How much do you know?"

"I saw you cast the curse," Yuki said. "You're the one who killed all of us. All these years, it's all your fault."

Reyna closed her eyes, sighing, and she propped herself against the wall. "Yes. It's my fault. But it wasn't me."

"I saw you," Yuki accused. "I saw you kill Snow with your magic, I saw you cast the curse."

"There's more than one curse at work," Reyna said, looking at Yuki. "They wanted me to pay for what I did, so I made them pay in return. Now we're stuck in this cycle."

"Them?" Yuki asked. "Who are you talking about?"

Reyna opened her mouth, but no sound came out. Yuki felt the magic change around the room, as if the air itself was snuffing out Reyna's voice. Yuki had never felt any magic at work beside in the books and her own body, but here it was again.

"I can't." Reyna's voice was small, defeated. She slumped on the floor, and Yuki didn't want to pity her, but her rage was waning.

Yuki was tired. She wanted to go to sleep and not wake up for a long time. She wanted to stop fighting everyone. She didn't know who she was fighting against anymore.

"I sacrificed my magic," Reyna said. "As payback."

"Payback for what?"

"For what else?" Reyna said. "For the curse, of course. The curse isn't yours."

"But we die!"

"Yes," she said, "but it's never you who gets hurt the most. When you die, I'm the one who's alone. I'm the one who has to watch you die again and again and again."

Yuki stared at Reyna. The one person she'd always had, the one who had always watched over her, the one person who was so much like her that it hurt. There was a reason Reyna was in all of the memories.

Reyna was always with her.

"I'm the cursed girl, Yuki," Reyna said. "Not you. Never you."

Yuki felt her heart slowing and her shoulders relaxing, as if she felt this truth was coming for a long time. She was so close to the answers now.

"I broke the rules," Reyna told her, looking straight at her. "Magic is an old thing. You don't understand what you're dealing with." She looked at the ice surrounding Yuki, and then shook her head, a small smile escaping. "Or maybe you're the only one who does. In all my years, I've never seen anything like this before."

In all her years. Because the curse was old, maybe two-hundred, three-hundred years of age, and Reyna was still standing, feeling its effects.

"Why were you cursed?" Yuki asked, protecting her heart, not wanting to give in to a moment of weakness.

"Because I wanted someone to love me," Reyna said. "Because I wanted someone I could love. Because I read the old stories, the old fairy tales, and I messed with something I shouldn't have."

"Stop with the nonsense!" Yuki shouted, and the room exploded into snowflakes again. "I've had enough! I want to know the truth!"

Reyna looked at her, tears in her eyes. "I—I can't." She opened her mouth again and choked, the same snuffed sound taking away her voice. "I played with forbidden magic. I created something. And so now I pay the price. Now I watch you die," Reyna said. "That's all I ever do, Yuki. I live, and you die, and it stays in the same cycle, until I learn my lesson. Until I learn that you were never supposed to be born in the first place."

"What about the others?" Yuki asked, her mind stumbling over Reyna's words. "What about the other girls?"

"They are only a consequence," Reyna answered. "I meddled with the stories, with the book of fairy tales." She looked like she wanted to say more, but again, her voice was held back. "The curse is too powerful. I couldn't destroy it."

That's why Reyna hadn't broken it. She couldn't, not by herself.

The girls were but a passing consequence. They were in the book, but Reyna had not brought them out. They were merely following the patterns, the girls reborn into the same cycles.

Yuki got up, trying to sort out the anger and the darkness that seemed to come back full force and gnaw at her heart, feeding her rage, but she didn't want to let go. She wanted to find a way out.

"If I kill you, the curse ends."

Reyna didn't answer. That was also the truth.

Yuki picked up the shard of the mirror again, tightening her hand, ready to swallow her heart, bury it deep again where no one would find it. She walked up to Reyna, every step determined, every breath steeling her body.

She stopped, hand raised in midair.

Reyna looked up at her, and Yuki saw the same thing she'd seen in Ella's eyes. The same acceptance.

The same willingness to die.

Yuki's knees shook, and she crumpled on the floor on her knees, and finally, after all this time, Yuki started to cry.

"I can't," she whispered. "I can't do it."

Reyna inched her hand as close to Yuki as she could. It was only a centimeter away, but Yuki still couldn't touch her. Still couldn't breach the barrier.

"It's all right," Reyna said. "There's nothing wrong with you."

Yuki looked up sharply, a sob shaking its way through. "Of course there is! Look at me! I—I tried to kill you! I *killed* Penelope!"

She said the words out loud, expecting her stepmother to turn away, to do what everyone should always do. Turn away from the monstrous, horrible thing that she was, even when this was all she could be.

"Your trauma and your darkness are a part of you," Reyna said softly, "but they're not all of you. You're so much more, Yuki. You're capable of so much more than destruction."

Yuki's sobs rattled her, the tears streaming down her face and falling, steaming and melting the ice on the floor. She felt the lump in her throat as she tried to speak.

"And what if there's nothing more?" Yuki asked. "What if this is all there is?"

Reyna smiled at her, kind and generous, and it made Yuki

315

feel warm and safe and terrified because no one looked at her brokenness and smiled. No one looked at the lonely and loved them for it.

"There's always a place for you here," Reyna said. "Whatever you want to become." Reyna's hand hovered next to her. "I can't break the curse because I'm too selfish. I refuse to learn my lesson. Not if it means losing you."

Yuki smiled through another sob, and finally Reyna looked up at the open door, at the mess around them, and there was fear again in her eyes. Fear of something that wasn't Yuki.

"You have to go," Reyna said, looking at the door as if she half expected someone to show up. "You know too much already. I told you all I could. It wouldn't be a surprise if..."

Reyna shook her head, stopping herself.

"You still haven't told me who cursed you, and why," Yuki said.

Reyna opened her mouth and tried to speak but only choked. Her hands flew to her throat, but the necklace was already gone. "I can't. I can't tell you more. I'm already putting you in risk."

"I can't. My friends are in danger—"

"And so are you, if you stay," she said. "I can't tell you who you are. But you *must*, you *must* learn. You must remember the rest." Reyna reached out as if to touch her, but drew back her hand again, her eyes misty from the tears. "I'm so lucky to have seen you grow up again. But you have to go. Please."

Yuki got up, her knees shaking. Reyna quickly packed a bag for her with clothes and money, and Yuki watched numbly. Reyna put the bag on the floor and Yuki took it, her hands still shaking.

She didn't want to leave. Everyone was still here. Everyone had been drawn here, toward the curse, toward their fate.

"It was you, wasn't it?" Yuki asked, realizing finally. "You brought all of us here."

Reyna tightened her lips, nodding. "I know the curse can't be stopped. But I wanted you to have a good life, while it lasted. It's all I could offer. To give you something good, before it's over."

Yuki had seen and known enough—she was nothing but a pawn in a bigger game of witches and curses and magic. It was like the stories, good versus evil, except that Yuki wasn't sure which was which or if both weren't tainted with the other.

But Yuki was a girl from the stories. Yuki had been born from that; it was written across the thin lines of her veins, in the tips of her eyelashes, in the way her fingers curled with power and hungered for more than she had.

As Yuki ran from Grimrose, she vowed to find a way to break her mother's curse.

CHAPTER FIFTY-ONE

NANI

Nani dropped down on her bed, looking up at the ceiling of the empty room.

No Rory. No Yuki.

Yuki's things were as she'd left them that afternoon, but there was no sign of her. Rory's side was the same mess as always, everything in a disarray, and it almost felt like she was going to come back at any instant to throw herself on the pile of blankets and clothes.

Except she wasn't. Rory was asleep in the hospital wing, and no matter what anyone else said, she doubted very much that the girl was going to wake up. Not unless they broke the curse, not unless they did something.

Nani didn't know what there was to do anymore. She almost wished she could go back to the beginning when she didn't believe in this stupid curse, when she hadn't come to this castle to look for her father at all.

She picked up the letter she'd taken from Reyna's room last night. Her father's name and Grimrose's address. She felt relieved there was actual proof that he'd worked there, that he'd spent the past year somewhere that had existed and that he hadn't just vanished beneath the surface of the earth. By now, Nani had grown used to the idea of his absence, the idea of a father who came back every once in a while and inhabited only her dreams. She had stood for hours looking at the letter, not brave enough to open the envelope. After the news of Rory, she knew that whatever the letter contained, it would change everything.

She turned it over in her hands, ready to open it, but not before she heard a knock.

Nani jumped out of bed, running to unlock it. It was Svenja, her face looking gaunter than usual, brown eyes blinking at Nani.

"Hey," she said.

Nani flew into her embrace, hugging her tight and not letting go. Svenja seemed shocked for a minute, but she melted into Nani's hold, her arms wrapping around her round waist, their heads leaning against each other's shoulders. The fight was already forgotten and unimportant considering the circumstances they were in now.

"Guess that answers my question on whether you're okay," Svenja murmured.

Nani didn't want to admit that she wasn't fine; she was supposed to be fine. She wasn't the one who had succumbed. Instead, she felt numb, her body distant, as the rest of Grimrose unraveled around them.

She'd felt the same after her mother's death. Nani had always liked to read, but after her mother died, reading became all she had. She devoured one book after the other, retreating into her shell, not uttering a single word. Not being able to recognize herself in mirrors anymore because there was a clear line of who she used to be: a girl with a mother, and now, a girl without one. She felt the sadness and numbness take over her body, until she was so far away from it all that she might as well live in another realm.

She held on tight to Svenja, trying to ground herself. She didn't need another of those episodes. She couldn't afford to fade away.

Svenja broke the embrace to close the door to the room, looking around to see that they were truly by themselves. She'd never come inside, and suddenly, Nani was self-conscious about the place where she slept, at her disorganized pile of books, and she wanted to rearrange everything she owned, even though it wasn't much.

"How is Rory?" she asked.

"Asleep," Nani answered. "They don't know how long she's going to stay like that. She had a pretty bad concussion."

Svenja nodded and didn't say anything else. Nani sat down on her bed while Svenja looked at the spines of her books, tilting her head slightly to read the titles. Her presence was both comforting and keeping Nani on edge. Nani wanted to talk about what had happened before, when she stepped away from Svenja, thinking she had a good reason to. Thinking it was best.

Svenja spotted the letter on Nani's bed, picking it up and sitting by her side.

"Isaiah Eszes," she read out loud.

"My dad." Nani's reply was small.

Svenja lifted an eyebrow, waiting for the explanation, and Nani looked at her girlfriend without knowing where to start. All the lies, all the things she'd kept, all the things that isolated her even more.

"He used to work here," Nani said. "I came here thinking I'd find him. But he was already gone, just like he always was."

Svenja's face was undecipherable. "Why didn't you tell me?"

"Because I thought that as soon as I found out what happened, I'd leave," Nani replied. "As soon as I knew where to find my father, I'd leave Grimrose behind, and not look back."

The silence filled the room between them both, and Svenja handed her the letter.

"Open it," Svenja said.

Nani looked at her surprised, but Nani felt suddenly glad for her company. Her fingers were shaking slightly as she tore open the envelope. She realized that it wasn't a letter from the school. Instead, it was a diagnosis from a laboratory in Switzerland.

She read the exam papers, trying to decipher them. Svenja had gripped her left hand, and they both sat side by side, hands intertwined, as Nani read the words again and again.

"What is it?" Svenja whispered.

Nani put the letter down and adjusted her glasses as a strange dread crept over her. She read the last bit of diagnosis again, looking at the evidence that had been staring her right in the face all along, the answers she wished she hadn't been so busy to realize.

Her father had left, but not on purpose. He'd arranged for her to come to Grimrose because he'd promised her an adventure, and he had given it to her. He'd kept his last promise.

Nani shoved the paper in Svenja's direction. "It's a diagnosis. He has terminal lung cancer."

CHAPTER FIFTY-TWO

ELLA

Y uki was gone.

There had been no sign of her in the bedroom, no answer to their messages, no note left behind. She'd disappeared into thin air. Ella and Nani had shared their worries with one another. Ella thought about asking Reyna, but Nani cut her off immediately. Reyna was the primary suspect in Yuki's story.

They couldn't trust anyone.

The library felt empty without the other girls there.

Ella stood in their meeting place with no one to greet her but Mephistopheles. He was sitting in Yuki's usual spot at the window under a streak of sunlight. He turned his belly up when he saw Ella, meowing. Ella tickled him.

"You miss her too, huh?" she said, even though Yuki had been gone no more than a week.

She'd vanished with nothing else than the last words that

they'd spoken to each other. Ella saying that she'd do anything for Yuki to get her happy ending even if she had to give up on herself.

She turned around when Nani entered the library, rushing up the stairs, checking to see that no one was following.

"Any news?" Nani asked, her tone hopeful.

Ella shook her head. Rory was the same, and Yuki hadn't sent even a message. Nani's face fell, and she adjusted her glasses, stepping back when she saw the cat on the table. Ella was comforted by the fact that some things never did change.

"What about you?" Ella asked. "Any news of your father?"

Nani shook her head. She'd told Ella about the lab results, but Nani had no idea where to look for her father now.

"I do have something else, though," Nani said, taking her phone out of her pocket. "I'd messaged a rare book dealer in Munich who has a book in his collection that sounds a lot like ours. It seems that your guess was right about them being one thing."

Ella's eyes widened, taking Nani's phone to read the email.

"It's only one volume," Nani said. "And almost all of the fairy tales match. I gave him a list of what we had."

Ella blinked, catching Nani's tone. "What do you mean, almost?"

"There's a single tale missing from his book," Nani said.

"'Snow White'," Ella took a guess, something in her stomach turning.

Nani nodded. "I don't know why it's missing. He sent me pictures of his volume, and it just confirms what we know.

The tales themselves match, the order, everything. And in most of the endings, although they're not exactly the traditional happy ones, the girls still survive. It's like our books were split into two extremes."

Ella thought there was still something missing. Snow White's tale wasn't in the other book. It had to mean something.

"And you're sure the book matches our own? How old is it?"

"Late seventeen hundreds," Nani said, and Ella could only open her mouth and stare. "I'm pretty sure that if we start tracing the curse as far back as that, we'll still see the patterns."

"But why Grimrose?" Ella asked. "Why here?"

Nani shrugged. "Maybe Grimrose is just another side effect of the curse. As much as we are."

Ella stroked Mephistopheles' back. She thought of Yuki disappearing down the stairs. Ella knew Yuki was safe, wherever she was. Yuki was indestructible. In all their years together, Yuki had remained untouched, unhurt.

Two books, one piece still missing.

"Look, I know Yuki didn't want to think it," Nani said carefully, interrupting Ella's inner thoughts, "but we've got to consider the options we have here. The obvious option."

Ella's eyes met Nani's, and they both knew they were talking about the same person.

"She's the headmistress," Nani said. "She knows everything about the castle. She had my father's letter hidden all this time. Besides, we know Yuki's different from us. There is a reason for that. Maybe she knows."

"But this curse has been going on for hundreds of years," Ella said. "Maybe more. Reyna is young."

"Maybe she's a vampire."

"Now you've gone too far."

Nani snickered, but Ella knew she wouldn't simply drop the subject. Ella clutched the cat harder against her chest, and he didn't protest.

"All we've been doing is making up answers to fit the theories we have," Ella said quietly, "but none of them are real answers. We still don't know how to break the curse. And the hearts, I..."

Nani frowned, and then she snapped her fingers. "It's the necklace," Nani said. "It has to be."

Ella looked at Nani doubtfully, but Nani was already pacing the library carpet, to Mephistopheles' unhappiness. "What are you talking about?"

"Reyna's necklace. I saw her wearing it the day Rory fell. It reminded me of the hearts we saw down in the vaults. I didn't—I didn't want to get close to her, but I don't think we have another option, Ella. What if it's the last object we're missing? What if we put the necklace together with the book, and we can break the curse?"

Ella could almost hear Yuki's voice: *That's a lot of ifs.*

It's what she would say. She would want explanations that made sense. But Yuki wasn't there, and they had nothing else to guide them. They'd lost their bets, lost their time, and now they groped blindly for a way out of the dark tunnel. They wished for any answers they could find, hoping it would lead them to the end.

Hoping it would lead them into the light.

"So what do we do?" Ella asked.

Nani's face hardened. "We have to steal it."

CHAPTER FIFTY-THREE

RORY

CHAPTER FIFTY-FOUR

NANI

On the Monday before graduation, Grimrose had been transformed once again. As if the rest of the students ignored all that had happened during the school year—or else made a conscious effort to forget—the preparations for the final ball had redoubled. A queue of helpers carried flowers and lace and tablecloths up and down the corridors. Three boys from the year below carried an enormous tree with golden apples down the hall as Alethea barked her orders.

"Set it straighter!" she said. "To the left! A little to the right! No, it's off by one centimeter, *everybody* will notice it!"

By her tone, Nani wouldn't have dare dispute this declaration.

"What's the theme?" Nani asked.

Alethea turned to her, hands on her hips, a big smile full of flashy white teeth. "Fairy tales, of course!"

Nani felt the nausea rising to her throat, and she stumbled

away from the corridor, going straight to her classes. It was strange to see the empty seats where she expected to see Yuki or Rory, and only Ella was at their table at lunch. Her vegetarian poke bowl wasn't the same without Rory there to complain about it.

"Do you know what to do?" Nani asked Ella at lunch. It would look too suspicious for Nani to go to Reyna's tower again. It'd have to be Ella.

"Yes," Ella said simply, looking like the light had gone out of her, her hair limp and her cheeks pale.

"It's just this one thing we need," Nani said, trying to sound confident. "Once we have it, we'll have the answers."

Nani wished she could believe her own words, because even once they had it, something could go wrong. She was sure the necklace was the key. She was in a panic, but she couldn't have mistaken its glow for anything else. And Reyna had to have the answers. Reyna had to be the villain in the whole story.

"Did you tell your grandmother what you found out about your father?" Ella asked.

"No," Nani said. "I don't have any more information besides the diagnosis. And even then..."

She didn't know what to think. The only clue she had was that her father was very, very sick.

They spent the rest of lunch in silence, trying to pretend that life was normal. Once classes were over for the day, Ella went to check on Rory at the infirmary as she always did, and Nani went back to her room, trying to avoid hurried students from the council who were filling the halls with decorations.

At the entrance hall stood an enormous rose arch that had been set against the main door, blossoms the color of blood. The thorns and bushes had been sprinkled with silver paint, but the flowers were vivid and enchanting all on their own.

Nani spotted Svenja when she turned around. Svenja smiled when she saw Nani, but there was something odd about the way she did it; it looked forced. As Svenja approached, Nani tried not to let her thoughts get carried away. Svenja was carrying papers, and she hurried to Nani's side as more students passed by with decorations.

"It's really going to be something, isn't it," Svenja said, looking at the roses.

Nani nodded, numbly, still thinking that it was a cruel joke fate was playing on all these girls, when more than half of them had their destinies tied to a book that only offered tragedy.

Unless they could stop it. Unless they broke the cycle.

Svenja kissed her cheek, handing Nani the envelope she was carrying.

"What's this?" Nani asked.

"A gift," Svenja said simply.

Nani noticed the way Svenja had tensed, the way her smile didn't quite reach her eyes. She hesitated then ripped the envelope open with her thumb.

On the page inside was an address for a hospital in Zurich and her father's name. They weren't complete medical records, far from it, but there he was again. With an address.

In a hospital. Nani's eyes widened, looking up suddenly at Svenja, her whole body still.

"Where did you get this?"

"My mom works for a health insurance company. They keep track of patients in hospitals," she said. "I just had to give her your father's name. He's there, Nani. Your father is there."

Svenja's voice changed a little at the end of the sentence, strangled and high-pitched. Nani didn't know what to say.

Suddenly, she understood Svenja's fear.

She was giving Nani her key to the castle. She was giving Nani a way out.

And Nani couldn't just not take it. It wouldn't be fair. She had come all this way to find her father. She closed the envelope again, her fingers trembling as she held the papers close to her chest.

"I'll be back," Nani said.

Svenja didn't answer, her lips pressed together. Helpless. She knew that in Svenja's mind, this might be the last time they saw one other. Nani couldn't help but think how wrong this all was. She shouldn't leave, but it was the only thing she could do. Even Svenja understood that.

Nani turned to the gigantic rose arch that covered the entrance. She picked out a single red rose, snatching it from the bush, prickling her finger on one of the thorns. It was real, alive.

She handed it to Svenja.

"I'll be back before that dries," Nani promised. "I always keep my promises."

Svenja looked at the rose in her hands, and Nani could almost imagine the petals starting to wilt and fall away. But she wouldn't take long—she had to be back soon. If Ella managed to take Reyna's necklace, then she might break the curse, and they'd all be free. She had to believe that.

CHAPTER FIFTY-FIVE

ELLA

Ella had gotten Nani's message when the bell rang to announce classes were over.

Svenja found my father, it read.

It was all Ella needed to know. She didn't need to ask questions or beg Nani to stay. It would be too cruel, too selfish of her to even ask. Nani had come to the castle wanting one thing, and now that she'd found it, Ella wasn't going to hold her back. Ella would give anything to see her father again, to spend more moments with him than what she had.

Ella had messaged back. Go. Be safe.

And that was all.

Ella needed to finish the plan for all of them. She needed to do what she'd discussed with Nani but still didn't have enough courage. After class, she'd gone to the only place where she thought she could find some.

Rory was still in bed. Pippa was there by her side, her arms crossed over her uniform, her hair loose. Pippa's curls fell long, almost to her waist, a mass of dark coils. She looked up when she saw Ella come in and made a move to step away from the bed.

"You don't have to leave," Ella said. "I just came to check on her."

Pippa nodded, quiet. Ella approached, thinking the same thing she always thought when she saw the bed: Rory was going to wake up. She was just asleep, it was part of the tale, not the final way of the curse. She was still alive.

As much as Ella dreaded it, when she looked at Rory, all she could see was death.

"She told me the truth," Pippa said quietly, looking up at Ella, interrupting her thoughts. "And I didn't—I didn't think she meant it for real. I thought I was only going to be a diversion, and I wouldn't be able to change anything in her life."

"She's going to wake up," Ella said. "And then you two can fight about it as much as you want."

Pippa snorted, brushing the backs of her hands against her eyes, her mouth thinly pressed. Ella recognized the universal gestures of holding back tears.

"I should have known better," Pippa said. "She wasn't scared of anything."

Ella looked at her. "Of course she was," said Ella, sincerity and kindness in her voice. "Everyone is."

"She never showed it," Pippa said. "It was just—she insisted that she could do everything alone."

Ella snorted, real laughter escaping her lips. "No one can do everything alone."

Pippa eyed her like she was seeing an entirely new side of Ella. Maybe that was all people saw when they looked—useless, patched up Ella.

"You never have to do anything alone," Ella said. "If you have friends...well, you're never alone."

It's what friendship meant. That they would do things together, and no matter how hard it became, they would still be there. It was not about proving a point that you could do it on your own—that was just stupid. Besides, it wasn't about accepting help. Friends didn't help you because you needed it or out of charity or pity. They helped because they loved you. They helped because that's what friends did.

So no one would take the journey alone. Friends cared, and they *chose* to care.

"You never told her that," Pippa said.

"Some lessons you have to learn on your own," Ella said, smiling. "Besides, if Rory had listened to me, she would have kissed you a long time ago."

Pippa turned her eyes down, hiding embarrassment. Ella looked at Rory again, fast asleep. Rory wouldn't have hesitated the way Ella was now. Rory would have done what she needed.

And for Rory, for Yuki, for Nani, Ella would do what she had to.

Three days before the ball, Ella went up to Reyna's tower.

She'd taken the two books with her, hoping that there

was a connection to the necklace, so the three pieces could magically break the spell when brought together. Ella wished the curse was as straightforward as curses were in the tales— broken by something as simple as true love's kiss, or the slaying of a witch, or the willingness of a sacrifice.

Of course, real life could never be that simple, no matter how much she wished.

It was no use waiting for Reyna to leave—Ella had never seen her without the necklace, if she remembered it right, in all the years she'd seen Reyna either addressing the school or talking to Yuki. Ella saw that the door was open, but she knocked anyway.

Reyna looked up from her phone and frowned at Ella.

"Ella. I wasn't expecting to see you here. You know this isn't my office."

It was more statement than question, her eyebrow raised. Ella hesitated in the doorway, and she noticed all the things that were off—there was no sign of Reyna's mirror anymore.

And Reyna wasn't wearing the necklace.

That stopped Ella in her tracks. Her eyes searched the room as she tried to calm down her breathing, trying to find something to focus on, a series of numbers that could save her anxiety from spiking even higher.

"I know," Ella said, her breathing labored as much as she was trying to hide it. "I came to ask about Yuki."

Reyna's eyes were storms all on their own, undecipherable. She lowered her phone on her lap, and Ella took another breath, focusing on cataloging every bit of the room around her. Three glass vases. One portrait. Eight books on the shelf, which she didn't like, eight was a strange number that prickled the back of her mind. A set of keys, twelve of them, and that made it slightly better.

"I wanted to know where she is," Ella said. "How she is."

Reyna got up from where she was sitting. Ella never realized how tall the headmistress really was. She was almost as tall as Yuki, the same kind of imposing posture that forced Ella to not ignore her.

"I thought she'd told you," Reyna said, her voice careful. "She left earlier for a college interview."

"Oh." Ella looked around the room, trying to find another clue, something else to hold onto. She doubted that Yuki would ignore her messages if it was something that simple. "She didn't tell me."

"It was very last-minute," Reyna said. "She's fine, I promise."

Reyna reached out to touch her, and on instinct, Ella shrank back, her knee jerking. The sudden gesture made her drop her backpack. It fell open on the floor, and Ella froze, seeing the two books fall out. Ella got on her knees to retrieve them at the same moment Reyna did.

"Here, I'll help you with those."

"There's no need," Ella said quickly, but Reyna was already kneeling down.

Ella picked up the Black Book first, and it was then that she saw the broken glass.

Reyna had cleaned most of the room, but Ella's eyes were clinical. She could see bits and pieces of mirror on the floor that Reyna had unsuccessfully tried to sweep under the rug. She noticed the leg of the table had deep scratches and its glass top was brand new, still with the protective film over it.

And finally, under the table, a broken piece of a necklace clasp.

These were signs that a storm had hit, leaving only the smallest fractions in its wake. Fractions that Ella couldn't miss.

She looked up at Reyna, who was picking up the remaining contents of Ella's backpack. Reyna's hand hovered over the white cover of the White Book, and then she drew back sharply as if her hand had been burned. She looked up at Ella, startled.

Before Ella could panic any further, she took the book, shoving it and the Black Book back into her bag, zipping it up.

"Sorry to bother you," she said to Reyna, whose jaw was set, her eyes dark. "I'll see Yuki soon."

"Yes," Reyna said slowly, "you will."

Ella bolted out of the door before Reyna could stop her, her heart hammering against her ribs. She'd shown Reyna her hand. Even if she grabbed the books quickly, Reyna had already seen them. But she didn't have the necklace. Reyna didn't have the last piece of the puzzle.

She was sure Yuki had gotten to it first.

CHAPTER FIFTY-SIX

YUKI

Yuki had dreamed of running away throughout her childhood.

She imagined running across the world to someplace where there were no doors like the ones at home, no pictures of dead mothers, no fathers who deemed they were never enough for their daughters. Someplace where she would be wild and free, to race with the wolves, to get lost in a forest and come back a monster—if not in shape, then in mind.

There were no wolves in Munich. It was as far as she'd gotten, blending in with the tourist crowd. The weather was nice, the spring fresh with its bright flowers. She'd brought Reyna's necklace with her. Picked it up from the floor, feeling the pulse of magic that seemed to echo her own, which she didn't understand yet. Reyna hadn't fought back with magic—hadn't any magic of her own, except she had stayed alive all this time, reliving the curse as her punishment.

Yuki hadn't found the answers, but she'd found the book-shop Nani had told her about.

It was a collector's shop, an antiquary dealing with old volumes. Heavy books lined the walls, the pages yellowed with age. The old attendant had eyed her curiously, and Yuki had said that she was doing research on her thesis. It hadn't been a lie, exactly, but she hovered in the back, looking at a section where no other students would look. These were the old books and manuscripts on fairy tales.

She hovered near the shelves as she spotted a book spine that looked familiar.

Gingerly, she took it out, looking at the same cover she'd stared at for the past year. The apple tree, the crows, the roots.

"You have a good eye," the salesman said in German, and Yuki turned, her fingers icy on the cover. The old man smiled at her, and Yuki forced herself to stay calm. "That's one of our rarer volumes."

She knew what it was. There was a reason why she'd come here.

"Come to the light," the old man gestured. "You can examine it better."

He shuffled toward one of the old tables and placed the book on a glass box. He clicked on a lamp with a soft glow and turned the pages with a gloved hand.

"It's not just Grimm's," Yuki said.

"Oh, no," the salesman agreed. "A worldwide collection of fairy tales, compiled by an unknown press. Only ten were ever made. See the binding there?"

Yuki saw where he pointed, looking at the tales that were so familiar already. There were no images in the book, but the order of the tales was an old friend. She looked at page after page, but then she stopped.

There was a mistake.

"Wait," she said, and he stopped. "There's no 'Snow White'."

"That's correct," the old man agreed, looking up. "A peculiar choice to leave out, since it's one of the most popular ones, especially in Europe."

Yuki put her hands on the glass table. "And this is the original?"

"Yes," the man said haughtily, his posture erect. "We would not alter it in any form. This book is the only preserved and intact copy that we know of."

Both the White and Black Book had the "Snow White" tale. The cursed books held her fate, written in their pages. Nani was right that Yuki was different.

Yuki wasn't just someone in the story.

Yuki *was* the story.

The answer had been staring at her all along. It was because she had magic. Because she could see the other versions of herself. Because the book had told her the truth all along.

Wasn't Snow White's story about someone wanting a child so badly that they would sacrifice anything for it? Hadn't Reyna admitted she had messed with the fairy tales, that the curse was punishment for her act of creation? And what crime would warrant a hundred lives, a hundred payments?

Only if what Reyna had said was true, that Yuki hadn't

meant to be born at all. She was untouched; she couldn't be hurt by anything but magic. She wasn't *anything* but magic, raging inside.

A girl born of the stories, a girl born from someone's stubbornness to find their own happy ending, a girl born from the pain of loneliness. A girl born of yearning: skin as white as snow, hair as black as ebony, lips as red as blood.

She thanked the man quickly, and he put the book back on the shelf. Yuki's mind was racing as she searched for her phone, and the moment she had it in her hand, it rang. Yuki stared at it, heart thumping in her chest. The number was unidentified. She hadn't told anyone where she was, not even Reyna. She hadn't answered any of Ella's texts. She didn't know what to say that could fix what had broken between them.

It wasn't Ella. She felt dread in her stomach as she answered. "Don't turn your phone off, dear." Mrs. Blumstein's voice was clear and sharp. "You must come home. Back to the castle."

"I'm not going back."

Yuki was safe. She was far from the inevitable moment of her death, the instant the curse would hit her. She was the only one safely away from Grimrose. The only one safe, anywhere. She looked up at her reflection in the window shop, but all the other versions of her had faded once she knew the truth. There were only her familiar features, the ones she'd grown up with in this lifetime.

How many others had Reyna seen? How many daughters had she lost?

Yuki had watched so many of them die in the memories,

in the piece that she knew was her heart. Dying like all the other girls in the tales, lost to the oblivion of the curse. If Reyna had picked the book of tales, if she'd wrenched it open with magic, then it had all rippled to the other tales as well. To other girls who had no idea magic existed, who were bound to the curse without ever understanding why.

Magic was dangerous. Yuki knew it, in her soul.

"I'm going to break your curse," she spat on the phone, her eyes were dark in the reflection. "You're going to pay for what you did."

Mrs. Blumstein didn't seem affected by Yuki's threats. How many times had they already gone through this? How many other times had Yuki remembered a part of herself, or found that she was still in the game? How many times had she approached the end, only to die again?

Not this time. She wasn't going to lose this time.

"You can't save their stories," Mrs. Blumstein's voice was even. "It is too late for that. It might be too late for Ella."

Yuki froze on the spot. "What do you want."

It came out as a hiss, not even a question. Only a demand.

"Come home," the teacher's voice repeated. "There is another way to end this."

Yuki knew what it was.

She'd thought killing Reyna would end the curse, but there was another way. A way where Reyna's mistake would be wiped away. A way where the curse could be undone if the sin was atoned.

"I'll see you tonight at the ball, then," Mrs. Blumstein said.

The line went dead.

Yuki stared at her phone. She'd run away, tried to find answers, but there was no truth but within herself. All the answers and endings were back home in Grimrose Castle.

All of her destiny had come calling, and the last page was turning.

CHAPTER FIFTY-SEVEN

Nani had left that same day she received Svenja's gift.
She'd taken a bus to Zurich, and she was at the hospital the next morning. Only two hours away from her father, all this time. She couldn't believe she'd waited this long to find answers.

The hospital was big. Her bag flapped against her as she walked; she'd packed a few changes of clothes and a sweater, along with money she'd guiltily borrowed from Rory's wallet. Rory wasn't using it, and Nani knew she wouldn't mind, but still. She stood on the sidewalk, looking up, wanting to go in but not quite managing it yet.

After months of no phone calls, of returned letters, of him vanishing into thin air, Nani wasn't sure if she could face what had been waiting all this time. After almost a year, she realized she had slowly given up on the idea of talking to him or understanding what happened.

Nani straightened her back and walked inside.

She was greeted with that ominous hospital smell—disinfectants and alcohol and something looming beneath it all. There was not enough disinfectant in the world to mask the smell of death.

Nani approached the main desk, and she didn't wait for the woman to look up.

"I'm here to see a patient," said Nani. "My father, Isaiah Eszes."

The receptionist looked her up and down, eyeing her clothes.

Nani didn't back down, thinking of all the other entitled girls back at the school who wouldn't let anything stop them. She thought of Alethea, and she raised her nose as high as she could. "I need his room number. I'll be waiting."

The receptionist nodded, checking the room in her computer. Nani's hands started to sweat, and she wiped them against her skirt.

"He's not receiving visitors at the moment," the receptionist said, looking up. "He hasn't listed any close relatives."

"You don't understand," Nani hissed. "I'm here to see him. Whether he wants to see me or not."

The receptionist looked at her, realizing Nani wasn't going to move. Nani adjusted her glasses sternly and thought of trampling some doctors along the corridor to make her point.

"His room number is 136," the receptionist finally said. "Good luck."

Nani turned without thanking her, following the signs on the walls. Her knees were shaking; her legs felt like they didn't belong to her body anymore. She could hear her heart thumping in her ears, the rhythm increasing steadily.

Nani stopped in front of the door. She knocked, but there was no answer. After waiting a second, she opened the door.

It was a regular hospital room. A single bed with white sheets, no flowers, only one window. She almost didn't recognize the figure on the bed.

Her father was slumped down, his eyes closed. His head was bald—not shaved, like he'd kept in the military. His rich dark skin was ashy, a papery texture. Tears sprung in her eyes.

Slowly, she reached for his hand. It shifted beneath her own, and suddenly, his eyes opened, grip strong on her hand.

Then he blinked, looking at his daughter.

"Nani?" he asked in a croaked voice.

Nani wanted to run. She wanted to stay. She wanted to close her eyes and never open them again.

"Yeah," she said. "I'm here, dad."

He gazed at her, at the school uniform, at her hair that had grown way past her shoulders now that she'd not cut it for a year. At her crooked round glasses.

"You're still the same," he said.

"You aren't," she said, sharper than she intended. Her nose was running, and she sniffed, wiping the tears.

Isaiah laughed. "Never one to keep quiet, are you?"

"You should have told me."

"I didn't want you to see me," he said, his voice coming out raspy.

Suddenly, Nani was angry again. As angry as she had been

with him all year. He hadn't called, hadn't answered a letter, had left his life behind and went somewhere she couldn't reach him, and now, he was headed to a place where she wouldn't be able to follow.

"You should have told me," she repeated. "I can't believe you sent me off to a school and then didn't tell me."

"I didn't want you to see any of this," he said, stroking her hand, caressing her fingers, and Nani felt like she was having an out of body experience, talking to her father after all this time. "I had left you already so many times. You would have grown up without having to remember this."

"I would have grown up without saying goodbye."

Her words were harsh again, but that didn't make them less true.

"I was being more kind to myself than to you," her father said quietly.

Nani stared at him.

Then she said words she never thought she would say to her own father.

"Oh, screw you," she said, surprised by her own vehemence, and then she burst into tears. Her body shook violently, and she launched into a hug, holding him as tight as she could without breaking him. Inside, she could feel her heart shattering, the ground disappearing from under her feet. Her father wrapped his arms around her, and it was the same as it always had been. "You don't get to choose for me. You always left without saying goodbye, and I always hated you for it. I'm not weak."

"Shh," her father whispered into her hair. She understood

what he'd chosen, but it didn't make it better. She understood
why he kept leaving, why he wanted to be in a place where he
belonged, in a place where there wasn't an empty space meant
for Nani's mother. She understood wanting the adventures,
wanting to see the world. She understood because she wanted
it too, but he had never allowed her to choose.

"I'm not a child anymore," she said, half sobbing. "You
don't get to leave me behind."

He stroked her hair, brushing her curls away. Nani's
glasses were foggy; she couldn't see a thing through them, but
she didn't let go of the hug.

"How are you here?" he asked her instead, and Nani had
to smile. Even though he had disappeared, she doubted that
he'd stopped checking on her.

Always far, but still near.

Always full of his promises.

"I'm in that stupid school. I made stupid friends. I'm
having the stupidest, best adventure of my life," Nani said.
"That doesn't excuse you for leaving me there. For not telling
me where you were. I miss you, dad."

Nani buried her face into his chest like she did when
she was a child, when she would hide from the sound of the
crashing and thundering storms.

"I missed you too, ku'uipo," he told her, his hands on her
curls. He still pronounced it outrageously wrong, and Nani
wanted to laugh. "But I'm glad you're doing it. I'm glad you're
writing your own story, love. That's all we can ever choose."

"Don't leave me again."

"I won't."

Nani guarded the words like a secret that had been whispered. She kept them close to her heart, to remember them, for the promise they kept.

Nani stayed with her father for the rest of the week. She'd brought a book to read with him, just as they did when she was a child and he came back from one of his trips. Nani told him about the school, about her friends, but she didn't mention the curse.

Isaiah didn't talk about his cancer, and Nani didn't ask. She understood the reason for lying, and even though she loved her father, she didn't forgive him. He had been a fluctuating force in her life, and while she hadn't chosen that, she could choose it now.

Friday arrived too soon. She had exchanged texts with Ella all week, but she tried not to think of the other inevitable thing. It was better if she enjoyed the remainder of days here because she wasn't going to have them for long.

They'd lost. The curse was upon them.

Nani was surprisingly okay with it. She looked at her father, asleep. He was still strong, but his treatment had left its marks. Nani stood and stretched then headed out to the hall to go to the bathroom.

Her phone rang, and Nani fumbled with it, but there was no recognizable number.

"Hello?"

A sudden, wrong, and raspy silence filled the end of the line.

"Nani?" a voice asked, familiar as always, but not warm. Svenja's. "Are you there?"

"Yeah, I'm with my dad. What happened?"

Svenja started to cry at the other end, and Nani was paralyzed.

"Something is wrong," Svenja said, sounding out of breath, half crying, her voice getting cut by the line. "I didn't mean—You have to come back. She gave it to me— She's going to—"

It cut again, and Nani cursed her phone, desperation growing in her limbs.

"Slow down," Nani said, trying to calm the panic she was feeling. "What's happening?"

"Odilia," said Svenja, and something banged on the phone so loudly Nani jumped. "Oh my god. She's going to kill me."

Her voice sounded more desperate by the moment, and Nani knew the story. She shouldn't have left Svenja there alone—not when she wasn't sure of Odilia's motives toward her cousin.

"It was a trap," said Svenja, voice breaking. "The address. So you'd leave. So I wouldn't—"

Sudden panic wrapped around Nani. She should have seen it coming. She should have known.

The thought of losing Svenja was unbearable.

"Lock yourself in," Nani said. "Stay safe. I'm coming."

Svenja's phone went dead, and Nani realized the call had

ended almost ten seconds ago. She dialed Yuki's number, but of course she didn't pick up. Nani tried to breathe, dialing again, but to no avail. She wanted to punch something.

She tried Ella's number but got a message that it was out of service. Something had happened. Something really, really bad must have happened. She cursed out loud, any words she could think, running her fingers through her scalp only for them to catch in her curls.

She leaned against the sink, staring at herself in the mirror. Maybe she'd made a huge mistake, and maybe she hadn't. At least there was still time to fix it before it ended.

Her father had told her to write her own story.

Nani went back to her father's room. He was still asleep. She tore a page from one of her notebooks and wrote a note. She'd be back for him. She didn't want to lie about that. But right now, Nani had to figure out something for herself—her true place.

"I love you," she whispered as she kissed his forehead. He didn't even stir in his sleep.

She'd be back. That was a promise she would keep.

But she had made another promise, one that felt more important now.

This time, it was Nani who left without saying goodbye.

CHAPTER FIFTY-EIGHT

ELLA

The rest of the week flew by too fast, and Ella was alone. Rory was asleep. Yuki was nowhere to be seen. Nani had left.

Ella was the only one still at Grimrose, and during her classes all week, she had expected something even worse to happen. Everyone around her spoke of only one thing: the graduation ball. The ball happening on the day before her birthday.

Every day that passed, she thought of what the books meant. Every day that passed, she was almost sure it was going to be her last.

And then Friday arrived, and Ella had finally crossed out the last day on her calendar. The last red X in all her five years of Grimrose.

Before leaving, Ella looked into the mirror. She didn't look any different from when it had started—same ash-blond hair straight at her shoulders, hazel eyes too wide, the pointed nose, and the hidden bruises beneath her skin. She didn't have a new dress for graduation, so she'd chosen the same one from the winter ball.

She didn't look like a girl going to her graduation party. She looked like someone about to make a last stand. In her bag, she was carrying both books, unwilling to let them out of her sight.

Ella tried her door and opened it carefully. It was a little before nine—it was late, and she wasn't supposed to leave the house. The twins had already left to go to the ball, and the house was quiet.

She went down the stairs one step at a time, stopping at the steps she knew might creak and give her away. The house was dark and silent, and not a sound was heard. When she got to the living room, she let out a small shaky breath.

Ella stepped toward the door.

A light lit up in the room, and Ella froze.

"Going somewhere?" Sharon's voice was as cold as ice. Ella didn't move. "You could at least talk before leaving. It would be the polite thing to do."

Ella slowly turned on her heels to face her. Sharon had her hands crossed over her lap, sitting in her velvet chair. Ella tried to find her voice, but it was stuck in a lump.

"I thought you knew the arrangements." Sharon's eyes narrowed. "You're not to leave the house except for school."

It didn't matter that the graduation ball was going to be at the school. Sharon wasn't interested in that. None of Ella's excuses had ever mattered.

"After all these years, Eleanor," Sharon sighed. "I thought you were better than my own daughters. Why would you disobey me?"

Sharon got up and Ella flinched. She wanted to run before something bad happened, but she knew she couldn't barge outside. Sharon had been waiting for her, which meant the gates were locked.

She knew Ella would try to leave.

Sharon stood in front of Ella, austere, her face impassive. She slapped Ella across the face, her fingers burning marks on Ella's cheek.

"Answer me. Or have you lost the ability to speak?"

"I didn't," said Ella, cheek reddening, but she didn't want to give Sharon the pleasure of seeing her cry. "It's the graduation ba—"

Sharon scoffed. "And now you care about such mundane things. Do you think I don't know anything that happens in this house? Don't you think I've wrenched it out of Stacie?"

Ella didn't let her face change, looking down. She couldn't blame Stacie. Couldn't blame the twins on a game where they were constantly pitted against each other and none of them could ever win.

"I've done nothing wrong," Ella said quietly.

"Are you calling my daughter a liar?"

Ella shook her head, the lump in her throat growing.

"Don't you know any better, Eleanor? Boys don't care about you. The best you can do is hide that pathetic little face of yours before anyone else sees you for what you really are."

Ella stood still; she couldn't simply run. She had only a few hours, and she wasn't about to spend them alone. She had to do something, anything at all.

"I'm going," she managed to say in a small voice.

Ella braced herself for another slap, but it didn't come. Instead, Sharon's hands went straight for her dress.

She heard the tear in her skirt before she felt it.

"Now this is much better," Sharon said evenly, and then her hands reached the sleeve of the dress, tugging it free. The sound of ripping fabric filled the air, and Ella stood completely paralyzed. "Now they'll see. Nothing but a dirty and pathetic girl who pretends to be more than she is."

Sharon grabbed her by the hair, and Ella felt the pull in her scalp as she yelped and stumbled. Sharon held more firmly, her other arm grabbing Ella's left hand to keep her from moving while she destroyed the dress Ella had created.

Ella couldn't stop the tears from running down her cheeks this time.

"Let me go!" Ella screamed as she tried getting away, but Sharon was strong, dragging her back upstairs by her hair, ruining every line of the dress Ella had worked so hard on creating.

Ella thrashed, but Sharon stepped on her foot, making her lose balance, and banged her head against the floorboard. Ella felt the flash of pain, and when she reached a hand to touch it, her fingers came out red and sticky with blood.

"Now, Eleanor," Sharon said forcefully. "Girls like you have no place at parties like that. You'll never belong with them, so there's no use going. I'm doing this for your own good."

She threw Ella through the attic door, and Ella fell on her knees, her dress in tatters, tears streaking her face. The contents of her bag scattered on the floor. Her phone was broken, the screen glitching lamely. The books were spread open, pages folding at odd angles, and Ella crawled over to them.

She looked up at Sharon, who was holding the doorknob, key in hand.

Her stepmother smiled thinly. "Think of it as mercy."

She shut the door, and the lock clicked. Ella crawled over and tried to open it, but she knew it was locked from the outside. She sat with her back against the door, cradling herself and shivering. She didn't even have enough courage to bang on the door and ask please.

CHAPTER FIFTY-NINE
RORY

#

Nani's heart beat so hard against her chest that it unnerved her to the point where she wished it would simply stop. Night had fallen, and it was a little after eleven when she finally arrived in Constanz. Her phone battery had died on the way. She'd made the journey in what seemed to be record time.

As she hopped off the bus, she could see the distant light from the castle—there were floodlights and fireworks, all of it like a grand and rich party. If she tried hard enough, she could imagine the music that was playing, all the students enjoying their last day of school.

She wasn't dressed for a ball, but she had no time to lose. She almost ran off the bus and had started up the road to Grimrose when another figure emerged from the darkness to greet her.

Nani's heart gave a leap of joy as she saw Svenja. She

ran forward to embrace her, starting to smile, but then she froze midstep. She recognized Svenja's white dress, the same makeup she always wore, but there was something different about the eyes.

Odilia's smile spread lazily across her face.

Nani stepped back. "What are you doing here?" she demanded, her heart returning to a frenetic rhythm.

Wrongness twisted inside Nani as she realized it was all part of the curse.

"Well, you had to be here," Odilia said. Her voice sounded so close to Svenja's. Nani didn't understand how she could do it. "Can you blame me for calling?"

Odilia grinned, amused. When the smile spread across her face, Nani could see another darker shadow.

"It was you," Nani said, accusingly. "You tricked me."

"Isn't it funny?" Odilia asked. "I just wanted to prove a point to Svenja. And you couldn't even tell the difference."

Nani didn't know if she should run. Maybe Svenja was safe and had no idea what Odilia was trying to do. And as long as Nani was with her, Odilia wouldn't be able to hurt Svenja.

"Why don't you tell me why you want to hurt her so bad?" Nani asked. "Why do you hate her?"

Odilia gave out a shrieking laugh, her small shoulders shaking. Everything seemed amiss—Nani needed to be with Svenja. Needed to help her friends, to be back at the castle. She felt her time ticking on the clock tower, her heart speeding up.

"Oh, no," said Odilia. "You've got it all upside down. I don't hate her. She's family. I feel sorry for her."

"Why?"

"Because I'm better than she is." She leaned against the wall, crossing her arms over her chest. Under the moonlight, she looked pretty and innocent. As pretty as Svenja. A chill ran up Nani's spine. "Wouldn't you agree, Nani?"

Odilia stepped forward, and even the scent of her perfume was the same.

"Right then, weren't you fooled?" she said sweetly, and Nani could almost forget who she was talking to. They were so alike it seemed impossible to tell the difference. In the dim light, with her old glasses that needed changing, it all became harder to tell.

But there was one essential difference that meant she knew who was who: One she loved. The other she didn't.

"Tell me, Nani," Odilia said, standing right in front of Nani, her breath cool on Nani's cheek. "Isn't it exactly the same thing, but so much better?"

Odilia leaned in, her lips brushing against Nani's mouth, first soft, and then harder, crashing against Nani. Nani took a second to register what happened, and she pushed Odilia away. Odilia smiled knowingly, as if she'd already won.

"There you go," she murmured softly, the smile still on her lips, triumphant in a white dress that didn't belong to her. "I told you. I'm a much better her than she is ever going to be. She's always going to have to prove herself, to the world, to you. But me, I was born exactly right."

Nani opened her mouth, horrified and disgusted, her hateful comment toward Svenja sinking in. Her lips tingled, and Odilia grinned. It wasn't just about taking her place but pretending that Svenja wasn't who she was.

"You're repugnant," Nani whispered. "Svenja doesn't need to prove anything to me."

"Then you better tell her that," Odilia said, gesturing to the cell phone in her hand, which Nani hadn't even noticed. A photo of their kiss shone on the screen. "Or else she'll be really disappointed."

Odilia's smile stretched from ear to ear. She didn't have to say anything else—it was done, and Nani wasn't going to be able to take back that kiss.

Nani turned back to Grimrose castle.

"You can start running now," Odilia shouted to her back. "See if you can catch her in time."

Nani ran and didn't look back.

CHAPTER SIXTY-ONE

ELLA

Ella was on the floor for what seemed like hours.
Her head had stopped bleeding and her knees,
although bruised, were fine. The pain was still throbbing, but
there was little she could do about that. Her dress was completely destroyed, the ragged fabric hanging and barely covering her torso. The butterflies she had so carefully sewn were
ripped wings and shapeless tufts of the skirt.

Ella could imagine what the books were telling her—she
wasn't going to the ball, couldn't help her friends. In the end,
she had tried and come up empty, just like it felt empty waiting for someone else to save her.

Sometimes, there was no one there but yourself.

Ella stood up, shaking at first. She took off her torn dress
and found an old blue one with a Peter Pan collar that she'd
worn many times. She put it on, tying her blond hair back. Her
face in the mirror was clean, now that the tears had been wiped.

She found an old pair of ballerina flats whose fabric was so worn that they were transparent in places. She wasn't going to give up.

And if she couldn't bring herself to save her friends, then she wasn't worthy of her name.

There was a noise at the window, and Ella jumped. There was a rattling against the padlock, and Ella stood paralyzed until it swung open.

In the window, there was Stacie's face, pale like moonlight. She was hanging in the tree, her ball dress tied up around the waist.

"Come on," she said. "We have to go."

Ella's mouth hung open. "What are you doing here?"

"Fetching you," Stacie said, seemingly annoyed at Ella's slow uptake. "We weren't going to leave you here. Quick, before Mum notices."

Ella didn't wait. There was a cool breeze in the night air that ruffled her bangs as she climbed down the tree, landing softly in the garden. Silla was waiting there, dressed exquisitely, pulling Carrots' harness forward. When the horse saw Ella, it whined, and Silla quieted it down.

"You take the horse," Stacie said, undoing the knots of her dress as if this wasn't a big deal, as if this didn't violate every single silent treaty they had forged throughout the years. "We're going through the front door saying Silla forgot her wallet. That way, she won't hear you slip out."

"Do you think she'll believe that?" Ella asked, taking the harness in her hands.

"We just need to buy you time," Silla replied, her voice

367

certain. "We've already enjoyed enough of the ball. Just take it and go."

Ella blinked, her throat bobbing as she looked at the twins facing her. "Thank you," Ella said to them.

"Don't thank us." Stacie's voice was sharp. "It's not much."

"Still," Ella said, reaching out for Stacie's hand, warm against her own, giving it a squeeze. Ella took the reins and pulled Carrots along, the three of them walking toward the gate, and it was then that the dark figure of Sharon emerged.

"Where do you think you're going?"

The three girls froze in place, but Ella was ahead of them.

"I'm going to the ball," Ella replied firmly. "And you're not going to stop me."

Sharon looked aghast with the combination of words that came out of Ella's mouth, the assertiveness that they carried.

"So the dog bites back," she hissed. "I thought you'd learned your lesson."

Ella stared at her, and she leveled her gaze with her step-mother, feeling calm. "Let me go, Sharon. Or you will regret this."

Sharon looked at the three of them, her gaze falling on her daughters.

"Both of you," she spat. "To the house. Now."

"Don't move," said Ella.

Sharon laughed. "Oh, now you think to give them orders as well. They only took pity on you because they're weak."

Stacie's hands curled into fists, but she didn't leave Ella's side. She didn't follow Sharon's orders, either.

"They're not like you. No matter how hard you tried

making them be." Ella's hold on Carrots' reins tightened. "You have done everything in your power to degrade me and to make me feel unwanted, but I'm not scared of you anymore."

In the distance, Ella heard the chiming of the hour. The Grimrose clock started resonating its powerful sound throughout the town, and each stroke echoed within her heart.

She counted them. One, two.

"All I did was try to help," Ella said. Three, four. "I never hated you, not even once."

Five, six, seven.

Ella remained fixed on her stepmother. "I would have forgiven you."

Nine.

"Why would I need forgiveness?" Sharon asked, looking Ella straight in the eye.

Even now, Sharon couldn't see. Ella knew she had too much hate filling her heart, and she wouldn't understand. All this time Ella thought she was hated because she was worthless, a burden, but that wasn't the truth. It was because of what she could be—what she could become someday.

Ten.

"I'm sorry, Sharon," Ella said, and she meant it, every single word.

She was sorry for all of them, for all the years trapped in a home she couldn't leave, forcing herself to work to compensate something that wasn't her fault. And if Ella could, she would stop every single girl who thought she was worthless and make her look in the mirror.

As Ari had done with her. As Ella could see for herself now.

Eleven.

Maybe she wasn't perfect, but she would never be. But she was still worth something—she was worth a thousand possibilities.

"Now it's too late," Ella said quietly.

Twelve.

Twelve chimes of the clock. Another day. All the masks and covers Ella wore had come undone by the simple fact that now she could see herself for who she was.

Ella mounted the horse.

"You can't go," Sharon roared, seeming to not understand why Ella wasn't standing down, why she wasn't backing away and making herself invisible as she had always done.

"I can," Ella said. "It's midnight. Midnight of my eighteenth birthday. I can do anything I want."

I'm free.

She looked at Stacie and Silla, who both nodded, their faces determined. Whatever would come next, Ella wouldn't have to be alone. Sharon wasn't winning again.

Silla ran to open the gate, and Ella rode alone toward Grimrose.

Ella arrived at the castle panting but glowing.

She almost couldn't believe that she was finally, finally free. She could taste it in her mouth, the sweet scent of the breeze and the flowers blooming for the spring. It was everything she imagined it could be.

But she wasn't finished. Not yet.

She left Carrots at the stables. She still had the two books with her in her bag, and somehow, she could feel their echo in her own heart, as if the magic was escaping the pages. She could hear the bubbling of the ballroom, where she imagined hundreds of students waltzing and laughing, oblivious. Oblivious to the fact that if Ella couldn't end the curse, they would all soon be dead.

Ella's footsteps echoed on the infirmary stairs, her muscles hurting from the lack of practice in running.

"Give it a rest!" Ella snapped impatiently, shaking her head, the weight of the books slapping against her back.

She opened the door of Rory's room, and to her relief, Pippa was there. She wasn't wearing an expensive ball gown— only jeans and a T-shirt, sitting next to the sleeping Rory, holding her hand. She looked up.

"What are you doing here?" Pippa asked, her voice creaky.

"I don't have much time," Ella said, closing the door and taking the White and Black Book out of her bag. "I need you to take care of these."

Pippa frowned. "What is this?"

Ella couldn't explain them, not in a way that made sense. She didn't have time to make Pippa into another believer. She needed to keep the books safe while she went looking for a way out. She couldn't meet Reyna again while she was wielding them.

"Please, just keep them safe," Ella said. "For Rory."

Pippa set her jaw, and then she nodded. Ella turned to Rory, a serene sleeper amongst the destruction. She wished she had the time to sit down, to talk to her friend, or even wait to see, hoping for one last miracle. She squeezed Rory's other hand.

"Rory, I'll be waiting," Ella said. "Maybe you don't need me. But I do need you."

Ella kissed Rory's brow. Pippa watched the scene, and Ella took a deep breath, ready to leave, and then she noticed something outside the window of the castle.

Ella frowned, and Pippa turned.

"What the hell is that?" Pippa asked, her voice rising.

Outside the window, the rose bushes had grown, though grown was describing it poorly. All around Grimrose, a forest of thorns had advanced, covering the gardens, the windows, the outer walls. Magic, pure and unaltered.

It's ending, Ella thought.

Ella leaned out of the window to see that the castle was fully surrounded, thorns and vines covering every window and entrance to the school, leaving no way out. The magic was obvious, and she knew what that meant.

Yuki had come back.

Yuki was in Grimrose again.

Ella ran out of the infirmary, back into the throbbing heart of the castle, in the direction of the music. If she was building a barrier, that meant Yuki was outside. Ella could tell her about the book Nani had found online, and they could go back to the infirmary to break the curse with Rory.

Ella went down the steps two at a time, passing by the door of the ballroom, the music loud and echoing. She headed toward the outside door before she was stopped.

"Where are you going?" Miss Bagley asked, and Ella's head whipped around.

"I need to find Reyna," Ella replied, saying the first lie that came to her head. "Where is she?"

"This is not the time to bother the headmistress," Miss Bagley crooned. "Go to the ballroom, Eleanor. You've done more than enough."

Ella took a step back, careful. "I need to go."

"The ball is this way, Ella." Miss Bagley's voice was firm, but Ella couldn't obey it—simply because she could feel something happening outside, a change she didn't understand.

Yuki was out there, waiting, and if she was back, that meant they had a chance to find a way out. As long as they had each other.

A wave of wind washed over Ella, a trembling sensation that seemed to change the world. Miss Bagley stopped, feeling it too, and then suddenly, her eyes were glowing bright, and she extended her hands.

All the sound around them seemed to mute, and Ella could feel that a curse had just been broken. She just didn't understand how.

Miss Bagley smiled, but her smile wasn't kind anymore.

She took Ella's hand, and then her fingers landed on Ella's cheek. They felt hot, as if Miss Bagley was burning from the inside, and the pain was searing into her soul.

Ella couldn't get away.

"You've done enough," Miss Bagley said, her voice seeming to crawl its way into Ella's core, burning. Ella suddenly felt dizzy, mist clouding her vision. She had to find someone. But she couldn't remember why. "Enjoy the rest of the evening. We'll fix everything."

Ella nodded again as Miss Bagley vanished from sight, disappearing through the door that led to the garden. Frederick burst through the ballroom door, frowning when he saw Ella standing there on her own.

Ella heard the voice, somewhere always in her head, trying to guide her, but the mist was thick, and nothing else seemed to matter. She was warm and happy and there was nothing she needed to worry about.

"You all right?" Freddie asked, then he noticed she wasn't dressed for the ball. "What happened?"

"Everything is wonderful," Ella answered, her doubt dissipating.

She took Frederick's hand to go to the ballroom, knowing this was where she was meant to be. Dancing with her prince, nothing at all on her mind.

CHAPTER SIXTY-TWO

RORY

At first, there was darkness.

A well of nothing, a void of blackness that engulfed her, a silence where she couldn't even hear her own heartbeat.

Then came the pain. It was searing through her body, lacerating her muscles, and she couldn't move, couldn't breathe, couldn't turn, couldn't open her eyes and beg for it to stop. Her body was completely still, and yet, every single one of her bones was undoing, shattering and breaking, the veins expanding as they took with them the pain that pushed further than she had ever felt.

There was darkness, there was pain, and there she was in-between, trying to stay alive somehow, even knowing she was dead, knowing that if she closed her eyes, truly closed them, it would all be over.

Except she couldn't. She couldn't let go. She didn't remember who she was, didn't remember her purpose, but there was something she needed to do. Something that called her, deep in the locked secrets of her heart, deep in a part of her she wasn't aware of before. Now she knew every searing end of her body, every single atom that kept her imprisoned in the stillness, and she knew only one word.

Weakness.

She was weak, and she couldn't wake up. She was merely existing, trying to breathe when there was nothing there, using all her strength to keep herself afloat even when the darkness was begging to swallow her whole. She was weak.

She couldn't do it on her own.

And then, in the darkness, in the pain, there was a voice. She wrestled against her captivity, against the ropes around her body and mind. She fought herself, her body, as she'd always done.

She had fought this battle all her life, and she'd kept winning. Every time she woke up, she won.

Every time the pain came through a fog, stilling her mind, she pushed herself further.

A voice was calling her name, and it was familiar and warm.

Rory, I'll be waiting.

Rory struggled, grasping her name and making it her own again, commanding her body from the inside. She was not part of the darkness; she was Rory.

I do need you.

Ella's voice. She knew it, felt the brush of skin against her own, and for a moment, she had a grasp on reality. She had almost managed to open her eyes, but then the darkness called her back, placing its tendrils around her arms. Rory opened her mouth to scream, but no sound came out.

She tried finding a path in the darkness. She had to wake up. She needed to wake up. Her fingers were as still as before, and in the silence, there was the faint sound of her heartbeat, the only sign that she was still alive.

Another hand, wrapped around her own. The skin-on-skin contact was electric, carrying its own jolt through Rory's heart, and it was a different type of pain. The fingers were sure.

"Maybe you were right about this," a voice said, and she couldn't place it, but Rory knew it was important. "Maybe I am the idiot."

Rory wanted to laugh because she knew it was the right response. Wanted to squeeze the hand that was squeezing hers, keeping her tethered. A stream of light amidst the darkness, a respite from the pain.

Rory couldn't do it by herself. It was a betrayal—all this time, she thought she was only independent and strong as long as she could do everything by herself. As long as she could prove she could stand alone.

But loneliness wasn't strength.

"I was so scared," the voice said again. "I was so scared that you were going away either way, that I thought confronting you was the best option. That it was better to fight because what else could I do?"

The voice sighed, and Rory wanted to reach out.

"I'll be here for you," the voice continued. "When you wake up, I'll be here. I always tried to keep you on edge, trying to push you away because I thought you didn't want me the way I wanted you." Rory felt her heart heaving, her muscles tearing themselves again, and this time, she steeled herself against the bout of pain. It didn't matter anymore.

"There's only one thing I can control," Pippa said, and Rory remembered everything, "and it's that I'll be here when you want me to be."

Pippa let go of her fingers, and Rory felt her own heart weakening, the darkness closing in again, burning. She didn't want to be alone again.

She wanted to scream for Pippa to come back, to not leave. She didn't think she could bear it, when all this time she had been all Rory wanted and craved. *Please, don't leave.*

And as if Pippa heard Rory's own heartbeat, her desperation that she would be left to the darkness, Pippa picked up her hand again.

"I'm not going anywhere," she said softly. "Not without you."

Her fingers brushed Rory's forehead, the same place where Ella had touched.

There was pressure, and Rory reached out. She reached out into the stream of light, through the pain, through everything, and when she did, someone was holding her.

Slowly, painfully, Rory opened her eyes.

Pippa gasped in surprise, and Rory didn't lose one moment, still too afraid that she'd lose control of her body, afraid that she'd be sucked again into the darkness. She jumped on Pippa, pressing her mouth against hers, her chest thumping in response. She didn't even care about the hospital dress or that her body had turned into jelly and that every single one of her muscles was protesting. Rory held on tight, and Pippa held her back.

When Rory was out of breath, she let go and opened her eyes again, relieved that Pippa was still there. That Pippa had always been there.

"You scared me," Pippa said, breathing in her ear, and Rory could sense Pippa's voice tingling all through her spine to the farthest outreaches of her body, waking Rory up.

"Don't tell me you were going to miss me."

Pippa laughed, and the sound was beautiful, and Rory wanted to hear it again and again and again, for the rest of her life. She put her forehead against Pippa's, closing her eyes and breathing deep, feeling the safety it carried. The certainty that this was what she wanted and she'd been lucky enough to be wanted back.

"This is going to sound cheesy," Rory said, "but I don't want to go anywhere that isn't with you."

"I like it when you're cheesy," Pippa said, laughing, and Rory wanted to kiss her again, curl her fingers around Pippa's face, feel the reality around them both, their heartbeats matching. "Makes me feel stronger."

"I'm still stronger than you."

"In your dreams, Rory."

Pippa kissed her again, and Rory felt her heart melt in the best way possible. Instead of the searing pain, it was all back under control. With Pippa there, she felt stronger. Rory had waited so long for this that she didn't even believe it was ever coming true.

"I don't care who I have to fight," Rory said. "If you're with me, I'm going to fight them all. I'll figure out a way, whatever it takes. I'm not scared anymore. I'm not letting you go that easily."

Pippa squeezed her hand. "I'm not letting you go, either."

"Good," Rory said. "Well—except maybe right now. I have somewhere to be."

Pippa frowned, starting to protest, but Rory jumped out of bed. She landed on her two feet, cracking her knuckles, and then she saw the bag at the end of the bed. She picked it up, looking at both books.

"Shouldn't I call the doctor?" Pippa asked. "You shouldn't be walking around yet. You hit your head really hard."

"I'll be fine," Rory said. She could hear the party going on downstairs. Graduation night. The fact that the doctors weren't around just went to show that everyone had quietly left her there, silently giving up.

Except Ella. Except Pippa. They hadn't given up on her.

She breathed deep, remembering it all. They were all in danger.

Rory had to go find her friends. She had to find Ella. The books were always the key. Penelope had known that. She'd outright *told* them. She had known who was to blame.

"Ella left those," Pippa said, pointing. "Look, the nurse should be back soon, I could just call..."

Pippa's voice trailed off, and Rory followed her gaze to the window to see the enormous forest of thorns that had taken over the school grounds.

"Oh shit," Rory muttered.

"What's happening here?" Pippa asked, her eyes searching Rory's face for answers. "You sure you should be going out there?"

Rory reached for the bag and looked for clothes that fit her in the infirmary. Luckily, someone had kept a change of clothes for her in the bedside drawer. She found a shirt and pants, putting them on. Then, a pair of old tennis shoes. She could feel the fog still rolling around her mind, her thoughts struggling, but her purpose was clear.

"Do you trust me?" Rory asked.

"I do," Pippa replied.

"Then go back to your room," Rory said. "I'll find you later. And then you can call the doctor and I'll sit here for three hours while they check out my head."

Rory couldn't bring herself to say goodbye, not after all this. Maybe if she could stop this mess, she'd be able to tell her the truth. After this, they would have all the time in the world.

If she could do this one thing.

If she reached Ella in time.

If they found a way out, together.

CHAPTER SIXTY-THREE

YUKI

Yuki arrived at the castle a little after midnight. She heard the clock chiming in the distance, an ominous gong foretelling a dreadful future. She felt her own insides turning into water. The gardens were dark as she crossed them, as if all the light had been cleared out, leaving only the shadows to surround her.

She didn't go in. The ballroom was lit up and she could see people inside. She wished she could stop for a moment more, feel the air around her, see the girls one more time.

Those were only wishes, and she felt the heavy air surrounding her as she looked up, her black hair whipping in the wind behind her.

"You came," a voice called to her, and Yuki turned around to face Mrs. Blumstein. "Just in time."

Yuki didn't let herself feel intimidated. The necklace in her pocket throbbed in the teacher's presence, as if everything contained there wanted to be released. She curled her fist around it, icing the necklace with her own magic.

Mrs. Blumstein didn't seem to be aware of it.

"What do you want?" Yuki asked. She wasn't afraid; she'd put the rest of the pieces together.

"To save them, of course," Mrs. Blumstein replied, gesturing with her head to the castle above. "It's time this comes to an end, Yuki. It has gone too far."

"Because we're so close to breaking the curse?"

Mrs. Blumstein laughed, and in her pale face there was scorn marking her wrinkles. She had an old power that distinguished her. One that Yuki should have seen a long time ago if she were only paying attention.

"You have never come close to breaking it or even understanding it," Mrs. Blumstein said. "What do you truly know, if Reyna couldn't tell you?"

"I know the curse is in the books," Yuki replied. "I know that you were the one to cast it, after she broke the rules."

"The rules?" Mrs. Blumstein said. "The rules! Magic is more powerful than *rules*, girl. It's old, it's ancient, and it does not bend to a simple wish."

"And yet it did," Yuki said, and there was a flash of hate in Mrs. Blumstein's green eyes. "Am I not here? Didn't she create me?"

"You are a mistake," she said. "An error to be punished. What are you, but words written on a page? A piece of paper, nothing new to add, still too tied to your own roots. We only have to look at your face to know."

Yuki didn't have to look at her face. She'd spent so long looking, wondering if something was wrong with her, why she was different, why she felt that need to pretend everything was fine even when it wasn't.

This witch couldn't insult her.

Yuki knew herself inside and out, and the magic that throbbed within her wasn't unnatural. It was a part of her, and it made her real. She was as real as any of the others, had lived and died as many times as the rest.

"So you're punishing Reyna for something you consider a mistake," Yuki said, her voice even and rage hidden, but still sharp as a blade. "Three hundred years of the same cycle. Aren't you tired?"

Mrs. Blumstein didn't even blink. "For all magic there must be a sacrifice. And when she couldn't face her own mistake, she cursed us all to oversee the infinite cycles."

"And she took away your magic," Yuki said, taking the necklace out of her pocket. "I know what this is."

Mrs. Blumstein stepped forward, but then Yuki held the pendant forward, feeling the wave of its magic push the teacher back. Yuki held it out to touch her, and Mrs. Blumstein tripped, almost losing her balance.

Yuki laughed. "I know you can't touch it. That's part of the magic, isn't it? You can't touch the thing you've been cursed with."

She'd been too oblivious to see it before, her own part in it. Of course she was the curse—she was the very reason the curse existed.

Reyna had created Yuki out of nothing, and Yuki was now Reyna's punishment under the witches' curse. To see her reborn and die again, never to touch her. To be present, and yet never alter the course of destiny. And Reyna, in anger, had wreaked her own retribution—forcing them all to witness the same cycle, and no one had any magic to stop it.

"You're as stuck as she is," Yuki said. "Why do you think you're going to win? You can't offer me anything I can't take for myself."

Mrs. Blumstein leveled her eyes with hers.

"I can offer you your friend's life," she said, and that changed everything.

Yuki stopped, the pendant still in her hand.

Mrs. Blumstein smiled again. "Will you let them get stuck inside this curse, Yuki, because of you and Reyna? Are you so selfish that you are not willing to trade your pain to spare the others?"

"You made the curse," Yuki spat. "It was your will in the first place, dragging all of us into it."

"You came from the book," Mrs. Blumstein answered. "The others were a consequence, their lives taking the shapes that were in the pages, all because the book came to life. But you can stop it."

Yuki wanted to scream.

Her rage bubbled inside her, and she felt something else grow around her in the gardens—not the ice-cold magic that she had, but something else. Grimrose, flowing through her magic, the bushes and gardens growing, trying to fight back.

Growing into a forest of thorns.

Mrs. Blumstein blinked, looking at Yuki again, but Yuki wasn't really making the roses grow—she was only fueling a part of it. It was the castle doing it—the castle which had seen all of them suffer, had known their deaths intimately, had witnessed the fulfillment of their fates again and again. Yuki was giving Grimrose its freedom because Grimrose itself was a part of the story too.

"What do you want?" Yuki shouted again. "What is your word worth?"

"If you break the necklace, I'll have my magic again," Mrs. Blumstein said. "If you break the necklace, I will free them of this curse."

"What's the catch?" Yuki asked, too aware they had come to a standstill.

Meanwhile, the curse was still working. It would eventually get all of them. It was a rigged game, built by the witches to make them win. Penelope had bargained her own secret for it, trying to get a happy ending, but not even the villains got those. She had done it all for nothing.

"The catch is that you die," Mrs. Blumstein said. "You were right. We've all grown tired of this punishment. I want to be free of it as much as you. To end the curse, you die. For the last time."

The curse would be over. And her life, forever.

She wouldn't have a new chance to see Reyna. To see her friends.

But she'd die knowing they'd escaped, that they had a new path ahead of them. A chance at a happy ending.

The tales had taught her well.

Sacrifices were always worth something.

She fingered the necklace in her hands, turning over the ruby heart. She knew it was part of her own heart—or maybe Reyna's. It didn't seem to make a difference. Sometimes, Yuki really wished she had been born without a heart. It would have saved her the trouble.

She wanted to laugh. She wanted to cry.

She wanted to burn the whole world through her tears and her anger and her pain, because she was here, she was alive. She had never felt truly alive until this moment, but when she looked up at the castle, she knew what she had to do.

There were other girls who were as alive as she was, and who deserved their own happy endings.

And wasn't that what she'd wanted, anyway? To protect them, no matter the cost?

Maybe that was all she had been good for. Maybe her pain would be the sacrifice they all needed. Pain was all that was left for her. She'd made her mistakes. She'd lashed out. She had done all of it wrong. Now she could fix it, her own chance of redemption.

She'd burned all her bridges, and it was time she faced the fire.

"I'll bind you to your word," Yuki warned. She'd find a way to come back if the witches lied. She'd hunt them down, no matter what it took, because it was a promise worth her future. A promise worth her oblivion. "What do I do?"

"It's very simple," Mrs. Blumstein said. From the inside

of her coat, Mrs. Blumstein took something out. It was red against the moonlight, as red as the roses that had bloomed and made their way around the castle, with their terrible thorns. It took a moment for Yuki's eyes to adjust and understand.

A red apple.

She reached out for Mrs. Blumstein's hand. It weighed nothing, but it was luscious. Perfect. Delicious. It was her fate, all along.

She looked up through the forest of thorns around the castle, and for a moment, Yuki could have sworn she saw Ella through the window. She smiled, taking a deep breath, knowing that this was the right thing to do. That this was the only choice she could ever make.

She'd swallowed her heart. Her pain was worth nothing.

Yuki crushed the necklace with her magic, and a wave of wind hit them, the magic of the curse dispelling. She looked over at Mrs. Blumstein and watched as the witch regained her power, how it flowed from the necklace and back into her hands, curling in its darkness, matching Yuki's own.

Without further hesitation, Yuki took a bite.

CHAPTER SIXTY-FOUR

ELLA

Eleanor swirled around the room, her right hand in Frederick's, his other hand around her waist while they danced and danced and danced. She felt light as her feet traced the marble floor, quick as she went around the room again and again. The room shrank down to only the two of them, and with her head leaning on his shoulder, she felt she was truly happy, and everything was right.

Except things weren't right.

Ella ignored the voice in the back of her mind that tried to break through her bubble, and she wanted to scream at it. She wanted to be happy, and she *was* happy, for once.

She was free now, even though there was a memory that kept trying to break through.

This was where she was supposed to be. Right here, right at this moment, in Frederick's arms. He'd promised to take her away, to keep her safe. Her hand was on his shoulder, the warmth of being so close to him almost intoxicating. She felt she might stop breathing at any minute, her lungs shrinking, not caring that she was out of breath.

She saw only what was right in front of her.

Frederick looked up suddenly, stopping the dance. "I think there's something happening on the other side of the room."

Ella didn't want to hear it. "It's probably nothing."

Frederick frowned. "Let's stop for a minute."

"Now?" she half whined. "We should keep dancing. I don't want to let go."

She smiled, the happiness bubbling to the surface, and she was almost delirious. She wrapped her arm around his, dragging him to the balcony. Frederick shook his head, but he followed her all the same.

"Come with me," she breathed, and he didn't protest any further.

She spun around, dragging him away, half-drunk on Frederick's company, amazed that she was allowed to be at the ball at all. How she'd longed for it. Her heart was light and a little jittery, even though she'd had nothing to drink.

There was something she needed to remember; she was sure of it. But even as she tried, she couldn't grasp it. Maybe it was what had always been—her anxiety, trying to edge its way through in her moment of happiness.

She refused to let it ruin everything.

"You look different," Freddie said as they stepped out on the balcony. The night air held a breeze, and the strong scent of roses carried through.

Again Ella's mind stumbled, remembering something, but not yet.

"I'm free now," Ella said simply, her shoulders dropping.

"Right," he said, and the smile reached his eyes. "I knew I was forgetting something."

The balcony was impossibly dark, but it didn't worry her. Frederick was there, and he locked eyes with her, touching her cheeks, caressing her face with his thumb.

His lips were soft, but Ella was demanding. She opened her mouth to his, hot and hard, feeling the change as his tongue slipped inside her mouth as she stumbled back against the balcony railing. Ella gripped his shirt, pulling him closer, not caring whether she was ruining his clothes, her mouth pressing firm as her breathing grew more ragged.

Frederick kissed her lips, her neck, her jaw, and Ella felt her breath slip each time and pressed herself harder against him. She could feel every part of him against her body, and she whispered his name, softly.

"I still can't believe you came tonight," he said in her ear. "How are you feeling?"

Ella didn't want to talk. She tugged his mouth to hers again, and she felt her entire body pulse in the same frequency of her heart.

"El," Freddie moaned as she nibbled at his ear, and she felt her own power over him, the way that she could make him melt if she wanted to. And Ella wanted to because nothing else in the world mattered. "I hope you're ready for your presents."

"I am," she said, kissing him again. This time, Freddie

stopped talking and pressed her back against the balcony. Ella felt herself slip, his hands at her waist keeping her upright. He lifted her against the balcony railing as she wrapped her legs around him.

Something prickled the back of Ella's neck.

A rose thorn.

She dropped her feet to the floor again, her hand flying to the place where she'd been hurt, and her fingers came back red with blood. Freddie kissed her neck, unaware.

He kissed her lips, and Ella trembled, because there was the snap of memory again, the spike of her anxiety rising. Frederick stopped, looking into her eyes.

"Is something wrong?"

"I—" Ella hesitated. It wasn't until a moment ago. She felt her happiness again. If she looked up to Freddie's eyes again, if he kissed her, she knew she'd put it all behind once and for all. "I don't know."

He looked at her quizzically, his hand still on her waist. "It's okay. You don't need to do anything for me. I'm just glad you're enjoying the party. It's..." He stopped, ruffling his hair, giving out a short laugh. "I can't even believe I didn't say it."

"Say what?" Ella asked, still looking at the blood from where the thorn had prickled her, slowly waking her up.

"Happy birthday."

And suddenly, Ella remembered.

Her birthday. The thorns around the school. The missing pendant. The end of the curse.

Yuki.

Ella jumped, letting go of Freddie's hand.

"I have to go," she said. Her head was spinning, as if a part of her was still trying to draw her back into the dream. But her own heart was hammering inside her ribcage now, her body rebelling as the anxiety pressed in her lungs, and she was suddenly aware of everything around her.

"Now?" Freddie asked, puzzled, but Ella didn't answer him.

She'd already wasted too much time, distracted by whatever magic had been making her mind hazy.

"I'm sorry," she said. "I have to."

Ella ran through the crowded ballroom and out of the back door to the gardens, Frederick running after her. Ella reached the stairway and as she ran, the shoe on her right foot slipped off and fell on the steps.

Freddie stopped but Ella kept going, turning just enough to glimpse at him picking the shoe in his hand. It looked almost transparent under the light. Crystal clear.

Ella ran and didn't look back again.

CHAPTER SIXTY-FIVE

NANI

Nani entered the ballroom and right away noticed the thorns growing outside the windows. It didn't look like any magic she had seen before, and she wondered if the thorns were meant to keep people out or to keep them in.

A shudder ran through her body.

She searched people's faces, pushing through the crowd, but she didn't see Svenja. The best place she could be was here, in a room full of people. Nani didn't see her anywhere. Odilia had challenged her to raise the stakes. To her, this was fun—the tension, Nani's growing desperation. To her, all of this was a game.

All Nani needed to find was one person. She searched the faces, but they all seemed to melt into a blur, her glasses foggy from the sweaty air. Nani's heart beat hard in her chest, her lungs constricted, as she tried to keep herself centered.

If she lost Svenja, she'd lose the one person who told her to stay.

It was that simple. Nani had been waiting for someone who would do what her father had never done—stay.
Someone who liked her enough to want her to stay too.

Nani blinked, and like a mirage, she spotted Svenja—the
girl in white standing in front of her, hair wrapped in a tight
bun, eyes dark with makeup. Svenja smiled.

"Hey," Svenja said. "Why didn't you tell me you were
coming back?"

Something was off. This didn't feel right—Nani couldn't
understand. The girl in front of her was the same one from
the bus stop. Odilia.

Nani shuffled back, stumbling on her feet.

"How did you get here so fast?" Nani demanded fever-
ishly. "Where's Svenja?"

Svenja frowned. "I'm here. What happened? You look sick."

"We have to go somewhere safe," Nani said, the air slipping
out of her. "It was all a trap. She's going to try and hurt you."

Svenja's look was blank. "Nani, calm down."

Svenja embraced her, and Nani let herself get buried in
her shoulders for a moment, feeling the soft skin scented by
the perfume she was wearing. But something piqued Nani's
senses again. This wasn't Svenja's perfume. Nani pushed her
away, confused.

When she stepped away from the embrace, Nani looked
up, and in front of her was another girl in the same white
dress and dark makeup as the girl who had hugged her.

"Nani?" the other girl asked, and for a minute, Nani's
mind went blank.

The two girls looked exactly the same, their likeness blurring together, and she couldn't tell the difference. And as soon as she thought this, the girl in front of her snatched her glasses, making everything clouded.

The not-Svenja stepped back in a hurry, but without her glasses, Nani's vision was only a blur of colors and streams of light. She narrowed her eyes, but the two girls looked exactly the same—their faces just out of focus, enough that she couldn't see the details that would set them apart from one another.

The two girls stood perfectly still, expressionless. One a mirror of the other, doubled in a strange vision.

"It's me," said the Svenja on the right, desperation on her voice. "Why did you come back? I thought you were with your father!"

"She's lying!" the one on the left shouted. "I called you to come back. She wants to kill me."

Nani looked from one to the other, her vision misty, the fog of the ballroom making it all worse. She remembered enough from the story to know what would happen if she picked the wrong girl.

"Please," pleaded the girls together.

"Don't believe a word she says."

"She's the one who set it all up."

"Please, it's me. You know me, Nani."

The girls stepped forward together, glaring at each other. Nani felt her desperation growing, her panic rising as she tried remembering distinguishing marks. She had spent all this time with Svenja, and none of it had been enough.

Because Ella had been right.

Nani hadn't been open to Svenja. Nani was never *here*. She was so frightened that someone would truly know her, know all her fears and her thoughts and still turn away from her, that she'd closed herself off to the experience.

Because Nani Eszes was a coward.

And now it was too late, and she had to make a choice.

"Nani, remember your promise," one of the girls in white said. "Remember the flower?"

"The flower you gave me?" said the other, and Nani realized that even the most intimate moments between her and Svenja had been watched, stolen. "Well, it dried up. You didn't come back in time."

She had to choose.

But did she?

Nani closed her eyes. She couldn't choose the right one. Partly out of fear that she'd choose wrong, but also because she felt she shouldn't *have* to do it.

Nani was a coward, yes, but she was also stubborn as hell. And no one would corner her into making a choice she didn't want to.

Nani stepped back. "Svenja. I know you're afraid. Whichever is the real you. And I know you're hoping that I'm going to choose, but I can't do it."

"Don't you know the difference between me and her?" both of them echoed at the same time, and Nani shook her head.

She wasn't feeling desperate anymore. She was calm, her eyes unfocused.

"I know we've had this conversation before," Nani said. "And it's the truth. I didn't let you in. I like you, but I never really opened myself to you. And what does that even mean? I can't choose, because all this time, I don't really know you."

Admitting it felt like a knife to the gut. She'd lost the battle, her heart wrenched from her chest. She liked Svenja, but Nani had never opened herself enough for this thing between them to grow. She hadn't given it water or nourished it; she'd let it merely survive.

Surviving wasn't enough for love. It had to bloom.

"I can't save you," Nani said, willing the other girl to believe, to see the meaning of her words. She wanted to let the light in. She wanted to open her heart to Svenja, to let herself fall, and if she broke, then she'd break, and that was that. She wanted to be known for who she was. "But you can save yourself."

And as one of the girls stepped forward, and the other stepped back, it was as simple as that for Nani to tell them apart.

"You're the worst girlfriend I've ever had," Svenja told her, and Nani laughed.

It was then that Odilia realized she'd made the wrong move. She took something out of her dress, something sharp and reflecting, and Nani pushed Svenja away on instinct as Odilia attacked.

"I'll have your place," Odilia screamed at Svenja, directing the knife at her cousin. "If it's the last thing I do!"

Svenja yelped, scrambling back, and Nani jumped in front of Odilia to stop her frenzy as Odilia raised her arm a second time. Odilia growled as Nani pushed back, the blade catching her arm and a red cut appearing down it, plunging the room into the smell of blood.

Odilia tried to jump past Nani, but Nani stood her ground. Odilia smiled, and then Nani saw that Odilia's first attack had been successful. Something red was coating Svenja's dress.

Her own blood.

People screamed around them, realizing what was happening, but Nani couldn't falter. The world had shrunk to Nani trying to stop Odilia from murdering them.

Odilia struck again, kicking at Nani's calves, but Nani was stronger, using her weight against her opponent. Svenja was still on the floor.

"Stop this," Nani screamed at the Odilia.

"Over her dead body!"

She made another strike with her knife, and Nani slammed against Odilia, bracing her arms around the girl's waist, trying to stop her rage, pressing her back. Nani felt a flicker of movement behind Odilia, a shadow emerging, and as suddenly as she had started the fight, Odilia crumpled to the floor, her knife falling, clattering loudly.

Rory stood over the crumpled body, her short hair ruffled up, the book in her hand raised high as a weapon, and for a moment, she looked like a vision. It felt surreal, seeing her standing there awake.

"Christ," Rory uttered. "I fall asleep for two weeks and this place goes to hell."

Rory grinned at Nani, who didn't know whether to hug

Rory, hug Svenja, or simply start crying. Rory knelt next to Svenja, sparing Nani the choice.

Svenja's wound didn't look too ugly, but the blood was welling. Nani pressed the wound, and Svenja winced.

"Nice way out," Svenja said, trying to be funny.

Nani smiled, blinking away the tears. "You're not mad?"

Svenja groaned. "I'm pissed. At you. For taking so damn long to realize this."

"You shouldn't be talking."

"You'll hear me for the rest of your life," Svenja said pointedly. "When I'm done with you, when I'm done prying all your secrets and learning everything there is to know about you, Nani Eszes, then, and only then, will I shut up, because I'll be too busy kissing you."

Nani smiled again, and Svenja pulled her in for a kiss. Rory groaned loudly in the background, and Nani helped Svenja get up. The students had all heard the commotion, half the ballroom stopping to look at the scene.

"We have to go," Rory said. "Ella's in danger. And from the looks of it, so is Yuki."

Nani locked eyes with Svenja, who shook her head. Then, Svenja leaned forward and picked something up from the ground. Nani's glasses.

Svenja slid them back on her face.

"I'll be fine," Svenja said. "Nothing but a flesh wound."

"I like you," Nani whispered to her. "And I can't wait for this to be something more."

Svenja smiled and brushed her thumb against Nani's

cheek, their gazes locked together, and Nani didn't want to be the first to look away.

"Me too," said Svenja and kissed her again. "Go. You got other people to save, I assume."

Nani nodded, and Rory stood behind them.

Svenja would be fine. They would begin again, the right way. They would get another chance.

But before all of that, Nani had to help her friends.

For the first time, in the midst of this chaos, Nani knew where her place really was.

CHAPTER SIXTY-SIX

YUKI

CHAPTER SIXTY-SEVEN

ELLA

Ella ran through the forest of thorns.

They cut deep into her skin while she tried to break through, her hands and arms blocking the worst of the blows from reaching her eyes. Her arms and legs were covered in scratches, and one thorn had cut straight through her right cheek, a red line forming amidst the freckles.

Still, Ella barely felt them as she rushed, her dress tearing as some of the fabric stuck in the thickets. She hurried, unstoppable, until she was out of the prison and into the garden again.

She stopped, still wearing only one shoe, and the first thing she saw was the fallen body, the apple next to it.

"No!" Ella screamed, but it got caught in her throat, and then she was running forward, her heart so loud that she couldn't hear anything else.

She dropped on her knees and cradled Yuki, pulling

Yuki's head in her lap. Yuki's eyes were closed, and her chest didn't move. Ella felt her entire body shudder, tears falling freely down her cheeks.

"No," Ella whimpered, holding Yuki against her. "Not you too. Please."

Ella choked on her words, trying to bite back the tears, trying to find air within her lungs, but Yuki remained limp. Ella's shoulders fell as the whole world was taken from beneath her feet.

She didn't wipe her tears. She could barely think—and Yuki was—Yuki was—

"Shut up!" Ella roared loudly, her anger rising. "You can't say it! It's not true!"

She wiped Yuki's hair out of her face, sliding the black strands behind her ears. Yuki looked so peaceful that Ella wanted to laugh. It was so unlike her. A sob caught in her throat, and when she looked up, Reyna was there, stopping in her tracks when she saw Yuki's body. Shock came across her face, but Ella knew better than to believe it.

"You," Ella accused. "You did this."

Reyna opened her mouth, but no sound came out.

Ella got up, carefully leaving Yuki's body in the grass. Inside her bag, Ella found one of her knitting needles. She held on to it, fists clenched, the closest thing to a weapon she had.

Ella wanted to laugh at the ridiculousness of what she was doing. A girl who couldn't fight, trying to protect the only thing that she had left. Ella stood in front of Yuki, weapon raised, and didn't let Reyna step forward.

"Eleanor, listen to me," Reyna started, but Ella shook her head. She wouldn't listen. She had enough—all her friends were lost to this curse.

Ari. Rory. And now, Yuki.

No more.

"I hope you're happy," shouted Ella, her mouth tasting the bitterness of bile mixed with the salt and blood from her face. "This is what you wanted."

"This was never my intention," she said, her voice breaking, her eyes welling. "Yuki is my girl. Don't you understand?"

She stepped forward, and Ella raised her knitting needle.

"Don't come any closer."

"Let me see her. I need to—*please.*"

Someone else came from the shadows of the school, but Ella wasn't surprised to see Mrs. Blumstein there. By her side, there was Miss Bagley and Ms. Lenz, the three of them with the same bright green eyes.

"We're sorry," Mrs. Blumstein said quietly, her voice even. "No one wanted for it to happen this way."

Ella shook her head, her arm still raised.

What did all of them know of the loss she was feeling? What did they know of missing half their hearts? What did they know of being young and having nothing to hold onto except this one good thing, even when it could turn terrible, even when it could have killed her?

Ella would have died for Yuki. A thousand times. As many times as it took.

Reyna stepped toward Yuki once again, but Ella didn't falter.

Maybe the damage Ella could inflict wouldn't be much. She'd inevitably fail—she could see the magic hanging in the air. The curse, the cursed, and Ella. She was the weak link. She wasn't brave and bold like Rory, smart and determined like Nani, or protective and true like... She couldn't bring herself to finish.

She had no magic.

She was completely and terribly ordinary.

"Step aside, Eleanor," Reyna ordered. "This is not your fight."

"Yes, it is," Ella said firmly, although her knees were shaking, and her bare foot was trembling. "I won't let you. You've caused enough pain."

"Ella," Reyna said, her voice calm. "You're going to hurt yourself. We can still fix this. I won't touch her. I *can't*."

"Eleanor, only you have the power to finish this," Mrs. Blumstein's voice called.

Ella's gaze turned to her, and suddenly, with a wave of the teacher's finger, green mist enveloped the needle in Ella's hand, and it became heavier, longer, the shape rippling while she held on to it.

When the mist dissipated, Ella was holding a sword.

"May it strike true to your enemy's heart," Mrs. Blumstein said.

And as if the sword itself was guiding her, Ella knew what she had to do. She'd watched Rory enough times to know, so it was simply an imitation. She raised the sword above her head, and Reyna shielded herself with the air.

Ella clashed against the invisible barrier, making Reyna back away, letting the sword do the work by itself.

"Eleanor, you have to listen to me!" Reyna shouted as the sword crashed against her side, as she raised an invisible shield to stop the blow. Ella couldn't stop, her muscles moving on her own. "They are controlling you! We can still save her!"

Ella didn't falter on her determination, her body moving quickly as she stepped forward, as she moved with a force other than her own. She felt the same strange, hazy mist around her mind, a blur that overcame her thinking capabilities, trying to numb her, propelling her toward a single goal.

She slashed the sword and Reyna raised her hand, pushing Ella back. Ella tumbled, getting up again, sword raised, and this time, she hit Reyna even faster. Left, right, left and left again. The blade crashed against the air as Ella's rhythm increased, and she was starting to strike before Reyna could block her attacks.

Ella cornered her against the palace wall, her anger and loss driving her.

Reyna tried to get back up, but she stumbled against the stone wall, falling to the ground. She was cornered, defenseless, scrambling.

"Kill her!" Mrs. Blumstein's voice rang through the garden, and for a moment, Ella stopped, the sword pointed right at Reyna's throat. "End this!"

Ella looked at Reyna's eyes, her tears choking.

"Please," Reyna murmured, looking up. "She's the only thing that I have."

Ella held the sword tight, willing herself to push through.

Reyna's eyes were wide, and Ella could see the same thing she felt reflected on Reyna's own face—helplessness, fear, and most of all, grief, something that couldn't be explained or spoken by any who hadn't felt it. A grief no one would ever comprehend. An inherent sadness at their loss, and Ella realized she couldn't do it.

There had been enough deaths. Enough grief. She wouldn't add more suffering to this terrible story.

Ella lowered her sword.

"I said kill her!" Mrs. Blumstein shrieked.

"No," Ella said calmly, and then her body was free of the sword's spell, of the magnetism of her rage.

She sunk the blade into the grass in front of her. She wouldn't pick the weapon again.

She turned to Mrs. Blumstein.

"Enough," Ella said, her lungs aching, her tears threatening to fall again. "I've had enough. I don't want to be a part of this cycle."

She turned around to look back at Yuki. Ella fell on her knees again, not having the strength to get back up. Her muscles were sore, her lungs tired, her body aching, but worse of all, there was an emptiness inside her chest that would never be whole.

She didn't care who had been cursed. She didn't care why. All she felt was the aching pain of her heart.

A cackle in the sky echoed like thunder gathering, and Ella saw that the three teachers were facing Reyna, still crumpled where she'd fallen, her eyes wide as she continued to look at Yuki.

"It's time to end it," said Mrs. Blumstein.

And suddenly, Ella knew she had gotten all of it wrong.

CHAPTER SIXTY-EIGHT

RORY

Rory went in first, wishing she'd brought her sword to cut through the forest of thorns. She knocked them out of the way with the Black Book, trampling every obstacle in her way as if she were a tank. Nani walked behind her with the other book. Rory knew not all battles required force, but this one felt right.

Rory's breathing was labored, her muscles tense from her sleep. She knew what would be waiting for them in the garden, and she hoped it wasn't too late. For the first time in her life, Rory worried that she wasn't going to save everyone. She'd thought she didn't need anyone before, and she had been so, so wrong.

"So what you're telling me is that it was the teachers?" Nani asked behind her as Rory smashed another inconvenient rose bush that stood in their way. The path looked used, as if someone had come through here only moments before, but the thorns seemed to be growing back swiftly.

"Yeah," Rory agreed. "And I think Penelope knew it was them too. She was working for them all this time."

"They knew she was an imposter," Nani mused, and Rory could almost hear Nani's mind racing with the possibilities. "She was blackmailing them. She kept the book, and in exchange they wouldn't tell who she was or that she'd murdered the real Penelope. As long as she'd help them."

Rory shook her head, concentrating on the path ahead. They couldn't know all of Penelope's motives for doing what she did, even when she was just protecting herself. She'd killed Ari only to keep her own ending, and Rory wasn't going to forgive that easily.

"And they want the books back," Nani said again. "Which means the books really are the keys to breaking the curse."

Rory risked a look behind her to look at Nani. Her curls kept catching on the thorns, making them puff around her head even more. They both had small scratches on their arms, but Rory had longed for this—she didn't want to go to sleep again. She wanted to feel alive.

"I think so," Rory said. "But I don't know if we have all the pieces right."

"They're the ones responsible," said Nani. "But why?"

Just then, there was a scream from the garden. Nani's eyes widened, and Rory raised her head in alarm. She recognized the voice.

Rory broke into a run, breaking through to the garden to see a strange scene in front of her—Yuki on the ground, not the final way of the curse. Ella stood over her, wearing only one shoe, and Mrs. Blumstein stretched her hands in the direction of a figure that seemed to be floating in the air, and only then Rory realized that it was Reyna.

She ran forward.

"Let her go!" Rory roared, and Mrs. Blumstein turned around.

Ella turned too, surprise and shock on her face.

"You're awake," the three teachers said in unison. They stepped forward in her direction as if they shared only one mind. Reyna crumpled back to the ground, her face red. "You shouldn't be."

"Fuck yes I'm awake," Rory said. "And you can bet I'm fixing this mess."

Ella rushed over to Reyna's side. Reyna's eyes were closed, and there were red marks around her throat. As Rory stepped closer to join Ella, she noticed the sword in the ground. Just then, Nani caught up with them, emerging from the thorns. Rory took a deep breath, and she exchanged one look with Ella, hoping they were all together in this.

Yuki was still on the ground, and Rory prayed that she was just fast asleep.

"You cannot fix this," the three teachers said, their eyes glowing a bright shade of green. Rory didn't flinch; she'd come all the way, and she wasn't scared of magic tricks. "This is not your curse to break."

Rory understood that now. It had never been theirs.

She looked at Reyna, trying to comprehend how the rest of the puzzle fit together. She didn't know if she felt relieved or not, or even if it mattered who was at the center of the curse.

"You won't stop us," the teachers chanted in unison, their eyes glowing.

"Well, maybe not me," said Rory, shrugging. "I kind of always knew I wasn't going to be the one to do it."

And just like that, Rory threw the Black Book to Ella and stepped over to the sword. Ella stood behind Rory and next to Nani, who held the White Book.

The three teachers started glowing, the strange green mist wrapping them, and, as if they were only one entity, they started melting into each other—they changed color and shape, their necks stretching upwards, their faces changing. A roar echoed across the garden, the earth trembling as they grew, amber eyes glowing, with long snouts and wicked glares.

Rory was standing in front of a three-headed dragon.

"You cannot break the curse," the dragon said, the three heads speaking together, their voices echoing through the thorns. "You will not interfere with the ways of magic."

The two girls behind her faltered, stepping back as the dragon rose, and Rory stood paralyzed. The adrenaline rushed through her hands, and she didn't move.

Rory knew somehow, although her destiny had always been uncertain as she was always scared of becoming the ruler she was meant to be, that the roles she played didn't matter in the end. Because now she saw that no matter what her role was, she was always going to do it. No matter what it was. Rory *faced* it.

She wasn't weak for faltering. She was strong for going through with it no matter how scared she felt.

Rory grabbed the hilt of the sword and pulled it from the ground, raising it in the air above her head, feeling all her muscles stretch, letting all that she was settle into place. She was going to do what she needed to: protect her friends and change the course of their destiny together.

She would do her best.

The dragon roared in front of her, menacing, frightening, impossibly big. She felt the sword in her arm, its magic fueling her body and casting a protective barrier around her—and the magic felt like Ella, like Yuki, like Nani. Like coming home.

"What are you waiting for?" yelled Nani behind her.

Rory turned her head over her shoulder. "I was really hoping for a She-Ra makeover. Fuck this."

Rory swiveled to the dragon, a wicked grin spreading across her face. She flexed her fingers on the handle one by one.

She wasn't afraid.

She charged the dragon, sword in hand.

CHAPTER SIXTY-NINE

Rory screamed as she charged the dragon, the sword swinging in the monster's direction. The dragon was a humongous thing, and Nani could barely believe it wasn't her mind playing tricks. She'd wake up any minute now, and instead of dead girls, dragons, and curses, she was going to find herself one of the chairs on the beach, passed out from sun exposure.

One of the dragon's paws smashed the glass dome of the castle's conservatory, the forest of thorns coming undone before its feet. One of the heads turned to face Rory, breathing a stream of fire. Nani watched as Rory maneuvered around the flames, unfazed and unhurt. The sword, somehow, was protecting her.

Beside her, Ella held the Black Book, watching as Rory battled the dragon single-handedly.

"Will you two hurry the fuck up?" Rory screamed as she

leaped around the garden, rolling to avoid a dragon's maw. "I haven't got all night!"

Somehow, Rory was keeping its full attention, and it didn't turn even one of its heads in the direction of the other girls.

Nani looked around wildly. Reyna was still on the ground, bleeding from her wound, but there was no time to worry about that. Nani knelt next to where Yuki lay, grabbing her hand as her father had taught her, as she tried to drown out the noise around her.

Ella fell to her knees on Yuki's other side. Yuki looked hauntingly beautiful, so close to her story counterpart that they could be one and the same.

"The book is the key," Nani repeated under her breath, trying to figure out what they'd been missing. Yuki didn't seem to be breathing. When she opened Yuki's hand, there was Reyna's broken pendant.

So it wasn't part of their curse, after all.

Nani looked from Yuki to Ella, and then to Rory, who was still fighting, relentless, a brush of red hair contrasting with the darkness around them. The dragon roared, and Nani's heart tightened. They had only one chance to end it all.

The necklace looked devoid of life, as if its inherent glow was gone. But then again, maybe it had. Maybe that had been what Nani had felt: the magic going back to Grimrose, returning to its rightful owners.

"I don't understand," Nani said, her voice cracking. She felt like she could grasp it, the answers within her reach. They had spent months gathering evidence. But maybe that was the problem.

Magic wasn't logical. It didn't have strict rules; it flowed through everything. It was the great adventure that Nani had sought, and now that it was happening, she still didn't know her role in all of it.

Nani looked up and met Ella's eyes in desperation. Yuki was almost gone, and they had both books, and they still didn't know what to do. Nani wished everything could be simpler, but wishes meant nothing now. Wishes never came true.

"Something is missing," Nani said. "It's both books, and—and—"

She tried getting her brain to work, to think logically, her gaze landing on Reyna. And where she looked, Ella followed her gaze.

"There's one last thing," Ella said. "If it's Reyna's curse."

Both girls looked down at Yuki, watching her still body.

"It's the blood," Nani said, her mind cracking like a whip. "Yuki's blood. We have to bind the books together. They have to be united again. Just like the copy from Munich."

Behind them, Rory was fighting, the dragon shaking the earth. One of the heads was sneaking closer to where the girls knelt, but Rory was quick to slice across its neck, green blood oozing and falling to the ground. The blood burned the garden, smoke rising.

Just then, Nani felt the smallest stirring from Yuki's body.

"She's not dead," Nani said. "She's not gone yet, do you understand?"

Realization dawned on Ella's face. Nani couldn't wait for her to catch up with her frenzy of thoughts, so she took a page from the White Book, held its edge out, and drew it across Yuki's arm.

The cut was clean. The blood welled up on her pale skin, and the book's pages rippled together.

"What do we do?" Ella asked.

"Bind the books back together," Nani said.

Ella looked shaky as she took a needle and a thread from her purse. She smeared her hands in Yuki's blood, covering her hands in red.

Ella's hands were slick with blood, and when she moved to the book, ripping out a page, it tore with ease.

Nani repeated the process, dampening her hands with Yuki's blood, the smell of metal hanging in the air. She took the books apart, tearing out the pages and remounting them in order as quickly as she could, story by story, and then Ella took the needle thread, dipping it in Yuki's blood—same as their hands. The needle flowed through the thick papers as if it were water, the pages coming together to form a single book.

When it was done, Nani breathed, checking Yuki's pulse again, feeling it so faint even though she still couldn't detect her breathing. She seemed to be in a state of suspension so close to death.

Nothing had changed with Yuki.

"It didn't work," Ella muttered, so quiet that Nani thought she hadn't heard it.

Nani looked at the book, wondering where she'd missed a

step. She was so sure that the book had to be complete. That it had to be made whole, and if she could just grab it, just rewrite it, and then—

It was a book of stories, Nani thought. Stories that came true.

They had been following the book to the letter, their fates bound without change. It couldn't be destroyed—but it could be written anew.

Her father was right. All she could do was write her own story. It was the only thing that would break the cycle.

Except Nani didn't know how to do that, exactly— she'd been alone for far too long. She wouldn't know how to begin. But there was someone else who could do it. Someone who Nani knew would do a far better job than she ever could.

"You need to write another story," Nani said, handing the book to Ella.

Ella looked up. Her fingers were tapping unconsciously on her leg. Another roar echoed through the gardens, so powerful it made them shudder. Rory wasn't going to be able to hold the dragon back for much longer.

A breath of fire roared above them, and Nani rifled through her pockets until she found what she was looking for. A pen.

She handed it to Ella, who only stared back with her wide and frightened hazel eyes.

"Your turn," Nani said.

"I can't," Ella said. "I'm not—I don't have any magic."

Nani grabbed Ella's hand and wrapped her fingers around the pen.

"You can," Nani said. "Write us a new ending. I figured this out, but you have to do your part. All of us have."

"Why me?" Ella whispered to her. "I haven't ever done anything—that's not me, that's not what I do."

"You did everything, Ella," Nani snapped, because she knew all their roles, all the places where they stood. They all worked together to protect the same thing, to live through this. It had meant to arrive at this moment, and Nani's heart was glad that this wasn't a betrayal. She could still hope for the good ending. "You were kind, and you believed we could break it more than any of us. You never wavered. That's why you *have* to do it. None of us had the faith. You can change the book. You can write us another story."

Nani's hand was still wrapped around Ella's, and when she let go, Ella didn't drop the pen.

Even when there was darkness, there was still Ella's light. If someone could change things, it would be Ella. Even when Nani couldn't see a way out herself, even when all of them had lost, there was still someone remaining.

None of them were meant to break the curse because none of them believed they could.

Except Ella.

"It's time," Nani said. "Save us all."

CHAPTER SEVENTY

Ella's fingers fumbled with the pen as she raised her trembling hand. Everything around her roared—the fire, the dragon, Rory, and Nani, who was pressing her hands against Yuki's chest to check her pulse and keep her heart beating.

Ella felt the tears streaming down her cheeks again as she put the pen to the paper, staring at the pages on the newly bound book. It was Reyna's curse, and there was a part of her that knew why Reyna had been cursed. Why Yuki had magic. Why she wasn't in the original book. There was one answer staring at her: a girl from a fairy tale.

A girl who had been created from magic, like her fairy tale, which was a mistake that the curse had been made to correct. Ella forgave Reyna for it. All of them made mistakes— some bigger than others, and sometimes, they took a long time to atone.

For all that Reyna did, Ella thought that hundreds of years was penance enough.

Maybe it hadn't started with the girls, but only one girl, and that was enough. And maybe, by being brought to the castle by the curse, finding each other had given them new strength. Reyna couldn't break her curse because she was alone.

But Ella wasn't. Ella had never been alone.

"Stay with me," Ella muttered to Yuki, breathing her words, dipping the pen in Yuki's blood. Her hands and dress were stained red, but she still held the pen firmly.

Ella wasn't alone because she had her friends. Yuki, Rory, Nani. And even Ari wasn't alone.

Now Ella would set them all free.

She picked up the pen, and—

"Shut up," she said to the narrator. "I'm the one telling the story now."

Once upon a time there lived a young girl who had made a terrible mistake. She wanted to be loved so much that she'd created someone to fill the place she thought was missing. The three keepers of magic had never forgiven her for it. She tried to tamper with life and death, and nothing could atone for the sin she had committed.

So she was cursed, and lived the rest of her days to see the person she loved die countless times.

Ella breathed hard. Yuki's blood made the pages of the

book light up, blurring her words, but she didn't care that her handwriting was ugly and that she couldn't see. The book was magic, and it would understand. She was pouring all of her will into it.

Once upon a time there lived a girl who was born of magic. She had done nothing wrong but still she had to pay for her stepmother's sins. She had been doomed to die by the hands of the curse, over and over again. She was scared of dying either way, so she embraced the parts she thought no one would love so that when she was gone, no one would miss her.

Ella didn't stop there. She would rewrite everything—she had to. She had to make all of it right, and she was the only one who could. They were trusting her with it. The girl who couldn't fight. The girl who couldn't stand up for herself.

Once upon a time in a real-life kingdom, there lived a young princess who thought she could do everything by herself. Maybe she could, and maybe she couldn't—and out of fear of failing and being weak, sometimes, she wouldn't even try. She shut herself inside her own body, until one day she had shut it to the point where no one could bring her back to the living.
She fell asleep and nobody could wake her.

She kept writing. The page was alight. She kept dipping

the pen back in Yuki's blood to write, holding the book. The light started radiating from the page, embracing the world around them in pulses.

Once upon a time in a kingdom far, far away there lived a young girl who wanted a home and a place to be herself. She wandered and wandered, crossed the borders of all kingdoms, but she could not find a cottage, a mansion, or a castle that offered her what she wanted. She crossed oceans and mountains, but still she was alone, because the walls she'd built were around herself, and no one else was going to tear them down for her.

Write the truth. Release it. The light was covering the gardens now, streaming.

Once upon a time in a kingdom not so far from here there lived a young girl mistreated by her family. She thought it was her own fault that she did not deserve her freedom, that she was unimportant enough that her life didn't matter. So she didn't do anything to change it.

And it was time.

Once upon a time in a kingdom right here and right now there lived hundreds of young girls who led different lives, and all of them were dragged into a curse. They lived their lives oblivious to their timed deaths, the circumstances that brought them together to live out their fate. None of them could be saved because they did not matter—they were only collateral damage. They could not be saved because their lives were insignificant.

But that wasn't true. Ella gripped the pen tighter, the world a blur of brightness around her.

Once upon a time there were four girls who mostly had nothing in common except that they had all been cursed without their knowledge. They were all different, but there was something that bound them together, something that was stronger than magic or curses, something greater than any other force in the world.

Once upon a time, these four girls believed in each other but not in themselves.

Ella's tears had long stopped bothering her, but now she wasn't crying because of her situation or how deep she had sunk. She was crying for what she always had and would always have with her. The invisible bond between them—their laughter on a sunny day, the way they could link their arms in the corridor, and the way they chose to care.

Her friends.

Once upon a time there were girls who believed they could destroy a curse. A curse that was not theirs and was not in their power to destroy. Once upon a time there was no balance between light and dark, life and death. Once upon a time there were four girls who stepped up to the curse that wasn't theirs, and they laughed in the face of Fate.

Once upon a time, Fate watched as the four girls laughed in its face and let them get away with it because they had power that extended beyond its realm.

Once upon a time, there were friends who stood together and made a promise to save each other.

Ella could almost see the end now, her muscles starting to relax, because now the darkness was past. Ella could only see light from the book that had cursed their lives because she was changing it.

Ella was doing magic.

Once upon a time, there was a girl with skin as white as snow, lips as red as blood, hair as black as ebony, who gave her life to end a curse in the name of her friends.

Once upon a time there was a girl with hair the color of the morning dawn and as fierce as one of Arthur's knights, and instead of waiting for her true love to kiss her awake, she woke herself.

Once upon a time there was a girl as beautiful as the waves of the sea and with a taste of adventure, and she found that after searching for so long, there wasn't one place where she belonged. She belonged to no one but herself, and her home was her own heart.

Once upon a time there was a girl with ash on her face and rubble on her clothes, worthless, sad, and broken beyond repair, who believed she could save everyone but didn't think she was worth saving herself. Until the day she looked and found that she wasn't broken at all.

A white glowing force emanated from the book as more of Yuki's blood poured into the pages. The glow started circling around the garden, tendrils of light touching the ground, the thorns, the castle, and spread into the air, the night glowing ablaze. It was too bright for Ella to see, but she didn't care because she had a task.

And she'd be damned if she wasn't writing a happy ending.

Once upon a time, there were people who would tell all girls that they meant nothing and that friendship wasn't going to save them, but all of them were wrong.

Once upon a time, it was believed there could be no happily ever after.

Once upon a time, there was a girl who didn't care about living happily ever after—only that she lived.

Once upon a time, there were friends who believed.

And they believed in everyone, in every single girl who was ever cursed, that they could all be forgiven. That

*they could mend themselves. But most importantly, all
of them believed they could live.*

Live, live, live...

The world flashed in blinding white light, taking over everything. Ella dropped the pen, and winds whipped from her hands. The book rose into the air, and the pages started shredding themselves, a storm of paper raining down from the sky. It was over; she'd done it.

There was only one thing that was left for her to do.

Ella needed to believe.

And so, she did.

CHAPTER SEVENTY-ONE

YUKI

Yuki could feel the change as it swept over the gardens, a light that blazed through everything in its path, tearing down the very fabric that the world had been built on, shredding it into pieces as the book itself was torn apart. Yuki could feel it in her bones—the change in the magic so obvious the world had to be dead not to feel it.

Suddenly, her body convulsed, sucking away the rest of the darkness, and just like that, her lungs were filling again with air, the magic surrounding her made from the same substance as she was. Even though she was flesh, no doubt, there was still a part of her that seemed to remember that the magic came from the words.

Yuki opened her eyes.

There was rain falling from the sky, and it took a moment to realize it wasn't rain at all. It was fragments of the pages, from the books, falling endlessly through the breeze. She blinked, and the first person she saw, kneeling by her side, was Ella, her hands slick and covered with blood.

Ella had broken the curse.

Yuki propped herself on her elbows, trying to make her body work again. Ella turned to her, ghostly pale, tears and dirt and blood caked on her face. She opened her mouth, and no sound came out, and Yuki felt a lump in her throat.

"You're alive," Ella whispered, as if afraid that the spell might come undone.

And then Ella tackled Yuki into a hug, falling back on the ground, arms tightly wrapped around her. Yuki hugged Ella back, her muscles hurting from the strength of it. She was afraid to let go, closing her eyes tight as Ella laughed and cried on her shoulder.

She didn't know who let go first. It didn't matter. Yuki said, "You broke it."

Ella smiled. "We did."

Around them, the world had collapsed. Yuki noticed it now: the gardens trampled, the smell of burning in the air. When Yuki turned her head, she saw that Rory was pointing a sword at Mrs. Blumstein's neck, the other two teachers fallen by her side.

Yuki refused to feel sorry for them. They had caused endless pain for so many generations, had caused death in the name of protecting something that they didn't understand.

Yuki got up, feeling the magic still searing through her, still with her, despite herself. It was over now. Yuki walked with Ella and Nani by her side, all of them in silence as they crossed the garden to where Rory was standing.

Mrs. Blumstein eyed Rory's sword. Rory was bruised and dirty, with scorch marks on her clothes, but her grip was firm, her blue eyes intense. The other teachers seemed to recover their consciousness after the magic had ripped through them all. Yuki looked around for Reyna but didn't see her.

Mrs. Blumstein raised her chin as Yuki approached.

"Is this the time to plead for mercy?" she asked, her voice still on edge, the magic still wavering behind her eyes.

"Mercy is for Ella to have and me to ignore," Rory snarled. "Tell me one reason to lower this sword."

Ella didn't contradict Rory. For the first time, Yuki saw how Ella's features had hardened, as if she was becoming another person. Still, Yuki saw the softness in her eyes that had always been a part of her.

"If we spare you, we get nothing," Nani said. "No guarantee you won't do it again."

"The balance of the world—" Ms. Lenz started saying.

"There's no balance," Yuki interrupted, speaking loud and clear. She was taller than her friends, standing apart, and Yuki felt the weight of the broken curse on her shoulders. "A mistake shouldn't be paid with the price of a life. Not anybody's life."

Yuki gestured around herself. The ground scorched, the gardens destroyed, and she couldn't see the point of all of it.

"I gave my life so the cycle would end," Yuki said. "And you did nothing. You changed nothing."

"I—"

"Enough!" Yuki screamed, and the scream echoed through the birds, making the trees shiver, and all around them, the magic glowed alive. Alive because she was one with it. She wasn't simply using it anymore; it was all a part of her. "Stop making excuses. All of us made mistakes. It's time you own up to yours."

Yuki wanted this to end. She was tired of all of it, but still, she kept going. Now she knew the nature of the curse, the nature of how far they would go to protect themselves, to perpetuate another cycle of punishment for the one thing they considered wrong.

Except Reyna hadn't been wrong.

Reyna had wanted someone to understand who she was, someone to be with her, because she didn't want to be alone. Yuki could understand that best of all, as she was still scared that all her jagged edges were pushing people away.

But they hadn't. Ella had saved her, she had saved Ella, and this cycle kept on running because this one was a good one. No matter how many times it happened, they would find a way to save each other.

"You didn't only curse all of us to live like this," Yuki said, and the teachers didn't dare to speak a word. She felt her magic growing and expanding, crushing things in its path. It was freeing because it wasn't an oppressive sort of magic. It was the freedom of letting it all go, of accepting things for what they were. "But it was your own insistence for the curse to work, for no girl to escape. One single life beyond your

432

grasp would be too much. Better for Reyna to know that no one could live happily, that not a single girl could escape the curse, make her think that it was all her fault."

Yuki didn't know what else to say, her mouth going dry as she thought of the countless girls that came before them, wrapped up all in the same story and having to die, not getting a chance to find a way out. Even for Penelope, who had tried getting her own happy ending the only way she knew, and even then, even after her tale was over, still fallen prey to it.

But even when the curse had doomed them, it had also given them a way out. In its strength lied its weakness. The infinitely repeating nature of the curse always allowed another chance. They only had to do it right one time.

"But this wasn't on Reyna," Yuki finally said. "You cannot blame the victim for the way of the curse. All these girl's deaths, all this cycle, it's all on you. All of it."

Even with the sword pointed right at her chest, Mrs. Blumstein's face of scorn was fearless, and then she started to laugh.

"What are you going to do, child?" she asked. "You're only a figment of a story. You were one of the vessels we used for the curse. How long do you think you will survive it now that the book and the curse's magic is destroyed?"

It was Ella who spoke. "She'll survive because I believe in it."

Mrs. Blumstein sharp eyes turned to Ella, but Ella didn't falter. Ella seemed relaxed, calm after the storm had passed. Yuki turned her head just slightly, and Ella's eyes met her own. Ella offered her hand, and Yuki took it, squeezing it tight.

"You made a promise," Yuki said. "I bound you to your word, and you broke it. You had no intention of breaking the curse even after I sacrificed myself because you were still righteous in your punishment. I'll not hear your excuses because there aren't any."

Mrs. Blumstein started to speak, and Yuki felt the magic that was trying to regain control there, but she wasn't going to let it. She gathered all of it around her, from the breaking of the curse, from the light inside her, from her own creation and existence, because she hadn't *learned* magic. She had been born from it; she lived it.

"Silence!" Yuki said, the words echoing again around them as the world changed and the curse was buried, as everything old started to wither, as they finally, finally swept the rest of the curse away and made a new world, full of possibilities.

Yuki faced the three witches, and she didn't yield.

"Who are you?" Mrs. Blumstein asked, fear in her eyes as she realized what Yuki was truly capable of.

"I am my mother's child," Yuki said simply, the only answer she had to that question. "And you're going to pay for what you did to her."

Yuki took a deep breath, and the magic bent to her will.

"I curse you," Yuki said. The words made her shudder as she held on to the whole world around her, because the world was her vessel, the magic boiling beneath the surface of her skin, inside her blood. "I curse you to live with the knowledge that what you've done was your choice. I curse you to live with the consequences of your actions."

A scream broke through the silence as Mrs. Blumstein's skin started to burn, as she started shifting her shape again to come for Yuki.

Rory stepped in before she moved. And Ella. And Nani.

A human barrier protecting Yuki.

Something Reyna had never had. Something Yuki could do differently now.

"I curse you to pay back in the same coin," she said quietly. "Not one thousand times and a thousand-fold, but only once. You only need to pay it once."

Another scream echoed throughout the garden, a terrible, terrifying gurgle of a soul that was burning. The three women before them stumbled back, disappearing into the forest of thorns, back into the shadows where they'd come from, the shriek still chilling the air.

Yuki felt weak as she finished.

But she didn't feel sorry.

She stood in the silence left behind, the magic still burning through the grounds of Grimrose. Yuki was burning with it, finally done with all the pretenses.

CHAPTER SEVENTY-TWO

RORY

They'd broken the curse.

Rory couldn't believe it. She looked around the trampled gardens, at the bruises she'd been collecting from the moment she'd woken up, and she knew how sore she would feel when she rested again. She didn't want to go back to sleep, not after facing what she'd faced.

Holding a sword, fighting an entire dragon.

"Not to be dramatic," Rory said, "but this was the best day of my life."

Ella gave her a scathing look. Yuki sighed, turning, and asked, "Where's Reyna?"

They found her where she'd been left, leaning against the side of the castle, looking almost as pale as Yuki. Nani knelt next to her, putting a hand to her wrist.

"You hit her pretty hard," Nani said to Ella, whose face went red.

"I didn't mean to," she replied. "It's the sword."

Rory had felt it when she used it, making her strokes more powerful, her blows forceful, as if the sword was driving itself.

"Speaking of which," Rory said, and as she handed it back to Ella, the sword disappeared, and in its place was a simple knitting needle. "Are you kidding me? The witches turned your needle into a sword?" Rory turned to Yuki. "Okay, when am *I* getting a sword?"

"You already own plenty of weapons."

"But Ella got a new cool one."

"Because I'm not going to use it."

"You do know using it is the point of swords?"

"No one else is getting a sword," Yuki said emphatically.

"Will all of you shut it?" Nani said, putting an end to the squabbling, and Rory was almost glad to see everything back to normal again. They had won the battle. They had broken the curse. And although everything was different, everything was still the same. "She's coming around."

They all went quiet as Reyna's eyelids fluttered. Rory narrowed her eyes toward Reyna, wondering what they would see once she woke up.

"Yuki?" It was the first thing to come out of Reyna's mouth as she opened her eyes. "You're alive!"

Reyna motioned to get up, but Nani held her down, not letting her.

"Ella broke the curse," Yuki said, her face straight, and Rory could see there was a turmoil of thoughts behind Yuki's dark eyes. Rory could still feel the magic that surrounded them, ashes in all their clothes from the burning thorns, and Yuki was at the center of all of it. "They're all gone."

Reyna blinked, as if understanding at last. Rory really wished she could do the same. It felt too surreal, too wild. All of Ari's notes, all the deaths, everything over, just like that.

"Thank you," Reyna said, turning to Ella. "Breaking the curse..." Reyna's voice broke, and Rory understood that she'd felt the weight of it all. For the first time, Reyna didn't look like their beautiful, irreproachable headmistress. She looked as young as they were, scared and alone. "I cannot ever repay you."

Ella's face blushed, and she looked down at her feet, one still bare. "It's nothing, really."

"It was," Reyna said. "A debt I owe all of you. You have saved my life. And you..." She looked at Yuki as she said the next sentence. "You have saved everything I care for."

They felt the echoing of the silence.

"If there's anything I can do," Reyna said. "Anything in my power."

They all looked at each other; they hadn't done it to get repaid, not like the knights in the tales who always sought a reward.

And Rory, for that, was glad of it.

She didn't want to be rewarded for doing the right thing. The right thing, breaking the curse and being free, was enough. They had done it together. Each of them playing a different part, they'd done it hand in hand.

Rory looked up at the castle, and then it hit her.

"Actually," she said, "there is something."

Reyna turned to Rory, examining her face. For the first time, Rory didn't feel like turning away, trying to hide her face and who she was.

"I don't think they need to remember," Rory said, gesturing to the castle and thinking of Ari, of Penelope, of all the people in the castle who were under the curse's influence. "I mean, they definitely have heard things by now. There was a dragon in the gardens. It's not like we can hide it. But it's not fair to them. They'll think they have been played their whole lives, and..." She felt the words catch in her throat. She couldn't remember the last time she'd spoken this much or if someone had been listening so intently to her. "We know about the curse, and it was our burden to bear. But they deserve better."

Rory took a deep breath, and when she met Ella's eyes, Ella was smiling kindly at her.

"They'll forget," Reyna promised. "By morning, everything will go back to normal."

Rory inclined her head, lips tight, and she thought of everyone in the castle. "I have to go."

"I'm going with you," Nani said promptly. "I have to check on Svenja."

"I guess Pippa needs an explanation on why I ran like a lunatic," Rory sighed.

"Isn't she used to that already?" Ella asked, eyebrows rising, and Rory glared at her.

"I'm staying," Yuki said. "I'll get Reyna inside. All of you can go."

They all looked between each other, and Rory glanced at Yuki, but she didn't look restless. She was peaceful, but still standing a little farther apart from her stepmother.

Eventually, Rory would get all the answers, fit in all the little pieces. But for now, she was glad that they were all whole, that they had all survived, and that they were standing stronger together.

Rory stepped away first, Nani with her, and then, finally, Ella, and they all headed toward different parts of the castle.

Rory found Pippa exactly where she thought she would.

She wasn't in the infirmary or her own room, and Rory was not going to waste time in the chaos of the ballroom. Instead, she went to another place, as if her gut feeling was guiding her. The moonlight shone through the large paneled windows of the training room, the black and white floor looking almost liquid under the filtered light of the glass.

"Hey," Rory said in what she thought was a charming tone, and Pippa turned so abruptly that Rory faltered.

Pippa blinked as if she couldn't believe Rory was really standing there. They stood in silence for a long time, and Rory didn't want to move, afraid that Pippa was going to run the other way.

"You're really awake," Pippa said, her voice small. "I thought I'd dreamed it."

"You seem to dream an awful lot about me," Rory said,

strutting toward Pippa, crossing the training room floor as she'd done so many times. It belonged to Grimrose, but it belonged to them so much more.

This was their realm. On this ground, they'd shared everything.

On this ground, Rory thought she was weak for denying her feelings, for trying to do everything on her own, for trying to prove herself when proving herself wasn't what she really wanted. It wasn't what she needed.

Pippa didn't laugh, and it was only when Rory was standing in front of her that Pippa finally moved, her fingers reaching delicately to brush against Rory's cheek, to push back her short hair that was still unruly.

"Still doesn't feel real," Pippa said. "I thought I saw a dragon outside."

Rory wanted to crack a joke to brush it all aside, but she didn't want to disregard Pippa's worries, didn't want to make it seem less real. Because all of it had been real, even if she wouldn't remember it next morning.

Rory wanted to give her a choice.

From the moment she knew who Pippa was, she wanted Pippa to choose her. She didn't care about fairy tale destinies, about what was written and who was who. Rory wanted Pippa for who Pippa was and not because it was written in some stupid book or because that's how it was meant to go. It was more than destiny.

It was a choice.

"You don't need to worry anymore," Rory said, holding

Pippa's hand in her own, keeping Pippa's fingers close to her face. "Do you want to pick up a couple of swords and beat me up? Is that going to make this more normal for you?"

Pippa laughed, and then she grabbed Rory's face and kissed it. The kiss still felt like Rory's insides were burning through fire, Pippa's fingers gripping her skin, her lips and tongue pressing against her until Rory didn't feel her body anymore. She was a jumble of thoughts and hands and mouth and touch, and Rory thought she was growing weak from it when in fact she was only becoming stronger.

"Sometimes," Pippa said, and Rory could feel her smile on her lips against her own skin, and she was about to melt, "you're really stupid."

Rory laughed, a happiness that bubbled from her chest that seemed to fill her entire body from her toes to the tips of her hair. She looked at Pippa as she considered how lucky she was. She didn't have to stand alone; she never had.

She had her own strength—not that of her body but that of her soul, and she knew that she was going to need that in the future; her fight had only just begun.

"You ready for what comes next?" Pippa asked, as if reading her mind, a hundred different questions hovering between them.

Rory didn't know what the future held for her, but she wanted to become herself. The best version she could be. The version that wouldn't back down when she was afraid, the version that wouldn't hide anymore. One who knew how to ask for help when she needed it, without feeling weak if she did.

The version of her which knew how to be herself. With more tattoos, maybe, and a cooler haircut. The version of her who would hold Pippa's hand.

"Baby," Rory whispered to her love, "I was born ready."

CHAPTER SEVENTY-THREE

ELLA

Ella crossed the gardens to go back to the castle. She kept glancing behind her to see Yuki, standing tall and helping Reyna inside. Nani and Rory had both gone inside to tide things over and evaluate the damage. Everything felt conjured up as in dream.

But her hands were still stained in blood, her face hurt, and it was all real. They were all free.

Ella found Frederick sitting on the steps of the main courtyard, his red hair contrasting with the white marble. The moonlight and the castle lights made it all seem bright, and Ella gently stepped forward, showing herself.

Freddie looked up. In his hands, he was still holding her shoe.

"You left this," he said.

Ella smiled, and Freddie smiled too, but his smile didn't

really reach his eyes. Ella felt her stomach twist as she walked forward, stopping at the bottom of the stairs.

"Guess I should have known all along." He nodded thoughtfully. "Are you going to tell me what any of this means?"

If he was going to forget again in the morning, did it even make a difference?

"It's obvious, isn't it," Ella said, gesturing to the shoe. "What would you say if I told you everyone in this castle was somehow caught up in their own fairy tales?"

Freddie's brown eyes met hers. "I would say it isn't the weirdest thing anyone has ever said to me."

Come morning, he would forget the coincidences. Come morning, he would forget the shoe, and whatever he'd heard or saw. But he would still remember Ella standing in front of him, talking.

"So, was it too good to be true?"

Ella shook her head. "It was true. Fairy tale or not."

"So what now?"

Ella shrugged. He got up, still holding the shoe in his hand. He sauntered down the steps, stopping in front of her, lowering his head. Ella could see his freckles, the light reflecting in his brown eyes, but at the same time, she knew it was inevitable. Not because of him, but because Ella had finally understood what she wanted, what she had ahead of her.

"I just wanted to say thank you," Ella whispered, looking up at him, touching his face with her fingers. The blood was already dry, and he didn't comment on her scratches or her face streaked with dirt. "For everything. You've made this year possible. You've made it bearable. And you've made it great."

She wasn't lying. She'd suffered many losses, but there were so many things she had found along the way. Much more than she'd ever dreamed.

"But it's over now," Frederick said quietly, catching on to her meaning.

There were things she did know and things she didn't. Her excuses not to think of the future, not to hope for it, were over now. It was right ahead of her, bright and inviting.

She didn't know what she was dreaming of yet, but she wanted to wish them all true.

"I realized that I can't rely on other people to come and save me, to depend on them always," she said. "I thought that the future would be with you because it was a good alternative to Sharon. But I don't want just an alternative. I don't want to simply follow into the next safe thing. I don't want to give up the choices I can make. And I don't want you to give up yours."

Frederick nodded but was still silent, his lips thin. Ella brushed her thumb against his cheek, and her heart, though sad and heavy, wasn't breaking. Some things ended abruptly, and some were meant to end from the very beginning.

And maybe that was the way they had to be. She had to follow it to find out where it would lead. Now there was a new path, a new beginning.

"I wouldn't be giving up anything," he mumbled.

"I would," Ella said sincerely. "I never thought this day

would come. I dreamed of it, but now, it's all so real. It's the first time I'm *free*. And I wouldn't give that up for anything in the world."

Freddie's eyes looked to hers again, and Ella knew he was as sad as she felt. They'd shared so much, and Ella had found peace with him—she wanted him to understand how important all of it had been, how much it had meant. That she loved him, but this wasn't the love story that she wanted. She had deserved his affection, but there was so much more beyond this. So much, and she was only beginning to dream of it.

"I understand," he said quietly. "I don't want to take anything from you."

Ella blinked, surprised to see that she could still find tears even after the night she'd had. Freddie closed the distance for one last time, his lips soft against hers. It wasn't a passionate or demanding kiss, but one that would stay in memory. A kiss to say goodbye.

He stepped away first. Ella smiled, feeling young, free, careless.

"Do you want me to put this on?" he offered her the shoe in his hand. Ella eyed it, the simple slipper that represented too much.

It wasn't glass, it wasn't gold, it wasn't silver. It was a regular shoe, but still it seemed to shine under the moonlight. After all, maybe it meant something.

"No, thank you." She picked up the shoe from his hand. "I can do it myself."

She slipped the shoe onto her dirty foot, and it fit

perfectly, because it belonged to her. Old, used, comfortable, but still standing. Still resisting.

Still prepared for what the future might hold.

For the first time, Ella could see that everything was bright.

CHAPTER SEVENTY-FOUR

NANI

Nani thought the castle was going to be in an uproar, but she was wrong. There seemed to be nothing out of place, as if no one had bothered to look out of the window and see a battle being wrought outside. There'd been fire and a dragon and a world ending, and no other student had been there to see it. When she passed by the ballroom, there was still loud music, students sweating, and a part of Nani was glad to see that the world went on despite the chaos. That there were still people focused on celebrating and living their lives.

Nani found Svenja in her own room, her chest bound in wraps and bandages where the knife had gone in. She didn't look any paler than usual, her sharp brown eyes staring out of the window until Nani came in. She turned immediately, her strong gaze still.

"No offense," said Svenja, "but you look like you're the one who got a knife to the gut."

Nani broke into a smile, rushing forward to Svenja's bed. "How are you feeling?"

"Great," Svenja said. "I really recommend the experience of getting attacked by a psychopath on graduation night. I'm going to audition for final girl roles."

"It's a brilliant start to your career," Nani conceded. "Shouldn't you be at the infirmary?"

"Nah," Svenja dismissed it. "They stitched me up and it's all fine. Besides, I think they're keeping Odilia there. The security guards ended up getting her out, but she hit her head pretty hard."

Nani nodded, feeling the end approaching. The release she'd waited for.

Nani's eyes met Svenja's again, and although they'd already kissed before, and Svenja had all the right in the world to be angry, there was still something that felt unfinished. She looked at Svenja's bedside, and she saw the rose there. It had withered, the petals falling on the floor, but there was still a single petal holding on.

"How was your father?" Svenja asked, her voice interrupting Nani's thoughts.

"He was...well, he isn't good. But I think he's holding on with the treatment for a little longer."

Svenja nodded, and there was more silence. More space for Nani to say the things she wanted to say but didn't know how. She'd gone through all of her story and was only now realizing what she'd gotten wrong. Grimrose was the prison castle, but it wasn't the students or even Svenja keeping her there.

That had been Nani.

Nani had always been her own monster in the story, her own fears and unwillingness holding her captive, tearing apart anyone who tried to get too close. Refusing to open herself up, believing always that it was best if she stayed on her own, inside the world and walls she'd built, never realizing what she was truly missing.

"I'm sorry," Nani said, looking up from her hands. "I know you were trying to help and I kept pushing you away. I'm not...I'm not good at this kind of thing."

Svenja tilted her head, and then slipped her hand into Nani's, their fingers intertwined. Even then, Nani's first reaction was to build another wall, to push away the gesture, but she didn't want to be caught up in that cycle anymore.

She'd looked everywhere for a place where she really belonged, and yet, she had refused to fit into at any place that was offered. But now she knew that there was only one place where she'd always be welcome, where she'd find the right thing—her own heart. And that's what she had to trust.

"You don't have to be good," Svenja said. "You just have to keep trying. I'm not the best at advice, but maybe if we talked, you know. That would help."

"Can you stop mocking me for five whole minutes?" Nani demanded.

"Where's the fun in that?" Svenja said, sitting up, slipping her left hand under Nani's neck and pulling her closer to kiss her.

Nani didn't protest, and it felt like the first time again.

Svenja's lips against her own in desire, her mouth exploring the sweetness, the delicate grip of Svenja's hand on her neck, the way Nani's body seemed to curl to the edges, even her toes feeling the warmth that spread throughout. Svenja let go of the kiss, hovering just a few centimeters away.

"I understand why you didn't choose," Svenja said. "And I understand if you want to walk away from all this because it was our last year in school and now things change. But I want you to know that if you want, we can try this."

Nani didn't need to think about it for too long. "I think I'd like to try again."

"Good," Svenja said. "I hate wasting time meeting new people."

"Me too."

"You don't say," Svenja said sarcastically, and Nani broke into laughter. If this was what it was—if love was someone taking your hand and pointing out your flaws but still loving you despite them—then Nani wanted to give it a chance.

She wanted to be better. She wanted to tear down her walls and see the world not behind books or words but with someone by her side, someone to help her get up when she was falling. Nani could break her own curses, but she wanted to share their burden too.

She wanted the next adventures.

Nani looked sideways and saw that the last petal had begun falling from the stem.

Nani grabbed it before it hit the floor, catching it between her fingers. The curse was broken. She wasn't stuck in the castle, wasn't waiting for someone else to break her curse, wasn't waiting for anyone to come and find her. She'd found herself.

The world opened up before her, and Nani, both girl and beast, felt welcome to embrace all of it with her whole heart.

CHAPTER SEVENTY-FIVE

YUKI

Yuki took Reyna up the tower, carrying her mother with magic. She felt it pulsing beneath her veins, the sensation that she was one with the world. It didn't feel cold anymore, as if in breaking the curse, there had been some restoration, some magic that had been released back into the world, and it was going to be there for anyone who looked for it hard enough.

It felt comforting; its rhythm was the same as her heart.

Yuki put Reyna to bed after checking on her head again, but there was no bleeding. She sat down on the edge of the bed, her heart a turmoil.

Reyna's hand reached up, hovering centimeters away from Yuki's face.

"The curse is broken," Yuki whispered. "It's over."

Reyna's hand hesitated a little longer, but then she bridged the gap, her fingers cradling Yuki's face, and Yuki realized that this was the first time her mother had ever touched her. She felt the tears welling as she leaned into the touch, closing her eyes. Then Reyna was laughing and crying, and then they were both hugging each other, so tight that Yuki couldn't feel the air coming into her lungs. Reyna held her like she was never letting go, and Yuki didn't mind it. She wanted it.

"I'm so proud of you," Reyna whispered, her hands running down the length of Yuki's black hair. "I'm so, so proud of you."

Yuki felt a sob catch in her throat, but she didn't let go; she only kept her eyes tightly shut and felt the touch she didn't know she'd been craving.

"I was always so afraid of losing you," Reyna continued, her words coming out in a rush. "I'd seen it happen so many times, and still, the only hope I always had was of finding you again."

She let go of the embrace, but she held Yuki's face in her own two hands.

"And because of the curse, I always did," she said. "And I'd promise myself that I wasn't getting attached, because I knew it'd come to an end, and I knew you were going to die, but I never could help it. I pushed myself away, trying to keep myself safe, but it didn't matter. I'd find you, and the promise would break just like that."

Reyna sniffed, and Yuki had so many questions still about the curse, about magic, about how all of it had started, and how the ending still felt so raw, so abrupt.

"How did you know where to find me?"

"I think you always found me first," Reyna said through

a smile. "I'd meet your father, or your mother, depending on how the story wanted to go. And then they would tell me they had the most beautiful little girl in the entire world. It was always like that, and I could never turn away, because I could never deny myself the few moments I'd get with you." Reyna kissed her forehead. "My little snow child."

Yuki didn't hold back the tears this time.

"Don't you regret it?" Yuki asked, finding her voice to ask the question that had lived with her all this time.

Reyna looked straight at her, eyes dark and unrelenting. "A part of me regrets giving up on finding another way out," she said slowly. "On not trying harder to keep the girls safe. But if I had to condemn a hundred, a thousand other girls so I could love my daughter, then it was a fair price."

In Reyna's eyes, there was the same turmoil as Yuki's—the same fire that burned too bright, the same hunger. Yuki pulled her mother into an embrace, shivering at their reflected souls.

"I could have broken it myself. But I was always too selfish," Reyna whispered into Yuki's ear, "because I didn't want to learn my lesson. I love you. I created you, and you are a beautiful, terrible thing, Yuki. You are just like me. I never regretted you."

Yuki felt the pain squeezing tight in her heart, the same pain of loneliness that she'd felt, hoping that she wasn't going to feel it again. Except now she knew that Reyna had been the same. Reyna had risked everything for her, had created her, and that had been no different than other mothers who bore their children. Reyna had made her the only way she knew how: through her magic, through her loneliness, and now they were bound together, and Yuki was here.

Yuki was here, with the curse broken, with her mother, with her magic, and she was never going to be alone again.

With Reyna asleep, Yuki felt like the weight of the world had finally vanished from her shoulders. She didn't feel the pressing of the curse, and her magic had slowed into a dimness. She watched the window, at the light that was coming in early because summer was starting, and she saw a lonely figure on the edge of the lake.

Yuki flew down the stairs quickly. She found Ella in the garden, near the lake, sitting down on the grass and staring out into the water.

She sat down next to Ella, their backs to the castle, the breeze a gentle touch to their faces.

"What are you doing here?" Yuki asked, breaking the silence.

Ella didn't turn her head from the water. "I didn't know where else to go."

Yuki watched her friend's features and suddenly remembered that it was still Ella's birthday. It was still the day she was set free, and she couldn't imagine how many plans she still had or didn't have.

"Why did you take the bite?" Ella asked.

Yuki looked down at her shoes, still scared to speak of

457

things she didn't entirely understand. She still felt it deep inside her, a darkness that would never truly go away. The doubt, the hunger, the want, the loneliness, all things that were terrible but still hers. She didn't push them away because accepting herself meant she dealt with all of it.

"I thought I was saving you," Yuki said. "After all I did, I wanted to make up for it."

"By *dying*?" Ella said, incredulous. "What a dreadfully stupid thing to do."

Yuki snorted a laugh, and Ella shook her head.

"I thought it was going to fix it," Yuki said, tracing her fingers on the grass. "If I died willingly, there'd be no more curse. If I died, all of you would survive. You deserved your happy ending."

"Not more than you."

"But I did something awful," Yuki said, looking out to the lake, seeing Penelope's body fall into the water as if they had just finished the act. "Ella, I need you to understand, really understand. It wasn't something other than me. I wasn't possessed by magic or cornered, or anything else. All of it was me. I wanted her dead, so I killed her."

A pause, and Yuki hovered, wondering if the worst was yet to come. If she was safe from the curse, only to have her heart broken in pieces now.

"Ella, say something."

Ella sighed. "I don't know how to live in a world where I don't love you. And I don't think I want to."

Yuki looked over, and Ella was smiling at her, and Yuki

felt her heart leap. If Ella understood and she wasn't leaving, then there was still hope.

"I don't know what to do," Yuki said truthfully, still thinking about Penelope, still thinking about all the hurt she'd inflicted on the others and on herself, how she had moved on so quickly from that. How she could rely on all her jagged and broken pieces to remind her that they were a part of who she was, that she didn't really have to be whole.

She didn't owe anybody wholeness.

She didn't owe anybody perfection. She could be loved even by making mistakes. Even when she felt like redemption was beyond her.

It never was. There was always time.

"There's not an answer I can give you, no easy way out," Ella said. "You'll probably think about it for the rest of your life. I just know this: I love you. I'm not going to stop loving you because you've made a mistake, because of who you're struggling to be. I love you, always will."

"And what if I can't make up for what I've done?"

"The important thing is that you're going to try," Ella said, squeezing her hand. "And honestly, that's all we can ever do."

Yuki leaned her head against Ella's shoulder, and Ella leaned hers in as well.

"I love you too," Yuki said quietly, as they united their hands together, squeezing tight.

Yuki was forgiven, and most importantly, she forgave herself.

CHAPTER SEVENTY-SIX

ELLA

Ella and Yuki stayed by the lake for a long time.

Ella thought of Ari and Penelope, of Molly and Ian and Micaeli and Ivy and Annmarie, and all of the girls who had lost their lives to the curse of Grimrose, and all those who had lived long enough to survive it.

The castle was quiet, the party over, the garden trampled. It was still in the early hours of the morning, maybe five or six, so there wasn't a soul awake to see them. Come morning, all traces of it would be gone, and the thing that remained would be their memory.

It was dawn when Nani and Rory showed up, and they each sat on a different side, Rory next to Ella, Nani next to Yuki, watching the lake and the mountains.

"So," Rory said, "it's over now."

"Yeah," Ella answered, her voice coming out a little hoarse.

"I'll be honest, I didn't understand like, one third of what was going on."

That made all of them burst into laughter. It was that moment, when Rory impelled all of them to laugh, that Ella somehow knew that even though the future was uncertain, whatever was going to happen, she would have her friends. That this was a love story, after all. Her love story.

"So next step is what, Rory's coronation?" Nani asked.

"You take that back!" Rory snapped. "Fucking nightmare. I'd rather fight another dragon."

Ella turned to her friend, smiling, and she pulled Rory closer to her. They were safe there, all of them under the protective shadow of the castle that had both kept them under a curse but given them the means to break it.

Ella knew she couldn't have done it on her own. As long as they stood together, there was hope.

Nani leaned back on her elbows, but she didn't shift away. "So what now?"

It was a genuine question, and Ella had no answer to it, except that thing which she had been thinking since the clock had struck midnight. She was free.

"Anything we want," she said.

The future was uncertain and unwritten, but there were some things Ella knew.

That there could be a hundred worlds and a hundred lives, that they could try again, but all that mattered was this one they were in now and how they lived in it.

That kindness would always ripple forward.

That love and forgiveness were always the key, no matter what else happened.

That loving someone and being kind and being bold and brave enough to claim yourself was the only way.

That trying was the only thing they could ever choose to do, again and again and again, because one day, they would get it right.

That fixing the world alone was impossible, but she was not alone.

That there was no happily ever after, but there was an ever after.

"Happy birthday, Ella," Yuki said as the four of them watched the sun rise together over the mountains, illuminating them and the towers of Grimrose castle.

There was no story to repeat anymore.

They would create their own.

ACKNOWLEDGMENTS

This book would not have gotten to this happy ending without the following people:

My family. Thank you for the support since the very beginning.

My agent, Kari Sutherland. Thank you for fighting for these girls every single bit of the way.

The Sourcebooks publishing team. Thanks so much for all the work you've done with this series, it has been an incredible journey. Wendy, thank you for taking care of book two with all your heart. Madison, thank you for all the creativity and effort you've put into promoting this story.

My friends. You all know who you are. We are more than friends, we are *amigos*. A special thanks once again to Solaine, for reading this book for the umpteenth time, and still loving the Grimrose girls as if it were your first. Franklin, for the notes encouraging me to see that it wasn't so bad as I initially thought. I owe both of you a lot.

Sofia, for existing in my general vicinity.

Librarians, booksellers, and reviewers who have read and

recommended the first book, who were as excited about it as I was. Special shout-out to the B&N team, for promoting the book beyond the far reaches of my imagination.

And finally, to readers, wherever and whenever you are. There is magic in telling a story, but it's only worth it when there's someone on the other end listening to it. See you on the next one.

ABOUT THE AUTHOR

Laura Pohl is the Brazilian New York Times Bestselling author of *The Grimrose Girls*. Her debut novel, *The Last 8,* won the International Latino Book Awards. When not taking pictures of her dog, she can be found curled up with a fantasy or science-fiction book or replaying *Dragon Age*. Her favorite Disney princess is Cinderella, and her favorite Disney prince is Kylo Ren. You can learn more about her on her website at onlybylaura.com or reach her on social media @onlybylaura.